QUEEN

Elk Lake Publishing, Inc.
Queen: Realms of the Infinite, Book 2
Copyright 2015 by R.J. Larson
Requests for information should be addressed to:
Elk Lake Publishing, Inc., Plymouth, MA 02360
Create Space ISBN-13 NUMBER: 978-1-942513-23-0

Cover and Graphics Design: Katharin Gramckow and Kacy Barnett-Gramckow
Cover Model: Brianna Anderson
Editors: Deb Haggerty and Kathi Macias
Graphics and Interior Design: Anna O'Brien, Melinda Martin
Published in Association with Hartline Literary Agency

QUEEN

R J Larson

Plymouth, Massachusetts

For Shoshi

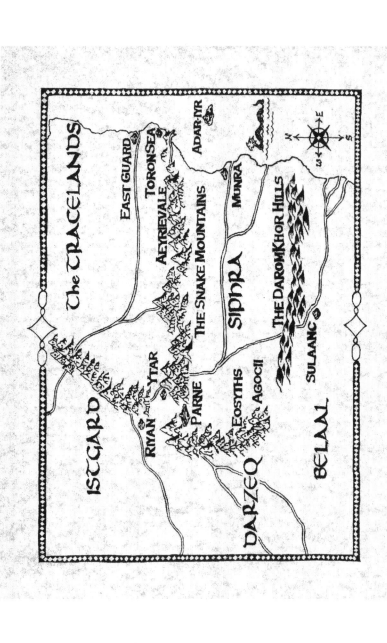

Chapter 1

Araine, prophet of Belaal, opened her eyes in the silvery moonlit chill of a nighttime garden. The king's garden. Alone. Her feet bare and cold in a puddle on a stone path, and her cloak askew over her shoulders as if she'd donned it while sleepwalking.

Well, she certainly wasn't asleep now. No ordinary dreams of fiery crimson monsters lurked, calling her to the shadows of darker realms. Nor did death threaten her yet again, promised by a golden ligature dangling from her father's own hands. Instead, she shivered on the rain-sodden path, her heart thudding as her very soul trembled.

"Infinite, beloved Creator, why am I here?" In the king's private garden. *How* had she bypassed the guards? "Does this mean that the king is…"

Yes. Her Creator's quiet affirmation stilled the question, even as she formed it. Even as light appeared within her clenched right hand, scaring her, producing the tall, fragile-seeming staff of the prophet's branch. The branch…its wooden grain glowing and silvered, shimmering with power, ever-alive as if lifted by her Creator from an eternal tree within His realm.

Wobble-kneed, Araine huddled on the wet stone path and pressed her face against the gleaming branch, praying beneath her breath, "Infinite, thank You! Bless Your name! Let Belaal's god-king wake as a mortal and call to You! Let him become a mortal and *live*!"

***

Bel-Tygeon sucked in a grass-scented breath and opened his eyes, jolted, looking up into a calm violet-blue morning sky…sane.

Clear and true thoughts filled his mind, even as air filled his lungs and returned him to life as a human. Flesh and blood encased his soul. Nothing more. Nor less.

Infinite, bless You! "Thank You!" He turned onto his belly in the cold grass and wept, burying his face in his arms as sobs shook his body.

He—Belaal's arrogant, willfully self-deluded fool of a god-king—didn't deserve mercy. Yet his Creator had granted him this second chance at life. "Infinite, do as You please! Whatever happens, I'll praise You, for I am no god, only Your servant! Be with me now, forever!"

At last, Bel-Tygeon lifted his head and wiped his bearded face with his…claws. While stirring his shockingly long beard, he nearly gagged at his own stench. Matters didn't improve as he surveyed the remainder of his body. Moisture, soil, grass, leaves and a mixture of filth that he didn't dare consider, all matted his beard and his hair.

Just as Araine had warned, he'd become a beast.

Worse, however—far worse—were the unfamiliar folds of roughly cut new leather wrapped and tied about his body. Some poor wretch had recently *seen* him and tended him in his odiferous animal-like state. But who?

Where was he?

Straightening, Bel-Tygeon studied the vast, unfamiliar landscape. Craggy, snow-dusted mountains encircled him majestically, framing this overgrown meadow that was sheltered by trees flaunting autumn's intense yellows and crimsons. Beautiful, but he was in the mountains. Not Belaal. Where was he, precisely? "Oh, Infinite, let me not be in Agocii lands!"

His flesh chilling with alarm, Bel-Tygeon shoved himself into a wary crouch, almost feeling Agocii chains about his hands and feet, with an Agocii warrior's spear piercing his heart. Or perhaps he'd suffer a more lingering torment—to be recognized and eventually handed over to his own traitor-general, Siyrsun. He'd be hacked to pieces. And then Siyrsun would seize control of Belaal, if he hadn't done so already.

Impermissible!

Siyrsun's squared, battle-scarred face glowered within Bel-Tygeon's thoughts, and Ty tensed, visceral rage welling, his heartbeat quickening, ready to fight. As if he could pull some nonexistent sword on his traitor-lord-general from this distance.

A ludicrous reaction, because judging by the length of his hair, beard, and fingernails he and his enemy were separated by a chasm of months, perhaps years.

Yet according to Bel-Tygeon's own perceptions, the general's betrayal *had* just occurred. Mere breaths ago, Ty had stood within his vast palace gardens, condemning the traitor-general, and himself as he screamed, "I am yet Belaal's god! … Sacrifice yourself to me!"

That instant, he'd been seared by a spiritual shock of self-induced terror—just before darkness veiled his mind. His last clear memory was of Araine's lovely, anguished face. Her blue eyes wide, stricken, *knowing* that he'd condemned himself with those arrogant, hateful words.

I am yet Belaal's god! … Sacrifice yourself to me!

Ty shuddered. Araine had warned him, begged him consider his true self. Yet, he'd been so determined to remain Belaal's god that he'd rebelled against his gentle prophet's fearful counsel. He deserved his punishment. He deserved death for condemning so many others.

Blessed be the Infinite for sparing him.

Bel-Tygeon crouched within the sheltering thicket of drying grasses, loathing his own arrogance. And his own filth. Scowling down at his long, begrimed, twig-like fingernails, Ty mentally listed his priorities. He must be sure that Araine and his sister and his friends were safe—and that his kingdom was secure. He needed weapons. Clothes. Food. Allies. Plans. But first… He licked his dry lips. Water. To drink and then to scrub the filth from his flesh, and to soften his grotesque predatory talons so he could hack them to civilized neatness.

He listened warily, inhaling and scenting moisture in the air. The muffled rush of a stream beckoned from beyond the autumn-hued trees at the base of this meadow, and he darted from his meager sheltering thicket of grass, praying for his Creator's protection.

***

Serena paused at the entrance of her lady-mother's darkened alcove within the tent and she peered inside, breathing the mingled scents of cedar, wood-smoke, and medicinal balm—which was worrisome. Adelia, wife of Tsir Andris, lord of Clan Darom, never used medicinal balm and she never slept in late. "Mother?"

"Serena." Adelia sighed. "I'm so glad you're here. I was just thinking of you. Come in."

Serena crept into the alcove and knelt beside her mother. "Should I light a lamp for you?"

"No need. I must rest today. Perhaps tomorrow as well—which is why I'm glad you're here." Adelia shifted on her pallet, then lifted one hand and offered Serena a decoratively sheathed dagger, accompanied by a stream of anxious maternal commands. "Guard this until I've recovered. Tend your brother and sisters. Hunt up some eggs, check the snares, and harvest more nuts and seed pods. Don't forget to bank the fire, and keep everyone—"

"Keep everyone busy adding to our wood piles and preparing for winter. I'll remember," Serena promised. Yet she couldn't blame Mother for fretting. With the first snowstorms threatening to swoop down upon them, Mother wouldn't shirk harvesting unless she was truly ill. Her touch feather light, Serena checked Adelia's soft face and forehead. Cool—not the least hint of a fever. Which could only mean...

A pang hit Serena, making her stomach sink as if she'd jumped from a terrible height. Please, not another miscarriage! "Is it the baby?"

Her words tender, wistful, Adelia murmured, "The baby flutters like a little bird. Just...nowhere near as much as I wish, so please pray. I'm also having pains, but they're lessened if I remain still. Therefore, you're in charge." She patted Serena's hand. "I trust you to rule the household with your own good sense and my training. Meanwhile, it's past dawn, so please hurry."

"Of course." Serena bent and kissed her mother's forehead. "I'll bring you some food and something warm to drink."

"Mint, please." Adelia smoothed the fleece coverlets, as if her request was trivial. But she disliked mint and drank steaming mint-water only when she was queasy.

Another troublesome sign.

Reining in her fears, Serena pushed through the felt-shielded doorway into her family's central tent where they gathered for meals, and where she and her siblings slept. The fifteen-year-old twins, Tessi and Kari, were already awake and kneeling on their padded sleeping mats, their dark-braided heads bent as they played their favorite game—tossing and gathering sheep knucklebones while communicating with their secret twin-language of hand-flutters, nods, and light grimaces.

Oblivious to the game, seven-year-old Ayden slept nearby, one leather-clad arm flung over his eyes, his black hair adorably tousled. Equally inert, two-year-old Miyna lay nestled in her corner of Serena's mat, working her lower lip as she slept. Quiet for now, which was a relief. Mother needed peace for the baby's sake and her own. Complete tranquility.

Mother had asked her to pray for the baby.... Serena sighed. Praying was all well and worthy if one believed. But she did not. What good had Utzaos, the lord-god of the sun, done for the Eosyth clans in the past two years? Nothing! Nor had his consort, Atzaia, goddess of the heavens and all life. Even Father's new deity, the Mighty One, the Creator, the Infinite of Parne, had done nothing to lessen their burdens and stave off the perpetual threat of starvation since father had destroyed the altars of Utzaos. Didn't the Infinite see His followers? Would He never defend them against the Agocii warriors who too often harassed Eosyth tribes and stole Eosyth animals?

Well. Serena straightened her shoulders. Enough unspoken whining. They'd survived last year, hadn't they? And, this year's harvest was promising and more varied—their usual caches in the lower valley caves abounded with the promise of adequate food and drying wood for the winter. She must content herself by adding to those caches at every possible instant. She would *not* face another winter watching her parents become thinner by the day, and hearing her siblings whimper for more food. Perhaps Mother wouldn't be in danger of miscarriage now if she'd not been half-starved last year.

If Mother lost this baby…if Mother died of the miscarriage, being so weakened…. Serena's throat tightened. No. She'd cry if she allowed herself such fearful thoughts.

Rot that wretched god-king, Bel-Tygeon, for demanding that famine-inducing tribute last year! If he were here now, she'd claw him half to death. She'd—

Enough. Why waste precious strength hating a tyrannical god-king?

Lips pressed tight, Serena slung Mother's ancient black and gold family dagger over her head and mentally stepped into her role as temporary queen of the household. Time to put fear and fury to work. She eased another split log beneath the central hearth's iron grate and checked the open kettle above it. Lazy tendrils of steam curled upward from the hot water. Perfect. She tossed a generous portion of dried mint leaves into a round clay pitcher, poured in water, then doled fruit, nuts, and grain-flecked flat bread onto a broad wooden dish, then carried them in to Adelia.

Attempting a good mood, she teased, "Are you ready for the storm? I'm about to wake Miyna."

"She's so much like you." Mother's beautiful smile and her sparkling eyes shone even in this dim light. "What fun you were! And what a comfort you are now."

"Why, thank you." More or less. Had she really been such a little wild woman as Miyna? Serena winced at the thought. Actually, she'd probably been worse than Miyna. And if that was true, then her parents were marvels of patience for not leaving her on a cliff somewhere before age three. She set down the food and the steaming pot of brewed mint, and then kissed her mother's soft cheek. "I love you! Eat and relax. I'll tend chores and return a bit later with more food. And I'll tell Father you're resting."

"What was I saying about comfort?" Mother smoothed Serena's hair. "May the Infinite bless you, my sweet girl! Now, get busy."

"Yes, lady-mother."

Bracing herself, Serena stepped into the central tent. The twins, Kari and Tessi, were humming softly and playing their game of knucklebones. The youngest ones slumbered on. Serena deliberately set aside her fears for Mother, then smiled and clapped her hands. "Get up, everyone—in *good* moods! We've work to do!"

She knelt beside Ayden's mat and jostled him awake, loving his mussed dark hair and the dimples around his small mouth as he grimaced. Ayden opened his brown-green eyes, then groaned, "We're not having any fun today, are we?"

"Of course we'll have fun. I'll take you with me to check our snares and fish traps as soon as we've finished morning chores."

Her brother brightened at once and he pulled his treasured leather quiver of small arrows from beneath his fleece coverlet. "I'm ready! If we see the monster, I'll shoot him!"

"He's not a monster, and no, you won't shoot the poor creature."

"But—"

"No." Serena shook her head. "Our lord-father commanded us to protect the madman, and it's only right that we do. We're Eosyths, not Agocii savages."

Ayden's wry expression suggested that, just for an instant, he'd prefer to be Agocii. "I guess."

A tiny huff, followed by a toddler-whine announced Miyna's unhappy welcome of their morning. To fend off full-blown wailing, Serena hurried to pick up her youngest sister, snatching a bit of crisp flatbread along the way to use as a Miyna-muzzle. She hugged Miyna and whispered conspiratorially, "Good morning! Will you talk to me today? Teach me Tessi and Kari's hand-signs; I know you understand them! Talk to me…"

As Serena cajoled Miyna, she combed the toddler's dark hair and twined it into a pert feather-like spray at the top of Miyna's head.

Overcome by the charming effect and her own success thus far, Serena kissed her baby sister, then lifted the toddler onto her hip and began to measure portions of food to her siblings. To the twins, she said, "Mother's not well today, so we're going to keep things calm and quiet for her. I'm depending upon you two for help with Miyna today."

Tessi dropped the knucklebone game pieces with a delicate clatter, and Kari flinched. The two exchanged a series of hand-flutters, grimaces, and pouts, and then Tessi faced Serena and resorted to using actual speech, her voice light yet mournful. "All day?"

"If you complain." Serena smiled at the pair, but kept her gaze stern, willing them to obey. "I want you to talk to Miyna today, as well as using your hand-signs—and I want you to teach me your hand-signs too, since Miyna prefers your language above ours."

Kari's expression went bleak, and she scooped the knucklebones into an embroidered leather pouch, then handed the pouch to Tessi. Together, the twins rolled up their sleeping mats, combed and braided their hair, and eyed Miyna as if facing their doom.

With her siblings temporarily conquered, Serena forged ahead. They'd eat their morning meal, bring in fresh water and firewood, check today's food supplies, and then the twins would take Miyna outside, perhaps visiting with their aunties in the encampment while she led Ayden through their morning round of checking traps.

Eyeing a small mountain of leather bags piled at the back of their tent, Serena smiled. By her reckoning, those bags of pine cones had been drying for nearly a month. Later today, she would set the twins and Ayden to bashing those bags on the floor mats and picking out the pale pine nuts, allowing them each to consume one handful as a reward.

Later. She charged through the chores, sent the twins and Miyna to inform Aunt Betiya and Uncle Zeddi that Mother was resting, and then she smoothed back Ayden's hair and tied it with a cord. Finished, she shouldered a collection of leather and mesh bags and led her little brother outside. As she crossed the encampment, a young man's cheery voice hailed her. "Serena! Good morning.

I'm going down to help with the herds. Do you want me to take a message to your father?"

Detzios. Father's cousin and scribe. Serena muted a sigh. He still made every excuse possible to talk with her, though she'd been kindly discouraging him for months. Years, actually. A pleasant, cheerful man, but…not for her. She intended to eventually help lead a clan. Therefore, she must follow her older sister's example and marry the heir of an Eosyth clan's lord. Which meant that she had only two choices.

Lije, son of Tsir Mikial of Clan Tsahfon, or Josias, son of Tsir Davor of Clan Ma'rawb.

Of the two, she preferred the solemn, steady, admirable Josias. Thankfully, according to a courier note from Clan Ma'rawb, he'd recently returned from more than a year's captivity in Belaal and her plans could now proceed. Fond as she was of Josias, no doubt she'd love him eventually.

Therefore she spoke pleasantly to Detzios without smiling. "Thank you, Detzios. Please tell him that Mother's resting today, and she placed me in charge—we'll see him this evening."

Detzios grinned, his teeth big and white amid his broad, dark-bearded face as he approached. "If he's delayed, I'll bring you word later. Perhaps you'd like to—"

Oh, no. Whatever his suggestion was, her answer was no. Before the young man could say another word, Serena turned Ayden about and rushed him toward the nearby woods. "Thank you, Detzios!"

Ayden brandished his miniature bow at her and grumbled, "Hey, quit pushing me!"

"We need to hurry," Serena excused herself. "We're behind with our work."

She marched Ayden along the narrow woodland path toward their line of fish-traps and snares, watching for scat and other signs of wildlife. Bears and deer lived in these woods, and large spiny-crested lizards haunted the nearby cliffs and caves. At least the clan wouldn't have to fear untamed herds of monster-destroyers until they settled in the lower valleys this winter. Just thinking of those troublesome beasts made Serena clutch at Mother's dagger. As if the dagger were any help against such—

The creature stepped into the shadowed path so swiftly that Serena gasped and drew the dagger.

Ayden screamed.

Chapter 2

Bel-Tygeon lifted his hands, glancing from the yowling little boy to the thin russet-haired young woman's shocked gaze, then down to the oiled black iron dagger in her surprisingly steady grip. Undoubtedly, she'd had some training to wield that dagger so intuitively. Soft-voiced to ease her alarm, he pleaded, "Forgive me for frightening you, lady and young sir. I intend no evil."

The boy's alarm lessened, but only enough that he turned defensive. He lifted his miniature bow and fitted it with an arrow, faltering a bit with two spares in one small fist. Ty eyed the child's stance, his distinctive native apparel, and the unique archery method he was obviously still learning. All pointed to one horrifying, potentially lethal conclusion.

Infinite…no. Let me be wrong!

Moistening his lips, praying the boy wouldn't accidently puncture him with a chance arrow, Ty asked, "Are you Eosyths?"

The young woman lifted her chin, but didn't lower her dagger. Like her hand, the woman's voice remained steady. Feminine, yet controlled and subtly inflected with the same calm efficiency as Ty's own Eosyth scribe, Nikaros. "We are. And who are you?"

The boy stared straight along his small arm as he aimed at Ty's face. Clearly regaining his usual spirit, he piped up, "Are you Agocii? Your beard's not long enough if you are. And you're not a very brave one, either, because you don't wear the—"

The woman gently but firmly placed her free hand over the boy's mouth and stifled his chatter. He snorted through her long fingers and glared up at her, mercifully lowering his bow in the process. The young woman's fear eased visibly, though her tone remained cold as she surveyed Bel-Tygeon. "*Are* you Agocii?"

Remembering the hostilities between the Agocii tribes and Eosyth clans, Ty allowed his true indignation to show. "No! I'm not Agocii. But more than that, I cannot say."

Her large hazel eyes glittered forbiddingly, drawing Ty's admiration even as she challenged him. "Cannot, or will not?"

"Both." Would she ever lower that dagger? Knowing that the Eosyth clans had recently trusted the Infinite following the disastrous siege of the ancient city-state of Parne, Ty added, "Nevertheless, I pledge that I won't harm either of you, for fear of our Creator, the Infinite."

The young woman raised one dark auburn eyebrow, not the least bit pacified. "I suppose I'll believe you. For now. Even so…" She scanned his snarled hair, the wild beard and then grimaced in obvious revulsion. "No doubt you need our help, but I can't allow you to walk into our encampment looking like the madman you've been. Wait here."

Those last two commanding words could have been carved in ice. And she actually walked backward down the path, holding the dagger level, prepared to attack despite the growing distance between them. As soon as they were a safe distance away, the little boy abandoned his defensiveness and capered around the too-thin young woman, clearly pelting her with questions, which she answered with inaudibly hissed words.

Whatever the young woman said, it made the child laugh and fling an impish grin at Ty.

Not terribly reassuring—the boy's glance nor the young woman's polite hostility.

Alone again, Bel-Tygeon shivered on the path, and then crept into the trees and hunkered down in the forest's undergrowth, feeling naked despite the leather wrap and his own overlong hair. He was among the Eosyths. How had he—in any beastly fashion—managed to cross the plains and hike up into these highlands?

At least he wasn't among the Agocii. With their spiritual fears and scorn of weakness, they would've butchered him long before now. Nevertheless, he must not reveal his true status to anyone. He must escape and return to Belaal. *Had* Siyrsun seized the throne? Was his sister, Dasarai, still alive? And Araine… He dared not think of Araine or he'd recall her sorrow once more.

Perhaps his sworn Eosyth servant and former captive, Nikaros, had managed to help Dasarai maintain order in the kingdom. But no matter what had happened, Bel-Tygeon must return to Belaal, and his palace in Sulaanc. He must find Araine and his sister.

Infinite, by Your great mercy, rescue me!

The young woman and the child returned sooner than Ty expected. As he crept out of the trees, she set a heap of leather garments between them on the path. "Here. I trust you've been civilized enough in more sane times to clothe yourself."

"Thank you, yes." Actually, his attendants usually fastened his pins and sashes. And they combed his hair. His servants also prepared his baths—though mentioning his attendants and slaves here might ultimately betray his identity. However, he'd managed a brief icy dousing in the stream this morning while blessing whoever had provided him with the leather wrap.

Ty inclined his head toward his Eosyth benefactors, and then stepped behind a tree to guess at the surprising intricacies of lacing on Eosyth leggings. The felted foot coverings and battered too-large leather boots felt oddly stifling. And donning the split leather tunic with its multiple leather ties and broad crimson wool sash proved equally challenging, yet he deduced their configurations. Undoubtedly the first of many small and ordinary accomplishments. Nevertheless, the garments weighed heavily against his arms and legs. Ty warned himself to not tear them off.

Had he been unclothed for so long that his limbs had forgotten the sensation of wearing garments? Horrifying thought.

Finished, and with hitherto-unknown awkwardness, Ty stepped onto the path again.

The little boy was amusing himself by aiming at pretend targets. However, the young woman was watching for Ty. She studied him warily and then pressed one hand to her forehead, apparently fighting a headache.

Ty smiled.

She frowned.

He paused, confounded by this new conundrum. His smile had failed to charm her. Odd. And disturbing. Without his usual regal trappings, was he actually a man who might be … resistible? He sighed at his own vanity. Of course, what woman would look at him now with his matted hair and beard, knowing he'd been mad? "My name is Ty. And yours is…?"

The young woman stared as if debating the wisdom of saying another word to a former madman. But the boy lowered his bow and grinned. "My name is Ayden. She's just my sister Serena."

Before Bel-Tygeon could thank the child, Serena pointed up the path. "When my brother and I reach that far tree with the drooping branch, you may begin to follow us to our encampment. But I warn you that if you make even one troublesome move, I'll scream murder. And every man in the encampment will come running."

Was that so? Why, then, hadn't she brought several men with her to subdue him? He *was* a madman after all. Undoubtedly, she'd threatened him with a self-protective bluff—for which Ty was grateful. If Serena had brought a troop of defenders, they'd have left him with bruises at the very least.

She tapped her little brother's shoulder, urging him to walk ahead with her. But the child lagged farther and farther behind, finally asking, "Aren't we going to check the snares and fish traps?"

Serena halted, almost mid-step, and bowed her head and shoulders in clear frustration. She turned and stalked back down the path, one hand on her dagger as she warned Ty, "Sir, step aside and wait here until we return."

Bel-Tygeon complied. But as Ayden passed him, half-heartedly turning the toy bow and arrows against the madman, Ty asked beneath his breath, "Is your sister always so…" Officious.

Overbearing. Commanding. He chose a word he'd often applied to his own sister during early childhood, "…bossy?"

Ayden shrugged and whispered, "Oh, *I* can scare her."

Two steps later, the little boy pitched himself over a slight rise in the narrow path, face-first—bow and arrows scattering as he fell. And he yelped, "Augh!"

Ty hurried to help Ayden to his feet. Serena turned and rushed back to them, her lovely eyes wide with panic. "Ayden!" She knelt beside him, hands trembling as she turned him over and checked his face.

"Ha!" Ayden jeered, instantly pointing at her. "I scared you!"

Serena jumped and then swatted his shoulder. "Don't *do* that! And don't point at people." But she laughed, clearly relieved.

Ty stared. Her smile…was dazzling. At this instant, relaxed and laughing, with that dark red-tinged hair, delicately determined chin, and her high cheekbones, she was as beautiful as any lady in the Women's Palace in Sulaanc—even Araine. Before Serena caught him staring, Ty looked down at Ayden and warned, "Young sir, beware. Older sisters usually take cruel revenge upon errant younger brothers."

"You use such big words," Ayden complained.

"My sister's fault," Ty explained. But the child had voiced a point to consider. He must choose his words carefully here lest he somehow betray his identity. By now, Serena was staring at him, and she was clearly no fool.

Her gaze curious though still wary, she asked, "Who is your sister?"

To distract her and deflect the question, Ty smiled warmly, admiring her as he murmured, "No one you've met, lady. And I'm sorry you haven't."

Serena drew back, and her eyes widened all the more, enchanting Bel-Tygeon. Had he ever seen such eyes? Darkest moss-green rimmed and flecked with brown….

Ignoring Ty's stare, the young woman scooped her little brother into her arms and stood, jostling him. "Ayden, since you can't walk without falling, I'll have to carry you."

As she settled Ayden onto her hip, he protested, "I'm not a baby!"

"You stumbled like one," Serena pointed out, beginning to walk away.

Ayden struggled in her arms. "Wait! My arrows!"

Ty laughed at him. "What was I saying about cruel revenge, sir? I'll guard your weapons until you return."

Miniature weapons, but weapons nonetheless. Ty grinned as he picked up the small bow and its arrows. Excellent craftsmanship, despite their simple lines. Why, with these, he could at least take out a dreki's eye.

Just before the beast killed him.

Unnerved, Ty stepped from the narrow path, braced his back defensively against a pine tree, set the miniature weapons, and waited for Serena and Ayden's return.

***

Serena set down Ayden and stalked along the path, scowling as she surveyed the pines, shrubs and ferns left and right. What a perfect day for the madman to turn sane! Mother needed to rest, the children must be kept busy, and she was supposed to establish herself as temporary queen of Clan Darom. This madman could disrupt everything.

And how disturbing that the madman was not only sane, but... if she must admit it...fascinating. Stupid of her to even contemplate his appeal, much less be intrigued by it. Though all her instincts told her that this man wasn't violent, he might be plotting thievery to provide for himself. Well, he'd gain nothing except Father's oldest garments—which Tsir Andris would have offered him no matter what—and Ayden's bow and a handful of arrows.

At most, that Ty-creature could stun and catch a few birds with those arrows.

However, he'd voiced belief in the Infinite. The instant Father heard of the man's views, he'd welcome Ty like a long-lost relative and invite him to stay the entire winter.

Perhaps this Ty wouldn't eat too much—a wasted hope, no doubt.

Her frustration grew as she and Ayden descended into the small ravine and hiked along its stream to check their traps. One after another, empty yet mangled fish-traps and snares greeted her— several snares with fresh scat and scuffling marks about them, as if an animal had been trapped earlier. Had someone deliberately raided and ruined her traps?

When she reached the final snare, Serena half-knelt beside the bubbling, sparkling stream and showed the snare's braided leather cords to Ayden, teaching him, even as she vented her aggravation. "Look! See how evenly cut those edges are? No four-legged animal did this—these cords were cut with a blade. And look at that supporting limb." She nodded toward a snapped sapling. "*That* is green wood, not rotten. It was folded down until it broke!"

No one in Clan Darom would do this. Food was shared whenever true need was present. Everyone toiled and guarded each other's supplies for their own survival. Life in the mountains was too hard to not work together as a clan. Worse… she eyed the scuff-marks and boot prints around this snare. Those prints were still fresh and damp. Serena caught her breath. An enemy was near.

An uncomfortable prey-being-stalked prickling crept along Serena's arms and shivered its way down her spine. A nearby rustling of leaves and scuffling noises justified her alarm.

No. Don't run.

She gathered the sliced cords, grabbed Ayden by one hand and whispered, "Let's go. Quietly."

"We can't forget Ty," Ayden reminded her softly. "He's wearing Father's clothes."

"We won't forget Ty."

Ty had no cutting blade—no way to protect himself. Her stalkers, however, undoubtedly possessed blades. Daggers. Swords. Hatred…

Straight-backed, mastering her panic, Serena stood, gripped Ayden's hand and looked around. Within the trees, shadows moved. A rough-hewn Agocii chieftain stepped haughtily into her line of vision like a living wall, his breadth and height avowing his strength. And those countless gold bead-clasps and bands garnishing his intricately-braided brown beard attested to his acts of courage and his human kills. So many kills…

Be calm, Serena reminded herself. She must be as composed as her name.

Slow and deliberate, she raised her hand to Mother's dagger, showing this invading chieftain that she would fight if need be— despite no hope of victory.

Chapter 3

The Agocii chieftain's full, wide lips curved, revealing his scorn of her defiance. Yet his coppery eyes gleamed with interest, and his low voice was smoothly accented as he deigned to speak to her. "Young fool-woman, why do you and your child enter these woods unguarded? Are Eosyths so ignorant?"

Clearly offended by his tone and words, Ayden retorted, "Don't talk to us like that! These are my lord-father's woods and *she's* my sister!"

The chieftain's expression hardened, his nostrils flared, and he glowered down at Ayden, his contempt an almost visible force. Particularly as six other warriors emerged from behind various trees, encircling them. Ayden backed against Serena's legs and she felt his small body tremble as the Agocii lord snarled, "Youth does not speak until it has wisdom and enough strength to defend itself! One more word, boy, and I'll cut a notch into your tongue and feed you your own flesh! Fool-woman, answer me!"

Serena curved an arm around her brother, pressed her fingers into his shoulder, and whispered, "Please remain still and silent." As Ayden gripped her hand in mute obedience, Serena returned the chieftain's glowering scorn. "Agocii lord, I am Serena, daughter of Tsir Andris, lord of Clan Darom. These woods are ours, and I'm familiar with most of the animals here. Except the two-legged ones. Why have you and your warriors entered Eosyth lands?"

For one long breath, the Agocii chieftain stared at her, eyes narrowing as if he longed to repay her for daring to hint that he was an animal. But then he shook his head. "I've no time to waste on females and children. I answer only in tribute to your courage, daughter of Tsir Andris. We seek a demon-man who invaded our lands and terrorized our families. Have you seen such a one? Answer me!"

Ty. They were referring to Ty. Serena spoke what she hoped was the truth. "There's no demon-man here. I'm sorry for your trouble. What did your families suffer?"

"Our cattle were frightened away—some lost completely for fear of his evil. His blood must be spilled to release my people from his spirit and his curse."

Superstitious Agocii!

Serena stared down at the mute Ayden and stifled her disgust. Not for anything would she disclose Ty's presence. Inconvenient as his existence might be, he was in Father's lands, and as temporary ruling lady of the household she must protect Ty as their guest.

Father himself had decreed that because the Infinite allowed the madman to enter their lives, then undoubtedly if they sheltered him, a blessing would follow. But she didn't believe in such blessings. And neither did these Agocii warriors. They had their own gods—gods no longer worshiped by most Eosyths. Bowing her head slightly to offer some respect for their beliefs, Serena said, "May your god Utzaii protect you as you search in the light of his sun. There's no demon-man in Eosyth lands, so leave us in peace."

Now, to escape… Shoulders back, chin up, she marched past the Agocii chieftain. He swept one big hand at Serena and gripped her face, making her stumble and flinch as Ayden gasped.

Hating herself for betraying pain, she glared up at the man. He narrowed his eyes, yet he seemed darkly amused as he muttered, "A time is coming when the Agocii will no longer endure insults from Eosyths who betrayed us at Parne and abandoned Utzaii. Warn your lord-father to guard his lands and his belongings!"

He shoved Serena away and turned his back on her, displaying the utter contempt of a victor who has spared a despised captive. He was practically inviting her to stab him in the back. Though if she dared, the chieftain's warriors would certainly repay her. She and Ayden would be tortured and cut to pieces.

To herself and Ayden, she whispered, "Say nothing!"

She must not cry. How horrible to feel so weak. So helpless and unable to protect her little brother.

Exhaling, she planned her course as she trudged out of the ravine. Ayden needed her to be calm. And so did Ty. If the Agocii captured Ty and killed him, Father would be shamed—perhaps forced to attack the Agocii in retaliation.

Their clan couldn't afford such losses.

To avoid calling attention to Ty's presence, she slowly climbed the slope up from the stream, crossed the narrow trail, and entered the woods beyond, planning a wide meandering circle. Hoping above all that the Agocii chieftain would consider her unworthy of tracking.

***

Keeping his gaze on the path, Bel-Tygeon retreated deeper into the woods and sank down among golden fronds of bracken and coarse shrubs to hide and wait. Surely the young woman, Serena, would return soon with her talkative little brother.

Yet time grated by until Ty's legs ached from the stillness, and his stomach rumbled its want of food. Where were they?

At last, hearing a subdued rustle among the trees and bracken to his left, Ty turned. Serena and Ayden approached, both of them looking troubled and ashen, as if they'd suffered some crisis. The boy was actually clutching his sister's hand. More troubling, when Ty stood and offered the miniature bow and arrows, Ayden snagged them as if clutching for rescue.

Before Bel-Tygeon could frame a single word of concern, Serena pressed one slender finger to her lips, requesting his silence. Two braided leather cords dangled from her fingers. And three livid crimson scratches stood out on her thin left cheek. Ty motioned to the scratch marks and lifted his hands and eyebrows, questioning Serena silently. She shook her head and then led the way through the trees.

Bel-Tygeon matched her hushed yet quick pace and her vigilant glances as she crept over the forest's damp uneven carpet of fallen leaves, pine needles, and fading bracken. Golden sunlight touched Ty's face, and he tensed, glimpsing Serena's destination through the trees—a broad sweep of comparatively level open space far larger than the meadow he'd awakened in this morning. Numerous round fabric-padded dwellings such as he remembered from the Eosyth encampments at the siege of Parne dotted half of the pasture, while small herds grazed beyond.

An Eosyth encampment.

Infinite? Can this truly be the place You would have me go? To take shelter among people I've harassed and humiliated? Yet, if it must be so, I'll praise You...

While he prayed, Ty followed Serena and her brother toward the encampment's center, watching for the men she'd claimed would defend her. Instead, children's laughter, feminine chatter, and muffled rhythmic thuds echoed around him—warm, reassuring sounds.

Until they saw him. Clearly, his madman presence alarmed them all.

As one, the Eosyth women stopped their varied tasks of beating fabric, grinding grain, tending fires, and sorting a variety of foods. They studied Ty, undoubtedly trying to decide whether they'd help him or pull their daggers on him—and every adult female in the camp wore a dagger. Those weapons, and the women's heavy, practical leather and wool clothes, rich but sensible dark braids and their sharp bright gazes all informed Bel-Tygeon that he could not trifle with Eosyth women even if he'd cared to.

The encampment's youngest children—most ruddy-faced from playing—stopped their games and stared, wide-eyed, and suspicious. Unnerved, Ty offered them all a grin.

An older woman abandoned the roll of fabric she'd been beating and stood, arms crossed, displaying the club as a weapon. Her hair was the same dark red-tinged brown as Serena's, and her leather garments were edged with bold crimson embroideries. Her voice matched her attitude, stern and ready for trouble. "Is this our guest, Serena?"

Serena nodded. "He is. Aunt Betiya, everyone…this is Ty. As I said earlier, he's sane and civilized enough, for now—don't worry. Aunt, how is mother?"

"Resting. I didn't tell her about our guest."

Was Serena's mother so ill that she must be protected from disturbances such as stray madmen? Ty hated to ask. Moreover, Serena was speaking to Betiya. "Thank you, Aunt. I'll tell her soon. Before then, please, let's send someone to fetch the men, and while we're waiting, help me to tidy our guest's hair and beard. We need to turn him into an Eosyth. The madman must no longer exist—the Agocii want to kill him."

Bel-Tygeon stared at Serena. "How do you know that the Agocii intend to kill me?"

She met his gaze, admirably steady. "I know because they raided and cut my traps and snares, and then confronted me near the stream. They're seeking a demon-man who crossed their lands, frightened their families, and caused their cattle to stampede."

Betiya snorted. "If I were in an Agocii's herd—cattle or human— I'd run too. No demons needed! I'll send your cousins to ride down to the valley and find your lord-father."

She called to two boys, who were seated before a nearby tent, both busily punching awls through broad squares of leather. "Siyos! Iared! Forget the saddlemaking for now and ride down to the men. Ask your lord-uncle to return to the tents."

Still ashen, Ayden finally spoke. "The Agocii chieftain threatened to notch my tongue and feed it to me. And he scratched Serena."

Forgetting himself, Ty growled a half-prayer, half-threat. "May the Infinite strike the man as I was stricken!" He looked Serena and Ayden up and down. Apart from the livid scratches welting Serena's face, they seemed unhurt. "Any other wounds? Threats?"

Serena tilted her head, staring at him oddly. "No. But I've said enough." Turning, she called to the other women, "Who has a comb? And we need shears."

She retrieved a felted brown mat from a pale tent, unfurled it on a patch of grass, and then nodded to Ty. "Please sit."

"What was the chieftain's name?"

Serena huffed. "I don't know. We weren't introduced. *Sit.*"

Like a trained beast, Ty sat. Within a breath, the other women surrounded Ty, producing combs, cords, and a pair of gleaming round-backed iron shears that grated unnervingly as Serena snipped at his matted beard. Finished, she knelt behind Bel-Tygeon, to brave the appalling task of restoring order to his wildly knotted mane. After a few tentative snips with the shears, she murmured, "Aunt, what is *that?*"

Ty froze as Betiya leaned down, paused, then muttered, "Don't worry. It's dead."

"Of course it's dead." Serena gave Ty's hair another cautious snip with the shears. "Flattened as it is, I really couldn't tell what it was…"

A dead, flattened creature was buried in his hair? Ty's once-divine pride sank to a new low of mortification.

"Oh." Betiya whispered, "It's a field mouse. Cut it away and give it to me."

Bel-Tygeon's empty stomach knotted as Serena snipped away more of his hair. The spasm worsened as the intrepid Betiya swept past him and dropped a surprisingly small snarl of fur and hair into the nearest fire.

With the last tattered shreds of his former conceit.

Softly, he whispered to Serena, "I'm sorry."

She remained quiet, alternately combing and snipping at his hair. But at last, she murmured, "Things could be worse."

"I hope not." Trying to lighten her mood, he added, "But, please, don't tell me if you find any more flattened creatures in my hair—I must have saved them there for food."

Serena half-laughed, half-sobbed as if the morning had been too much to endure.

While she worked and the other women returned to their chores, Bel-Tygeon sat perfectly still and quiet, watching the youngest children play.

How good it must be to know nothing of the world. He'd been cruelly robbed of such childish joys at too early an age...

Young Ayden approached and sat beside him, bow and arrows abandoned. Drooping a little he said, "I think that Agocii chieftain wants to kill us."

So much for knowing nothing of the world.

Deliberately calm and self-assured—as if he could protect the child against the entire Agocii nation—Bel-Tygeon said, "We'll be sure he fails."

He must rid the Eosyths of his dangerous presence lest the Agocii attack. He needed weapons. Supplies. A horse.

Infinite, Mighty One, let me trust You to supply what I need to save our lives!

***

Nikaros, former captive of Belaal, and son of Levos, high-lord of the Eosyths, flinched and covered his eyes against the early light. A distant morning in the far-off mountains filled his vision, becoming reality. Bel-Tygeon, almost unrecognizable with a full beard and hair grown far past his shoulders, sat on a rustic mat, garbed in the heavy leather apparel of an Eosyth. Behind him a pale leather and fleece tent shone in the morning light, and he was talking to a gloomy little boy, also clad in warm Eosyth attire. The little boy was Ayden, son and heir of Tsir Andris, Lord of Clan Darom!

Ayden's small familiar face and the glimpse of the Eosyth tent woke Nikaros fully, though he didn't open his eyes. As the dream-sight faded, he begged silently, Infinite, let me step into that vision and live there! Let me take Araine and return to my people!

A wound, raw and unseen, abraded his heart, and his soul ached with what he'd lost, even as he rejoiced at what was gained. The king was alive and in familiar lands. Yet how could it possibly be true? "Infinite? Am I mistaken?"

His wife's voice, loving yet despondent, answered from the opposite side of their bedchamber. "You're not mistaken, my lord."

Alarmed by her mournful tone, Nik sat up in their bed and stared, temporarily setting aside the implications of his dream. "What's wrong?"

Araine, prophet and slave of Belaal, sat in a chair near a small stand of guttering lamps. Completely dressed for the day. Even her long, gold-streaked ash hair was perfect, softly pinned back, revealing her sweet lively face. She stood and carefully replaced one of her precious scrolls of sacred verses in its storage chest. "My love, if something is the Infinite's will, then it cannot be wrong, even if we fear it."

"What do you fear?"

"What I cannot see. And…what I can see."

Such a cryptic and prophet-like answer. Never mind. He'd draw the truth from her soon enough. Wondering, Nikaros touched her side of the bed. A chill met his fingertips. "Have you been awake all night?"

"Most of it. I've been praying and I didn't want to disturb you." She crossed the chamber and bent to kiss his bewhiskered cheek. Then she nodded toward a silver flask and a full silver cup near his side of the bed. "I brewed mint for you."

Slight tendrils of steam curled upward from the flask, indicating that the brewed mint—a traditional Eosyth beverage—was a perfect drinking temperature. Wary of her fine garments and gold filigree hair pins, Nik tugged Araine into his arms, cherishing her softness and her sweet spirit. "Thank you. I'm so predictable that you should be bored with me by now."

Araine laughed and hugged him. "Never! Your calm predictability is perfect, and I adore you!" She hugged him again and then scooted from the bed, mischief adding a sparkle to her clear blue eyes. "We're about to be summoned, by the way. You'd better don your sandals and fresh robes at once, and drink your brew."

Nikaros grinned and reached for the cup. "Thank you for the warning. What an advantage—to be married to the Infinite's own prophet." He sipped the brew, then dressed. Araine offered him his sword-belt, and Nik accepted it with a kiss to her soft lips. "I must make plans to retrieve the king as soon as it's safe—a covert scheme."

"You'll have to tell him that we're married."

By order of the king's sister—the Lady Dasarai. She'd been adamant and rightfully so.

As the Infinite's prophet to Belaal, Araine was a political danger to the infatuated Bel-Tygeon. Indeed, Bel-Tygeon's priests had already attempted kill Araine for practicing heresy within Belaal by worshiping the Infinite, instead of their god-king.

How long would Bel-Tygeon's infatuation have allowed him to tolerate Araine's rebellion against his god-king status? Not long. Indeed, Araine wouldn't have been Bel-Tygeon's only victim condemned to death for religious rebellion. Ultimately, Sulaanc's streets would have been stained crimson with the blood of the god-king's disbelievers—Nik's included.

Moreover, Araine's own misgivings had been verified by another renowned prophet, Ela of Parne. The Infinite had sent Ela to warn Araine and the king that Bel-Tygeon must never take Araine as a wife—not even as a lesser wife. His reign would not have survived their union.

Nik grimaced as he pinned his mantle. He must not delude himself: he and Araine might not survive their own royally-arranged union. Would Bel-Tygeon forgive them?

Araine crossed the chamber, sedate and beautiful, her sacred Prophet's branch in hand, its faded vinewood contours fragile— hiding its strength and hers. She paused at the chamber's door, her delicate hand hovering just above the latch, and she shot Nikaros a beguiling, rougish smile, imploring his silent complicity in her mischief. He grinned. An instant later, she flung open the door, calling, "Come in, Ebatenai! We're waiting for you!"

Ebatenai, Belaal's chief steward of the royal household, stumbled inside the chamber, his big hand moving downward with the strength of his disrupted knock. Straightening his portly frame, he huffed at Araine, his eunuch-high voice piping his not-quite-stern indignation. "Prophet! You've no need to be frightening me so—I'm getting too old for this! Lord Nikaros…" He cast a chiding glance at Nik. "Can you not control your wife?"

"No more than I can control our Creator. They're both untamed, I'm sorry, good sir." Nik grinned at the flustered royal steward. "Even so, we're ready. Where's the Lady Dasarai?"

"In her private garden." Mollified, Ebatenai bent and allowed Araine to kiss his round cheek in apology—doting on her like a fond relative. Straightening, he intoned thinly, "Our princess had a terrible dream last night…"

Araine tugged the eunuch's formal blue and gold mantle into tidier folds over his big shoulders, and then patted his arm. "At least *some* people in this household slept long enough to have dreams. Lead away, dear Ebatenai!"

Nik clasped his wife's free hand, and they followed the royal steward through one gold and blue corridor after another, until they reached the Women's Palace, a vast, eerily echoing sweep of rooms built to house the kings' unofficial royal wives.

Nikaros shivered as always when he entered this exquisite gilded and carved wing of the palace. A year ago, he would have been executed the instant he set foot here. But now the rooms were empty, for Bel-Tygeon had freed his unofficial wives, paid their dowries, and sent them all to their families or homes of their choosing. Only the Lady Dasarai resided here.

How could she endure the chilling, abysmal hush about this place?

The Lady Rethae Dasarai, solitary Princess of Belaal, waited in her garden, seated in her favorite cushioned chair, her stiff courtly robes glittering with embroidered gold vines and blue gemstone flowers— her hair piled high and pinned with countless gold filigreed birds and blossoms. She watched them approach and bow, her delicate oval face unmoving as a mask, though her dark eyes were wide, silently expressing her worry. When they'd knelt on the cushioned mats at her feet, Dasarai stared at Araine. "Prophet, I know you interpret dreams. What can you tell me of my dream last night? Where is my brother?"

"He's sheltered amid the Eosyths, lady. He was restored to sanity this morning. But your dreams were troubled for a reason …"

As Araine faltered, Nikaros added quietly, "Before waking, I saw him within the Clan Darom's main encampment. I assure you, Princess, that because he is their guest, they will protect him with their lives. Unfortunately, due to his circumstances, we cannot retrieve him immediately."

"Furthermore, lady…" Araine interposed, her usually light voice weighted with the Infinite's own warning, "Before we even attempt to rescue our lord-king, the Infinite warns that Belaal must prepare for war."

Chapter 4

Araine watched the Lady Dasarai's exquisite oval face drain of color, her fear becoming almost tangible. "What? Why will Belaal go to war?"

Araine paused, praying. *Infinite, though she doesn't trust You, grant the princess wisdom to heed Your warning!*

Feeling her beloved Creator's strength sweep about her like a mantle, Araine tightened her grip on the fragile grayed vinewood staff and willed the princess to not issue any hasty and irreversible commands. "Lady, I'm unsure. It could be Siyrsun, or the new ruler of Darzeq, or the Agocii."

"Those boors!" Belaal's princess shut her lustrous dark eyes, clearly seeking calm. "Belaal should never have become so dependent upon the Agocii for slaves and gold! They're not even loyal amongst themselves!"

The instant Dasarai opened her eyes, Araine continued, "Indeed, Lady. Either way, be it Siyrsun, Darzeq, or the Agocii, we'll face a threat by spring. To prevent an invasion, and to save the king, we must prepare Belaal's army within the next few months, while the Agocii are still hidden within their tents and valleys for the winter, hatching their schemes."

Dasarai clattered her formal gold-filigree fingernail shields together, her agitation visibly heightened. "Can we not rescue the king now?"

Nikaros shook his head. "In my dream I recognized the land itself. We are in autumn here, Lady, but from what I saw this morning, and from my own childhood in those mountains, I can tell you that snowstorms will soon descend upon the Eosyths. Within a few days—before we could ever hope to reach the king— the storms will isolate them in their central valleys. Because it's Eosyth tradition to protect all guests, they will prevail upon our lord-king to remain with them until it's safe to descend to the plains—which will be late spring for us."

Dasarai looked pained. "Such a long time…"

Araine sighed. "I understand, Lady, and I wish it weren't so. However, I prayed for our lord-king most of last night. The Infinite hasn't saved Bel-Tygeon of Belaal only to cast him directly into a tomb."

As the princess cut a sharp glance toward Araine, Nikaros straightened. "With regard to the Agocii and our former general, Siyrsun, we have the advantage of time. I'll alert the commanders to prepare our forces and I'll order supplies today. I'll also send notes to our contacts in Darzeq requesting information on their country's possible plans for invasion. Whomever our enemies might be, it's best to thwart their plans at the start. Otherwise, Belaal might be at war for years."

The Lady Dasarai flexed her gold-tipped fingers, claw-like. "You *will* keep me informed of all of Belaal's plans, Nikaros of the Eosyths. If you fail us and my lord-king dies, then there will be no mercy for you or the Infinite's prophet, despite all her prayers."

Araine suppressed a rebellious glare. Dasarai's severity was understandable—Bel-Tygeon was her only sibling, and the only living person she loved. Even so… How easily Belaal's princess had threatened one of her most trusted and honorable advisors, Nikaros, and her highest ranking female slave over some yet-to-exist catastrophe.

Araine matched her husband's bow of acknowledgement and forced herself to speak gently. "Believe us, Lady…it's the Infinite's wish and our own to bring good to Belaal and its king despite the coming troubles."

Dasarai waved a dismissive hand, her whole posture and attitude that of offended royalty. "The Infinite will have my regard when my lord-brother is safely returned to us! Until then, I warn you both that there will be no refuge for you anywhere if he is harmed because of your advice to delay. Now, go. Make your plans for his wellbeing, and then report to me again."

As they retreated from Dasarai's offended royal presence, Araine felt her husband's fingers entwining with her own, his grip protectively tight. The instant they were out of earshot, Nikaros muttered, "She had no need to threaten you! If I weren't pledged to serve the Infinite and my people as one of Belaal's officials, I'd snatch you up and we'd escape this place!"

Araine squeezed her husband's hand, loving his protectiveness and the warmth of his touch. "Dear lord-husband, I'm a mere slave who must serve the Infinite in Belaal for the rest of my life. The princess is worried."

"We're all worried." Nik halted and stared down at Araine, his forest-dark eyes deathly serious. "Will the Eosyths become involved in this conflict? Are my people in danger?"

She swallowed, hating to tell him. "Because the Eosyths turned to the Infinite at Parne and abandoned their mountain gods, the Agocii have sworn to spill rivers of Eosyth blood in this coming war."

"Infinite…" Nikaros allowed their Creator's Name to trail off in an anguished one-word prayer. He kissed her hand, and they departed the desolate Women's Palace in silence.

Why say what they both knew?

The first Eosyth clan to suffer attack would be Bel-Tygeon's refuge, Clan Darom.

***

Bel-Tygeon remained statue-still as Serena finally tied back his hair and murmured, "I think that will do. Aunt, what do you think?"

Seated nearby, Betiya unfurled the roll of leather she'd been clubbing, revealing a length of thick tawny-cream felt. Casting a brief glance at Ty, she nodded and returned to her work. "Yes, he might be mistaken for an Eosyth. As long as he doesn't speak."

Ty shrugged, easing his shoulders. "Maintaining silence will be easy. I've little to say." Indeed, what could he boast of? He currently had no kingdom, no queen, no heir, no wealth, nor even a cloak of his own. How swiftly life's burdens had returned after such a joyous dawn.

A small child's shrill wailing cut through the air. Serena exhaled. "Miyna!"

As she stood, twin russet-haired adolescent girls—one lugging a squirming, wailing toddler—rounded a nearby tent as if they couldn't hurry fast enough. Serena stretched out her arms for the unhappy child and cooed, "Miyna, you're just fine, I'm sure! Tell me—what happened?" The toddler pointed, then flapped her hands about like a distraught fledgling. Serena huffed and eyed the twins. "One day, I'll understand her. Until then, *talk* to me! Where have you three been?"

The twins exchanged glances and then one protested, light-voiced, "We've been doing whatever Miyna wants."

"And going wherever Miyna wants," the second added, her voice mirroring the first.

"I think she wants food." Serena's severity eased and she smiled at the toddler. "Let's feed you and then get some work done. First, however, I must set you down while I prepare the food and check on Mother. Miyna, visit with Kari and Tessi. Talk to them…"

She kissed the child and gently set her on the mat near the twins, who began to play a game, tossing tiny squared bones in the air. The toddler stared at their pastime, clearly interested, and Bel-Tygeon watched the child, his amusement turning wistful. She looked quite healthy with those big bright eyes, rosy cheeks and tiny dimples showing around her grimacing little mouth. Not to mention the droll spray of hair fluttering like dark red-glinted feathers atop her small head. A beautiful, cherished toddler.

Infinite? Will You ever bless me with such a child? Just one healthy child, and then I will be satisfied.

But first, he must find his queen. Did she even exist?

The tiny girl reached for the twins' gaming pieces, but the girls blocked her chubby hands with their own hand-flutters, clearly conveying rebuke. Ty could almost read their silent language. No, Miyna. Wait… Stop!

Evidently unwilling to merely watch their game, the toddler pitched herself onto the mat and wailed at the top of her lungs.

Such an appalling temper for such a tiny body! And such a powerful voice. How could the others just ignore her? When Miyna hit an ear-stabbing pitch, Ty lifted her off the mat, held her at arm's length and growled teasingly, "What is all this noise? Explain yourself! Talk to me." She finally hushed, stared, then poked a small finger at his face and answered with a series of flaps, twitches, and punching motions.

Unable to translate, Ty pretended to snarl and bite toward her fingers instead, and then he grinned. The toddler chortled and poked toward his nose. He feigned another growl and snapped his teeth audibly. The child laughed, her small body shaking with hilarity.

Ayden whooped, finally regaining his spirit. "Bite her! She's such a pest!"

"No, young sir. Imagine her screaming redoubled."

Confusion played over Ayden's small face. "Redoubled?"

"Twice as much," Ty explained.

"That would be bad," Ayden agreed.

"Indeed. Furthermore, she's just as likely to bite me, and I fear she'd draw blood." He grinned at Miyna. "Wouldn't you? Charming little savage! Talk to me. Clearly you've much to say."

Miyna beamed. And mucous trickled from both of her small nostrils. Ty froze, appalled. Shouldn't that ooze be wiped off before it reached her mouth? Just as Bel-Tygeon prepared to voice his concern, Serena emerged from the tent, carrying a heavily-laden tray. She placed her burden in the center of the mat, swept the toddler from Ty's hands, and flung him a skeptical look. "Thank you, Ty."

After checking over the toddler, Serena snatched a rough, tattered-looking swatch of fabric from the tray, pinched the dual globs of mucous from beneath the Miyna's nostrils, and then folded the begrimed swatch and tucked it beneath Miyna's small chin.

Directly after handling the mucous-tainted fabric, Serena offered Ty a round of coarse flatbread. "We have meat, dried fruit, and some curds. What would you like to eat?"

Bel-Tygeon forced down his revulsion. He'd eat nothing.

Not a single curd.

Serena stared at him, waiting, wide-eyed as Miyna. Slowly, his empty stomach churning, Ty braved a bite of the bread.

***

By the end of their modest meal, Ty had managed to swallow enough food to avoid offending Serena, and she returned to the tent with the tray. Miyna—thankfully scrubbed clean—dozed in a small heap of fleece as the twins and Ayden busied themselves picking pale nuts from the centers of smashed pine cones.

A scarlet hawk screeched from the nearby woods. The other women and children chattered and worked around Ty until several Eosyth horsemen entered the encampment. Without exception, the women and children stood—surely in tribute to their lord, Tsir Andris.

Bel-Tygeon stood, as did the twins and Ayden, who appeared expectant and eager to greet their father. The lead horseman halted his dark, shaggy-haired horse directly beside the mat and dismounted easily, despite his formidable array of weapons—a long curved sickle sword slung over his back, a broad dagger, a round wood and bronze shield slung from his saddle, and a finely worked bow with arrows so perfect that Ty longed to steal them for archery practice.

Clan Darom's lord, tall, lean, and bronzed, smiled at his children, particularly at Ayden, who snatched the horse's reins from his father's hand and led the beast to a patch of reasonably thick grass.

Watching the little boy stand guard near the horse, Bel-Tygeon paused, musing. Not quite three years ago, he'd given orders for the capture of certain Eosyth hostages, namely the eldest son of each

Eosyth lord. Ayden was Tsir Andris's only son. The boy would have been about four or five when the hostages were taken. Why hadn't he been brought to Sulaanc with the other three Eosyth heirs?

Nikaros, son of High Lord Levos, had never breathed a word of the boy's existence. Yet Nikaros had pledged to always tell Bel-Tygeon the truth in everything. While it was most likely a good thing the boy hadn't been brought to Sulaanc, this omission compelled Bel-Tygeon to ponder Nik's character. What else had the man been hiding?

Shaking off his suspicion, Ty looked directly at Tsir Andris, who'd turned to greet him.

The Eosyth lord's eyes widened as if startled. Ty braced himself, ready to be denounced and attacked. Surely Tsir Andris had recognized Belaal's fallen king—Bel-Tygeon had once spoken directly to the gathered Eosyth lords at Parne. They'd been quarreling with the Agocii and remained separated from the central encampments. Their willful isolation had contributed to Belaal's humiliation during the siege.

Tsir Andris studied Ty intently and then his expression eased, revealing a quirk of humor. "Our wanderer. Welcome. You look much better than when I saw you last. How are you feeling?"

Ty exhaled, releasing much of his tension. Infinite, thank You. "I feel like a burden to you, my lord. Thank you for your concern."

Tsir Andris shook his head. "No. You're not a burden—we consider visitors as blessings. To care for the defenseless...I'm convinced it is the Infinite's will."

Another twist of fear unraveled in Ty's soul. Smiling at the mention of their Creator, he briefly bowed his head. "Whatever the Infinite's will, I'll praise Him."

Now the Eosyth lord grinned. "Then we're doubly blessed. What's your name?"

"Ty." He shouldn't have told Serena his true childhood name. It was too close to his formal name. However, the matter couldn't be undone now. "Thank you for the welcome, my lord. How I ended up here, I don't know...."

His words trailed off as Serena emerged from the tent, her lovely face tensed with apparent distress. She motioned at the twins and whispered, "Run for Aunt Betiya!"

The instant they fled, she turned to Tsir Andris. "My lord-father, thank you for coming."

He nodded, his lean tanned face grave. "What's happened?"

Serena untied the two leather cords from her belt and handed them to Tsir Andris. "The Agocii cut my snares this morning and they raided and ruined my fish traps. They're in our lands, searching for our guest, and one of their chieftains told me to tell you that the Agocii will no longer endure insults from the Eosyths, because we betrayed them at Parne and then abandoned Utzaii. You're warned to guard your lands and belongings."

Tsir Andris's mouth tightened and he clenched the cords in his fist. "What did this chieftain look like?"

"Tall." Serena clipped her words as if they were as unpleasant to say as Ty's hair had been unpleasant to groom. "Big enough to survive countless fights. Dark brown beard. Filled with kill markers."

Her father shook his head. "That could describe several I know of. How many warriors?"

"I counted six. As I said, they were seeking our guest to kill him."

"Then they'll have a battle. Is your mother inside her tent?"

"Yes, my lord. But…" Serena bit her lip, composed herself, then said, "She's having pains. I've sent the twins for Aunt Betiya."

The Eosyth lord winced. "Does your mother know I've returned? May I speak with her?"

"Yes, Father. She's waiting for you."

Tsir Andris hurried to the tent, ducking as he stepped over the threshold. As Serena checked the sleeping Miyna, Ty asked, "Forgive me, but what did you mean—that your mother is having pains?"

Serena paused, clearly mastering her emotions. But tears glistened in her eyes. "My lady-mother fears she's miscarrying a child." To the other women, she called out, "Prepare to decamp! We must move at once."

What? Ty stopped Serena as she reached for the small heap of pine nuts gathered by her siblings. "How can you possibly order the camp moved? If your lady-mother's in danger of—"

She lifted her eyebrows, seeming astonished by his protest. "Your life's in danger. If the Agocii are preparing for battle, then we're *all* in danger, including my lady-mother and the baby. She ordered this move. Do you think the Agocii will have pity on her condition? I promise you they won't! Therefore, we're traveling to a place even Agocii warriors fear."

Chapter 5

Bel-Tygeon frowned at Serena. "A place even Agocii warriors fear? How can such a place be safe, much less livable for an encampment of women and children?"

Impertinent as Araine, Serena flashed Ty a taunting look. Brisk, she packed away the pine nuts, then stood and began to unwind the lacings around the tent's entryway. "You'll have to trust us on that, won't you?"

The twins returned with Betiya, who entered the tent as the twins began to help Serena unfasten the tent's outermost lacings. Soon after, Tsir Andris emerged from the tent, his expression controlled and still—a protective mask Bel-Tygeon recognized all too well, having worn a similar expression to hide his most intense emotions throughout his life. Distress haunted Tsir Andris, betraying its presence in his silence and distant gaze.

And Ty himself had caused much of the Eosyth lord's sorrow. Ty bowed his head, accepting the role of guilty underling. "Tsir Andris, perhaps it would be for the best if I leave." But what would be his nearest destination that didn't require him to traverse Agocii lands? Parne? Or perhaps he could cut across the plains and then through Siphra—though he had enemies there as well. "How far are we from Parne?"

"Too far for you to make it there safely. But why go? Parne's a poisoned ruin haunted by scalns and serpents. And look at those mountains."

As Ty studied the majestic cliffs and peaks in the distance—all dusted with snow, Tsir Andris said, "The snowline's lower this morning. By the ache in my shoulder, the next storm will arrive within a day or two. Even if we supply you with a horse and weapons, and even if the Agocii don't find you first, you won't be out of our lands by then. You cannot survive one of our blizzards without a good shelter—surely you know this."

He knew now.

"Stay and help us," Tsir Andris urged. "Your blood is upon us if we don't return you safely to your home—which most likely cannot happen until spring—and certainly not before the Agocii have retreated from our lands."

"Until then, I'll be a burden to you all. A danger."

"The danger's less if you appear to be an Eosyth. How can I pray to the Infinite in peace if you die? Please, stay and help us." Tsir Andris narrowed his dark eyes, studying Ty intently. "What is your usual work among your people?"

Judging by that question, surely Tsir Andris suspected something. Yet the question must be answered. What was his most elemental skill as king? Bel-Tygeon grimaced. "I'm usually an administrator. But I'm also a trained soldier. I can fight. Swords, javelins, daggers, arrows—"

"Then stay and help us. I'll give you weapons and a horse. However…" The Eosyth lord eyed Serena and the twins, who were swiftly untying segments of the tent's pale, felted covering. "I must warn you to respect my wife and daughters, as well as the other women. Or else you won't survive—and I won't be the one to attack you, trust me. The women will. Even so, I request your word, on your honor."

"As I live, I'll honor your request," Bel-Tygeon pledged, meaning every syllable. Yet another new experience. Had he ever, from birth, been within another household and bound by their rules? Not that he remembered.

Much less ordered to respect and honor others, excepting his parents and sister.

Beneath his breath, Tsir Andris said, "Good. Wait here. I'll find a horse and weapons for you. If you know how to fight, then you can help us if the Agocii attack as we retreat."

Bel-Tygeon nodded, and pleaded in silence. *Infinite, help us as only You can.*

After Tsir Andris hurried off, Ty watched as the three girls tugged away their tent's outermost covering and rolled and tied the pale felt rectangles—neatly sidestepping the napping Miyna.

A woman crept from the diminishing tent, wan yet lovely with high cheekbones, big eyes and neatly braided hair all so like Serena's that she could only be Tsir Andris's wife. She nodded to Ty, but then turned away as Betiya emerged from the tent, scolding. "Adelia, at least sit down. The girls are perfectly capable of packing."

Her voice as smooth and in-command as her daughter's, Adelia nodded. "I know they are. Don't worry about me, Bet—see to your own tent."

"Don't worry?" Betiya huffed. "Tell clouds to not rain. Now, be a good little sister. *Sit*, and then I'll go."

Adelia drew her full robes about herself regally and knelt on the mat near Miyna. But she cast a glance at Betiya that scolded even as she obeyed. "There. Are you satisfied?"

Yet as Adelia spoke, Ty saw her tense, exhale, then draw in a long, controlled breath. Betiya reached for her, but Adelia lifted a gentle staying hand. Gradually, her tension eased and she said, "Please don't fuss, Bet. Just hurry. If we can leave before midday, we'll reach the lower camps and safety by nightfall. I'm sure we have time."

"You know I'll hurry. But if the journey becomes too much—"

"I'll be miserable wherever we are, Bet, so let's continue."

"Of course." Betiya pressed a hand to her sister's shoulder and then hurried away, calling orders to her adolescent sons who were already dismantling their own brown tent.

Adelia glanced at Bel-Tygeon. "I'm sorry that your welcome has been so hectic. Have you eaten?"

"Yes, Lady. Thank you." Remembering Tsir Andris's request, Ty bowed his head. "Please rest and don't trouble yourself on my account. Your children have been excellent hosts. Very well-trained."

"Thank you." Adelia gave him a thoughtful smile as lovely as Serena's, and then cautiously scooped the dozing Miyna into her arms. "My children are lovesome—especially when a certain child is sleeping."

As they waited in silence, Adelia gently checked Miyna's garments and then rocked her. Ty watched the Eosyth women and children swiftly dismantle their huge tents. Outer layers of leather and heavy felt were opened, revealing two central posts encircled by fence-like latticework, crowned with sloping, spoke-like wooden rods which were fitted into a peaked central hub and formed the tent's roof—all bound by cordage.

The girls arranged the coverings, posts, compressed latticework, and rods into orderly piles, which they then fastened onto the stocky, shaggy horses, or into carts now being led into the camp by the men. Most of the women, Serena included, were also fastening quivers of arrows and curved ready-strung bows from their high-built saddles. Ty blinked. Did Eosyth women fight alongside the men?

With the tents packed and the fires doused, each woman placed her family's larger items—kettles, carved wooden storage chests, and bags of grain into a series of two-wheeled horse-drawn carts that were evidently shared by the entire camp. Finished with the larger items, the women piled bundles of leather, fleece, garments, and foods onto the sturdy horses and into the carts, and then crowned these heaps with clattering utensils, assorted leather bags and, intriguingly, drums, harps and carved ram's horns. One cart's uppermost contents caught and held Bel-Tygeon's gaze.

Woven cages, containing birds—gray birds with crimson talons and dark-barred wings.

Courier birds! Ty almost said the words aloud. Were any of those birds trained to return to some town in nearby Siphra or even Darzeq? If so, was there a chance he might be able to relay a message to his sister in Sulaanc?

Would it be safe to relay a message to Rethae in Sulaanc?

A man rode up beside the cart and checked the birds with an air of familiarity that proclaimed the winged creatures as his. Seeming satisfied, he guided his horse toward Serena, who paused beside one of the carts and nodded politely, clearly eager to continue her packing. In the composed pleasant tones of a woman with nothing to hide, Serena asked, "Detzios, did you have a question?"

"Yes. I've heard about the Agocii. Are you well? Those marks on your face—"

Serena betrayed the slightest flicker of impatience, but her voice remained even. "Mere scratches, and I've cleansed them. I'm fine—thank you for asking."

He hesitated. "And…the madman?"

"He's sane and peaceable enough. See?" Serena extended one hand toward Ty.

Detzios turned and lifted an eyebrow, surveying Bel-Tygeon as one would a filthy dog.

Ty suppressed a growl. Doubtless he must forget sending messages by way of a courier bird. He managed a smile and inclined his head toward the man with proper courtesy. Inwardly, however, he bristled. Ridiculous, of course. He was behaving as if he had a right to resent Detzios. In reality, as a guest, he had no rights here at all.

Exhaling a deep, ragged sigh, Adelia stood cautiously, hugging Miyna as the twins rolled up the felted mat. Despite obviously her discomfort, she glanced from Serena to Detzios. Every bit the attentive mother, she said, "We're well enough, Detzios. Thank you for your concern."

Detzios nodded, bowed his head toward Adelia, and then turned his horse away.

Adelia motioned to Serena. "I'll need help settling onto my horse with Miyna."

"I'm here, Mother." Serena gave Adelia a tender hug, but her thin face tensed with anxiety. "Just tell me how you want to proceed—I don't want to add to your pain."

Watching Adelia hesitate, noting the strain etched between her eyebrows and at the corners of her tight-pressed lips, Ty loathed himself. He, not Serena, was responsible for adding to her pain with his uninvited presence.

Tsir Andris approached, leading a stocky shaggy horse over to Ty. A quiver of arrows was slung over the horse's high-built leather saddle, and a plain but well-polished bow rested at an angle aligned with the horse's left side. "Here. The bow is my second, but it's excellent wood—yew from the north. As for this horse, he's strong, calm, and familiar with the trails. You'll have to carry some of our household gear on our journey."

A horse and weapons.... Ty grinned. He still needed supplies of his own, and heavier garments to face the coming storms, but this was a start. "Thank you, my lord." Quietly, he added, "I'm sorry to cause you and your family such misery."

Casting a melancholy glance at his wife, Tsir Andris sighed. "Today would be a worrisome day for us no matter what else might happen. Don't blame yourself. My wife's thoughts and mine are all toward leading our people to safety. Including you."

"Thank you. Then, I'll hurry. What's the proper Eosyth way to lash gear onto a horse?"

If he must become an Eosyth, then he ought to learn quickly.

Ty copied Tsir Andris's packing methods and the Eosyth lord grunted his approval as Ty cinched the last knot. "That will do well enough—better than some I've seen." As Bel-Tygeon mounted his loaned horse, Tsir Andris turned and called to Serena, "Are we ready?"

"I'll double-check, my lord." Serena finished wrestling the squirming Miyna into a carrying pack on Adelia's horse and gave the toddler a bread-scrap.

Somber, she then walked up to the front of the procession and circled back, eyeing all the horses and their riders and loaded carts as well as the trampled encampment site. The twins straightened on their shared horse as Serena passed.

Like a soldier reporting for duty, Serena halted beside her mother's horse, where her father also waited. "All's ready. The boys have gone ahead with the herds and the camp is cleared."

Her parents nodded and Adelia said, "Thank you."

Tsir Andris kissed Adelia's hand, then retreated to his own horse and Ayden, who reluctantly handed over the horse's reins to Tsir Andris.

Evidently satisfied with her inspection, Serena swung herself onto a waiting horse and then motioned Ayden toward her. "Hurry—we're waiting on you."

Ayden protested, "But I want my own horse!"

Clearly unmoved by her brother's bid for independence, Serena reached down for him, her braid swinging with the motion. "You'll have to wrestle Ty for it later—he's riding our last horse."

Did last mean least? Even so, Bel-Tygeon grinned at Ayden. The boy huffed and accepted Serena's help onto her horse. Several young men—including Detzios—trailed behind Ty, ostensibly guarding their procession, but sending a tremor of unease down Ty's back. Each of the young men carried at least a dagger, and several wore swords strapped at their sides. Others boasted feather-garnished javelins, and all had bows and abundant arrows. He hoped they intended to protect their guest according to their traditions.

They rode single file toward the pasture's western slope, which led downward into a narrow shrub-edged trail overlooked by formations of red rock spires to their left, interspersed by rugged inclines of sparse grasses and stones to their right.

As the descent steepened and the spires to the left and right blended into cliffs and jagged overhangs, the young men following Ty traded harsh whispers. "Agocii! Look up to the left! Isn't that Sea-Boor? Set your arrows!"

Sea-Boor? Bel-Tygeon tensed. Did they mean Cziybor? "Infinite…"

Trusting his horse to know the trail, Bel-Tygeon dropped the reins, lifted the bow and grabbed a fistful of arrows. Within a breath, he set the first arrow's nock into the bowstring and held the remaining arrows Eosyth-style, curved within his left hand while he gripped the bow—as he'd practiced for months with Nikaros.

Prepared to defend his hosts, Bel-Tygeon looked over his left shoulder and up at the Agocii warriors who surveyed them from a stone ledge.

Directly at their chieftain, Cziybor.

The craggy, stocky Cziybor stared down at him with all the hostile arrogance Bel-Tygeon remembered from Parne.

The Agocii chieftain had been one of Bel-Tygeon's allies in the siege against Parne, though not a welcomed ally. Ty had sent General Siyrsun to deal with him most of the time and Siyrsun's men brought disturbing reports of the Agocii warlord's activities. Cziybor enjoyed planning and inflicting intricate cruelties on enemies and lawbreakers. Physical and emotional cruelties that exceeded ordinary battle tactics or cold-eyed legal justice.

Rarely did Cziybor grant mercy.

Sweat prickled over Ty's skin as he imagined himself chopped apart, joint by joint. Beneath his breath, he whispered, "Infinite!"

Let Cziybor be duped. Don't allow him to recognize me...

Chapter 6

The Agocii chieftain and his six warriors stood along the ledge, their weapons readied, but not set. Cziybor stared at Ty, unblinking, clearly judging his potential willingness to fight.

Ty narrowed his gaze and allowed himself a subtle sneer at his former ally. To look away or to flinch in the least would call down Agocii scorn and further attention, marking him as weak—an easy target in a future battle. Moreover, he'd never glared or sneered at Cziybor in the past, nor had he worn a flowing beard, to Cziybor's erstwhile disgust.

Infinite, let Cziybor perceive me as an Eosyth. Let my beard and ordinary attire disguise me....

Cziybor turned his head, scanning this branch of Clan Darom as it proceeded along the trail. While the chieftain stared, his warriors gradually eased their stances, lowering their javelins and bows by the merest hair. Ty kept his gaze fixed on the man. Was Cziybor counting everyone in Tsir Andris's tribe?

Behind Ty, one of the younger men muttered, "We are too many for them."

"Only for now," Bel-Tygeon answered.

Detzios huffed. "They're afraid of our women *and* our madman."

Do not react, Ty warned himself.

He lowered his bow. As his view of Cziybor and his warriors was finally blocked by another ledge at a turn in the trail, Bel-Tygeon faced forward again, easing his shoulders. Ahead of him, Ayden continued to look up at the ledges, his young face strained. No wonder the boy had been so intimidated. Cziybor himself had threatened to cut Ayden's tongue. As for Serena, Ty's esteem for her courage, already considerable, soared. She'd faced one of the most fearsome Agocii chieftains and dealt with the aftermath effectively. Infinite, I beg You, shield her in the coming conflict! Protect Clan Darom!

Ayden nudged at Serena, obviously informing her that the Agocii warriors had vanished from view. She looked over her shoulder to eye the cliff, her profile a marvelous blend of feminine grace and strength.

Her anxious expression eased visibly, but she turned to check upon the riders following her—and caught him staring. Ty smiled and gave her the slightest admiring nod.

Her eyes widened, and she looked away first.

Now, Detzios spoke again, his mocking words carrying clearly. "*Madman*, you pretended well—handling your weapons like an Eosyth."

Was that a compliment or resentment? Ty raised an eyebrow and gave the man a pitiless stare he reserved only for unrepentant miscreants awaiting his verdict in Belaal's throne room. "Thanks to the Infinite, I'm no longer a madman. My name is Ty. As for my handling of weapons…I give you my word that I've practiced. If you doubt my abilities, test me."

Detzios grinned. Several of the young men guffawed. But some looked at him anew, clearly trying to recall if they'd seen him before. Bel-Tygeon gave them a determined-yet-courteous smile and faced forward again.

Had he given away his identity? Would they confront him?

He re-gathered his horse's reins, determined to avoid further suspicion. He must help these people to thwart Cziybor's coming attack—for knowing Cziybor as he unfortunately did, Ty knew the Agocii warlord planned to strike Tsir Andris's people.

When?

He must talk with Tsir Andris.

***

Serena exhaled, trying to collect her scattered thoughts. How infuriating that Ty should smile at her so brazenly! He was almost rude. Almost.

Well. If he didn't know quite how to behave, at least she did. She must ignore him and remain dignified. She adjusted her horse's reins, then her toe-holds in the saddle's stirrups, the leather creaking and the horse's ears flicking in reaction to her movements.

Ahead of her, Mother briefly lowered her head, then straightened, rubbing her back. Still in pain. Would she truly lose the baby? Please, no. She'd miscarried once before Ayden, and once before Miyna. They'd mourned as Mother's songs were silenced within the tent. Must they face such sorrow again?

Let her keep this child!

Serena repeated the plea over and over within herself, to no one.

***

Seated on embroidered cushions before her low writing table, with sunlight slanting down over her work from her chamber's high windows, Araine dipped her ivory writing stylus into a fat little rock crystal inkwell and copied the next verse from her aged Books of the Infinite onto a fresh parchment. Through each verse, she held her breath and wrote the words with exacting, excruciating care.

If she made the least mistake…one dot too many, then she must scrape the blotch to spotless perfection or burn the parchment. Without crying over wasted time and ink, she hoped.

As soon as she finished this copy of the Infinite's sacred verses, she would hand it over to other scribes, who'd pledged to faithfully copy every single dot, bar, and character of each verse. Afterward, they would send copies to the faithful throughout Belaal.

A daunting task—frightful, even—yet she cherished each ancient, golden verse. Her favorite verse was still the first she'd ever read. … *you are forever in My sight, precious and honored, because I love you.…*

She smiled, seeing the words in her thoughts, golden, flowing and alive. Beautiful enough to turn her giddy. "Infinite, how could I live without You?"

A thud resounded at the door. Araine jumped. Panicked, she lifted her stylus from the parchment and checked the verse for damage. None. She exhaled and set the stylus in a tray. Weren't her attendants able to lift the door's latch? Araine stood and hurried toward the door. "Jemma? Inae? Come in."

The door opened and a woman entered, throwing back her lavender veil to reveal a lovely face, flawless skin, large dark eyes accentuated with cosmetics, and glossy black curls, perfectly tended. Bel-Tygeon's former favorite, Zaria. She smiled, unusually tentative. "Prophet. I trust you've not forgotten me."

Could anyone afford to forget an enemy? "I've not forgotten you, Zaria. Please be seated." She motioned to floor cushion. Zaria wouldn't be able to attack her easily while seated. Araine returned Zaria's cautious smile and then settled herself more than an arm's length away, eyeing her guest.

Infinite, advise me, please. Why is she here?

Memories of Zaria paraded through Araine's thoughts. Ever prideful. Bejeweled and spoiled. Empty of everything but her overwhelming ambition to become Belaal's queen. Not a servant. Never a servant to minister to Belaal's king and people.

Infinite? What would have happened if...?

His tone that of a Father comprehending her thought before she formed it, He murmured, *Ask her.*

Gently, Araine voiced the question. "Zaria, what would you have done if you had become queen? Once you'd gained the crown, what then?"

Zaria blinked, then widened her eyes. "What should I have done? Don't you mean, what will I do? I'll enjoy my place as queen. I'll be above all other women, and I'll do as I please. Not even the Lady Dasarai will interfere with me then."

"Does the Lady Dasarai know that you're here today?"

"Of course not." Zaria flexed her fingers and eyed her flawlessly-tended nails. "I still have influence here, you know."

Obviously. But what sort of influence? And with whom? Araine stared down at her own short ink-stained nails. "Why are you visiting me?"

Pleating her veil in demure folds, Zaria smiled. "I've heard that the king will return. I want to know when."

"Interesting that you're so well informed. We've just heard this news ourselves."

"I do have a few friends within these walls." Zaria shook out the veil's folds and her smile faded as she mocked, "Why are you so uninformed...for a prophet?"

Because she hadn't asked her Creator. Araine held her stare toward Zaria, but asked silently, Infinite, will Bel-Tygeon take back Zaria? What will happen?

A warning current of images swept into Araine's thoughts, warning her, and halting her questions. The Infinite whispered, *Does she believe I have changed? She will destroy herself if she continues to do as she wishes.*

Evidently taking Araine's listening silence for acquiescence, Zaria continued, "I've been living respectably and quietly while biding my time. You cannot criticize my behavior."

"I wasn't criticizing. You questioned me, and now I'm answering—and it's a kindness. In fact, it's sincere *love* to tell you that the Infinite is concerned by your behavior as much as your pretenses. He warns you, Zaria, that He hasn't changed, nor will your situation."

A small muscle twitched near Zaria's left eye. Gently, Araine continued, "Consider my own situation. I've been married to Lord Nikaros for a year, yet I've no child. Neither will you. This palace remains a barren place, Zaria, and you will never be its queen. If you try, you will destroy yourself."

Zaria's delicate nostrils flared. "Others disagree. And they'll help me in any way possible."

"Including conspiring yet again to kill me?" Araine watched closely as she asked the question. Something flickered over Zaria's face. Zaria's memory of conspiring with Belaal's priests, perhaps. Followed by their written collusion with the traitor General Siyrsun. Offenses she'd never fully confessed—not even to herself.

Araine stood. "Your conspiracies placed the king's life in danger, therefore the Lady Dasarai regards you as an enemy. You won't escape notice today, so you'd best leave now before she learns that you're here."

Zaria stood, but she tensed, aggressive as a dog scenting prey. "When will the king return?"

"When the Infinite wills his return. Ask your informants."

Her lips tight with compressed rage, Zaria swept the veil around herself once more and, garments rustling, she flounced from Araine's chamber.

No doubt to complain to her current informer.

Sighing, Araine pressed her hands to her face and paced through the chamber. Too tired to write, but too distraught to rest while she waited for the Jemma. After a time, a familiar tap sounded on the door. Bracing herself, Araine called out, "Jemma, come in."

The maidservant entered, her arms heaped with snowy folded linens. She kicked the door shut and flung Araine a pert smile. "Really, I must change my way of tapping on your door."

Controlling her voice, Araine added, "And you must cease to be an informant in everyone's pay. In this case, I'm referring to Zaria. You're one of the few people who knew I was still here this afternoon."

Jemma's usually lively face stilled and turned ashen. But just as quickly, she mustered her defense. "Zaria threatened me. You know how she is! She—"

"If such a thing happens again, Jemma, come to me. Tell me. Also, if you need money…"

The maidservant lifted her chin. "If you must know the truth, yes. I need money. I want to buy my freedom if such a thing is possible. Would you help me?"

"Jemma, I'm also a slave."

Jemma blinked as if she'd forgotten that little fact. Araine offered her a weary smile, adding, "I wish I weren't, but this is my situation. Yet true freedom begins in the heart and the soul. Even if you are freed, you'll carry your spirit of discontent with you."

"You're wrong. I'll be perfectly happy."

"Doing what? Jemma, you can't possibly—"

Her heart is like flint, the Infinite chided. *She will not listen.*

Infinite, thank You. Araine drooped, surrendering. "I'll ask Ebatenai if there's a set price for you. Meanwhile, for your own safety, be patient and don't give in to Zaria's bribes. By taking her money you help her cause. Or rather, her destruction."

"Then I'll enjoy a double gain. My freedom and her ruin." Jemma dropped the linens onto the nearest storage chest and flitted from the room as if she'd gained a victory.

Stomach knotting, Araine stood. To replace the linens, to pray, and to meet with Ebatenai

Infinite, why am I so distressed? Why is my soul so fretful when I should be rejoicing today? Thank you for protecting the king. Please, calm my fears, I beg you…

***

Throughout their gradual descent to an interior valley, Bel-Tygeon felt watched, as if the Agocii continued their stealthy pursuit. Obviously, the entire group shared his fears. Like Ty, all the adults kept their weapons readied. And with the exception of the youngest children and the bleating herds of goats and sheep, everyone in the procession had remained hushed for most of the journey.

At last, amid approaching dusk, the clan's mood eased. They entered an autumn-misted meadow rimmed by a mixed forest and they set up their encampment so swiftly that Bel-Tygeon blinked. It seemed that one instant he was unloading carts and walking horses to their grazing areas and the next he saw tents standing draped with their heavy wool and leather coverings. The women laughed and called to each other as they carried their bricks, grates, and three-footed portable iron ovens inside, then gathered wood and kindling to burn within their central hearths.

As plumes of smoke drifted upward from the tents' crests, Ty helped Tsir Andris and Ayden peg down the last few ropes to tether the grazing horses. Finished, he straightened. In adjoining fields, farther upslope, youngsters were goading the sheep and goats into stone-walled enclosures, which they roofed with coarse, lightly-entwined bundles of uprooted shrubs. Throughout the encampment, family members were calling to each other, and laughter echoed here and there between the tents—a marked change in the clan's mood.

Ty asked Tsir Andris, "Why do you and your people feel safe here? What is it about this place that makes you certain the Agocii won't pursue you?"

Tsir Andris straightened and ruffled Ayden's dark hair as the little boy leaned against him. "This valley is where we Eosyths have traditionally mourned our dead. Each year, for generations we've hidden in these hills and wailed our laments for those who've departed. Generations of Agocii have heard the songs' echoes and fear for their souls if they dare approach. Even their warriors halt at the borders of this valley, leaving us in peace. Tomorrow, we'll go up to the caves and you'll understand."

"Tomorrow?" Ayden echoed. He grinned and stifled a small whoop of celebration. "Can we take food with us?"

"That's your sister's decision—she's managing the supplies." Tsir Andris nodded to the young men who were building a fire and preparing for the night's watch, telling them, "I'll return later."

He led Ty and Ayden to the large, pale tent in the encampment's center. But instead of simply stepping inside, Tsir Andris rapped sharply on the carved door frame. "Does our guest have your permission to enter?"

"Yes, and welcome," Serena called back, ceremonial and dutiful, if not exactly overjoyed. The Eosyth lord nodded at Ty, stepped over the threshold, shook one of several leather bags hanging near the door, and then explained, "These are goat milk curds. By shaking them, you will help mix some of our winter food supplies."

"I'll gladly help in whatever way I can." Copying Tsir Andris's motions, Bel-Tygeon stepped over the threshold and shook the second bag, which sloshed thickly, near-quenching his appetite. Inside the tent, the twins were playing with Miyna, who was giggling and bright-eyed—clearly pleased to be freed from her carrier.

Near the hearth, in the low, flickering, gently-snapping firelight, Serena rolled out thin rounds of dough and slapped them onto the flat surface of a portable, three-legged iron oven. The dough rounds swiftly puffed and Serena flipped them using the edge of a dagger. She nodded to her father, her voice lowered, mournful. "Mother's outside walking with Aunt Betiya. She won't eat with us tonight— she asked us to remain here."

Had the Lady Adelia's condition worsened? As Ty blamed himself yet again, Tsir Andris exhaled, scooped Miyna into his arms and then sat down on the mats. "While we wait for the food, we'll pray."

Ty sat with his host and bowed his head as Tsir Andris prayed. And prayed. For his people, his wife, his children—including the unborn child. For a dear one named Tiphera. And…resting a hand on Bel-Tygeon's shoulder, the Eosyth lord prayed, "We thank You for our guest. We beg Your ceaseless protection as a shield about him! May he be blessed by his time among us as if he were cherished by his own family."

Lifting his hand once more, he added, "Mighty One, Creator, we continue our prayers for the safety of Nikaros, son of Levos, and health and wisdom for Belaal's king that he will deal with Nikaros— and us—fairly and with continued mercy."

Ty held his breath, incredulous. They'd been praying for him ever since he'd ordered the hostages taken? —Nikaros among them?

Guilt dropped over Bel-Tygeon like a sodden, smothering cloak.

He deserved no prayers. He—a fool-god-king—had heaped hardships on these people. He was to blame for their losses. Their privation of the previous two years, with the loss of all their gold and revenues. The need to move this morning. The Lady Adelia's additional sufferings. And the coming battle with the Agocii. All these things were his fault.

Infinite? You are more than fair. I was not. I deserve my fate... being here among these people.

Whatever its cost to me, let Your perfect justice be served.

Chapter 7

In the pre-dawn darkness, Serena placed the tray beside her mother's pallet and bent to kiss her and hug her tight. "Mother, I'm so sorry!"

Though she couldn't see her mother's face, Serena felt Adelia shake with silent sobs, as tears dampened her cheek. "It was a boy," Adelia whispered. "Another Ayden!" Unable to continue, Adelia wept and held Serena close.

At last, when Adelia's grip eased, Serena straightened and rubbed a hand over her tear-streaked face. She must control herself. Mother was depending upon her. She squeezed Adelia's hand. "I love you! Call for me—I'll be preparing the morning meal. I'll bring you some food." She would bring the last two preserved eggs simmered in broth, served with fresh bread.

Adelia sniffled moistly. "I'll recover eventually. Your aunt will check on me today, you *know* she will. So…" She smoothed Serena's hair. "Take your brother and sisters up to the caves this morning and…think of the baby. Cry the Lament for him."

"I will." If she didn't break down and cry for their loss. Serena's throat burned. Silent, she kissed her mother's wet face and then stumbled from her section of the tent. Miyna stirred on Serena's pallet and then sat up, doubtless soaked. Serena scooped up her toddler-sister, coverlets and all, hugging her tight, swaying, grieving for the baby brother she'd never held.

***

Emerging from a dreamless sleep, Bel-Tygeon opened his eyes. The tent's interior, softly lit by hearth-light, surprised him yet again with its spaciousness and comfort. Particularly when he glimpsed Serena swaying gently, lulling the bright-eyed Miyna with tender, broken humming. A charming formless lullaby to match the tranquil scene.

Ty shut his eyes briefly, feeling like an intruder. However, the sight of Serena cuddling little Miyna was too beguiling to ignore, and he studied the sisters through his lashes. Infinite? Will I ever wake to see my wife, my queen, holding our child?

The sight would be worth all of Belaal.

Nearby, Ayden sat up, blinking, his hair wild. He looked around, then scrambled from beneath his coverlets, clearly pleased it was morning. "Are we going up to the caves today?"

Serena knelt nearby and set down Miyna. Her voice low and controlled, she said, "Yes. After morning chores."

Ayden frowned at her. "Why are you crying?"

Was she crying? Ty propped himself on one elbow and stared. Serena swallowed visibly and busied herself with cleaning Miyna. "Mother miscarried last night. The baby's gone. We…must be quiet today."

Ayden's frown deepened, revealing his confusion. But sobs lifted from the twins' shadowed portion of the tent. One of the twins piped up, her tone a whimper. "Was it a girl?"

Serena swiped fresh tears and sniffled as she tended Miyna. "The baby was a boy."

Both girls covered their faces with their hands, sobs redoubling. Ayden froze, then wailed, "I wanted a brother!"

Ty hastily retreated from the tent.

***

"Come with us." Tsir Andris beckoned Ty from where he was brushing the family's horses—another new accomplishment he'd acquired from watching the other men during chores. Low-voiced,

Tsir Andris added, "You should see the caves and pray with us as we mourn our losses. Today's and this past year's. It's tradition."

"I'll follow, my lord." Ty bowed his head and then gave the horse a final swipe and a promise. "I'll return to you later. Don't roll in the dirt!"

Tsir Andris strode ahead, calling to the others. A number of men and women emerged from the tents, shouldering scuffed leather bags. Detzios followed Tsir Andris. Ty readied himself mentally for the man's hostility, but Detzios ignored him, staring ahead. As Tsir Andris passed his family's tent, the twins emerged, carrying heavy leather bags, their steps quick, their eyes still reddened.

Serena followed the girls, carrying Miyna in a sling on one hip and a leather bag of supplies over her opposite shoulder. The girls walked silently. Even Miyna caught their mood and regarded Ty solemnly from the confines of her leather sling, her brown-green eyes wide.

Only Ayden seemed somewhat recovered from his mourning. The little boy fell into step with Ty and looked up at him. "Serena packed bread and cheese."

Bread and cheese? In Sulaanc, the royal cook would have been flung in prison for serving him those two stark ingredients. Now, however, Ty's stomach growled and his mouth watered in anticipation. Choosing small terse ordinary words, he said, "Sounds good."

He walked with the others to the base of a nearby cliff and then halted. Tsir Andris and the other men were crawling down a slide of gravel and dried leaves that tunneled beneath an archway of rock barely higher than his knees. His knees! Ty fought misgivings. Should he crawl through that child-sized fleapit? No!

Bel-Tygeon was about to say the word aloud. But Serena and the other women were waiting for him to move. He snorted. "Who was the first madman to crawl down there?"

Her voice beautifully controlled and sardonic, Serena asked, "Don't you trust us?"

He surrendered and knelt, grateful for his heavy leather tunic and leggings. A short gravel-jabbing crawl beneath the arch led him into a cavern. Into a different world. Ty gaped at the series of high, natural stone chambers that apparently followed the crests of the cliffs above. Here and there, thin beams of light shone down into the cave, illuminating the floor, granting life to a section of cave below. Leggy shrubs and autumn-gold deciduous trees flourished here in contrast to the evergreens beyond this cave. Though the trees looked bizarre, their tall thin trunks mostly bare, crowned with flourishes of golden leaves at their crests that stretched for the light high above. Contrasting with this broad patch of foliage, the high stone walls stretched in broad, unyielding lines, striated in water-like patterns that almost dizzied Ty.

Serena and the other women were crawling beneath the low entrance arch, handing the smallest children through to each other. Then, while Tsir Andris and the other men hacked dried shrubs from the fringes of the concealed wilderness, Serena cleared an evidently ancient, much-used stone hearth that had been carved into the cave's floor. Her movements assured, she struck flint and stone into a lightly nested handful of dried grass and kindled a tiny fire, blowing into the grass nest to encourage the flames. A useful skill Ty didn't yet possess. And its lack would have doomed him on any solitary journey.

Infinite, how right You were to keep me here! I've so much yet to learn….

"Ty, look!" Ayden nudged Bel-Tygeon and lifted one small hand, showing Ty a bug. Pale, shimmering, it curled up tight in the boy's palm, resting there like a pearl.

A colorless woodlouse? Ty grinned. He'd loved playing with the insects as a child, but hadn't thought of them for years. "I've never seen a clear one before. Are there more?"

"Yes, over here." Ayden lifted a rock in the shadows beyond the fire pit. "My lord-father said it's the darkness here that makes them pale."

"No doubt he's right." Bel-Tygeon crouched beside him, marveling at the bugs' almost iridescent gleam in the firelight, and toying with them until Serena called to him and Ayden.

"It's time to pray and eat." She offered Ty flatbread topped with melting cheese, accompanied by handfuls of dried fruit and pine nuts.

Some of the younger men were already eating dried fruit and spitting the pits into the shadows—a skill Ty hadn't mastered. His cooks had never dared to serve him fruit with pits for fear he'd choke and they would suffer his sister's wrath. Furthermore, Rethae forbade spitting.

Ty saved the fruit and ate only the bread, cheese, and pine nuts— preferable to explaining his ineptitude at spitting. However, he ought to learn. If she saw him, Rethae would pretend to faint. Or swat him with her fan.

Which brought up one of Ty's earliest god-king conundrums.

A perfect god wouldn't need disciplining and certainly wouldn't tolerate an older sister's fan-swats. Ty had struggled with this perplexity as a child and finally dismissed it for the sake of his own sanity, which was another puzzlement altogether. A true god wouldn't suffer insanity.

Tsir Andris led the prayers, and Ty winced inwardly again at the guilt-inducing mention of Nikaros and of Belaal's king.

A god-king fool!

To his sister, he thought, *Rethae, we were wrong to unquestioningly accept my role as Belaal's god. The siege of Parne would have cured me... if it weren't for my pride.*

Ty shuddered remembering his Creator's power displayed before Parne's broken walls, that mighty fist-like storm of wind-hammered rocks and sand, upswept by the Infinite. He'd refused to acknowledge the Infinite at the time, but he'd known the truth. That instant in Parne had been the first true fissure in the stonework of his god-king status, and deepened his unadmitted hard-fought reservations concerning his supposed divine nature. In truth, he'd concealed many doubts.

Insufferable statesmen never vanished when he willed them to be gone. True happiness never appeared when he'd longed for it. And despite all his power and his desire to see justice done, villains thrived in his kingdom while the weak suffered, even as his own selfish nature often hindered matters.

Furthermore, he'd been bound by *mortal* laws and legal codes. Yet Rethae had proclaimed the rightness of abiding by mortal laws and reaching to mortals on their own terms to win their hearts, while Ty—as a teenager—would have preferred to bash more than a few miscreants who'd failed to win him on his own terms.

Fool. He'd known.

Subdued laughter scattered his self-recriminations and brought him back into the present, in the cavern. Around him, the Eosyths were visiting. Talking. Grateful they'd escaped the Agocii. Pleased with the harvest. Praying for the herds to thrive and replenish themselves this year. Ty listened to their talk and dutifully ate every morsel of food offered to him.

The twins began to hum during the meal, odd considering their grief. And yet the humming matched their thin, solemn faces— sweet, melancholy notes, amazingly fluid and harmonized.

Serena, rocking Miyna, added her lullaby-hum to theirs, her tones full and rich, warm, yet endlessly mournful as if through them she expressed grief for her mother and baby brother. At last, one of the twins leaned over and plucked at Serena's sleeve, and Tsir Andris nodded to them. "Go ahead. This year, you lead the Lament."

"Yes, Father." But Serena looked away, as if she'd rather be anywhere else. The twins hopped up and scurried off. Serena followed them slowly, adjusting Miyna in her carrying sling. They walked toward a recessed area within the huge cavern, where Ty could just glimpse their faces amid the shadows. There, Serena lifted her voice, the humming lullaby now a vibrant, mesmerizing croon that echoed through the cavern and stole Ty's breath with its sheer enchantment.

Serena's dirge needed no words. Tender, melting notes merged into a sorrowful keening that gained power with her every breath. Despite himself, Ty leaned forward, watching Serena's shadowed form. Such an astonishing voice! Strong, controlled, with a range worthy of the best in Belaal—and he'd heard and rewarded the best with gold and royal patronage. Serena surely ranked among Belaal's finest soloists.

Strengthening her mourner's tones, Serena stopped swaying, took another breath, and sent her unaccompanied notes soaring toward the cavern's roof. Ty shivered as her wordless hymn lifted from mourning to anguish, filling the entire cavern with her expressively fluid wail. Her song's final breath spiraled upward, conveying excruciating torment—a piercing death-cry that lifted every hair on Ty's scalp.

In Serena's arms, Miyna squawked, clearly frightened, and several onlookers exhaled as if they'd been holding their collective breaths. Bel-Tygeon exhaled as well. Any Agocii warriors who'd ever climbed the cliffs above and heard such wailing death cries would presume these cliffs and caves were haunted by murderous spirits.

The twins picked up Serena's wordless dirge, their young voices full of promise, though Ty doubted they'd ever match Serena. If she had appeared in his court, he would have granted her true wealth. If she'd been one of his own slaves, he would have taken her as an unofficial wife.

No. Ty abandoned that thought the instant it crossed his mind. He'd pledged to honor this young woman and her family. He must never touch her nor think of her as he had the women in his palace. However…. He leaned toward Tsir Andris and whispered, "Her singing is the most amazing I've ever heard."

Clan Darom's lord grunted. "She has the lungs for it. Just like Miyna."

But Tsir Andris's eyes shone in the firelight, revealing a father's quiet pride, which changed to despondency—reflecting unspoken grief for the child he'd lost.

***

Moving softly past her sleeping family, Serena carried the tray beyond the heavy curtain, into Mother's section of the tent. Surprisingly, Adelia was seated on her pallet and wearing her outer cloak for the first time in ten days. She gave Serena a tiny smile and whispered, "I'm feeling better. I believe I'll move about outside today. How is our guest?"

"I don't know. He's not awake yet." Which was perfect, because the instant Ty opened his eyes and crawled out of his pallet, he was too captivating for Serena's own good. She must rein in her besotted foolishness because Mother would notice Serena's fascination with their guest. And Mother would be rightly concerned.

Even now, after several weeks, they knew little of the man except that he hadn't coat nor colt to his name—and that was only part of Serena's unease. She set down the tray and whispered the thoughts that had been troubling her. "Mother, I'm convinced that Ty's *someone*. He has to be. He's very intelligent, but he hasn't a clue about ordinary life. At mealtimes, he handles food like a fussy woman, and he stares at every new task as if he's never worked before—though he does learn quickly. It's as if nothing ordinary has ever been demanded of him."

Adelia pursed her lips delicately. "So...what are you asking of me?"

"Only watch him, please. Tell me if I'm wrong. Ayden said that Ty spits like a little girl—or he did last week. What sort of man doesn't spit? Outside the tent, I mean. He's not...ordinary."

"I'll watch him," Adelia murmured, though she looked amused. "But first I'll eat. I'm hungry this morning."

"It's about time." Serena kissed her mother and crept out into the main area of the tent. Father snored in the far side of the tent near Ayden. Kari and Tessi were just stirring. Miyna squirmed, whimpering. Ty coughed in his sleep. A remarkably rough cough. Was he ill? She eyed his shadowed form.

Seeming upset by Ty's cough, Miyna sat up in Serena's pallet and gave Serena a pitiful, spotty-faced look as she motioned her irritation using the twins' silent language. No wonder she was unhappy; those blisters looked miserable. Did Miyna have the milk-pox? Serena touched Miyna's blistered face. The poor baby was definitely warm.

Ah, well... Serena sighed. She'd tended Ayden with his pox three years past. She could manage Miyna. She hoped.

Ty coughed again, turned onto his back and lifted one long hand to his red-blotched face. Serena stared at his blistered cheek and groaned, "Oh-no!"

***

Bel-Tygeon opened his eyes to find Serena staring at him. The sight would have been lovely, but she seemed horrified. And he felt as if he'd lost a battle with a venomous scaln. He touched his face, its blistered, itching roughness quickening his heartbeat with agitation. The last time he'd been stricken with such blisters, he'd nearly died. He cast a worried glance at Serena and when he spoke, his voice rasped from his raw throat. "What's this? Do I have a rash?"

Serena knelt beside him and huffed, "*How* could you not have had milk-pox before your baby teeth fell out?"

"What are you talking about?"

"This." Serena plopped Miyna beside his pallet and the tiny girl wrinkled her sweet blister-splotched face at him. "You have milk-pox, both of you."

"I have milk-pox?" Ty studied Miyna's inflamed liquid-filled blisters and recoiled. "Ugh! No wonder I feel awful. Are you certain it's not fatal?"

"Of course it's not fatal—we've all had milk-pox. Though it's certainly uncomfortable." Serena pursed her beautiful lips and then asked a dangerous question. "Weren't you around other children while growing up?"

He gave her the only possible answer. "Not much."

Actually, the only children he'd been allowed to associate with were those who didn't cough, spit, possess runny noses, or scheme outrageous mischief—and who were gifted with perfect manners and practiced absolute obedience toward a certain fledgling god-king.

In other words, he'd been denied association with the entire race known as children. Lack of scheming outrageous mischief had been his most appalling loss, not to mention simple joyous companionship while hunting for hapless woodlice in his secluded royal wilderness.

Serena sighed. "Well, since you two are sharing the same sickness, will you guard Miyna for me while I prepare some broth for you both?"

"Yes." Even if he had to wipe Miyna's splotchy, runny nose. Miyna sneezed daintily, then drooped against Ty's arm and coughed. Next, she'd be wiping her nose on his sleeve.

Ty winced, resigned to his own blistered, runny-nosed fate.

***

Ty drew a deep waking breath and opened his eyes to humid mineral-scented dimness. For the first time in almost two weeks, he felt rested and able to breathe freely—a blessing wrought by the steam tent ordered by Serena and her mother, his lovely and fretful dictators.

Alarmed by his cough, they'd dug a small pit in the soil beneath the tent's far side, lashed together a slender sapling frame, covered the structure with layers of felt, and then coerced Bel-Tygeon inside, just before they poured water over heated firestones in the pit beside his enclosed pallet. He'd been convinced he would smother, until he realized his cough had eased and that a slight current of fresh cool air seeped in beneath the steam tent. He'd slept soundly.

Shaking off his languor and cautious of the now-cooled pit, Ty lifted the frame and crept from beneath it to find the twins absorbed in their usual morning game of knucklebones.

Adelia nodded to him from beside the small central oven. Ayden was dressing—until Miyna hauled at his long red sash and chortled when her brother tugged it away. "Miyna, stop!"

Ty grinned at him. "At least she's laughing." And she, stalwart child, had recovered from the milk-pox far more quickly than had Belaal's king. Rueful, Ty donned his felted foot coverings and then his boots. As he grabbed his heavy new fleece coat, Bel-Tygeon eyed its seams. Sure enough, Serena and her mother had added more sinew stitches and crimson felted edgings. Ty bowed toward Adelia with just the right amount of respect. "Thank you, Lady."

"Of course, you are welcome." She waved him off with self-depreciating grace and then snatched up Miyna and kissed her. "Let's feed you, little mischief-maker!"

Ayden tucked in the crumpled end of his belt, then eyed Ty. "Are you going to the trench?"

"Yes, and then I'll take a walk before we eat." Ty ducked through the entryway and braced himself at the chill, amazed as always at the Eosyth tents' effectiveness at closing out frigid winter air. Snow and ice laced the ground, and a frozen path traced the way to the men's waste trench at the edge of the encampment. Ayden hurried past him with an almost brotherly shove. Ty groused, "You're in a hurry."

"I'm hungry!"

Wary of aggravating his cough, Ty followed at a more leisurely pace, going through the men's morning ritual of visiting the trench, then briefly scrubbing near the watch-fire. Finished, he caught up with Ayden, who was scanning the encampment. "Well, young sir, let's move along with the morning inspections!"

As they walked down the encampment's eastern edge, Ty caught sight of a small gold object half-sunken into another man's icy boot-stomped footpath. He bent and picked it up and sucked in a sharp breath that sent him into a coughing fit. An Agocii warrior's gold kill band—unmistakably the sort flaunted by the ruling chieftains as beard markers.

Here…in this supposedly safe valley.

Sucking in a hoarse breath, Ty rasped, "Ayden, hurry! We need to find your lord-father."

Chapter 8

Her breath rising cloud-like in the frosty air, Serena lifted her meagerly-moistened wooden milk pail and nudged past the inquisitive, winter-shaggy does to scoot from the goat pen. She lashed the gate, counted the goats again, and then looked around, baffled. How had the yearling escaped? None of the woven fencing was dislodged or worn—she'd mended it the day after their arrival. The pen's covered area of wattle and brambles rested undisturbed. If the creature had become separated from the herd, it would be bawling loud enough to—

Serena stopped, her booted feet sinking into a small drift as she stared at the tracks. A man's tracks by the size of his boot's wide imprints. The singular trail led up to the very edge of the pen's covered area, where the tracks skidded and blurred as if the man had briefly slid and struggled to maintain a foothold.

While stealing a healthy yearling goat?

Serena's heartbeat thudded at a runner's pace. She anchored her pail in a snow drift near the pen and then rushed down to the paddocks where Father usually finished his morning rounds. Father was indeed there, standing beside the stone and timber fence with a number of other men, including Ty and Ayden. Truly, something must be wrong. The men were all death-somber and staring at an object in Ty's outstretched hand. As she approached, Serena heard Ty say, "It must be Cziybor."

Father straightened, and his eyes narrowed. "How do you know Cziybor?"

Ty's handsomely-bearded face tensed, faintly sneering. "Let's just say that I've had the misfortune to deal with the man while he was tormenting others. Of all the Agocii I've met, Cziybor is the most brazen and malicious. The question now is, do we search for him or leave the valley for fear that he's planning an attack?"

"We take up weapons and we search," Father said. "If it appears that the thief has departed from our lands, then we remain here until the next gathering. If we catch sight of other Agocii, we'll depart today."

"Father," Serena interposed, "One of my yearlings is missing. It looks as if she was lifted from the pen, and she was not a tiny creature. I can show you the tracks if you'd like."

Tsir Andris nodded and rested a hand on the dagger secured within his wide belt. "Yes, I want to see them. Also, Ty, show me where you found the gold. Perhaps we'll find more indicators of our Agocii visitor's identity. Meanwhile—" Father lifted his voice. "Everyone!—whatever happens, we'll increase the night watches. No one should leave camp alone."

Standing at Tsir Andris's left, Detzios said, "I'll send word to our kindred tribes, and to the northern clans, that the Agocii are spying upon us, and we request that our kindred use care if they visit. Do you wish to add anything, my lord?"

"Thank you, Detzios, yes. I send my greetings to the others. Tell them that we look forward to seeing them again." To all the men, he added, "Tell everyone what we've found, and that a yearling was taken from Serena's milking pen. All the animals should be counted and guarded with additional care. We'll keep watch over each pen for the next few nights."

As the men dispersed, Ty muttered to Serena, "That does *not* include you, Lady."

His tone was so overbearing. As if he had a right to command her. Serena snorted. "What doesn't include me?"

"Keeping watch over your goats at night—that duty will be mine. You've lost enough sleep tending invalids for the past few weeks."

As if she had no choice in guarding her own property? The herd was vital for adding her share to her family's food supply. She faced

Ty toe-to-toe and stared up at him, willing him to back away. "I'm fine, but you're sounding too controlling for a guest."

"Yes. Brutish of me, isn't it? You'd think I'm a monster." He allowed her a grin at his own irony, and his smile was anything but monstrous. She couldn't think of another Eosyth man half so good-looking. Serious again, Ty continued, "Think of me as an exceedingly concerned...older brother. If our spy is Cziybor, as I fear, then he's liable to repay you for defying him during your last encounter—for which I blame myself. My own failings have produced this Agocii menace which is now arrayed against you."

"That's taking a mighty portion of credit for the situation, isn't it?

"Not if it's true—and it is—so pay heed, Lady, as any wise leader would."

His stern tone and commanding glance strengthened her certainty that he was *someone*. She could envision him in elaborate lowlander's garb. Bright and lordly robes that proclaimed his authority as he rode through his lands—with all the women avidly watching his progress, their hearts foolishly aflutter as hers was now.

Foolishness or not, she would not allow him to command her. He must honor her place in Clan Darom. One day she would be an Eosyth clan's ruling lady, like Mother and, perhaps, her older sister, Tiphera. All the more reason to resist admiring the man.

Ty was *someone*, and he would ultimately leave Clan Darom.

Stabbed by a pang at the loss she hadn't yet suffered, Serena affected a gracious nod toward their guest. Father approached, and she smiled, hoping she appeared unruffled. "Thank you for being concerned, Ty. I'll remember what you've said. Meanwhile, may I see that gold?"

Ty lifted and opened one hand—an almost perfect hand—and revealed the rather chunky gold band resting in his palm. A kill marker, embossed exactly like the ones she'd seen in Cziybor's awful beard. The very sight of the band riled Serena's memories and set her stomach churning. "Yes. That looks like one of his markers."

"Which is why you must be careful, Lady. Undoubtedly Cziybor hasn't forgotten you—it's no coincidence that one of your goats was taken, believe me."

He sounded worried. As if he cared for her in a more-than-brotherly way. Was she imagining Ty's unspoken affection? Serena nodded again. Before she could muster more polite words, Father said, "Ty, show me where you found that thing. We'll scour the area. If he's anywhere near, I want him caught."

Ty nodded. "Certainly, my lord."

But Serena glimpsed a flicker in his dark eyes, and a brief twist of his lips that revealed his true opinion. Cziybor wouldn't be captured. Instead, the mighty Agocii chieftain would hunt the Eosyths. And she, a proud and disrespectful female, was one of his targets.

As was the madman, Ty.

Serena's entire being fluttered its distress, and she scowled at herself. She *would* become infatuated with a madman—a stranger who'd arrived without coat nor colt of his own. Even if he was fine-looking and beloved to her most secret heart, she was stupid to think of him. She'd made her plans, and it would not do to upset her entire future for a someone who'd ultimately leave Clan Darom.

She wouldn't be such a fool.

***

Masking his royal longing to grab Serena and coerce her to obey him, Bel-Tygeon followed Tsir Andris to show him where he'd found Cziybor's battle token. Undoubtedly this bit of gold had been hacked from one of Cziybor's victim's beards, for the Agocii gloried in defacing their kills.

For all her courage, Serena must practice caution and forget her pride. He could tell her about ruinous pride.

A small, cold hand clasped his wrist. Ty looked down at Ayden—he'd almost forgotten the boy. "What are you thinking, Ayden?"

The little boy's face was altogether too pinched and fretful. He hesitated, clearly working up courage for his question. "If Cziybor finds me, will he cut out my tongue?"

Cziybor might do worse if he could get away with it. Ty scowled. "If Cziybor comes near you or your family, I'll kill him."

Or willingly die trying. Ty smoothed his expression, but frowned inwardly, evaluating his feelings. When had Tsir Andris's family become so critical to him? Such a vulnerable, vital part of his soul? This likeable boy was much the son Ty had ever longed for. As for Serena...

Ty didn't dare look at her while they hiked through the heavy snow. He wanted to surround Serena with a fortress and an army of servants and guards. He wanted to kill Cziybor for her sake.

Infinite...my Creator...do I love her?

Love would certainly answer his current war of emotions. Not even Araine, for all her beauty and impertinent sweetness, had so captivated him. How would Serena react if she knew that Belaal's king was mesmerized by her very glance? Elated by her laughter? And so contented in her presence that he couldn't bear to think of losing her?

If she were wise, she'd run.

But then he'd chase her...his love.

Catching his breath at the thought, Ty jostled Ayden. Playfulness would shake off his own gnawing worries and some of the little boy's fear. "When we've scoured the camp and searched for Cziybor, we'll practice at archery—with your lord-father's permission, of course."

"Of course," Tsir Andris agreed, his tone thoughtful as he shot Ty a glance from beneath his black eyebrows.

Did Clan Darom's leader finally suspect who he was sheltering? The tall, solemn Eosyth lord betrayed nothing. Truly, he was as adept at concealing his thoughts as anyone in Belaal's courts.

Ty crushed down his own emotions as he returned with the others to the tent for their bows and arrows. Whatever happened, he was indebted to Tsir Andris and Clan Darom for protecting him so diligently. He'd repay them with his life if need be.

Before they left the tent, Ty held up the chunk of Agocii gold. "Let this be Cziybor's compensation for the goat he stole and because he threatened Serena and Ayden."

Tsir Andris studied him for a long instant, and then nodded. "We'll have their Uncle Zeddi put that accursed gold through fire and hammer it into pendants. I'll consider the gold as legal repayment to my children. Come, let's search for any signs of the Agocii."

* * *

His bow and arrows readied, Ty followed Tsir Andris and Serena as they cautiously entered the narrow cave near the cliff's crest. A thick, stomach-curdling death stench assailed Ty, making him grit his teeth and hold his breath. Tsir Andris lowered his sickle sword and crouched beside a dead hearth. He nudged at the charred wood and growled an echoing opinion. "If it was Cziybor, then this is where he stayed. But he's long gone—the hearth's cold. He must have allowed himself one fire each night to stay warm. Whoever stayed here, he's an animal, living in this cave with those rotted remains of his kills. Yet even Cziybor wouldn't brave winter here alone, trapped and knowing we'd discover him eventually."

"If he's gone for now, then I'm grateful." Ty retreated to the path again. As he sucked in untainted air, Tsir Andris and Serena joined him.

Softly, Serena said, "He was so close. Perhaps for weeks—spying upon us."

Her distress made Ty long to embrace her. To protect her forever. Instead, he urged the Eosyth lord, "Tsir Andris, let me help keep watch each night—we must be vigilant. Perhaps even consider a strategic retreat to unite with your kindred clans. Would the northern tribes join forces with you?"

"They would. Moreover, the other clan lords'll be here at the first sign of spring. Until then, we will be vigilant as you say. But now that I'm certain he's gone, we must begin our winter's work."

"Which is?"

Tsir Andris affected a wry frown. "How are you with a hammer and chisel and breathing dirt all winter while you guard against starving cave-dwellers?"

Standing behind her lord-father, Serena widened her eyes as if Tsir Andris had gone insane. Ty could only presume he'd just been challenged to a winter's worth of work. He hid a smile at Serena's protectiveness and nodded to the Eosyth lord. "Show me what to do."

Chapter 9

The beasts emerged from a green-black sea, immortal giants, their colors garish beneath sullen storm clouds lit by lightning. A golden-winged aeryon, a crimson-hued scaln, a black lindorm, and a crested blue dreki, all arrayed against Araine as an undying army—until the scaln raked the wings from the aeryon, then viciously turned upon it, eating the aeryon alive. The lindorm joined the feast, but the scaln savaged the giant serpent, tearing it to bloody shreds. Yet the scaln finally weakened as the dreki grew, its darkening claws becoming mighty talons, its teeth like rows of merciless blue azurnite blades, glinting as the beast turned its bloodied gaze toward Araine, and the souls sheltered within her care.

Araine leaned against her writing table and covered her eyes with her hands, drawing in deep breaths of warm gently humid springtime air. "Infinite, bless You! Let me ever serve You… But what does this dream mean?"

The vision faded, and unbidden unwelcomed memories opened within her thoughts. So real that she sprawled, almost feeling her father tightening the ligature around her throat as he wept. She struggled to breathe—and fought to save the Books of the Infinite from destruction. "Infinite no!" Hands gripped her shoulders and she struggled against her noble accuser, Corban Thaenfall. Betrayer! Murderer… "Infinite!"

"Araine!" Nikaros held her now. But his embrace was too similar to Corban's possessive grasp. Araine flung off his arm and sat up straight.

"Infinite, why am I reliving this again?"

Nikaros leaned over Araine and rubbed her back gently, as if she were a frightened child, his handsome face tensed with worry, the love. "Araine, what's wrong?"

"I'm unsure." She stared into her waking vision as it shifted, revealing death. Innocent victims in Darzeq—a massacre she'd predicted to the disbelief of a Darzeq prince. For his skepticism, the royal family of Darzeq was all but destroyed.

Araine put a hand to her throat, trying to breathe without weeping. Why was she seeing this carnage again? The massacre was almost two years past.

Silent, Araine pleaded, Infinite…? How was Corban involved with the massacre?

Hearing His answer, Araine leaned into her husband's arms and wept. As he smoothed her hair and held her, she pleaded, "Pray for me! The Infinite commands me to speak to Corban once more."

His voice tight with protective disapproval, Nikaros said, "I'll go with you. When?"

"I don't know." Never, she wished. A futile desire indeed. And… she must go alone.

***

Holding the prophet's branch, and clad in her finest gold and blue tunic and mantle, Araine bowed, ready to follow the Lady Dasarai from the Women's Palace out to Belaal's throne room. But the great lady—resplendent in golden robes and a blue-jeweled tiara—lifted a hand, her gold-shielded fingernails gleaming in the light. "Araine, you've been crying. Are you ill?"

"I'm distressed, Lady. I've received troubling news. Soon, I must face the nobleman who killed my grandfather."

A flick of surprise crossed Dasarai's exquisite features. "The noble Thaenfall who sought your death? Is he coming to Belaal from Siphra?"

"Lady, I don't know where he is, but our Creator warned me in a vision that I must speak to him."

"One hopes the man will not incite chaos within Belaal." Dasarai tapped her gilded palm fan against Araine's sleeve. "I won't be merciful toward him, even if Siphra's king should send a plea for clemency."

"If he visits Sulaanc at all, Lady."

"If he doesn't appear in Sulaanc, then you cannot possibly speak with him," the princess murmured. "Therefore this matter is of no consequence."

"As you say, Lady." But did the Infinite agree? Araine followed Belaal's princess into the long, gloomy main corridor of the Women's Palace, and through the enclosed formal central garden to the palace entrance. There, four eunuchs waited, guarding two golden carrying-chairs to transport Dasarai and Araine to the throne room. Araine settled into her chair and leaned against the branch, praying. "Infinite? If I must speak to Corban...." She halted mid-thought.

Did she expect to make demands of her Creator? She started again. *Infinite, what are Your thoughts toward Corban—and his toward You, that I must speak with him?*

He is my own child, whom I love.

A knot tightened in Araine's stomach. Remembering her grandfather's crumpled body, his death-stare, she swallowed. The Infinite loved the man who'd killed her dear Grumps.

Loved him!

Was she supposed to fathom such a mystery? *Infinite, grant me Your understanding. Can I forgive a man who's caused me such torment?*

Did he not rebel against Me and wound Me by killing My beloved child?

Grumps... Araine sniffled. Infinite regarded Grumps as His beloved child. Corban too. Nausea welled, and Araine mentally pushed away the vision.

His voice the merest thread amid her thoughts, the Infinite asked in gentle rebuke, *Are you My servant?*

Yes. But obviously some things were beyond her mortal abilities. "I pray You grant me strength." She pulled the branch closer, praying fiercely until the eunuch-porters halted before the throne room's entrance.

Nikaros was waiting, and he clasped her hand before she set foot from the chair. Low-voiced, his forest-dark eyes troubled, he asked, "How are you?"

"Better. I hope." Changing the subject, she eyed the gilded rectangular case beneath his arm. "What do you have there? It must be important if you're guarding it personally."

He smiled, setting her heartbeat a-skitter with his appealing warmth. "You'll see, Prophet."

Blaring trumpets within the throne room announced the beginning of the royal audience. Araine rested one hand on her husband's arm and they followed the princess and her attendants through the throne room, crossing the glorious crystal-starburst floor, and then bowing before the lowest step at the gold throne's base. Dasarai ascended the first broad step and sat upon a cushioned bench.

In deference to her absent brother, she never set foot on the higher steps, but no one doubted her authority. Guards—investigated and chosen by Nikaros for their loyalty to the king—flanked the throne, their bronze and blue shields and weapons glinting dangerously in the sunlight that streamed from the windows far above. A respectful hush fell over the throne room.

Dignitaries approached the throne one after another, bowing to Dasarai and offering gifts and flattering words to Belaal, which the princess accepted on behalf of Bel-Tygeon. The ambassador from Darzeq was particularly effusive and held his bow longer than any others—the showy humility of a man seeking favors for his nation. When he finally stood and retreated, the ambassador slipped into the ranks of visitors, but Araine felt his gaze. She cast an oblique glance over her right shoulder and the ambassador's eyebrows lifted, silently questioning her.

What did the man wish to ask? Darzeq had become an accursed place within less than two years, and surely its current ruler had nothing to say to a prophet of the Infinite.

Yet the ambassador stared at Araine until she shivered.

Infinite, I beg You, enlighten me!

A sense of waiting enfolded her, and she allowed the plea to rest. Particularly as her beloved husband bowed beneath the Lady Dasarai's sharp-eyed glance and her delicate, imperious voice. "Lord Nikaros. You wish to publicly disclose the results of your investigation against the traitor-general, Siyrsun."

"I do, Lady." Nikaros bowed again, then strode to the center of the throne room, where he bowed again. "Let all of Belaal understand that General Siyrsun planned his rebellion more than a year in advance, accruing funds by accepting bribes, by skimming ransoms for hostages, and by redirecting military funds. If he is captured and brought to trial, he cannot plead ignorance—he wrote or signed most of these documents himself." Nikaros opened the gilded box and displayed the loose parchments and scrolls inside. "Here are the originals of each available document and all recorded testimonies and allegations placed in evidence against the general."

Stepping forward, Nikaros handed the gilded box to Ebatenai, who officially accepted the documents for Belaal.

Dasarai nodded to Ebatenai, who quietly closed the box and stepped back from the throne, bowing. The princess lifted her elegant voice, enunciating each syllable so all could hear. "In addition to this written evidence, I have seen and heard the general's own treasonous words and actions. Today, we add to our previously offered reward. Whether he is captured and brought to trial, or if he is cut down in battle, his estates will go to the one who brings him down."

She motioned from Ebatenai to Nikaros. "See that official notice is sent and proclaimed throughout Belaal and all neighboring lands. Let Siyrsun be eliminated."

Nik stood beside Araine once more, and the royal audience wore on until Araine's feet were numbed with inactivity and her empty stomach threatened disastrous audible growls, or worse…hiccoughs. She smothered a sigh of relief when the last petitions and gifts were received. Until the Lady Dasarai lifted her hand toward the crowd.

Ro'ghez, high priest of Belaal's god-king cult, emerged from the crowd and made his stately way to the front of the throne room, the gold threads in his dark blue robes glittering in the light. He bowed to Dasarai and then retreated slightly and raised his pale hands to pray aloud.

Nikaros cut a questioning glance at Araine, and she shook her head at him. No. She hadn't known that Ro'ghez was invited to pray today.

Why was he still in favor after fomenting plots that had ultimately added to Siyrsun's rebellion?

Araine frowned remembering the black dreki talon he'd sent her. A death-pledge he likely still hoped to fulfill. To herself, she grumbled, "Infinite, spare me!"

A breath-like current skimmed past, ruffling Araine's veil. In her hand, the prophet's branch flashed its silver-white fire. She gasped and closed her eyes as the current strengthened, swirled around her and swept her away.

***

Araine opened her eyes to a smoldering, lowering fire set in a crude stone hearth, and to the mingled scents of burning pine chips and dank woolen garments. Harsh-muttered exclamations and the sounds of metal rasping over metal made her look up.

Two men stared at her—one not much older than herself with intense long-lashed golden eyes and handsome bronze dark-whiskered features. But the other man retreated a step, his sword drawn, its blade aligned with his haughty, sternly attractive face—too familiar despite his overgrown whiskers and ragged hair. "Corban."

It was indeed Corban. But his eyes…his ever-chilling gray eyes were no longer cold.

He gazed at Araine and shook his head. "This cannot be true! Araine?"

She swallowed, willing herself to stand her ground. He would *not* intimidate her. The branch gleamed in her hand, reminding her of the One who'd brought her to this place. To... "Infinite, where am I?"

Darzeq. Speak to these men, My own children of dust.

Araine drew a breath, bracing herself. "Your Creator sees you both. Do not think that you are forgotten."

A flash of rage and pain crossed the younger man's face. But tears hinted in his vivid yellow eyes—the same color as a Darzeq prince, now dead. Like that prince, the young man doubted her. He shook his head. "What are we to think? All hope's gone! Who are you, and how did you get in here?"

Corban interposed, his highborn voice equally harsh with alarm and disbelief, "Araine, are you actually alive, or a specter sent to haunt me for my failures?"

He'd truly changed. His expression was...vulnerable. Corban Thaenfall, the great and proud Siphran lord who'd sworn to ever love and guard her—before he tried to kill her—was truly vulnerable. Araine managed to meet his gaze with dignity. "I'm alive, sir. Not some specter."

Corban stepped toward Araine, stirring all her old fears. She placed the branch between them, its base thudding against the building's dirt floor. "Stop! I've been brought here by the Infinite, but you will not touch me!"

Instantly, Corban knelt and placed his sword at the base of the glowing branch. "Forgive me! Araine, I promise you, I've thought of you every day since your disappearance from ToronSea. Wherever I've been since that night, I've remembered you! And your grandfather...."

Throat closing, Araine whispered, "I can't discuss him." She would cry. Already tears gathered, stinging her eyes. "Instead...the Infinite sent me to speak to you both. I am His prophet to Belaal."

Both men stared, aghast. Corban rocked backward, visibly shaken, clutching his hands close as if he'd been wounded. "It's true?"

The younger man recovered first. "*You!* You're the prophet who warned Sheth of the murders!"

"Yes. If he'd listened, he would be alive, and Darzeq would now be at peace. As for you…" She eyed the young man guardedly, comprehending his spirit through the Infinite's vision. "Matteo of Darzeq, why are you hiding?"

The young man gaped briefly and then shook his head. "Why do you ask, Prophet? Undoubtedly you know—just as you foretold Sheth's fate. We've lost! My wife…."

Araine frowned. "Did you ask your Creator?"

Matteo caught his breath, his fine golden eyes widening. "Does *He* dispute what's happened? Dare we hope for victory if we attempt an attack?"

Hope? Perhaps. But not on Matteo's terms. "The Infinite hears your prayers, which is why I've been brought here to warn you. Now, obey Him. Leave this place and fight or you'll be captured, both of you." She eyed Corban, wary though he hadn't moved. "And you, Corban Thaenfall, the Infinite sees your heart. Do what you know you must, and bow as His servant."

Motionless, he stared at her. But then his countenance changed, his eyes expressing his soul's plea. "Will you forgive me? Araine, please…"

She must. Wasn't forgiveness one of the main reasons her Creator placed her here? A sob threatened, and she nodded. "I…do forgive you. But you must go *now*. Both of you. Escape and fight!"

A warning current sent tendrils of hair skimming over Araine's face, and she bowed her head toward Corban as he stood, prepared to obey their Creator's command. Softly, even as the current closed around her, Araine added, "Seek peace, my lord."

***

Released by the air current, Araine steadied herself with the branch and opened her tear-filled eyes. Gasps surrounded her from every side of Belaal's throne room. But she didn't dare glance around, for the Infinite had placed her directly in front of Belaal's ascetic gold-clad high priest, Ro'ghez. He looked her in the eyes, his expression shifting from shock to seemingly tranquil composure, though he'd undoubtedly like nothing better than to cast her into a pool with a starved dreki, while cheering for the scaly water-beast to gnaw her into bloodied flotsam.

No, Infinite, please! First Corban, now Ro'ghez? Would a starved dreki be involved?

Ro'ghez finished his prayer with inspiring serenity, his hands upraised in blessing. "May all who hear, earnestly pray for your return, our god and king, our Prized of the Heavens. May you return to us swiftly, and grant us the joy of your presence once more!"

Finished, Ro'ghez cast Araine a gently forbidding look. Daring her to confront him.

Blinking back tears, Araine returned the priest's gaze while pleading with her Creator.

Send me a vision!

Chapter 10

Infinite, why Ro'ghez?

Remind Belaal's high priest that I have offered him My help. Ask him, 'When will you confess your doubts?'

Doubts? Araine eyed the dangerous, imposing man before her. Ro'ghez and the word 'doubts' didn't match in the least. Nevertheless.... She cleared her aching throat. "Ro'ghez, your Creator reminds you that He once offered you His help. Now, He asks, 'When will you confess your doubts?'"

Ro'ghez recoiled visibly, his gold-embroidered garments flashing with the movement.

From her place on the step above them, the Lady Dasarai asked, "Doubts? Ro'ghez, you are dismissed. You will send me word of your doubts at once. In writing!"

The high priest's face didn't so much as twitch. Yet Araine heard him vent a frustrated breath through his nostrils for all the world like a burnt-out dreki or a young scholar scolded by his teacher. He bowed to Dasarai and spoke with sublime calm. "As you wish, revered Lady. And may my concerns please you in regard to my changeless loyalty toward you and our lord-king."

Before he retreated, Ro'ghez chided Araine beneath his breath. "This is base of you, Prophet—trying to shame me before the entire court!"

Reassured that he might be unsettled, she whispered, "Compelling you to confess a truth isn't shaming—it prevents you from being a hypocrite! Furthermore, my rebuke hasn't reached *your* level of throwing me into a pool swarming with starved monsters!"

Ro'ghez answered with a vague shrug. "Your death seemed essential."

"Is it no longer?"

He didn't answer, for above them, the Lady Dasarai clicked her gold-shielded fingernails delicately against the stone bench. Ro'ghez glanced up at her. Belaal's princess motioned him away with a seemingly bored wave. As he retreated, Belaal's princess raised one eyebrow at Araine. "Prophet, why do you create such scenes? One hopes to tame you eventually!"

Araine worked up a smile, and—she hoped—the proper tone of lightness. "Forgive me, Lady. I pray for you to succeed—these unexpected transports are dizzying."

"Recover yourself and attend your duties this afternoon."

"Thank you, Lady." Bowing, Araine stepped backward, rejoining the royal servants. Nikaros clasped her free hand, obviously concerned. Warming her fingers with his own, he whispered, "What happened? Where did you go?"

"Darzeq, my lord."

He raised both eyebrows. "So swiftly... Did you speak to Corban?"

"Yes." Fearing she'd weaken, Araine looked away from her beloved husband as Corban returned to her thoughts. Pride personified, kneeling to plead with her. Corban Thaenfall had torn her world apart, nearly tempted her to destruction, and then killed her dear Grumps. Had she truly forgiven him? Let it be so. For she'd seen what would happen in Darzeq.

She'd seen.

Tears burned her eyes, turning all the light in the golden throne room to a fiery, sun-struck haze. Nikaros slid an arm beneath her mantle and hugged her, whispering, "You're ill. When we're dismissed, you must rest."

Could prophets ever truly rest in the mortal world? Everywhere she looked she saw danger for others' souls—the merest sliver of what her Creator comprehended each instant. Aching, she appealed to Him.

How do You endure it all?

My child of dust, His voice murmured in gentlest consolation, *Love endures. Be strong...*

Staring into a fresh vision-fragment, Araine gathered His proffered strength and then steadied herself. Obviously, her day wasn't finished.

***

Araine stood as her attendants entered the spacious central room where she and Nikaros received visitors. Inae edged inside first, all caution, carrying a tray of fruit, salted olives, fried meat patties, bread rounds, and a plain clay flask of steaming liquid—undoubtedly Nik's brewed mint.

Behind her, Jemma carried a small water pitcher and three folds of linen, appearing burdened as if she held a mountain. She lifted the folds of linen toward Araine. "Three. As requested, though I don't know why you'd need three. Do you intend for one of us to share your food?"

Softly, remembering her vision, Araine said, "Jemma, you've already had your share from our tray, in addition to your noon meal."

Inae flung her co-attendant a strained glance. "There! Didn't I warn you, Jemma? Why must you always do what you shouldn't? I'm forever being blamed by Cook for things that aren't my fault. At least the prophet can see what's happening."

"Cook is always too ready to blame others for her own pilfering," Jemma sniffed. "At least I'll admit to mine." She plunked down the pitcher and nodded to Araine. "Yes. I tested the bread and a serving of meat."

"Which means that you ate my serving," Araine observed. "We're expecting a guest—the ambassador of Darzeq. Please return to the kitchens and request another portion, then thank Cook."

Jemma cast her gaze toward the ceiling and heaved a long-suffering sigh. "Prophet, you don't understand..."

"I understand." Araine gave her attendant a stern look. "Jemma, your rebellious spirit will bring you to grief. For your own good, please restrain yourself. Your behavior reflects upon my character and the Infinite's because you've proclaimed yourself as one of His own followers. Do you think He doesn't see you?"

Jemma retreated, but then she paused at the door. "My intentions are good, Prophet. I'm sorry you don't believe me."

How could she twist matters so deftly? Araine shook her head. "Jemma, you know the truth. Please behave. And hurry, for our guest's sake."

The maidservant flitted away without closing the door. Inae placed the food on a low table. "Thank you, Prophet. I was afraid to say anything."

"Don't be afraid, Inae. If you're worried about something, please tell me."

"Yes, Lady, but *I* have to room with her."

Nikaros tapped the door and entered the chamber. "May I interrupt?"

Inae bowed and scampered out, closing the door as she fled. Araine hugged her husband, breathing in his fragrance of cedar and sandalwood—scents she'd mixed for him because they reminded him of the mountains. "You need never ask, my love."

He grinned and kissed her. "I know. Yet I'll respect your domain. Here, you rule." His handsome face sobering, he asked, "Are you well enough to receive a visitor? I've just spoken to someone who was mightily impressed by your disappearance and return this afternoon."

"The ambassador of Darzeq? Yes. I've requested food." She motioned to the tray.

Her husband's smile returned and he smoothed her hair. "How I love the Infinite's prophet! And Him. When will you tell me what happened during your brief foray into Darzeq?"

Could she? It seemed she must. For Nik's question, though gently asked, unmistakably expressed his deep concern. He would wait ages for her answer. Araine swallowed and gathered her Infinite-granted strength. "I spoke to Corban. And to a nobleman who waited with him. I was taken to Darzeq because they're in danger and the Infinite required me to warn them to escape and to take action despite their doubts. Which is why I must speak to the ambassador."

"He's on his way," Nikaros reminded Araine, swaying, rocking her soothingly. "He asked for an invitation to speak with you and he seemed distressed, so I agreed—knowing you'd do the same. Now, tell me how you dealt with Corban."

"He still frightens me, though I forgave him." Araine rested in the warmth and strength of her husband's embrace, grateful for his calm. Very soothing, that calm.

Dangerously quiet, Nik asked, "Did he threaten you?"

"No. In fact, he humbled himself and begged my forgiveness—I never thought I'd see such a thing. Surely the Infinite has reached him."

"After everything you've said of Lord Corban Thaenfall, his humility seems a wonder."

"It is."

"Our Creator knows the truth," Nikaros mused aloud. "It's for the best that I couldn't accompany you. I might have beaten the man bloody."

"I'm grateful you weren't there." Humility or no humility, Corban would have defended himself ferociously. Hadn't he drawn his weapon when she first appeared? He could have killed Nikaros. Araine's heartbeat doubled at the appalling thought.

A light tap at the door compelled Araine to step away from her husband and settled herself. The ambassador must remember that she'd been calm.

Inae opened the door and bowed their visitor inside. Slender and silvering, Lord Magni Ormr, Ambassador of Darzeq, entered with timidity quite unworthy of his name. Seeing Araine, he bowed, nervousness making his face twitch and his voice wobble. "Ah-um, Prophet. Lord Nikaros. Yes, thank you for receiving me."

"You are welcomed here," Araine murmured, meaning it. "Please, rest, and share our meal."

Jemma bounded in halting all pleasantries. Her thin face mutinous, she thunked down a tray, bowed, and swept out—closing the door with a hearty thud. Undoubtedly she'd had a scene with Cook. Araine offered Ormr a determined smile. "Did you have a pleasant journey from Darzeq, Ambassador?"

The question was enough. As they ate, he launched into a lengthy description of perfect weather, rude Agocii traders, a lame horse, disturbing servants, and greedy innkeepers. He finished with compliments to the delicious meal and gratitude for Araine's kindness in receiving him. She smiled and inclined her head. "Thank you, Ambassador."

Nikaros leaned back from the table, though he'd done more listening than eating. "You wished to ask my wife a question, Ambassador Ormr?"

"Eh, yes." The ambassador puffed out an uncertain breath. "Prophet, you foretold the disaster that overtook our royal family. In place of our noble princes, we have two usurpers."

Araine nodded. "When the honorable are ruled by fear, usurpers invariably conquer them. Now your fear becomes terror and rightly so. Because you follow the Infinite, if you don't win this current conflict you and your comrades will be slaughtered, even if you weren't involved."

Ormr blinked and dabbed his mouth with a linen towel. "Prophet…I know…my actions in Darzeq during this past year have been…less than commendable. Because of my cowardice… I have no right to ask the Infinite's help and yet…"

The Infinite's compassion threaded through Araine, gentling her rebuke. "Because you admit your failings and truly regret them, you've received your Creator's mercy. Nevertheless, sir, *where* is your courage?"

He shrugged. "I've none. Even as we speak, I'm eaten with fear. If it becomes known that I have spoken with you…."

A sudden glimpse—unwanted, unwelcomed—made Araine stiffen and plead with her Creator. Can't this be undone?

My child of dust, the choice has been made. Can you force others to heed Me?

No. Clearly she couldn't. Araine drooped. "This meeting will become known, Ambassador. There are spies within your household. If you don't act, then your 'disturbing' servants will betray you and you'll die the same day that you cross from Agocii territories into Darzeq—as will your son, unless you heed the Infinite's warning."

Ormr dropped the napkin, retrieved it, and then stammered, "I-I... P-prophet, it's known that our lord-prince Sheth ignored your warnings and died. I must protect my family. I will obey the Infinite with all my heart."

Araine straightened, conveying her Creator's sternness. "The instant you leave this room, Ambassador—without speaking to anyone—you will lock yourself in your private garden and personally send a courier bird to your son, ordering him to gather all your forces and fight."

"But..." Ormr paused, moistened his lips, dabbed his face with the towel, and then stood and bowed. "Very well, Prophet. Please excuse me and I'll go now—silent as the dead until I've obeyed my Creator."

Nikaros leaned over and kissed Araine tenderly, making her shiver as he whispered, "Sadly, love, I must go as well. I promised Ebatenai I would return to our work as soon as we'd eaten. I'll return this evening." He stood, adjusted his mantle, and then walked the ambassador out to the corridor.

Seated unmoving at the low table, Araine waited to face this day's last trial, praying. Jemma rapped on the door and then hurried in to gather the trays and dishes. Softly, Araine asked, "Jemma, where have you been?"

Not looking up, Jemma answered—just a bit too sharp. "Nowhere, Lady. I've been waiting for your guest to depart."

How easily she lied, despite her claim of following the Infinite. Sorrow tightened Araine's throat and words. "I warned you, Jemma. Why didn't you listen?"

Jemma rattled the dishes on the trays, stacking everything in a teetering heap. "Lady, I don't know what you're talking about."

"By the Infinite's will, I saw you. My spirit saw you taking a purse-full of money from the ambassador's servant. Didn't you know that he's a spy? Did you care that he wishes to destroy the ambassador?"

Jemma stared, her hands motionless upon the dishes. Araine stood and continued, mourning every pained word. "Because you've taken wealth in this manner at the expense of my honor and the Infinite's Name, all of Ambassador Ormr's fears will be multiplied and heaped upon you forever. Go, and never return to my service."

Trembling, her eyes huge, Jemma skittered backward and then fled as one pursued.

Alone, Araine shut the door. Her footsteps weighed and sluggish, she returned to the low table and sank down upon the cushions, staring at the pile of unwashed dishes.

Tears gathered, blurring her vision, and she cried.

For Darzeq's losses. For Corban's torment.

And for Jemma, who would never be truly free for the remainder of her mortal life.

***

Sweating in the meager lamp light, Ty readjusted his leather-mitted grip on the chisel, and eyed the dark, defiant chunk of crystal embedded in the cave's wall. He'd never worked so hard in his life as he had this past winter. And yet despite the grueling labor, mining fascinated him. He'd never imagined the toil involved in acquiring the gems and gold he wore each day in his palace. Gems and gold he'd taken for granted like air and water. No more. The Eosyths deserved kingdoms for their work here in these gloomy timbered tunnels.

To think that he'd been rude enough to shun such gems for gold when he'd demanded ransom for Nikaros, Josias, and Lije. To think that he'd been vengeful enough to take the young men as hostages in the first place. He loathed the god-king he'd been.

Let the Prized of the Heavens false god be forever destroyed!

Gritting his teeth, Ty set his chisel against the blue-striated rock and chipped it away from the dark crystal—which, raw though it was, gleamed tauntingly in the faint light. Most likely, as Tsir Andris had pointed out, the final cut and polished stone would be fit only for a minor nobleman of Darzeq. However, one spectacular gem could add richly to the clan's yearly provisions, and the hope was an irresistible lure, goading Ty onward. Perhaps this initial crystal was larger than it appeared.

Just beyond the edge of his lamp's light, perhaps twenty paces away, Detzios worked within the dim circle of his own lamp's light, his hammer and chisel ringing steadily as he chipped away the stone.

Grit and rubble fell clattering around Ty's boots, loosening his foothold. He kicked some of the fragments away into the darkness, and then lifted his hammer again…just as a low, primitive hissing raised the hairs on his scalp in prey-like terror.

Wielding the hammer and chisel as weapons, Ty pivoted, staring hard into the tunnel. Two liquid amber eyes flashed like fiery oil pools in the lamp-light, and a pale gleaming row of bared jagged teeth glinted—level with Ty's chest.

The flat and luminous eyes shifted in the darkness. Nearing with the clicking accompaniment of talons.

He had only one chance.

Growling at the shadow-cloaked beast, Ty lunged.

Chapter 11

Roaring, Ty swung his iron hammer down between those flat, luminous eyes, and then cuffed at the creature's head with his chisel, striking the beast aside just as its eyes closed. Blade-like sharpness lashed at Ty in the darkness, tearing at his bare forearms and then falling away in a feral thrashing of talons and limbs against gritty stone. Ty struck again with all his might, and heard the crack of bone beneath iron.

Infinite, let the beast be dead! Bel-Tygeon refused to perish from a fluke attack. Not daring to look away from the creature's vicinity, Ty yelled, "Detzios! Call the others! Bring your weapons—there's a beast in the cave! Perhaps more!"

Detzios bellowed down along the tunnel, "Tsir Andris! Bring your weapons and light torches—Ty's been struck!"

Detzios rushed toward Ty, carrying his clay lamp in a wavering circle of dim golden light—his hammer upraised to attack. If the man were truly vengeful, he'd strike Ty now and swear the beast had killed him.

Instead, Detzios leaned into the darkness, panting, his lamp outstretched, hammer readied to strike the beast again. Ty reached for his own lamp, lifting its warm clay contours and easing it toward his fallen attacker.

A broad tawny-to-gray beast sprawled lifeless in the lamplight, its crested head and tail ending in odd gray plumage that covered its winged, hook-like fore claws. Ty crouched beside the beast and exhaled his gratitude. "Infinite, praise You, it's dead." To Detzios, he muttered, "Might there be others?"

"It's possible." Detzios hunkered down beside him. "But congratulations. This was a good strike. And lizard meat's not horrible if it's pit-steamed for a day."

Eat that stringy animal? It surely had the flavor and dryness of mangled ropes. Ty rubbed at the oozing scratches the beast had raked across his arms as it fell. "You cannot be serious."

Detzios nudged his hammer at the carcass. "You talk like a man who's never faced starvation."

Well... "Obviously I've much to learn."

Headed by Tsir Andris, the other men reached them now, an Eosyth force armed with blades, hammer, torches, and lamps. Tsir Andris loomed over Ty and Detzios, his torch throwing light and shadows over the walls and the dead creature. The Eosyth lord studied the beast, and his stern face eased. "A crested lizard. Any injuries?"

Detzios grinned. "Mostly to the lizard. It was Ty's kill."

Tsir Andris nudged Ty. "Good work. Let's chase out any others and then carry this beast to the meeting cave for a feast tomorrow. Find some balm for your scratches, Ty—we don't want those to fester."

"Thank you, my lord." Ty stood and nodded to Detzios. "Thank you. I appreciate your swift response."

Some of the scribe's humor faded. "Men fighting for a common cause shouldn't battle between themselves."

He sounded so like Nikaros. Had the two men trained as scribes? "You're talking about more than the Agocii."

"Yes." Eyeing Tsir Andris, who'd edged further along the tunnel with several other men, the scribe whispered, "I'm also referring to Serena. It's clear that she loves you, though I'd wish otherwise. I want nothing more than her happiness. Therefore..." He narrowed his gaze at Ty, his words almost inaudible. "If you dare hurt her, I'll thrash you to pulp."

"There's no need for threats." Ty sobered. "I honor Serena. But if I return to my people, I cannot take her with me—the legal requirements facing my poor future wife are insurmountable for an Eosyth. I'd never expect Serena to make such extreme sacrifices."

The scribe's whisper turned grim as if believing he'd lost a battle. "You love her."

Was he so obvious? "Yes. But tell no one. Why cause turmoil when it'll lead to nothing?" Even as he spoke, Ty fought the elation of his own confession. Yes, he loved Serena as any ordinary man living an ordinary life should love a worthy woman. If only he could live an ordinary life.

Could he?

No. He shouldn't even risk the thought. Eventually he'd be recognized. Furthermore, his very presence among the Eosyths added to the dangers they faced. To protect Clan Darom, he must behave honorably and then leave as soon as the weather permitted.

Belaal might not need its fallen god-king, but he had to return to Sulaanc and help his sister. Infinite, Mighty One, keep Rethae safe! And Araine…

He hadn't thought of Araine for days.

She deserved better. In other words, not Bel-Tygeon.

***

Kneeling before the Lady Dasarai in her golden receiving chamber, Araine faced Ro'ghez. The priest's gaunt face settled into forbidding, blaming lines, and he actually glared at her. As if this situation was entirely her fault. He was the one with doubts.

Infinite, what is his role in Belaal?

No answer. Yet…she sensed His Spirit near. Waiting.

Why?

Araine rested her prophet's branch on the carpet before her and then squared her shoulders and studied the priest. Would he serve the Infinite? Would he survive such a conversion in Belaal?

The Lady Dasarai rapped Araine delicately with her gilded palm fan. "Prophet, you will control yourself and remain present as we talk. Matters must be settled between you two. Our lord-god must find his realm in good order when he returns. Do you understand me?"

Araine bowed. "Yes, Lady. I doubt the Infinite will remove me for another task today. Yet, if He does…I give you my word that I'm quite disturbed by my own disappearances. I've no control over them."

Ro'ghez pursed his lips, studying her as if doubting her veracity. "Is this so? Or is it sorcery?"

Sorcery. Did he think she'd been swept up in a whirlwind of her own conjuring? "Sir, I promise you—as I live—the Infinite sweeps me from place to place according to His will. I am only His servant and a feeble one at best."

"That's not my impression." Ro'ghez placed a scroll before her. "You called me to task publicly for my doubts, before our princess and all of Belaal and its allies. Here they are—and they ought to be publicly proclaimed. All three."

Dasarai prodded Araine with her glittering fan. "Read it aloud, Prophet. No one is near, and I want this matter settled peaceably."

"Yes, Lady." She reached for the scrolled parchment. As she reached, she saw the priest's hands twitch as if he longed to snatch it away. Araine stilled her hand just above the document, and she looked up at the priest. His thin, proud features didn't move. But his eyes…

Infinite, he's afraid.

My Child of Dust, his life is before you and before Belaal, to be judged and obliterated.

Could Ro'ghez die by these words? By his fear, it seemed so. Softly, Araine asked, "Ro'ghez, would you prefer that I destroy this unread? I will for your sake."

The man stared at her, clearly confounded. He paused as if considering her offer and battling within himself. But then he straightened all the more—as one gathering courage. "Destroying the parchment will not extinguish my doubts. Read them, Lady."

"I admire your spirit, sir." Araine opened the pale, crisp parchment and read three sentences. "One—'Belaal's temple vanishes like dust and the Infinite's prophets, though frail mortal specimens, conquer kingdoms and Belaal's own dreki, to our god-king's cost."

The Lady Dasarai shifted in her seat, huffing out an exasperated breath. Araine glanced up at her warily. Belaal's princess motioned for her to continue, though her dark eyes glittered dangerously. "We will hear his doubts and then decide his fate. Read on, Prophet."

"Two. 'When the Infinite's prophets declare what is to be—according to His will—then everything happens as He decrees—unlike the prophets and wise ones of Belaal." Araine swallowed, blinking tears like the frail specimen Ro'ghez deemed her to be. "Three. 'Therefore, is the Infinite the one true God above all?'"

As Araine lowered the scroll, the Lady Dasarai stood, her robes glistening as she struck Belaal's high priest with her fan. "Traitor! It's one thing for these unmanageable foreign girls to enter Belaal as the Infinite's servants—against our gods and Belaal—but it's quite another for *you* to question our Prized of the Heavens!"

Ro'ghez bowed, humble and silent as any slave. Dasarai struck him again, breaking her fan over his head. She flung away the fan's shattered base and sat on the bench once more, regally displeased. "What are we to do with you, Ro'ghez? By law you must die."

Araine snatched up her branch and the vinewood glowed, its silvered spiraling grain becoming palest fire in her hand. "Lady, I beg you to not destroy a sincerely-questing subject! Spare him, please!"

"You hush!" Dasarai snapped. "He tried to kill you and your husband. Repeatedly. And though you are foreign and devotees of the Infinite, you have been useful to Belaal and to our Prized of the Heavens! Whereas *this* man—" she motioned at Ro'ghez and actually spluttered her indignation. "He…he…ought to know better! By his doubts, he unsettles our kingdom! He dismantles everything he's served from the day of his birth!"

Now, the branch blazed, making Dasarai turn away and lift one bejeweled hand to her eyes. "Quench that thing!"

"The Infinite cannot be quenched, Lady." Eyes wide open, staring into the white fire, Araine prayed aloud, "My Creator, how I love You! Send Your beloved Spirit and guide my every word!"

Imagery opened before her and she closed her eyes, seeing His will. Infinite, if this is true… Araine summoned her courage, and her voice. "Lady, you know I'm your servant as well as the Infinite's. And I serve your brother as my king—you may kill me if I displease you with the truth." As the Lady Dasarai turned to her again, shielding her eyes from the branch's light, Araine said, "The Infinite has shown me that if you order his death, you'll condemn him for our lord-king's own beliefs."

"No!" Dasarai argued, "That cannot be. They will dismantle this kingdom!"

"The Infinite warns that this kingdom will be dismantled by Belaal's enemies if you do not support your brother."

From beneath her delicate hand, the princess stared at Araine as if she'd lost her mind. Araine persisted. "Bel-Tygeon now follows the Infinite. You must decide what you truly believe."

Dasarai motioned her to silence. "I have always considered you and Ela of Parne as sorceresses. Between you, in the name of your Infinite, you are destroying everything Belaal has built over generations to honor their god-kings! I tolerated you only because my brother wished for a prophet."

"A prophet whose words are never false," Araine agreed. "And so I am—but only by the Infinite's power. He declares the truth, I merely speak it. You may kill us if you please. But by doing so, you are denying your own doubts, and you are destroying two of Bel-Tygeon's staunchest allies in Belaal."

Ro'ghez. A staunch ally? Araine studied the silent man. Undoubtedly he'd ever acted according to the king's best interests. Never from malice. Why had she not discerned this before?

Infinite…I am such a fool.

My child of dust, can you know every heart? Or weigh each soul?

The branch faded to a gentle glow. Dasarai lowered her hand, looking like a badly ruffled, glorious little bird who didn't like being upset one bit. She pursed her lovely mouth, and her dark eyes glittered like dagger points. "Ro'ghez, you are removed from your place as high priest, and you are confined to your home until

I decide whether you live or die. If you attempt to flee, I will have you executed without a trial. Araine, for your impertinence, you are banished to your rooms, but spared for the king's sake. Now, leave! Both of you!"

They bowed and backed away. Dasarai glided from the room, kicking aside her splintered fan as she went. Ro'ghez exhaled and spoke softly. "Now I have nothing. Perhaps not even my life. Yet it's more tolerable than feeling like a fraud." He eyed Araine, wary. "What next, Prophet? Tell, me. Though, undoubtedly, to my own sorrow, you'll tell the truth."

She smiled. "Will it be sorrow, Ro'ghez? I think that decision is yours." She led him to the doorway and bowed him from the chamber. "While you're banished and bored, you'll need something to do. I'll send you some books to read."

"I might have known you would." He sighed and cast an imploring glance at the ceiling. "What can I lose if I've just set my own seal to my death sentence?"

They walked along the long palace corridor, their sandals clicking against the polished marble floor. Pondering their possible death sentences, Araine reminded the priest, "The first thing you should know, sir, if you chose to follow the Infinite, is that you'll most likely die early. Therefore, accept the possibility and go on."

He paused beside a gold-flecked blue marble pillar frowned at her. "You defended me to the Lady Dasarai, though I ordered your death last year. Why?"

"By attacking me you struck at my beloved Creator. Yet, the Infinite's forgiven you. Therefore, so do I." She offered him a wry smile. "In fact, He's deeply concerned for your sake, and He's awaiting your decision. Will you follow Him?"

Ro'ghez looked away and resumed walking. "Send me those books, and we shall see."

Araine smiled. She would send him the Book of Wisdom. Then the Book of Praises.

Ro'ghez would study the words that had first drawn her toward the Infinite

...you are forever in My sight, precious and honored, because I love you....

Infinite, let Ro'ghez trust You!

Her prayer faded as swift footsteps echoed behind them—the sounds of multiple pairs of boots stomping against the marble. Araine glanced over her shoulder and stifled a gasp. Six of the Lady Dasarai's burly eunuch guardsmen were stalking toward her and Ro'ghez, their expressions, cold, flat, duty-bound, spears held ready to run them both through.

Softly, Ro'ghez muttered, "Thus we are arrested. May your Infinite spare our lives."

As the guards surrounded them, Araine said, "He is your Infinite as well."

"Is He, Lady? We shall see."

***

Nikaros placed the scrolls within the box and slid the lock closed with his blue-corded square key. He slung the key around his neck and then faced his comrades: Commanders Utthreates, Seir, and Vioc. "Send any other requisitions for your troops to me and I'll tend to them at once. Are you confident in your army's readiness?"

Big, blunt and stern, Utthreates nodded. "We are, my lord. The drills will continue until the king's return. I want the men to be..."

His words faded into a blur and Nikaros lost them altogether as he turned, caught within a waking dream. The southern mountains of Clan Darom surrounded Nik—an inner valley of mixed woods still icy with the late-winter chill, yet beautiful enough to sharpen his long-suppressed homesickness. The pungent scent of pines mingled with aromas of smoke and food from tents in the snowy fields beyond. Nik stepped toward the encampment until two men approached. His scribe-friend Detzios and... "The king!"

Bel-Tygeon appeared to be wholly Eosyth now, wearing his long shaggy-edged goatskin coat over a roughened tunic. Myriad tools hung from his wide crimson belt and he carried his bow and arrows readied in his left fist as if expecting to use them at any instant.

Why did Bel-Tygeon appear so prepared for battle? Though he unhurriedly shook open his coat as if he were too warm. Beside the king, Nik's own scribe-friend, Detzios, shoved Bel-Tygeon, clearly joking and laughing—and clearly unaware that he was taunting a king.

Detzios, too, held his bow and arrows readied. Nik wished his waking vision would allow him to question the king and Detzios. Why were they ready to fight in a valley renowned as an Eosyth sanctuary?

Apprehension forced Nik to retreat into reality. Where Belaal's three commanders were staring at him as if fearing for his sanity. Nikaros straightened. "Forgive me, sirs."

Utthreates frowned, deepening the harsh lines in his face. "Are you ill, my lord?"

"No. But I've just seen the king, and I'm uneasy. Snow or no snow, spring is here. I'm leaving by morning to bring him out of the mountains. I need one of you to volunteer as the leader of his covert guards."

Chapter 12

Standing over her makeshift carved-stone worktable, Araine stirred the powdered cassia into the mixture of cloves, myrrh, and pulverized resins. Being imprisoned in her living quarters had blessed her with enough time to resume her former profession of creating incense, mixing tonics and ointments, and pressing pills.

Testing and blending spices was as comforting as visiting with old friends—not to mention a useful pastime that allowed her to pray as she worked. Disgraced slaves ought to remain useful. If only she knew more of…

A light tap sounded upon the door. Araine frowned. Who was bold enough to defy Lady Dasarai's imprisonment order against Belaal's disgraced prophet? "Who is it?"

A crisp feminine voice replied, "Never fear. It's only me." The Women's Palace physician, Cythea, hit the latch and entered—her thin arms laden with baskets and boxes.

Araine hurried to help her palace mentor. "Cythea! Welcome—I was just wishing for some good advice for my work—but how did you get past my guards?"

Cythea's calm narrow face crinkled with a smile and she swung a heavy basket into Araine's arms, almost knocking the breath from her lungs. While Araine wheezed, Cythea said, "I sent word to the Lady Dasarai that you're ailing—for by now you surely are. Boredom must have you clawing the walls."

"Not quite, but thank you. I'm so glad you're here." Araine set the weighty basket on her work table. "I'm preparing incense for the king's return."

"I see." Cythea nodded her approval and leaned over Araine's table, inspecting the aromatic contents of a spice mortar. Quiet joy lit her pallid face as she inhaled the fragrance. Cythea had tended Bel-Tygeon since his birth and loved him with a single-minded ferocity rivaled only by the Lady Dasarai's. "No doubt his rooms need to be freshened and all his garments checked for moths. We ought to fumigate everything."

Not bothering to hide her smugness, Araine returned to her spices. "It seems I've anticipated you."

"Further proof that you must train as my eventual replacement. Beginning now."

"Truly?" Wasn't it enough that she served as Belaal's troublesome prophet? "Do you have royal permission to officially train me?"

Cythea set down her boxes and began to unpack the basket, placing alabaster boxes and crystal vials in an orderly row on the table as she talked. "Not precisely, but I'll take the chance. I decided that if the Lady Dasarai refused to allow you medical treatment, then you were awaiting official condemnation. If she allowed you treatment then…" The physician shrugged. "She's ready to consider forgiving you."

"I hope so. Have you heard anything of Ro'ghez?"

"Yes." Cythea opened an alabaster box of yellow-green ointment— an olive-oil and beeswax concoction by the look of it. She set down the alabaster lid as if it might break at the least look. "He was beaten several weeks ago. I was ordered to send him some healing ointments, which indicates that the Lady Dasarai doesn't consider him to be condemned."

Infinite, thank You! "Good. I sent him copies of books, but I've heard nothing from him since we were arrested, and the Infinite has remained silent. I was becoming worried."

Cool and efficient, Cythea lined up an assortment of crystal vials. "If anything else happens, I'll send you word. Meanwhile, the king's shaving oil consists of myrtle extract, sandalwood extract, peppermint—"

The door opened. Nikaros stalked into the chamber, dropped a collection of boxes onto the bed, and then headed for the nearest storage chest. "Where are my old clothes? The ones I wore when I was first brought to Sulaanc?"

Thrown out. Araine almost teased him with the words, but he was entirely too serious. Before he could begin any ruthless foraging among their carefully organized storage chests, Araine rushed to a far corner of the chamber, her bare feet pattering over the tiles. "Your hunting gear and old garments are here. I didn't want to mix them with your newer clothes."

Nikaros hurried to help her open the chest and haul out his boots and a heavy, shabby old leather coat, which was brushed clean and redolent of cedar "My love, you're wonderful! Thank you!" He offered a hasty kiss, his whiskers scraping her cheek.

Behind them, Cythea coughed. "Prophet, send for me when you're ready to resume our work."

A flash of humor lightened Nik's green-brown eyes. "I fear that I am her work as she helps me to gather my gear. But I'll be gone soon enough."

As Cythea hesitated, clearly interested, Araine almost whooped. "You're going to retrieve the king?"

"Yes. I saw him in a vision. He's well, but the men are carrying their weapons as if they expect to use them instantly, which is unusual for my people. Beloved, I must leave at once. Commander Vioc and some of his men are riding with me, but we'll be clad like outlaws—a gang of rag-tags."

Dry-voiced, Cythea said, "We'll prepare plenty of delousing oil for your return, my lord. Meanwhile, Prophet...." The stately physician smiled. "Tomorrow, we'll start lessons in earnest. Be ready. My lord, I wish you a safe journey. May you return our lord-king swiftly and in good health."

Nikaros grinned, though he continued to inspect his old coat. "Thank you, Cythea."

The instant she closed the door, Nikaros dropped the coat and reached for Araine, sliding his fingers into her hair and then fervently kissing her lips and throat, dizzying her with his warmth. "How I'll miss you, my love! Listen—" He bent slightly, his green-brown eyes somber, yet appealing as a summer woodland. "Commander Utthreates and Commander Seir will remain in Sulaanc. They've asked that you serve as their civil contact with the Lady Dasarai for any vital matters. They trust you to speak on their behalf."

"I will. But I'm still guarded. I—"

Her husband grinned and lifted her in his arms nuzzling her throat. "I guarantee that you'll be returned to the Lady Dasarai's favor. By now, she knows I'm leaving to bring our lord-king home. You know she'll send for you, demanding information."

Before he could kiss her again, Araine briefly touched his mouth, stopping him. "Has anyone heard the least whisper of General Siyrsun's whereabouts?"

"No. Some say he's in Belaal, others vow he's taken refuge in Darzeq. But I fear that he's been hiding like a fox in his den through the winter and now he's prowling about in the mountains. Which is why I must hurry—if Siyrsun learns of the king's whereabouts, he will attack, and we don't know how many have fled Belaal to join the Old Dreki's rebellion."

"Hurry then, love. And we'll pray the king forgives us for marrying without his permission."

"Yes," Nik set Araine gently on her feet. "I don't enjoy the thought of prison."

Would Bel-Tygeon force them to separate? Araine shivered and clung to her husband with all her might, listening to his heartbeat, which sped now, racing as he held her and kissed her in prelude to their farewell.

***

Wearied and too warm after a day's work in the mine, Ty shook open his coat as he walked along the snow-edged trail. Actually, despite the dripping, melting snow, he didn't need his coat. He paused and loosened the garment's shaggy-fleeced edges from his broad belt.

Detzios shoved him genially. "Animal! Keep your clothes on."

Ty grinned and shoved the scribe in turn, making him stumble sideways. "Careful, bird-brain! I might yet bite."

Detzios righted himself and readjusted his bow and arrows. "Well, that would undoubtedly lead to blood-poisoning—though I must say I'm more fearful of a hammer-strike."

"It's tied to my belt, you fear monger. I don't know why you're concerned."

"I've seen your knots—they're feeble. That hammer could fall on my feet and I'd be limping for life."

Ty pretended a lordly sneer. "Scribes don't need to walk."

"Obviously you've never been a scribe."

Before Ty could shift the conversation from the dangerous topic of his possible past occupation, Detzios scanned the upper cliffs as they did every afternoon on their way back to the encampment from the mines. "Right now, however, I'd prefer to have wings and see if Cziybor's set any spies over us with the return of spring."

Ty muttered, "I agree. Let's run another search at dawn."

"I'll alert the others," Detzios said. "I'd love to catch Cziybor off guard and cut a few markers from his beard."

"You'd have to kill him first." Something Ty would gladly do if given the chance—though Cziybor wouldn't be an easy kill hand-to-hand.

How might the Agocii chieftain be most easily taken down? Detzios was obviously pondering the same, for they walked in silence, their boots splatting against the slushy path as they tromped down slope toward the encampment. As ever Ty admired the serenity of the view—Tsir Andris in the distance with the older men, checking the herds, while the women laughed and called to each other between the smoke-plumed tents as they finished their outdoor tasks for the day. No sign of Serena. When would he accept that he must give up hoping for her? She could never be his queen....

At the edge of the encampment, Ayden's jubilant voice cut through the air. "Ty!" He ran toward them, flourishing his miniature bow and arrows. "I've been practicing—I'm holding three arrows now when I shoot! Want to see?"

"Yes—and I'm waiting for you to beat my aim."

Detzios waved off Ty. "Go. I'll meet you at dawn."

"Dawn it is." Ty followed Ayden to his makeshift practice area.

Solemn with self-importance, the little boy raised his bow, set his stance and took aim, careful and sure as he drew three arrows in succession from his fist. Each small blunted arrow thumped and fell from the speckled old goatskin he'd draped over a rock. Finished, he grinned up at Ty. "See?"

"Excellent! Now try four." Ty crouched beside the little boy and reached for his cache of arrows, shaking his coat's sleeves away as he fanned out four small arrows.

Ayden frowned and took the arrows. "You've got another rash on your arms. Mother and Serena will dose you for sure."

Rash? This would be his third bout in four months. Ty studied his arms. Actually, this was no rash. Instead, a veritable constellation of pinpoint blood-red blisters showed between the dark hairs on his forearms. Had he been afflicted with another blood plague? These blisters weren't as spectacular as the ones he'd suffered nearly three years past, when he'd defied the Infinite. Nor as painful. Even so—*any* blood blister now evoked memories of the agony he'd endured as a result of his own god-king ambition.

Controlling himself, Ty shrugged. "They're nothing." He helped Ayden adjust his grip with the four arrows and applauded when the boy managed to strike the target twice despite his awkwardness with the added arrow. "Well done! Soon you'll handle a whole fistful just like your lord-father."

By now, the skin along Ty's arms itched with a crawling, stinging sensation he couldn't ignore. Excusing himself from Ayden's practice, he hurried to the white tent and rapped on the frame. "Am I permitted to enter?"

"Yes," Serena's voice lifted agreeably. "Welcome!"

Inside, Serena was laughing with her mother and sisters and Betiya as they laced a hide to a slender wooden frame. The sight of her halted Ty for an instant. Had any woman in his palace ever been so lovely? The radiance of Serena's glance as she looked up at him nearly stole his breath.

Overwhelmed, he turned away and focused on closing the tent and sealing out the cold air. By the time he'd finished his task, he was composed again.

And by the time he'd finished his task, all three women were staring at him, six if he counted Miyna, who peeked out from behind Serena's arm, and the twins who abandoned their stitchery to smile their unified welcome. Lovely ladies all, even Betiya.

Ty bowed his head slightly to honor them, but he growled at Miyna, "Meeenaaa!"

The little girl's dark eyes brightened. She squealed and charged at Ty, clearly and rightly certain that he'd welcome her reckless attack. Ty scooped up the child—Serena's miniature likeness at the same age—all mischief and winsome sweetness. He teased her briefly, then swung her beneath one arm and eyed Serena, Adelia, and Betiya.

"Forgive me, ladies." Ty leaned down and showed them his free arm. "I need your opinions. What is this rash?"

While the twins crowded him to study his arm, and Miyna squirmed, fluttered, and kicked within the crook of his elbow, Serena studied Ty's forearm. Her lovely eyebrows lifted above her widened eyes and she flung Ty a wonderfully worried look. "Do you have a fever?"

"No."

"Then," Adelia said, tranquil as settled snow, "it's nothing. You've just gotten overheated with working in the mine."

"Are you sure?"

Betiya sniffed. "Yes. Unless you take fever by sunset. Or, unless you've rubbed witches' moss over your arm, in that case no one can help you."

Ty winced inwardly and shook the sleeve over his arm. "May our Mighty One spare me *that*. Thank you, all. I will try to reassure myself with your opinions." Curious, he asked Betiya, "Witches' moss?"

"How can you not know about witches' moss?" The woman's polite derision informed Ty that he'd utterly failed in basic Eosyth life-skills. He smiled at the intrepid lady, allowing silence to rule. If he confessed ignorance due to not being born an Eosyth, which they all knew anyway, then her questions would begin. Much as Ty liked Betiya, she was nosy and bossy—as Ayden might phrase it. She gave her awl and a handful of leather lacings to Serena, who'd twitched as if to stand. "Finish my edge for me, Serena. Neatly, mind you! I don't want a sloppy screen in my tent for the next ten years. Ty, follow me. I'll show you a creeping of witches' moss I spied this morning. I suppose you can be forgiven for not knowing; you haven't spent a spring-season with us. Adelia, may I borrow a lamp?"

"Of course." Adelia leaned over the frame again and lifted her awl to punch more holes in the cured leather. "Kill the moss, Bet-dear, and alert everyone to any resistant patches."

"You know I will."

Ty leaned down to set Miyna on her feet, but the toddler howled and clung to his arm. Betiya shrugged and gave Miyna a doting smile. "Throw a blanket around the little imp and let's take her with us. We won't be long."

"Thanks!" Tessi breathed—clearly so moved by gratitude that she deemed speaking as vital. And Kari gazed at Ty adoringly as if he'd saved her from an intolerable task. He grinned at the gangly, freckle-nosed pair. Undoubtedly, they'd drag out their knucklebones game the instant he carried Miyna from the tent. And they would return to their silent, elaborate language.

Her lips pressed tight, Serena stood and retrieved a heavy felted coverlet for Miyna. But she flung her aunt a reproving look. Betiya ignored her, instead checking the oil and lighting the wick in a small bronze lamp. Guarding the flame, she led Ty outside and through the encampment to narrow ridge. In his arms, Miyna chortled as if she'd gained what she wanted—a walk outside. Betiya gave the toddler a toothy smile and crooned, "Ooo, you pretty little bug! Why couldn't I have a daughter? Just one?"

"I quite understand." Ty tugged the coverlet more firmly around Miyna. "I've always wanted a daughter or a son. Perhaps one day, the Infinite will bless me with children."

"Mm-hm." Betiya paused near a natural wall of stone. Dry-voiced, she said, "I'm sure He will. You'll be an excellent father, Ty, if you don't spoil your children. You've a winning way with little ones—and with ladies."

"I'd say thank you, but I'm not sure you're complimenting me as much as warning me."

"You're also quite clever." While they were beyond earshot of the encampment, Ty expected her to interrogate him. Instead, she motioned to a dim, green-gray puff of growth barely showing within a niche on the cold stone wall. "Did you touch anything like this?"

"No."

"Then you'll live. Foreigners from Darzeq and Istgard sometimes raid our lands for this moss and they turn it into poison to kill each other. Vile things—the moss and the thieves. This moss would have turned bright green within the next few weeks. Now, however, it's dry and easy to kill." She held the lamp's wavering flame near the stone outcrop and set the winter-dried moss afire. A peculiar green flame crept thinly along the stone leaving powdered gray ashes in its wake. Fixated on her task, Betiya touched the flame to all gaps in the stone, until every part of the formation within reach was laced with green fire. Satisfied, she stepped back. "Where did you say you were born, Ty?"

He smiled. "In a distant place. I apologize for so few details. I was too young to remember the event."

"Brash young men with secrets," Betiya shook her head at him. "May the Infinite chase your soul forever if you upset our Serena's purpose. She's to marry a future Eosyth lord."

Ty's invisible hackles raised with alarm and fury. He seized calm. "Who?"

"Josias, son of Tsir Davor. Or Lije, son of Tsir Mikial—they're much the same age as Serena. You'll meet them in a few weeks. The lords and their sons have planned a meeting to discuss the Agocii threat."

Josias and Lije? His own captives taken from the Eosyths' lands and enslaved in Belaal?

So they had been freed as he'd instructed in his written will. But he hadn't expected to awaken in Eosyth territories.

Ty schooled his face to well-practiced smoothness, but sweat beaded beneath his heavy garments, and his thoughts raced, frantic as a snared creature's thrashing.

They'd recognize him at once.

He must contrive to escape disaster.

Chapter 13

Finished with practice, Ty lowered his bow and motioned to Ayden, who was looking around at the clan's new encampment. "I'd say we've practiced enough for today. Do you agree, sir?"

"Yep!" Ayden all but swaggered as they marched toward their battered leather target. "I'm going to show my lord-father that I can hold four arrows now, and then I'll watch for our visitors. I hope they arrive today."

Visitors. The Eosyth clans' lords—which was why Clan Darom had moved north, into this broad mountain valley at the joint boundaries of Darzeq and Istgard. Though less sheltered, this new location was more easily reached by the northern clans. Yet Clan Darom wasn't beyond Agocii threats. Ty scanned the nearby slopes. Ayden grumbled, "You're slow as an old man!"

"And you're as impatient as a flea!" Ty shifted his bow and helped the little boy gather his arrows, grinning at Ayden's enthusiasm. He'd found a temporary younger brother in Ayden, complete with spitting contests, discussing wild-imagined plans for the future, and taunting each other over missed shots during archery practice.

Tonight, he would sit down near the hearth with the boy and Tsir Andris, and they'd make more arrows and then fall asleep early. Yesterday's journey here had been uneventful, but wearying.

Laughter and feminine voices drew Bel-Tygeon's attention. Serena's laughter in particular. He fought to conceal his admiration. Her beautiful smile, and the dark auburn gleam of her loose recently-scrubbed sunlit hair shone temptingly as she walked from the encampment with the twins. Serena met his gaze and her hazel eyes sobered a bit as she passed him, heading toward a nearby slope. Why were they hiking toward the slope? Even as Ty wondered, Ayden yelled, "Hey! Where are you three going?"

Serena turned and flung a bright smile at her little brother. "We're checking our stash of supplies to see if they've survived the winter here without us."

Ayden charged after them. "Wait! I want to go with you!"

So did Ty, but if he chased Serena in an un-brotherly fashion, others would notice.

Wiser by far to remain silent and help Tsir Andris with the horses instead—though he couldn't resist a furtive glance over his shoulder to once again admire Serena's glossy loosened hair and her lively pace as she hurried Ayden along. Even beneath her heavy winter clothes, her form appeared graceful, curved, and enticing. No doubt Josias and Lije would be competing for her attention when they arrived.

Infuriating thought. Yet what could he say if one of the other young men decided to court Serena and she agreed? He couldn't speak of his kingdom or wealth. Perhaps he had neither after all this time. Moreover, Serena would hate Ty for his past oppression of her people. Belaal's traditions, too, stood in his way. Serena met none of Belaal's legal requirements for a royal wife and she never would. But if only she could!

How much longer he could he continue to behave honorably toward Serena?

Forever, his conscience and heart argued. Yet the urge to touch her, to speak of his love for her, was becoming difficult to resist. He must find a polite excuse to move into another Eosyth's tent without insulting Tsir Andris and his family. And without alarming his prospective host.

Pondering his dilemma, he found the Eosyth lord to the north of the new encampment. Seeing him, Tsir Andris grinned. "Ah, a willing worker! The others are repairing the far paddock—this one's the least broken, so we've half the herd here. Ty, help me with this gate. I need to test the brackets. Then we'll deal with the stones." He nodded toward several stones that had tumbled from the massive paddock walls. "I would vow that this camp has been invaded during our absence—these walls and gates have never taken such a beating in less than a year. And by the tracks around these fields, a herd of horses was driven through here before our own."

"That's a disquieting thought." Ty braced himself and helped the Eosyth lord lift the sagging wooden-poled gate and then he held it within the brackets as Tsir Andris checked its heavy pegs and bars.

"I'm convinced it's true." Tsir Andris grunted as he shoved against one of the brackets, testing its strength. "At least our ungrateful guests—whoever they were—only took down the gate and the top-stones on this paddock. I must remind everyone to not become complacent here. As the weather warms, we may well become targets for raiders. Particularly since we've been mining this winter. In a few weeks, I'll go down to Kiyrem in Darzeq and trade the gems for more supplies. Perhaps you'd like to journey with me."

Kiyrem? Ty's thoughts sharpened at the name. According to Detzios, Kiyrem was the home of Darzeq's famed Master-scribe, Tredin, who'd schooled Detzios and Nikaros for five years. Detzios had laughed at the memory. "Worst five years of my life—living in that school. Master Tredin was a fiend in mortal form. But by the time he'd finished beating me, I'd learned enough to take my place as Clan Darom's scribe. Nikaros fared better, being a quick learner and the son of Lord Levos."

Remembering the conversation, Ty nodded to Tsir Andris. "Yes, I'd like to accompany you to Kiyrem." The journey would temporarily remove him from Serena—which was probably her father's intention.

While they finished repairing the gate and replacing the nearby stones, Tsir Andris talked of the prospective journey and the goods they'd purchase in Darzeq. Until distant whistles and a hunting horn's blare cut through the brisk morning air.

Tsir Andris straightened. Bland-voiced, he said, "Ty, please go check the other side of the paddock for damage."

Was Tsir Andris sending him away from the necessity of greeting their visitors? Away from potential recognition? Ty studied the proud man briefly. Had he guessed Ty's true status? He'd learn soon enough.

Ty bowed his head, so humble that he might never have been a god-king. "Yes, my lord."

Satisfying to watch the lord's gaze flicker with uncertainty. So the Eosyth lord did hold doubts about Ty. Interesting. And mortifying. Bel-Tygeon didn't deserve such protection.

Infinite, bless Tsir Andris, Your faithful servant. May I be equally honorable.

Ty squared his shoulders and walked alongside the ancient rock wall, away from their visitors' approach. By sending him away, Tsir Andris was only delaying the inevitable. Ty must seize the initiative and hopefully mitigate his two greatest risks—Josias, son of Tsir Davor of Clan Ma'rawb, and Lije, son of Tsir Mikial and heir of Clan Tsahfon.

Fresh splits and splinters stung Ty's callused fingers as he lifted the first stone. He'd have to ask Serena for some balm tonight to mend the raw splits on his thumbs. The dried skin was catching on everything he touched. Aggravated, Ty placed the stone on a hollow rimming the paddock and then gnawed at the ragged flesh on his thumb. He spit the skin tag with such ferocity that his sister would have pretended faintness just before rapping him with her fan. If she was yet alive.... Infinite, let Rethae be alive! Let her remain safe...

Another horn blast made him turn and watch the visitors approach. A brawny commanding man rode ahead of the others, his gilded sword, round shield, elaborate longbow and heavily embellished goatskin coat emphasizing his physique and his status. His brown hair and powerful, calm features startled Ty with their familiarity—though they'd met before at Parne. Levos of Clan Qedem—High Lord of the Eosyths, and the father of Nikaros, Belaal's captive.

Guilt swept over Ty like a wave, so physical that he stepped back. Infinite, I've wounded this good lord and his people beyond measure. How can I repay them?

How would they repay him?

Would Lord Levos kill Bel-Tygeon for taking his son hostage?

Ty retreated, but he flung another glance over his shoulder, scanning Clan Darom's guests. There, riding in the center of the band, were Josias and Lije—both looking older and almost like brothers, their dark hair longer, their beards winter-wild. Dangerous as the pair might be to him, Ty was almost grateful for their presence. If they didn't kill him, perhaps they had news of Belaal.

Keeping the visitors within his wary line of vision, Ty retreated to the far side of the stone paddock and peered through the milling herd of horses, watching for his chance to confront Josias and Lije.

The Eosyth lords greeted each other as kindred, with embraces and fist-strikes to each other's shoulders. Lije waved his hands dramatically and bellowed out a pretend-complaint, making everyone laugh, including Lije. Obviously the young man hadn't changed—he'd ever been the cheerful rattling jester, balancing Josias's perpetual air of stolid gloom.

Almost as one, the Eosyth lords walked together toward Tsir Andris's large pale tent while Josias and Lije and a sturdy adolescent boy unloaded the horses, rubbed them down, checked their hooves, and then guided them inside the stone paddock. Ty worked along the wall, retrieving and replacing rocks, slowly making his way toward the trio. The stocky youth ignored him with the single-mindedness of a starved person laboring for a meal.

Josias and Lije, however, laughed as they worked, obviously pleased to reach their journey's end. Or were they pleased to be within the same encampment as Serena?

Ty gritted his teeth at the thought and heaved another tumbled rock onto the wall.

As they unloaded the last horse, the big resolute young man said, "We're done. I'll haul off some of the gear." He shouldered two leather packs and a sleeping roll.

Lije huffed, "That's all you can carry? Ildros, you're a weakling! Or is it that you can't reach for more? Here…let me help you."

He settled two more packs over the young man's shoulders and stepped back. "That's better, isn't it?"

"Hardly," Ildros grumbled.

He lumbered off, and Josias chuckled. "We won't see him again until our work's done."

Or until he'd emptied several kettles of food, Ty guessed. He grinned, set another loose rock atop the wall and then without looking at his quarry, he deepened his voice and yelled, "Do you two need some help?"

Josias yelled back, "That's good of you—yes!"

As both men hunkered down beside the heap of gear, Ty strode toward them. Josias was saying, "Yes, there's enough for three to carry, if we make two trips each. Confound Ildros and his weak bladder!"

"I thought it was his empty stomach," Ty replied in his usual voice. "Welcome, Josias and Lije." As one, they turned, then gasped. Mouths agape amid their black beards, they backed off, mirroring each other's shocked expressions. Before they could say a word, Bel-Tygeon said, "Yes. It's me. By the Infinite's unending mercy. Among Clan Darom, I'm called Ty, and I am the guest of Tsir Andris. Though I suspect he's guessed who I am."

Lije faltered, still gawping and round-eyed as a fish, "And…he's allowed you to live?"

**

Her boots scuffing over the cave's gritty rough-stone floor, Serena halted and surveyed the remains of Clan Darom's late-winter cache in the lamp light. Now that she and the children had organized everything, she took true measure of the Clan's reserves, then swallowed as her stomach took a sickening plunge.

So little left after storing so much last year….

On either side of Serena, oblivious to her distress, the twins were now humming, their hands fluttering in a secret song all their own, while Ayden scooted toward the shadowed base of a wall, checking glints in the rock as if planning to mine for gems. If he'd been older, he'd be mining for gems to sell in Darzeq. The Clan needed to offset their losses.

How cruel of the unknown raiders! Clan Darom must now strictly ration their food until the harvest. She and mother would soon lose the weight they'd regained this winter.

Summoning the courage to break the news to her parents and the clan, Serena practiced on her siblings. "We won't be able to stay in this camp as long as we've planned, thanks to whoever raided our supplies. If we stay here, we'll starve."

Tessi and Kari stopped humming and Ayden looked over his shoulder at her, his small dear face wrinkled fretfully. "That sounds bad."

"It is. Come along, you three." She lifted the lamps and then eyed the twins, who were now flickering signs of agitation at each other. Seizing the chance to think of something besides near-starvation, Serena announced, "Tessi and Kari, tonight when we return to the tent, you'll show me some of your signs—we've delayed my lessons long enough."

The twins looked as if she'd slapped them both at once. Kari whined out real words. "Must we?"

"Yes, you must—you can't continue to close off most of your family by keeping so many secrets. And you need to share with Ayden and our parents as well."

The two traded desolate glances in the lamp light and Tessi sighed. "But sharing everything will take years."

"No it won't. Furthermore if you don't share, I'll confiscate your knucklebones game. You'll have plenty of time to share then." Serena handed her a lamp. "Come on." She led them through the cave's narrow funnel-like entry tunnel, with Ayden dragging his fingers along the walls while the twins moped.

Outside, Serena drew in a cool breath of air, and she scanned the hills and more distant crests above. No Agocii. As there'd been none all winter—thank goodness. The goat thief had surely been the chieftain Cziybor himself, as Ty insisted. Who else could vanish so quickly? Who else would have worn such amounts of gold in his beard that one fallen kill-marker had vanished unnoticed?

While she led her siblings down the slope, Serena clasped the small beaten-gold pendant dangling against the hollow of her throat. Undoubtedly, Cziybor wouldn't approve of his refashioned gold serving as a feminine ornament. Father had given her the gold in agreement with Ty that it should serve as repayment for her goat.

No one had mentioned the little tradition that a man who offered gold to a woman's family was asking that she consider him as a husband. Ty's ignorance of their customs must be excused. However, if he offered her a ceremonial dagger, she must gently correct him and refuse. To accept a ceremonial dagger was to accept responsibility for a man and his future family. As Aunt Betiya had needlessly reminded Serena, her plan to ultimately lead a clan allowed her only one of two choices: Josias of Clan Ma'rawb, or Lije of Clan Tsahfon.

They'd arrive here sometime this week with their lord-fathers and with High Lord Levos. They…were here now. Serena stopped and stared at Josias and Lije, her prospective suitors, who stood with Ty, starlings compared to an eagle. She almost covered her eyes at the sight.

Ty dominated the two—she couldn't help but notice. The Eosyth heirs listened to Ty, their expressions hesitant, almost meek as he questioned them. Not a fine sight for any woman gauging her future husband.

Unless her future husband was Ty. For a foolish instant, her thoughts rested with him. If only Ty could have intentionally given her parents the gold she now wore. She would have worked up their own tent alone if need be, felting the wool and binding the coverings… Foolishness indeed. She could not sacrifice her long-held dreams in favor of a man who might soon leave the mountains.

Her chin up, she led the twins and Ayden to her mother's tent and leaned inside, just in time to hear High Lord Levos muse aloud in his deep, full voice, "Yes, the Agocii are becoming too bold. We'll move the Clans southward to help you lest they attack."

***

"Where's Nikaros?" Ty demanded of Josias and Lije. "Did he remain in Belaal as I asked?"

Josias licked his lips. "Yes, Sire—Ty—he resides there still. Furthermore he obeys your instructions and the Lady Dasarai's with absolute loyalty. You'll be pleased, except…"

Lije yanked at his comrade's sleeve and interposed, "Except that the Lady Dasarai compelled him to marry your prophet, Araine. Or, rather, she gave Araine to Nikaros and he married Araine according to Eosyth customs."

Struck as if he'd taken an arrow to the gut, Ty stared at the two. "What!"

Josias flinched, adding, "Araine is still a slave of Belaal—that edict Dasarai obeyed. Yet it was a sad wedding. Araine mourned over your exile the entire day. We left the next morning."

"I understand." Ty turned away, enduring the emotional attack. His own sister had betrayed him and Nikaros had bowed to her scheme—though Bel-Tygeon had certainly left him with enough independence to defy such edicts. As for Araine… He wouldn't think of Araine.

He eyed his two former captives. "Have you heard anything of Siyrsun's whereabouts?"

Lije shook his head. "No, Sire. We've hoped he's dead."

"He's not; he's resilient and cunning as an old dreki. When the weather warms, I must leave the mountains and reclaim Belaal. Can I depend upon you two for assistance?"

***

"Tomorrow, we leave for Kiyrem," Tsir Andris informed Ty as they stood in the snowy, dawn-tinged pasture, watching their visitors depart. "The instant we return, we'll help pack out the clan and move north."

"Yes, my lord." Ty nodded, watching Josias and Lije ride away with their lord-fathers. They'd pledged to escort him from the mountains as soon as the weather warmed. And to his knowledge, they'd breathed nothing of his identity to anyone—nor would they. Nikaros had ordered them to say nothing among the Eosyths of what had happened in Belaal.

Why? Was Nikaros still working for Belaal? For the Eosyths? Or for himself now?

He *had* taken Araine, though she was Ty's own slave and cherished prophet.

This betrayal would require time and forgiveness. Yet Josias and Lije insisted that Nikaros remained a true friend. Could it be so?

Perhaps. If he could forgive such a personal betrayal. He must return to his kingdom, and then seek answers. Without Serena…

***

Nikaros halted his horse in the snow-edged meadow and nodded to Commander Rtial Vioc. "I'll wait for you here. Take half the men and ride over that ridge. You should find him in the encampment below—a guest of those in the pale tent. Tell him that his servant waits."

Vioc half-bowed in his saddle. "Yes, my lord. But won't you greet your own people?"

Nikaros closed his eyes and shook his head. "If I see my people, Commander, I won't be able to leave them. And I must return to Belaal."

Chapter 14

Done with his afternoon meal, Ty relaxed, waiting for Ayden to finish eating so they could return to work on the paddocks. Idly, he watched the twins continue their endless game, their delicate hands lifting, curving, and slicing the air as they argued in their silent, secretive language. He'd begun to pick up a few of their meanings. A small outward sweep for 'no' and an abrupt pat on a hand or on air for 'wait.' Their motions for 'eat' and 'drink' were easier, but he suspected the subtle fist-strikes were more complex than 'angry' or 'hate'. Did a fist-strike convey the negative emotion's intensity by the angle of its downward movement? Interesting.

Seated between Ty and the twins, Miyna finished the crisp seed wafer she'd been munching, and she lifted her chubby hand toward the twins to halt their game. Testing his theory, Ty gently swept his hand outward and then patted the air before Miyna. The little girl paused and looked up at him. To celebrate his victory, he smiled and scooped a seed wafer into a small dish of soft gamey-tasting goat cheese—which he'd learned to enjoy—and he handed it to the child. She accepted his offering, but thumped her tiny fist on her knee, her expression distinctively grumpy.

Ty almost laughed at her toddler-outrage. Almost. She'd soon begin to howl, and inside the tent, her voice was a true weapon, which was far from amusing. Interestingly, her fist-strike had a different angle altogether from the twins' motion. Hmm…

Serena, feeding another sliver of wood into the fire beneath the grate, murmured to Ty, "I saw that."

He grinned at her. Serena rewarded him with a dazzling smile, and then looked away as if self-conscious. From the other side of the hearth, Adelia glanced up from her mending and lifted her fine dark eyebrows at Serena—the expression of a watchful mother pondering her tactics.

As Ayden swallowed the last of his allotted food, Ty stood. "We should return to the herds." He bowed his head to Adelia and Serena. "Thank you, ladies. May the Infinite bless your afternoon's work."

Adelia allowed him a smile, but a corner of Serena's lovely full mouth skewed down slightly, as if she pondered his words and questioned the Infinite's abilities. Gently, Adelia said, "When you greet my lord-husband, please remind him again that he must eat. I'll help him gather supplies for your journey while he rests."

"Lady, I will." Ty bowed again. No doubt Adelia was grateful that he would depart for Kiyrem at dawn. "Indeed, I'll carry his gear myself."

"Thank you, Ty. If he—" Whistles and shouts from outside silenced Adelia. She stood, her eyes wide.

Ayden scrambled to his feet, his young face tensed. Did he yet fear that Cziybor would invade the camp to carve out his tongue? Would Cziybor attack so directly?

Heart thudding, Ty reach for his bow and the quiver of arrows he'd placed near the doorway. He fanned an array of arrows beneath his left thumb, curved his fingers around the bow's stave, and then stepped outside, prepared to defend Clan Darom.

Vioc—one of Belaal's most stalwart commanders—was leading one of Bel-Tygeon's own horses up to the tent. Vioc halted and bowed, clad in unremarkable leather robes, without a trace of anything from Belaal. Why? Ty summoned coherence. "You found me…"

Vioc grinned, transparent joy easing his squared face. "Yes, my lord, may the Infinite be praised forever—He granted us a vision, and we praise Him that we've found you safe and well! Please, you must come away at once. Your servant waits beyond that ridge."

"Yes…" Ty couldn't say more. Yet that one word was enough. With it, Bel-Tygeon watched his dreams of an obscure life with Serena die—vanishing like vapor in chilled air.

Apparently drawn by the commotion, Tsir Andris hurried toward them, his bow and arrows arrayed for a conflict. He looked from the men to Ty. "Do you know these men?"

Ty nodded, his words a bleak monotone. "They're my own men. I must go with them."

Caution darkened the Eosyth lord's eyes and he lowered his voice. "They are welcome to rest here for the night, Ty, being your friends."

Was the Eosyth lord wary of handing him over to men who might not be as friendly as they seemed? Ty shook off some of his own shock. "Thank you, my lord." He eyed Vioc. "What do you say, sir?" He longed to pull aside Vioc and question the man. Was Rethae well? Did Belaal still consider Bel-Tygeon as its king? Where was Araine? What about Nikaros?

Vioc bowed his thanks to Ty and then to Tsir Andris. "My lord, first I repeat my gratitude that we have found you safe and well. As for your host—you are Tsir Andris, are you not? May the Infinite bless you and your clan for your kindness in protecting our lord. Please forgive our haste, but we must leave as soon as possible."

His mention of the Infinite and his obvious sincerity in offering a blessing, not to mention knowing the Eosyth lord's name, set Tsir Andris at ease. His wariness faded, and he smiled, though Serena frowned from the tent's entry. *She* wasn't so trusting simply because some pleasant-faced man had spoken a blessing in the Infinite's Name. Yet Tsir Andris seemed convinced. He swept his hands toward all the men. "Why must you leave? Stay awhile and rest."

Listening, Ayden perked up, clearly no longer able to restrain himself. "Will we have a feast?"

One more meal with his adoptive family. A reprieve. Ty opened his mouth to accept, but Vioc hastily knelt.

"My lord," Vioc pleaded, "we beg your forgiveness and permission to depart. We've a long journey yet, and our lord is desperately needed in his…domain."

Fear slithered over Ty's skin and then coiled in his guts. What was wrong? "Vioc, is my sister well?"

Vioc blinked, clearly taken aback. "She is, my lord, but she holds a thousand threads in one hand while commanding your concerns with the other. She cannot rest until you return."

"Infinite, thank You!" Ty ran a hand over his hair and exhaled. "I'll depart at once."

He turned to Tsir Andris and gripped the man's bare hand. "My lord, may the Infinite—our Mighty One—forever bless you and your family for your kindness! I give you my word, I'll seize any chance to repay your benevolence toward me this winter."

The Eosyth lord shrugged depreciatively. "No repayment's needed. If I've served the Infinite by protecting you, then we're all rewarded."

Fighting to keep his words respectful, not commanding, Ty asked, "Will you move north soon?"

Tsir Andris exhaled, then nodded, clearly setting aside the idea of a trip to Kiyrem for the sake of his clan. "Yes, if it will set your fears to rest, we'll leave tomorrow morning before dawn. We'll shelter in a valley near the Kehb'el Caves. We should be safe there—it's our northern-most site and rarely used."

Ayden tugged at Ty's arm, his voice rising, young and pitiable. "You're leaving? *Now?*"

Ty knelt before the boy. "I must. My sister needs my help." He withdrew five arrows from his quiver and handed the remainder in the quiver to Ayden. "Keep these for yourself, and remember me. I've enjoyed our archery practice."

Ayden flung himself at Ty and hugged him, snuffling moistly as if fighting tears. His words almost inaudible, Ayden said, "At least I had an older brother for a while!"

"To me, you're ever my younger brother—therefore I'll sound like one now." Ty patted the boy, then shook him gently. "Keep watch against Cziybor and obey your parents and Serena. Hurry everyone north without delay. Promise?"

Ayden stepped back, blinked his tear-rimmed eyes, and then lifted his chin. "Promise."

The Lady Adelia had emerged from the tent and stood beside her husband, Miyna in her arms and the twins beside her. "Ty, you've been a most welcomed guest. A blessing to us all. Will you return?"

"I hope to. Yet even if I never return, Lady, I'll remember you and your family and Clan Darom. May the Infinite bless you and redouble your joys after your losses these past few years."

"Thank you." Adelia inclined her head, as regal and lovely as his sister in Sulaanc. To Vioc, she said, "If you and your men need supplies for your return journey, we'll provide them."

Clearly recognizing her status, Vioc bowed. "Lady, your offer is most gracious and appreciated with all respect and admiration. How good it was of the Infinite to bring our master to your tents! However, we have all we need." He motioned to two other men, who'd dismounted. They approached, carrying a small, heavy wooden box. Kneeling, they offered the box to Tsir Andris. Vioc said, "Please accept our gift, which expresses our joy in finding our lord safe. May our Creator multiply this treasure in your service."

Ty winced. Had his servants betrayed his identity with marked gold from Belaal?

But Tsir Andris shook his head and repeated, "No repayment is needed. When a guest has become a cherished family member, even a feather is too much reward. I can't accept this."

Seeing a way to leave the gift safely, Ty said, "Then I give it to all in Clan Darom. But you're forbidden to open the box until you reach the Kehb'el Caves." Surely the promise of a gift would hurry Clan Darom northward to safety, and ensure his own escape.

By now, everyone in the clan who wasn't guarding or tending animals was watching and listening. Their collective gazes mutely appealed to Tsir Andris to accept the reward and ease the loss of their winter cache. At last, the Eosyth lord yielded to his clan's silent plea, and nodded. Vioc offered Tsir Andris the key, and Ty's men placed the chest unopened before the pale tent.

The twins charged at Ty, crying and motioning their grief as they hugged him. Betiya and Zeddi followed, with their sons, then Detzios, and one by one, all present.

As the sunlight shifted, Ty turned away from the clan and touched Miyna's sweetly rounded face. Unable to speak to the silent, wide-eyed little girl, he motioned his unhappiness at leaving with a slight fist-strike, followed by a gentle patting-air motion. Wait.

Miyna moped at the sign, her sweet face perfectly replicating Serena's unhappy regard.

The instant Ty glanced at Serena, however, she turned away—motioning for him to wait.

Bel-Tygeon waited. Forever, he hoped.

Waiting meant that he didn't have to leave Serena.

***

As Ty waited, Serena blinked down tears and stifled her protest. What could she possibly say to prevent his departure? He was *someone* as she'd suspected. Each of the rough-clad men waiting on him looked ready to kill for his sake. She caught her breath, dizzied. Ty was leaving. No... But even as her whole being mourned, she reached inside the tent, removed Ty's goatskin coat from its peg and handed him the heavy garment. "You'll need this until you leave the mountains."

"I'll need this for all my life," Ty corrected gently. "Thank you, Lady."

He set down his weapons and donned the coat. Finished tucking in his crimson wool belt,

Ty turned to Serena at the tent's entry, his height blocking her from the others' avid stares. He gazed at her as if he could watch her forever, his expression so vulnerable, so anguished that she had to bite down tears—a wasted effort. She wiped her eyes.

Looking up into his beloved face, Serena willed her voice to work. "Who are you?"

"Your debtor. And forever grateful. The Infinite blessed me beyond measure by restoring my senses here." He admired her with his silent, eloquent gaze—she would have sworn that he was counting the very freckles on her nose. Ty clasped Serena's right hand

and held it against his heart. "Thank you for everything—you saved my life, and I'll never forget it! Please, save your family now. Hurry north! Remain vigilant and guard yourself!" He glanced away briefly, as if afraid to speak. But then, he locked his gaze with hers and whispered, "If I'd stayed as I wished, would you have married me?"

An invisible cord knotted itself about her throat. But she nodded and managed to rasp, "Even if we'd…had to live in a cave. But you aren't meant for caves…and you must leave."

"I'd plead to marry you now," Ty whispered. "But my future wife, whoever she is, will be bound by so many laws and expectations—" He caught his breath and persisted. "I could never demand such dire sacrifices of you—you could never fulfill those laws. Only know this: I'll never forget you!"

He kissed her fingers, bowed to her, and retreated, his footsteps weighted as if he walked toward some dire punishment.

Resisting sobs, Serena stared up at the chilly blue sky instead while Ty mounted his waiting horse. Then, composed again, she crossed her arms and held herself still as she watched him ride away with his men.

She *would* fall in love with a madman. A noble someone she could never marry. Now she must forget him, even if it took her entire life.

Her lifetime of marriage with… Josias. Or…Lije.

Serena sucked in a stabbing breath, enduring its pain. The instant she could politely do so, she bowed herself into Mother's tent, pressed her hands over her face and wept, rocking in silent grief.

***

When he was finally able to speak again, able to temporarily endure the memory of Serena's tears, Ty called ahead to his guardian and guide, "Vioc, what gift did you offer to Clan Darom?"

Vioc slowed his horse until he rode just slightly back at Ty's right. "I offered exactly what Lord Nikaros provided, Sire. He—"

"Sir," Bel-Tygeon corrected. "Until we reach safety, you and the others must call me, 'sir' and nothing more."

"Yes, sir." Vioc bowed his head and continued, "Your servant provided small, unmarked gold ingots."

Ty exhaled his relief. At least Serena would never know that the madman she'd tended, nursed, scolded, and loved was the despicable Bel-Tygeon. Even so…

He ground his calloused knuckles fiercely over his heart, as if physical pain could fill the invisible tormenting wound left by his parting with Serena and Clan Darom.

To no one, Vioc sighed aloud, "What a wondrous-terrible thing it is to possess a heart of flesh in this broken world. Infinite, bless You forever…."

Ty agreed in pained silence, focusing hard on his horse's flicking brown ears and smoothly combed mane as they rode up the slope toward a gently carved mountain pass. Raw-voiced, he asked, "Where is my servant Nikaros?"

"He's waiting for you, sir. Just beyond that ridge."

With an explanation, perhaps, for marrying Araine. Ty goaded his horse ahead, forcing his men to quicken their pace. Forcing himself to remain calm. Most of all he must not resent Nikaros for finding him so swiftly, before he could be certain of Clan Darom's safety.

Infinite, Lord of All, in my heart, I kneel and beg You to protect Serena and her family from Cziybor!

Chapter 15

Nikaros flexed his chilled fingers around his bow's stave as he paced, his horse trailing him and nosing the icy ground. What was taking Vioc so long? Infinite, let all be well. Let the king and Clan Darom be safe! Let us be as shadows escaping Agocii notice!

And Eosyth notice.

The longer he waited here, the greater his risk of being recognized, and he did not want his parents to learn that he'd been in Eosyth lands without greeting them—their hurt would be endless. Soon, if the Agocii threat could be suppressed, he'd bring Araine to meet his parents.

If the king approved.

If he didn't kill or imprison Nik for life for daring to wed Araine.

Turning toward the narrow mountain pass again, toward the early-afternoon sunlight, Nikaros glimpsed the first rider cresting the rocky divide. The king. Closely followed by Vioc and their troop of wary, leather-clad, weapon-wielding men.

As Bel-Tygeon rode toward him—composed as a stone carving— Nikaros knelt, placed his weapons on the frozen ground, and then bowed his head until the icy loam chilled his face. Above all, he was the Infinite's servant, and the Infinite had placed him in Belaal to work for the king. Therefore, he would work with all his might if Bel-Tygeon forgave him.

It didn't matter if a king followed the Infinite; the king was yet a man and vulnerable to every destructive mortal impulse, including vengeance—and Araine was worth the king's wrath.

Nikaros remained humbly bowed and still, his heart thudding, his breath and hands icy in the cold air. The king's chestnut horse drew near, its hooves sending small tremors through the soil. Bel-Tygeon halted the beast and dismounted, his boots crunching against frost and hardened patches of snow. For an instant, the king stood above him, silent as Nik slid a glance at his scuffed, battered Eosyth-style boots. Then, quietly, in the tone of a man guarding his words, Bel-Tygeon asked, "Son of Levos, why are you still bowed?"

"Because I've offended you and must beg your forgiveness. I married your prophet, your own slave, according to Eosyth customs."

Dry-voiced, the king said, "I know. I also know that you obeyed an order from my sister—though you could have resisted."

True. But Araine was Nik's mortal weakness—beyond resisting. Surely the king knew this as well. Only truth and coolness would serve them all now. "You know I love her. Yet she's been mourning for you these past sixteen months. We've all prayed for you."

"Indeed?" Nik heard the beginning of forgiveness in that one word. Bel-Tygeon leaned down and tapped him on the shoulder. "Stand. Let's depart, if we must."

"Thank you, Sire." Nikaros stood, facing the king, meeting his scrutiny. "If we stay much longer, I'll never leave these lands—and we must return to Sulaanc."

Bel-Tygeon took a quick breath, and his gaze flinched away, unspoken pain swiftly concealed behind a stern, regal mask of coldness. "I agree. We'll leave at once."

He mounted his horse again, looking every bit an Eosyth surrounded by a pack of formidable outlaws. Nik recaptured his weapons and his grazing horse and readied himself to travel. They rode east, silent except for the creaking of leather saddles, the occasional clinking of tack, and the thudding of narrow supply carts. All along the trail, Nikaros scanned the nearby ridges and trees for signs of Agocii.

He and Vioc had agreed to urge the king and the men out to the plains with all possible speed. Thankfully, Bel-Tygeon rode on, steadfast and silent, as if he fully approved their plan—though his bleak expression betrayed misery at their abrupt departure from Clan Darom.

That night, at the evening fire, Bel-Tygeon accepted the dried meat, salted broth and dense grain cakes offered by Vioc. Instead of eating, he looked around, his gaze resting briefly on each soldier as he spoke for the first time since their departure from the mountain pass. "Thank you, Vioc, and thank you all. Your courage and your service to Belaal will be remembered and rewarded, if the Infinite restores me to my kingdom." He looked up at the evening stars and prayed aloud, "Infinite, our Mighty One, may Your name be praised forever! We ask that You bless our meal and this journey as we return to Belaal. Above all, I beg You to protect Tsir Andris and his family for their obedience to Your will…"

Nikaros froze, unable to breathe as he comprehended the extent of Bel-Tygeon's transformation. It was one thing to know that the Infinite had spared the former god-king for finally acknowledging his Creator's might and his own despotic weakness. It was quite another thing to witness Bel-Tygeon's new-found humility and faith.

As one, all the men stared at their king, frozen by his open admission that he now worshiped the Infinite. That he was mortal, not a god, and not above pleading for favor from their Creator.

Air returned to Nik's lungs, and he twitched with the longing to whoop like a boy—to shamelessly exult over the king's words. If only Araine could hear Bel-Tygeon and know that the Infinite's faithful in Belaal need no longer fear their king's persecution. But perhaps as Belaal's prophet, she'd already seen and heard the king's prayer.

Infinite, there is no one like You! Who will believe that Belaal's god has become Your servant?

Bel-Tygeon studied Nikaros and then motioned for him to approach. "How did you know exactly where to find me? Did Araine see this in a vision?"

"No, sir. The Infinite granted me knowledge of your whereabouts. In fact, when you were first stricken, by the Infinite's will, I was able to track your path until you escaped the garden. Afterward, I watched for you in visions, so I knew you were here."

"You've been hunting me, then."

"No, sir. The Infinite has hunted you—in the best possible way."

Bel-Tygeon shifted as if this insight didn't rest easily within his thoughts. "Have you been able to see me throughout the year?"

"Only enough from time to time, to reveal your safety and location." Nik grinned, remembering his insight of the king walking with Detzios, the humble Eosyth scribe. "What do you think of Detzios?"

Bel-Tygeon almost smiled. "He's a good man. He became my friend after he realized I could not marry the young woman he's besotted with."

"Yes, Serena—my sister by marriage. He's loved her for years."

The king stared as if Nikaros had been the madman. "Serena is your sister by marriage? What are you talking about?"

Hadn't the king learned Nik's secrets by now? Evidently not. On his guard, Nik mentally approached the subject as if it were a viper that might strike. "Sir…did anyone mention Serena's older sister, Tiphera?"

"Yes, during prayers—with your name—and with mine. I was so discomfited at hearing them pray for Belaal's king and for your eventual release, that I never questioned them about Tiphera. I knew only that she was the eldest daughter and that she'd married a man in one of the northern clans and her parents wouldn't see her again for months."

"She married my older brother, Aleon—*he* is my lord-father's heir." While the king flung him an 'I-will-strike-you-down' look, Nik hurriedly explained, "Aleon remained at home during the siege of Parne to guard our herds and help my lady-mother rule Clan Qedem during our absence. Therefore, at Parne, I was evidently perceived as my lord-father's heir."

"And you allowed us to believe this lie!"

Aware of the other men and Vioc, all listening as avidly as women at a gossip-gathering, Nik shrugged and kept his voice smooth. "It wasn't *my* lie, sir, but Belaal's misperception. I simply kept quiet about the truth to protect others. Never tell a foe your plans."

"Then I must still be your foe—you've been remarkably close-mouthed," Bel-Tygeon huffed.

"A noose and imprisonment convinced me that silence was wise."

"Fair enough." The king chewed a chunk of dried meat, finally swallowed, and then admitted, "I'm glad young Ayden remained in Clan Darom. A boy needs his parents." Gloomily, the king stood and tucked dried meat within his coat. "You've all endured a long journey for my sake. I'll keep watch tonight while everyone sleeps."

***

Ty moved away from the lowering fire to better hear any sounds in the distance. Walking and keeping watching beneath the stars comforted him. He could pretend that he was yet in Clan Darom, guarding the enclosures that sheltered the herds while most of the clan slept. Where was Serena tonight? Had Clan Darom dismantled its tents and moved north? He prayed so.

Infinite, protect them! Thank You for bringing me into their care...

Someone stirred within the firelight. Nikaros cautiously stood, retrieved his bow and arrows, and crept away from the smoldering hearth and the snores of his comrades. He approached Bel-Tygeon, bowed, and spoke quietly. "Respectfully, sir, you should sleep awhile before sunrise."

"I doubt sleep's possible." He began to walk again to ward off the chill.

Nikaros followed him, clearly the inheritor of his lord-father's calm perseverance. "Nevertheless, sir—"

"Thank you, but no." Ty changed the subject. "By the way, I saw your lord-father a few weeks past. He's well."

Nikaros halted. And his voice lowered all the more. "Thank you, sir. It's good to know..." His words faded, betraying emotion. But then, he regained his composure. "Were you recognized at all?"

Ty smiled despite himself, remembering Josias and Lije. "I startled your former fellow-captives a few weeks past. They told me about Araine. If anyone else recognized me, they said nothing."

"Good." Nikaros gusted out a long breath, which lifted like smoke in the icy sky. "Sir, about Araine…"

"We'll say nothing more of your wife. Except that she must remain in Belaal as my prophet."

"As we both intend, sir."

How? Unable to contain his skepticism, Ty looked Nik in the eyes. "How can you possibly pledge such a thing? I've met your lord-father. I've lived among your people and honor them, yet you'll remain in Belaal—separated from them? Forgetting them? That's unlikely."

"Not if I'm permitted occasional journeys into the mountains, sir."

Impermissible! And yet… Ty loathed himself for his own envy.

Nik said, "Nevertheless, my place is in Belaal as your servant." Wry-voiced he added, "Tracking your whereabouts for the past sixteen months has convinced me that I'm right."

"Are you finished tracking me?"

"I hope so, sir. No offense."

"I'm more disturbed than offended," Ty complained.

"A reaction I shared. Sir."

"Should I be angered, or glad?" But he smiled again and forgave Nik. Why not? His heart was too raw, too devoted to Serena to think of another woman—even Araine. Unable to stop himself, Ty asked, "Were you ever a rival to Detzios for Serena?"

"No. I admired her. All of my unmarried friends admired her, but she was a bit proud. We'd heard that her plans never included marriage to a second son—not even the second son of the High Lord Levos." Nikaros shot him a quizzing glance. "Did she scoff at you, sir?"

"No. But like your friends, I admired her." Relieved to confess to something approaching his true feelings, Bel-Tygeon added, "I regret that I'll never see Serena and her family again." He paused, maintaining his composure. When he could speak again, he said, "However, as soon as we've returned to Sulaanc, I would like to send a small army of men here to intimidate the Agocii and drive them behind their own borders once more. The chieftain Cziybor has been harassing Clan Darom."

Nikaros bowed agreement. "That should be easy enough, Sire. Araine warned us months ago that Belaal must prepare for war."

"War? No…this won't be a war. Just a tacit defense of Clan Darom."

"Of course, sir. Now…may I suggest some sleep?"

Ty sighed, more wearied than he'd admitted to himself. He returned to the camp, watching every shadow. Wishing he was yet guarding Clan Darom.

***

Nikaros stared after the king in the darkness. So Bel-Tygeon wished to protect Clan Darom. He spoke as one inextricably linked to the clan. Why? Did he love certain clan members? More precisely, was Bel-Tygeon smitten with Serena? If so…poor man.

By now, as a clerical worker in the palace, Nik understood that every law in Bel-Tygeon's kingdom conspired against such an unsuitable, illegal match.

Infinite, I pray You swiftly send this king a beloved and loving wife. His true queen.

***

Wearied from their journey, and shivering in one of the Kehb'el Cave's gloomy storage chambers, Serena leaned forward beneath the stone chamber's fast-fading daylight hole as Father slapped the flat key into the small chest's lock. He slid the bolt aside and revealed the gift brought by Ty's men. Row upon narrow row of small, flat, distinctly yellow metal rectangles gleamed in this chamber's wan light.

Gasps echoed against the stone walls. Aunt Betiya actually faltered. "My lord, is…is it real?"

Father picked up one of the thin ingots and bit it. His molars left clear marks on the thin bar. "Yes, it's gold. All of it, judging by the weight."

Mother sighed, her beautiful eyes glistening with unshed tears. "This was unnecessary, but oh, what a blessing! This more than makes up for what the thieves stole from our cache. We'll be able to purchase food in Darzeq—and share with the northern clans!"

"I'll take some men and set off tomorrow with shares for the other clans," Father promised. "This will offset their losses in ransoming the captives."

Serena turned away to prevent her parents from seeing her tears. Oh, Ty! She would gladly trade all this gold to have him here. Would the pain of missing him ever heal? Would the hurt ever allow her to laugh or at least smile without regrets? All her glorious plans to be the queen of an Eosyth clan, to honor her family and strengthen their northern alliances…her plans were nothing. Mere dust flung away beneath the hooves of escaping horses.

If Ty's Infinite—Father's Infinite—truly existed, He surely laughed at her now.

As she stood facing the rock, two pairs of arms entwined around her waist, holding her tight. Tessi and Kari swayed with her and then motioned their unmistakable mutual sorrow. In her own grief, she'd forgotten theirs—they'd adored Ty. They signed to her, small flutterings of comfort and misery. Silent, she kissed the tops of their embroidered caps and tried to sniff back the threat of unshed tears. Perhaps someday, she would recover from loving Ty.

She must.

***

Feeling stifled in the largest cave, which was crowded with supplies and mildly bleating goats, Serena dropped her carrying pack to the rubble-strewn floor. Her siblings also dropped their packs off to her right, just beyond the thin rays of early sunlight slanting through the daylight hole above. To her left, several other women from the encampment were organizing their supplies and checking their goats, which had been sheltered in this cavern last night with Serena's.

Ahead of the other women and children, Mother turned about in the confusion, frowning, obviously remembering something. "Serena, we forgot to mix the milk grains before we left the tent—they need to start warming and brewing today. If you'd hurry back and prepare them, I'll care for the goats as soon as we've stored our provisions. Oh, and please check on Miyna. If she's distracting your Aunt Betiya too much, then bring her back with you."

"Yes, Mother. I'll herd out the goats as soon as I return."

Serena marched across the cavern, clambered through the cave's narrow, sheltered opening and then rushed down the tree-edged stone path to the encampment and Mother's tent.

The tent's rare silence made her pause briefly and look around within its cozy sheltering walls. If she'd had the morning alone here, she would have cut out new shoes for Ayden and Miyna, while daydreaming about Ty.

Nonsense! She must try to forget him. Serena shook a ration of dried fermented milk grains clattering into a deep bowl, tossed in dried fruit, added cool water, and then stirred the mixture briskly, willing herself to hurry. She must return to the cavern and help Mother and the children with the goats. If only the paddocks and pens had been maintained here! But Clan Darom rarely used this site, and portions of the wattle fences must be rewoven before most of the goats could inhabit their allotted spaces.

If Father were here to help her chop branches, Serena's task would be shortened. But he and Uncle Zeddi and some of the other men had departed with a majority of the gold just two days ago, and the wattle-fence wouldn't weave itself. Even so, she'd rather do the work alone than ask any of the younger men here to help her—it wouldn't be fair or appropriate to give them the slightest chance to flirt with her. After she repaired the fences, she must set a fresh line of snares. She'd take Ayden with her, and hope she wouldn't think of Ty.

She covered the basin of soaking milk grains with a wooden platter, then sighed. Time to rescue Aunt Betiya from Miyna. Or would she be rescuing Miyna from Aunt Betiya? Who could say? The only certain thing was that she'd rescue her cousins Siyos and Iared from Miyna. The little girl loved to chase and tease her older cousins.

Actually… Serena paused, listening to thin, shrill screams. Could she hear Miyna now? Odd. Aunt Betiya usually soothed Miyna quite effectively.

As Serena tugged on her coat and tightened her belt, the screams intensified. Women's screams. Children's wails. Men yelling deep, chilling war cries, signaling an attack.

Serena grabbed a knife and dashed outside the tent.

Chapter 16

Serena lunged from Mother's tent and fought down a wail. Agocii warriors—this far north!

Weapons readied, heavily bearded warriors were running through the encampment. Setting fire to tents, attacking the Eosyth men who hadn't snatched their bows and arrows in time to defend themselves—and hacking them down with swords and axes. The Eosyth men were outnumbered, and with each kill, Agocii victory-cries pierced the frosty morning air.

Detzios, stark-faced, bow in hand, had backed himself against Aunt Betiya's tent and was releasing arrows upon all Agocii within his range. An arrow-spiked Agocii's body lay between the tents, and Detzios felled another warrior—just before two Agocii charged him obliquely, knocking him to the cold ground. They fought, their collective breaths rising amid the scuffle. One of the warriors lifted his bloodied axe, and Serena screamed, "No!"

She started toward Detzios, but froze as a horribly familiar warrior charged into view, blocking her path. Cziybor.

He saw her and bared his teeth, his vicious sneer framed by his thick braid-tufted beard. Even as he shifted his bloodied sword and turned to pursue her, Serena fled, sweating beneath her long heavy coat, which was slowing her down. If only she could shed the coat. But she'd tied her belt too snugly. Faster! She must run faster. To where?

For one wild instant, her thoughts returned to Mother and the children in the cavern.

No. She would not lead Cziybor to Ayden. She must find a way to lose the chieftain and then return for Miyna, Aunt Betiya, and

Detzios. If only she'd snatched Father's oldest bow and arrows before leaving the tent—perhaps she could have shot Cziybor. Now, her only hope was to run faster.

"Please!" She prayed with all her might to the skies as her booted feet thudded against the stone incline edging this side of the encampment. Please let them survive! Let me escape...

Her breath coming in frantic gasps, she climbed the rock trail, nimble as one of her goats.

Surely Cziybor didn't know this territory—she must lose him!

But his throaty snarl roiled the air behind her, and his boots clumped hard against the stones below—closer than she dared to consider. She and her dagger were no match for the warrior and his sword. Panting, she goaded herself to climb higher on the stone slope. She could escape him once she reached the crest. There were fissures amid the cliffs above that led to...

Something—multiple somethings—pelted her boots and scattered around her like a shining golden rain over the high stone path. Kernels of grain rolled beneath her boots, loosening her footholds over the stones. Serena flailed for balance and then slid and fell against the incline. Her knees, hands, chin, and nose hit the stones in succession, leaving her stunned and prostrated on the path—and her knife thrown from her grip by the brutal impact of her fall.

Brought down by one handful of Agocii grain! Flung by Cziybor...

She shook off her dazedness and scrambled to regain her footing. Behind her, the Agocii warrior's stomping gait announcing his mastery of the path as he crushed the grain beneath his heavy boots. He tugged at Serena's coat, dragging her downward again as she screamed.

Cziybor crushed the breath from her with his own weight, and then he slid his bloodied sword beneath her throat. Regaining his breath, he tightened his hold around her waist and whispered harshly, "I could kill you now!"

Do it! She couldn't draw enough breath to form the words. If he intended to torture her before he killed her...best to rush him along.

Let her name become a tiny kill marker on his beard. She squirmed and reached back over her shoulder, grabbing a fistful of Agocii hair and wrenching it with all her might.

He retaliated, snarling anew as he pinned her against the path and twined his free hand viciously into her hair, tearing at it, making her yelp with pain. Then, he hissed, "We have that baby girl you're so fond of—it's nothing to me if she dies!"

Miyna. They had Miyna…

Serena opened her fist and slid her hand from his tangled hair. Faintness turned the stones and his bloodied sword to dark blotchiness beneath her gaze. Miyna.

Cziybor shifted his hold to Serena's arm and dragged her upright. As she took in a hurting breath, he muttered, "Descend with me quietly or she suffers."

Monster! Air, hatred, pain, and the taste of blood cleared her thoughts and sight as she descended the stony slope. On level ground again, Serena limped beneath Cziybor's grasp. He gloated, "However far you've fled, did you think I'd forget, daughter of Tsir Andris? I haven't! In fact, I've been planning this day since before our meeting. Now…" He jostled her as if she was a lifeless bundle of fleece. "Where's your lord-father in your time of desperation?"

Working up the voice to speak, Serena licked her lips and found her lower lip swollen and bloodied. "He's gone. Several days past."

Cziybor shook her. "To where?"

"The northern tribes—to meet with the other lords!"

Though he sounded disappointed, the Agocii chieftain muttered, "It's just as well. Whether I challenge him now or later will make no difference to you. To him, the torment of knowing he was too far away to help you will hinder him and speed my victory." Cziybor gloated, "His punishment will be multiplied!"

Punishment? "Why, lord?" She allowed humility and fear into her plea. "How did my lord-father offend you?"

"You Eosyths have offended *us*. Your men broke the alliance at the siege of Parne, shaming us. Then, your lord-father destroyed the sacred altars of Utzaii and his consort. What does he and his clan deserve but death?"

"Please, no!" By now, they were in the encampment again. Seeing the tents aflame, the paths edged with bodies, Serena wept. "Please… spare the survivors!"

He shook her again. "Hush! Where's that insolent little brother of yours?"

Ayden. He'd make Ayden's punishment part of Father's torment? She fought sobs. "He's g-gone!"

Ayden, stay in the cave! Oh, Mother, prevent everyone there from leaving! Where was Miyna? And Aunt Betiya?

Cziybor answered her unasked questions in disgruntled silence. He dragged her to the far side of Aunt Betiya's tent. To Aunt Betiya's blood-soaked body. To Detzios, whose death-calmed hands were yet-curled as if still gripping weapons to fight. And to Miyna, sitting silent and obviously dazed between them, her sweet little tear-streaked face speckled with blood. She'd seen Betiya die? Oh, poor baby. And poor Uncle Zeddi—to be met by such a terrible loss at his return. Betiya! Not Betiya…

Serena choked down fresh sobs.

Cziybor snarled, "Kneel!"

Kneeling, Serena took a deep, shaking breath. She must be calm. Control her grief and protect others where possible. Miyna was watching Cziybor now, her eyes huge, terrified beyond tears. Serena's heart thudded heavily with another squeeze of anguish. "Oh, Miyna…"

Risking Cziybor's fury, Serena scooped her baby sister into a hug. Tremors coursed through Miyna's small body. Unstoppable shudders of fear, one following another like the aftershocks of a mighty quake.

Cziybor, now commanding his men, didn't seem to care if Serena held her sister. One of the men dragged Betiya's younger son, Iared, over to Cziybor. The warrior forced Iared to kneel before Cziybor. The Agocii warrior dangled a pendant between his bloodied fingers—one of the thin gold ingots offered by Ty's men. "My lord, they've gold! We're finding gold on most of the bodies."

"Take it and search everyone, living and dead," Cziybor glared down at the scrawny, preadolescent Iared. "Where did your people find this gold?"

Serena begged in her thoughts, Don't tell him about Ty! Iared, they'll hunt him! Be strong!

The youth sniffled back tears and shifted his tormented gaze away from his mother's body. He swallowed, briefly glanced at Serena, and then up at Cziybor. "It-it was a gift of thanks from a c-clan…of the eastern plains." He snuffed again, adding, "Tsir Andris s-saved one of their leaders from death. We didn't know they had g-gold, but they g-gave it to us."

His words sharp as a blade of ice, Cziybor asked, "What clan?"

"We don't know that either, s-sir." Iared's thin freckled face hardened, framed by his dark wild, copper-tinged hair. "Tsir Andris refused to t-talk about it. But he shared the gold."

Lowering his sword, Cziybor bent and slid his callused fingers inside Serena's heavy coat, beneath her tunic, against her skin. Serena shuddered and Miyna whimpered softly. The Agocii Chieftain lifted the leather cord from its resting place around Serena's throat and then cut away her gold ingot and his own lost gold kill-marker, which Uncle Zeddi had thankfully melted and beaten beyond recognition. Gazing at the gleaming makeshift gold pendants, Cziybor smiled. "So, Clan Darom's people wear their own kill markers. Thus does Utzaii, ruler of all, reward his servants."

Utzaii, ruler of all. Was Father wrong about the Infinite? No… Serena lifted her chin. She would never place Cziybor's beliefs above her lord-father's. What, then, was left? She had nothing but prayers. Serena trembled, hugging and rocking Miyna.

She must measure a God by His true followers.

For honor's sake, Father followed the Infinite. Therefore… Serena rested her cheek on Miyna's dark hair and prayed silently. Infinite, God of my father, let his trust in You be vindicated! I bow to You. I'm captured and in despair…rescue me! With Miyna. With Iared and Cziybor's other captives. Shelter those who survive this Agocii's plans. I beg You…please, keep my mother and the other women and children inside that cave!

Several warriors approached and grinned as they set cages of courier birds near Cziybor. "We've found our evening meal."

Cziybor chuckled. Serena bit down fresh tears. Mother and the clan would be isolated for days—weeks!—unable to send messages to request help from the other clans. To the Infinite, she prayed, Protect them, please! Keep them safe and hidden…

She rocked Miyna and prayed with all her might until Cziybor gripped the back of her heavy coat and hauled her to her feet. He fastened a heavy leather strap around her throat like a collar and then tied it with a cord, swift and fierce. "Time to go, woman—and be sensible. Obey my every word, or the child will suffer." To his men, he said, "Bring that boy. But bind him well and put him on one of the horses. If he fights or tries to escape, kill him."

Serena slid a glance toward her young cousin Iared, silently imploring him to obey Cziybor and survive. A temporary surrender might ultimately yield victory.

Iared caught her look. Sullen-faced, he stood and affected a slouched, defeated posture as one of the warriors bound his wrists. Only Iared's clenched fists revealed his wish to fight. But then he gazed down at his mother's body, and his posture of defeat deepened. He choked on sobs as tears slid down his thin young face. In silence, Serena wept with him, her soul wailing an inward, hidden dirge.

Cziybor noticed Iared and laughed. "Are you the only child to lose a parent thus? Have courage or die, young green fool!"

While Cziybor led her to the waiting horses, Serena gave her aunt's and Detzios' stilled forms a final aching look and fought her own tears. The world swam and blurred around her, and she begged once more, Infinite, rescue us…save Clan Darom's survivors!

***

A shudder rippled through the ground, jolting Ty from a heavy sleep. Around him, the other men stirred and reached for their weapons as they studied the dawn-lit plains. A dark liquid splotch of distant activity raced toward them from the north. As Ty stood, the reverberations increased, jarring his body and his memories.

The last time he'd felt a similar quaking, he'd been commanding his troops before the walls of Parne. Until the united forces of the Tracelands and Istgard charged toward him, riding their monstrous giant black warhorses— "Destroyers!" He scrambled to gather his gear. "Pack out! Hurry! If they're wild and rampant, they'll overrun us as if we're dead grass!"

And if this was some army's cavalry, then Belaal couldn't afford for its king and his men to be captured and held for ransom.

His men doused the fire, snatched their gear, and hurried to their horses, who were stirring and whickering their growing panic. Ty lashed his gear to his horse, crooning to the beast with a calm he didn't feel.

Nikaros called out to the others, "If any of your possessions are lost, don't go back to retrieve them. Objects can be replaced—our lives cannot!"

Within mere breaths, they were racing east, clear of the destroyers' approach, though Ty almost wished he could watch the beasts from a safe place. If only Belaal had the natural resources to sustain and confine an army of those monster-warhorses.

Yet if he'd controlled such a force while he was yet a god-king, he would have certainly resembled those beasts—proud, tyrannical, and vicious marauders. From all he'd heard in Clan Darom, the beasts were uncontrollable unless they willingly submitted to a higher authority.

When they finally slowed their wearied horses and tremors no longer shook the ground, Nikaros said, "If this is the only difficulty we've experienced throughout our journey until now, then we've been blessed."

Behind Nikaros, Vioc echoed, "Indeed! May He continue to protect us!"

"May He indeed." Ty gave his horse a bit more rein, allowing the exhausted creature to graze. As he descended to check his horse for injuries or signs of distress, Bel-Tygeon grimaced. Hopefully the Infinite would tend him as well and mend this gash in his heart—this helpless, impossible longing for Serena.

Protect her, Infinite.

***

How much farther?

Measuring her footsteps against the cold winter-deadened slope, Serena looked ahead, watching her young cousin Iared trudge up a hill. She and Miyna and Iared were the only Eosyth captives taken. Had all the others in their encampment been killed? Please, no. She must tell herself that the others had escaped the encampment and were hiding. And Father, Uncle Zeddi, and the men who'd gone north were safe, as were the other women in the cavern, with Mother and the children.

If only they'd taken Miyna to the cave earlier... Serena drew in a breath and stretched slightly as she hiked, trying to ease her aching back. After the first two days, Cziybor had compelled her to walk as much as ride. Light as Miyna was, carrying her during this four-day journey had pulled every muscle in Serena's shoulders and arms. Two days past, she'd finally been permitted to bind Miyna to her with a makeshift sling that Serena fashioned from her wide sash in order to hurry her pace and rest her aching body.

Just ahead of her, Cziybor tugged her corded leash and muttered, "Hurry, woman. Do not make me regret my decision to spare you and the child."

Miyna stiffened at the sound of Cziybor's rebuke, and she peeked up at Serena, her eyes enormous, her fearful gaze seeking reassurance. Serena quickened her pace and curved one hand around her little sister's mussed dark auburn hair to console her. How much longer? She needed to rest—truly rest—and recover from her ordeal.

It wasn't just the long walk or her sweat-sodden rankness and Miyna's sour-urine stench—this afternoon, Cziybor had denied them time enough for Miyna to relieve herself—but Serena struggled with her other wounds as well.

Her fall against the sloping rock incline had left her knees and chin swollen. Also, despite several scrubbings at various streams, countless flecks of dark gritty rock embedded in her palms were beginning to fester. And her scuffed flesh had the texture of sueded leather where it wasn't crusted with oozing scabs. Added to this, her stomach was hollowed and growling for lack of food. If this journey continued for much longer, she could weaken enough that the Agocii would lose patience and kill her.

Miyna, too, seemed to be fading in spirit—each day sleeping more. Only Cziybor's voice drew clear responses from the little girl, and those responses were stark fear beyond utterance or even hand-signs of toddler-fury and hurt. Serena hugged her baby sister closer.

Infinite, God of my father, where is Your rescue? Save us and...

She allowed the prayer to dribble away to nothingness in her thoughts, replaced by bleak desolation. What was the use?

Following Cziybor, and chafed by the leash, Serena reached the crest of a slope. There, she looked down into an evergreen-edged mountain camp, sheltered by huge red rocky bluffs beyond. Garishly painted leather tents and shield-decked pikes informed her that she'd entered an Agocii encampment.

Cziybor lifted a ram's horn to his beard-framed lips, forcing out a blaring trump-call that echoed over the valley below. While Cziybor led his war party's descent, with Serena yet leashed, distant trump-calls welcomed the Agocii heroes. Cziybor's tribe hurried to cheer for him at the bottom of the slope as he entered the camp. He tugged Serena forward and bellowed, "I've returned victorious! Behold the captive daughters of the traitor Tsir Andris! Our enemies weep—they'll mourn this defeat for generations!"

Around the boasting Cziybor, his warriors grinned, silently bolstering his claims by flaunting the gold ingots they'd looted from the Eosyths. Cziybor's tribe greeted the news and the gold with yowls of victory that made Serena's filthy hair prickle along her scalp. In her arms, Miyna whimpered and squirmed.

Four women—one tall, one short, one broad, and one thin—paraded toward Cziybor now, haughty in boldly-painted robes and crimson and gold-twined braids. They offered Cziybor a brimming cup of liquid and their kisses of congratulations. But beneath the elated clamor of the people around them, one of the women said, "My lord, you've returned just in time. The Dreki Siyrsun sent word that he will arrive by sunset. He expects to receive the tribute promised to him by our tribe."

For the first time, Serena saw the Agocii chieftain's gaze flicker with dread, though he covered it swiftly with a sneer.

His wives were studying Serena, and the one who'd warned Cziybor of his unwelcomed visitor asked, "Will she be part of Siyrsun's payment?"

Cziybor frowned at Serena. "That wasn't my plan. However, when she's scrubbed and fed, send for me and I'll decide." He left Serena with the four women, who now glared at her as if she were a viper they intended to stomp and hack to death.

Chapter 17

Cziybor's wives watched her every move. Within the dark confines of their tent, Serena felt their hostile gazes knifing into her back as she knelt to bathe Miyna.

As if she was to blame that their husband had attacked Clan Darom, massacred her dear aunt and friends, and then stolen her away. Serena bit her lip hard. She mustn't weep. At least Miyna had evidently earned favor here with her lovable face and big dark eyes. One of Cziybor's wives had actually warmed a deep basin of water for Miyna's bath.

Unlike the icy bucketful they'd handed to Serena. She was still half-numb from the water's biting chill. At least she was reasonably clean and wearing a warm leather tunic that didn't reek of dried urine. She crooned to her sister, "Sit still…you're so good…."

Miyna fluttered one small hand in a twin-sign, causing Serena to swallow more unshed tears as she remembered her siblings. In desperation, she prayed, Infinite, do You hear me? Do I matter to You? Protect the twins and everyone in the cave, I beg You!

She scrubbed and rinsed Miyna and then patted her dry and clothed her in the surprisingly new crimson garments provided by Cziybor's wives. Seeming revived by the bath, Miyna offered a spritely hand-sign, clearly approving of the crimson tunic. "Pretty," Serena enunciated firmly. "Say 'pretty'. The tunic is pretty."

"Doesn't she talk yet?" One of the wives drew near, frowning.

"She can, but doesn't want to," Serena explained as she braided Miyna's damp hair. "Our twin sisters created their own language of hand-signs and Miyna prefers hand-signs to talking. However, when she's angry, she can yell louder and longer than anyone else in Clan Darom."

The wives didn't reply. Instead, they handed Serena a cup of fermented milk and two puffy folds of flatbread smeared with a paste of herbs and pine nuts, much like a light, hasty meal Serena sometimes offered her family. At once, Miyna sat, her hands on her knees, ready for prayers and food.

Serena bent and whispered Father's most repeated prayer to Miyna alone, "Mighty One, Infinite, our Creator, please…" she paused, fighting for composure, "…save our family and Clan Darom!"

She offered the cup to Miyna, and then the bread. Miyna drained the cup and ate as she hadn't since the massacre—leaving Serena with just over half of her own piece of bread.

"Such an appetite," one of the wives huffed in disapproval.

Sparing the wives nothing, Serena said, "It's the first full meal she's eaten since she saw our aunt butchered by your people. Miyna was splashed with her blood."

Whatever Cziybor's wives might have said was silenced by Cziybor himself. He entered the tent, growling, "Didn't I tell you to send for me when she was bathed and fed?"

His wives stood and backed away, and Miyna scooted right along with them, obviously agreeing with their collective impulse to remain beyond the Agocii chieftain's reach when he growled. Serena stood her ground. Cziybor must never think that he'd vanquished her.

An elderly woman followed Cziybor into the women's tent, her eyes keen in her soft-wrinkled face. She lifted one sparse gray eyebrow at Serena, then worked her thin lips over her gaping teeth as if muting a grin. Cziybor eyed Serena as well. And he quizzed her softly. "Tell me, daughter of Tsir Andris, is that child yours?" He pointed at Miyna.

Serena shook her head, warily. Why was he asking? "No, lord. She's my youngest sister."

"Have you ever given yourself to a man?"

Had she ever— "No! Of course not. I'm unmarried."

Cziybor's full mouth curved disdainfully amid his thick gold-flecked brown beard, and he turned to the old woman who'd followed him into the tent. "Mother Ataii, prove her words. If she's telling the truth, mark her accordingly."

He stalked out of the tent again, leaving Serena to stare after him, aghast. "Of course I'm telling the truth! I—"

All four wives grabbed her in unison. Serena struggled, twisting away from the short one and the thin one. The remaining two wrenched her to the tent's carpeted floor. Serena kicked at the pair and landed her fists wherever possible. This one's eye, that one's belly. Both women screamed. The short wife and the thin one rejoined the fight and beat Serena into submission as Mother Ataii laughed and Miyna cried.

***

Still furious enough to spit even if it hurt, Serena glowered at the floor as the Agocii chieftain reentered the tent. For an instant Cziybor paused, and then he laughed uproariously as if enjoying the best joke ever told. "Isn't this a fine sight! Look at the five of you. I haven't seen such black eyes and split lips since the last tribal gathering. Who won? I should make you all fight again to decide."

When his laughter was met with silence—except for Miyna's scuffling as she hid behind Serena—Cziybor hunkered down in front of Serena. Fingering the crimson cord twined around her abraded throat, he taunted Serena, compelling her to look at him, "So you were telling the truth. Very good, daughter of Tsir Andris. I have such plans for you!"

The tall wife with the black eye braved a question, her tone all bitterness. "Will you give her to the Dreki Siyrsun?"

"No." Cziybor smiled into Serena's eyes. "She's in no shape to be given to the general or anyone right now, thanks to your beatings. Siyrsun would be insulted and we must placate him with a bit of the gold and a few promises—the dog. However…"

The Agocii chieftain gloated aloud to Serena, "Your rebellious Eosyth-female arrogance will vanish soon enough. You'll cry for your lord-father to save you, but he'll no longer exist! He's my prey. You and the child are mere bait."

Serena closed her eyes. She must not spit on Cziybor; he would repay her in countless terrible ways, beginning with her vulnerable baby sister. Miyna huddled behind Serena, leaning on her, quivering like a trapped rabbit. Serena hoped her little sister didn't comprehend Cziybor's threat against Father's life.

Infinite, Mighty One…defend our father who worships You!

***

Stealthily working to loosen the cords binding her wrists and ankles, Serena lay in the shadowed curve of the women's tent near the drowsing Miyna. Despite her leggings and soft leather boots, her ankles were chafing from the cords' pressure. Her feet prickled numb-cold, and she longed to sit up and ease her bruised shoulders. At least they hadn't bound her wrists behind her back, but no doubt they'd notice if she tugged the cords with her teeth.

Perhaps if she pretended to scratch her face, and then rested awhile with the cords near her face—no one would notice if she cautiously loosened a few knots later tonight.

She flexed her fingers beneath her chin and then eyed Cziybor's two wives who'd remained within the tent to guard her. The thin one and the tall one. How silent they were. With the exception of Cziybor's gleeful cruelties, no laughter warmed this tent. Indeed, the only brightness here shone in the low central hearth and Miyna's small crimson tunic.

No doubt being Cziybor's wife would oppress any woman and rob her of joy. Serena tilted her head, listening as Cziybor's other two wives worked outside the tent, preparing food for their illustrious expected company—was his name Siyrsun? Cziybor was certainly striving to play the benevolent host. A false benevolence, considering his plans to delude Siyrsun and to kill her lord-father.

Father… Serena nearly wept to think of the dangers he and Clan Darom would soon face. She must find some way to warn Father of Cziybor's plans. But if she could escape, would she and Miyna survive the journey to reunite with their family?

They needed a horse. And the chance to safely flee—with enough of a start to evade Cziybor's pursuit. He would surely hunt her down and kill her or punish her somehow.

A beating or perhaps a maiming. Serena shuddered.

Would her family still be at the Kehb'el Cave site? Perhaps she could—

Cziybor's booming laughter reached Serena from outside the tent, scattering her thoughts like autumn leaves in a gale and waking Miyna from a sound sleep. How wicked that the Agocii chieftain could laugh after massacring an encampment of peaceable Eosyths—most of whom were women and children. When Cziybor laughed again, Miyna scooted over to Serena, dragging a coverlet with her. Glancing up at Serena, Miyna struck a small fist on her knee. Serena whispered, "I understand. Stay with me."

Miyna leaned against her, drawing her coverlet up to her chin, and then tucking her small thumb in her mouth—something she hadn't done in months. Serena curved her body protectively around Miyna's as much as possible and listened to a tumult within the adjoining main tent.

Men's voices, the metallic clatter of weaponry, several deep coughs, throat-clearings, and one distinct hacking of spittle. Obviously listening as well, Cziybor's thinnest wife huffed beneath her breath, "Did you hear that? They'll ruin the floor-coverings!"

Her resentful, swollen-eyed gaze upon Miyna, Tall Wife said, "Let *him* buy us new ones."

Serena closed her eyes, listening to the men. In braggart's tones, Cziybor said, "Lord-General Siyrsun, welcome to you and your men. We're honored. Rest—food is being prepared."

"Yes," a man's low, gruff voice answered. "Thank you."

Lord-General Siyrsun didn't sound pleased. Serena frowned, listening intently. A dull thud sounded within the tent, followed by a hush, then the fragile ringing of metal against metal.

Cziybor gloated, "While we wait, here is our tribute as agreed—all in gold! With this wealth, more weapons and mercenaries are yours. An empire is within our grasp!"

Empire? What sort of empire? Had Cziybor just given the lord-general gold from Ty's gift? Serena steadied her breathing, listening hard. Siyrsun's now-pleased voice turned brisk. "Indeed, it's a good beginning if the remaining tributes match this one. Lord Cziybor, where did you acquire these ingots?"

"From the Eosyths to the north." Serena's stomach clenched as Cziybor explained, "We raided an encampment to repay the Clan's leader for his betrayal at Parne, and we found this gold within the camp. A princely sum for the taking."

"With minimal risk?" Siyrsun's heightened tone betrayed his interest.

Cziybor gloated. "They hid well, but delayed our attack only for two days. We lost no one and suffered only a few wounds, quickly stitched."

Because he'd attacked an encampment of women and children, while the men were scattered during chores! To the Infinite, Serena pleaded, God of my lord-father, do you hear him? Let Cziybor be repaid!

"Hmm." Siyrsun's voice became a musing growl. "Might there be more gold?"

Another man's voice added, "My lord-general, this would be worth raiding more Eosyth encampments."

Rivulets of horror washed over Serena's flesh beneath her coarse tunic and coat. Her stomach knotted harder, threatening nausea as Siyrsun agreed, "Yes. If the encampments are such easy targets." Serena heard a thump—a decisive strike on the mat. "Send word to the others that we'll gather more recruits from Darzeq next month. As soon as the weather warms enough, the month after, we'll plunder the Eosyths to finance our conquest of Belaal with Eosyth gold."

At the cost of Eosyth blood! Serena tucked her face toward Miyna's small crimson-clad body. She must not panic. She must flee and warn Clan Darom that Cziybor's ally, General Siyrsun, was planning to attack.

While the men ate and plotted their strategies in the adjoining tent, Serena listened in silence. But her innermost being wailed. The gift brought in gratitude by Ty's men would provoke more Eosyth deaths! How could she protect her people?

She held her tears, pondered options, and prayed—only vaguely distracted as Cziybor's two absent wives finally reentered the tent and lured Miyna away with coaxing whispers and a tray full of food.

***

A rough hand covered Serena's mouth, waking her. Cziybor's tallest wife motioned for Serena to maintain silence and then removed the ties from her ankles. A journey to the privy pit? Yes, she'd welcome the chance to walk. Moving gently to avoid waking Miyna, she eased herself upright and nodded to the thinnest wife.

Despite her heavy coat, Serena shivered as she and Cziybor's wives crept through the adjoining tent, which was Cziybor's domain, and thankfully empty. The Old Dreki, Siyrsun, had taken his leave early, and Cziybor had evidently departed with him at dawn.

Please let him not attack Clan Darom.

"Move," the thin wife grumbled as the tall one nudged her through the tent and outside into the pale cloud-grayed morning.

When they'd finished at the women's pit, Cziybor's wives led Serena to a stream and allowed her to rinse her hands and face. Serena's breath misted in the early morning chill. She slid glances at her two unhappy companions. Both bore livid scratches and bruises from their earlier clash with her in the tent—not to mention the tall one's bruised left eye. She could beat these two again and escape.

If it weren't for Miyna, she could flee this instant while Cziybor's wives rinsed, filled, and tied leather water skins. She'd kick this glum pair head-first into the icy water and run. It was an appealing notion.

If only it could be true.

As they returned to the still-hushed encampment, both women handed the cold, dripping water skins to Serena. The taller one muttered, "Carry these."

Serena obeyed, but frowned as the two women steered her away from Cziybor's tent. Where were they going?

They cut across the camp toward the grazing area where Cziybor and his men had secured their horses. An Agocii warrior waited there, guarding her cousin Iared, and the boy cast a despairing glance at Serena...just before she noticed Cziybor standing beside his readied horse. Smiling.

Serena halted, horror seeping in with the realization. Cziybor was taking her away from Miyna. "Wait!"

Cziybor's wives tugged Serena forward and shoved her into Cziybor's grasp.

Holding her hair as he would a rope, the Agocii Chieftain slid one broad hand beneath his hateful gold-decked beard and produced her leather collar and its cord from the folds of his furred coat. "Daughter of the traitor Tsir Andris, may the gods bless me—I have such plans for you!"

Chapter 18

Jolted by the horse's rough gait, Serena unwillingly leaned forward and clutched Cziybor's broad leather belt. He grumbled and kicked his horse into a trot along the snowy base of a cliff, passing most of his men. At the front of the column, Cziybor slowed, and they approached the warrior who'd bound Cousin Iared backward on his horse. Three days of such backward riding left Iared wan and queasy.

Yet, as Serena threw him a worried glance, Iared hissed, his words emerging as vapor, "Serena! Where are they taking us?"

She shrugged and then shook her head. If only she could answer. But Cziybor only spoke to her when he could gloat or snap at her to hurry in the evenings as they built their camp sites.

At least doing chores kept her safely away Cziybor's stench. Seated behind him on his horse, however, she was stifled. The man took in pure air at one end and released foul air at the other as easily as he breathed—defying the early spring chill and half-choking her in the process. Yet Serena subdued her complaints. He'd probably double his stinking output and smother her himself if she mentioned her misery.

Her squeamishness heightened as Cziybor led their procession down a beaten trail and into a stark narrow rock passage amid the mountains—high inward-curving walls almost met at the passage's crest. A defile Father would have called it. Yet the defile's structure unnerved Serena. Cziybor's fumes notwithstanding, these confining walls worried her. An army could array itself atop this defile and rain arrows upon them. Robbers could gather at either end of this passage and wait to attack the unwary as they emerged from the stone channel.

Obviously Cziybor was supremely confident of his own safety. Either that, or he intended to kill all attackers with his foul releases. She averted her face again, studying the defile's walls.

At last, Cziybor finally led his men into the sunlight...and an unexpectedly broad valley. With an Agocii encampment. Serena swallowed. Was this their destination? She didn't dare ask.

When they reached the edge of the encampment, Cziybor—as always—flung one leg over his horse's long neck and dropped easily to his feet, swinging her down within the same breath. If Ty had perfected such a sweeping and audacious dismount from his horse, Serena would have melted. But Cziybor would never be Ty

Cziybor set Serena on her feet, then gripped her face with one big hand and smiled. "Do you wonder about my plans for you, daughter of the traitor Tsir Andris? Listen carefully, then. I promise that if you survive, you will bear enemies. Warriors who'll attack the Eosyths! And for however long or short a time you live, you will remain a loathed stranger among the Agocii."

She stared at him, speechless. He smiled, lifted his hand from her face, kissed his fingertips, and then flung the kiss toward the sun above. "I praise the gods, Utzaii above all, that I have captured a child of my enemy!"

As his men dismounted around him and began to lead away their horses, Cziybor draped a seemingly convivial arm around Serena's shoulders. "Tomorrow you face your destiny. But for now, set up camp. If you try to escape, I'll enjoy killing you."

He'd said nothing of Miyna. But when she glanced up at his smiling brown eyes...the threat shone there.

Muting her rebellious impulse to gouge out his eyes, Serena looked away.

***

Seated in her chamber before her writing table, Araine, Prophet of Belaal, straightened and dropped her pen into its tray. A living current washed over her skin and hair, and a vision entered her thoughts, sending her senses a-swimming. "Infinite, is it true?"

Even as she started to her feet, swaying, the prophet's branch lit like white fire within Araine's fingers, making her jump and laugh. Would she ever become used to this vinewood staff living within the Creator's will and beyond her control? Likely not. She could only laugh at her own foolishness. However, Inae wasn't as amused.

The gentle attendant gasped and clutched her sewing in obvious panic. "Lady, what's happening?"

"You're sending for a large tray of food, Inae—and plenty of hot water! That's what's happening. Hurry, please!" Abandoning her work, Araine swept up her billowing pink robes and sped from her rooms, not stopping until she reached the Lady Dasarai's royal apartments.

The burly eunuch-guards eyed the glowing branch warily, and rapped on the door. The Lady Dasarai called out in preoccupied tones, "Yes, what is it? Enter…"

Their timing well-practiced, the two guards opened the double-doors in unison, bowed, and then motioned Araine through. She sped barefoot over the carpet-padded floors and knelt before Belaal's only living princess, breathless. "Lady, our lord-king approaches! Let me follow you to meet him!" And Nikaros! Araine's heart skipped and her soul danced at the thought of her husband's handsome face and his beguiling presence, but it wouldn't do to mention Nik to Dasarai in the same breath as she'd mentioned their lord-king.

Araine dared a glance at the great lady. Dasarai's lovely brown eyes were huge. She pushed aside her official documents, and covered her mouth with her exquisite, gold-shielded fingers. But then she composed herself and lifted her chin. "How terrible that you're wearing pink—you know how much he loathes the color. Do I have time to re-pin my hair and don fresh robes? Where is my comb? Really, Araine, one wishes you would hurry!"

***

Sulaanc. Ty exhaled, surveying the glorious white and blue city gleaming above the rain-washed plains. His capitol city, his people, and his palace.

When had it become such a prison to him?

To gain one last instant of freedom, the last splinter of time that finished his life with Serena and Clan Darom, he gazed north at the distant blue-gray crests of the DaromKhor Hills.

Had Eosyths possessed those hills in ancient times? Before the rise of the Agocii, the Siphrans, and the god-kings of Belaal?

If they had, then Ty could comfort himself by looking toward those dark gray-blue shadows and imagine that he was close to her. Ty prayed, his words near-silent. "Infinite, You know how genuinely I love Serena! I entrust her to Your care, and bless You for the time I spent with her and with her family. Help me to endure life without her."

Forcing the pain off to the fringes of his conscience where it might remain manageable, Ty lifted his cloak's drab hood over his head, then took a bracing breath, looking down to conceal his identity while Commander Vioc led Belaal's now-sane king toward his palace once more.

He wasn't hiding due to shame. Indeed, he—Bel-Tygeon, the king turned madman—would proclaim his downfall and his return to the entire world, with endless praises of the Infinite. But not yet. First, he must greet his sister. He'd missed Rethae's maternal bossiness, which offered so many ways to provoke and torment her.

And Araine. His delightful prophet. Nik's *wife.* That would take getting used to, though he'd forgiven Nikaros and Araine. In truth, their marriage was a blessing, for it bound Nikaros to Sulaanc, and Bel-Tygeon wanted the Eosyth to remain in Belaal as his civil servant.

They rode over the magnificent canals—in need of dredging— then through the marketplaces, which must be inspected and most likely reminded of standards of weights and regulatory laws by his own royal writs. From the marketplaces, they rode past Belaal's sweeping temple site, which needed rebuilding as a place of devotion to the Infinite.

Ty grimaced at himself. His first ride through Sulaanc in eighteen months, and he was planning years of work. Good.

If he remained busy, then perhaps he wouldn't dwell upon being parted from Serena.

At the palace gates, Commander Vioc called up to the sentries in the gatehouse's massive blue tower, "Open the gates and send word to the Lady Dasarai that Lord Nikaros and I have returned! Send word to Commander Seir that we require his presence!"

"At once, Commander!" But the guard above hesitated. "Was your mission successful?"

Ty flung back his drab hood and straightened, giving the guard a stern look. "What do you deem successful, good sir? Open the gate!"

The guard gaped and then bowed so deeply that Ty feared he would fall over the embrasure. The man vanished and Ty heard a discordance of yowls and whoops. Were his guards actually celebrating?

Beside Ty now, Nikaros laughed. "Sire, I believe your return is being celebrated."

Why? Who would miss the tyrant god-king he'd been? "They're the madmen."

Unless they feared Siyrsun's rule in Belaal more than they feared Bel-Tygeon's return. Yes, that would explain everything. He, Bel-Tygeon, was the least atrocious sovereign.

The first gate's massive iron-and-gilded-bronze-shielded doors opened, and Commander Vioc led the procession through the long gatehouse and the vast courtyard beyond in a thunderous echoing of horse's hooves. Ahead of them, the second courtyard awaited—the gates fully opened and crowded as if the guards genuinely welcomed his return.

On the other side of the courtyard, the gilded blue entry door to the palace also swung open, accompanied by the high, full blare of trump-calls usually reserved for royalty alone.

Rethae? Ty dismounted and pushed one hand through his wild hair.

His sister emerged from the great doorway first, walking slowly, but clutching her ceremonial fan close as she did in times of distress. Araine followed, wielding her gleaming prophet's branch and wearing pink—frivolous prophet. Bless the Infinite that they'd survived his absence.

Ty walked toward his sister, closing the distance between them in the sweeping courtyard. Rethae's eyes became huge, and her pace faltered. What was wrong? Ty hurried to reach her. "Lady, are you ill?"

Rethae halted and put one hand to her mouth, evidently trying to cover her sobs. Ty hugged her. "Surely I don't look that monstrous! Rethae... Bless the Infinite—all's well!"

She wept. "I thought I'd never hear your voice—nor see you again!"

"And now aren't you sorry?" he teased.

"You look wonderful and utterly disreputable!" Rethae hugged him fiercely. "One would think you've been running with thieves!" She stepped back and wrinkled her nose. "One would also think that you haven't bathed in weeks."

"One would think you're right." To shock his sister, Ty told her the truth. "Actually, the water's been too cold for bathing."

Bel-Tygeon looked beyond her to Araine, who wiped her eyes, then laughed. Her voice and expression as sweet as ever. She bowed. "Sire, we've been praying constantly for your safe return—bless the Infinite!"

"Bless Him indeed." Belaal's prophet was so lovely—Ty could almost forgive her for wearing that ridiculous pink. Was she about to cry? Bel-Tygeon pretended regal impatience and waved her aside. "Lady, go greet your husband."

"Thank you, Sire!" Araine rushed to embrace Nikaros, who laughed and swept her up in an embrace then kissed her. Ty smiled. He'd missed Araine. But not as much as he longed for Serena now.

"A bath, at once." Dasarai was saying. With a nod to his coat and the gear his servants were untying from his horse, she added, "I'll order those garments burned."

"Not for half this kingdom!" Bel-Tygeon called to the servant, "Guard every bit of that gear as if it's gold, and carry it all to my chambers at once!"

Noting his sister's fan shifting and then fluttering with her exasperation, Ty explained, "The people who provided me with that coat and those weapons saved my life this past winter, repeatedly. I'll treasure those items until my final breath."

At once, Rethae's impatience softened. "Naturally, then, we'll save the coat."

Ty kissed her cheek "Thank you for everything you've done in my absence. Tonight, we'll share a meal and you'll tell me all that's happened. I—"

Ebatenai rushed into the courtyard now like a stout whirlwind, his pale garments and silvering hair disheveled, his plump face agog with joy. "Sire! It is you!"

Bel-Tygeon grinned at his ever-loyal steward. "You won't be so happy a week from now, Ebatenai, when I've buried you with work!" Before his elated servant could kneel before him, worshipful as if he were yet a god-king, Bel-Tygeon hindered the man with a fond cuff to one shoulder. "Haste, good Ebatenai! We've too much to do. First, I want writs sent to the markets…."

***

Araine paused to enjoy Ebatenai's delight in greeting the king, then she turned and hugged her husband once more, relishing his delicious warmth and strength. "Oh, how I've missed you, my lord! You look so tired."

"And you look as perfect as ever." Nik's green-brown eyes gleamed, and he bent to kiss her fiercely, his dark beard scuffing at her cheek.

Before he could ask, she said, "I've ordered food for you."

Nikaros almost lifted her off her feet again with his hug. "Have I told you how much I love being married to Belaal's prophet? Thank you. I'm starved, and I stink."

"Your over-all air is overwhelming, my lord, but I wasn't about to tell you so." She hurried Nikaros from the courtyard before the Lady Dasarai could issue any orders that might interfere with his meal and a bath.

Nik looped an arm around her and held her near as they walked to their rooms. Low-voice, he asked, "Has anything changed? Are we still preparing for war?"

Some of her joy faded, remembering her visions and her conversations with Commander Seir. "We are, my lord. No further details or rumors yet as to why, but I'm sure it's all to do with Siyrsun."

Nik bent and kissed her hair. "No doubt you're correct. I'd give the other half of our fortune to find that man and destroy him. Before dealing with Siyrsun, however, the king wishes to send a small army up to the mountains, to intimidate the Agocii and prevent an attack on Clan Darom. I must write his orders—even before a bath."

***

Serena jolted to alertness as Cziybor bellowed, "Awake! Now!" And—as he'd done each morning of the journey—he grabbed the flapping edges of her bedroll and yanked them violently, sending her bound form rolling helplessly into the musty, stifling folds of the tent he shared with his men. The few men who still lingered in the tent laughed with Cziybor, enjoying her humiliation.

Serena gritted her teeth as the Agocii chieftain untied her ankles and dragged her outside for morning duties. Seeing the dawn, he kissed his fingertips and then waved his hand toward the reddish cloud-hazed sun in homage to the highest of his gods, Utzaii. "Praise to you, Utzaii, bringer of light and giver of gold, for sending me the promise of treasure and vengeance!"

He eyed Serena and paused. Waiting. Let him wait! Did he truly think she would praise his god? Utzaii had been the Eosyth's most exalted god, as Utzaos, until they'd turned to the Infinite, their Mighty One, the Victor of Parne Infinite.

God of my father, please repay his trust and mine! Rescue me, Infinite…

Clearly displeased by her failure to worship Utzaii, the Agocii chieftain gave Serena a vicious shake that nearly rattled her teeth. His words low and malice-laden, Cziybor taunted, "Rebel-daughter of Tsir Andris, today we learn your fate, you and I. And how I will enjoy whatever befalls you. I'll laugh as you weep!"

Chapter 19

Serena walked obediently as Cziybor led her to the center of the Agocii encampment and then halted amid carts and makeshift pens of sheep and goats, and a multitude of horses and warriors. Wild-bearded Agocii warriors stared at her and then smiled...not kindly. Someone yelled, "What've you found, Cziybor?"

The Agocii chieftain laughed. "Are you interested?"

A weakening tremor shivered through Serena's limbs as Cziybor wrenched her to a halt.

Several of the men made insinuating comments, nudging each other—scoundrels scheming. Their eyes were so bold that she didn't dare look at them after one glance.

Instead, as her trembling heightened to panic, Serena looked up at the cold blue sky, pleading silently. Infinite, are You truly here? Do You see me? Save me, I beg You!

When she finally looked around the encampment again, a familiar face held her gaze. Her cousin Iared shrugged at her, lifting his eyebrows and shoulders to reveal his bewilderment, and his mouth framed the question, "Why?"

Serena shook her head. Why were they here?

The warrior handling Iared dragged him over to an empty cart and hefted him into it. When Iared knelt, the warrior bellowed, "Stand!"

Iared obeyed, all pre-adolescent coltishness and uncertainty. The warrior pressed a spear point beneath Iared's chin and yelled to the encampment, "Here's an Eosyth captive taken from Clan Darom! I spared him to honor his courage during battle—notable for such a raw-green youth. Throughout our journey here, he has never once complained. He is the nephew of Clan Darom's lord, and he can *work.* Ten years among us as a slave will either crush him or turn him into an Agocii warrior. Who will buy him or trade for him?"

Serena felt the blood draining from her face. She lowered her chin and took several slow, deep breaths. They were selling off Iared as a slave...

The warrior looked around the encampment, clearly seeking likely buyers. "Gufiyr? Vsevold?"

A cold-eyed man with a thick black beard liberally clasped with gold bellowed, "Two pieces of silver and three goats! His growing years are just ahead, and he will require a great deal of food."

"He'll work for his food," Iared's captor argued. "Vsevold, have you nothing to offer?"

A second warrior stepped forward, fraying the silvering braids from his grizzled gold-clasped beard as he frowned at Iared. The boy returned his stare, quiet and cold-eyed, his courage stealing Serena's breath. She must be this brave...

The contemplative warrior named Vsevold finally lifted his chin. "One colt and three pieces of silver."

When the first warrior-bidder stepped backward, shaking his head, Iared's captor nodded at Vsevold. "He's yours. May Utzaii bless his work for you."

As Vsevold led her cousin away, Serena cried, "Iared, remain strong!"

If she ever had anything to say in the matter, Vsevold must relinquish Iared soon. Please let them escape or be freed soon. No doubt Uncle Zeddi or Father would find some way to rescue them. Weak, infuriating tears slid down Serena's face.

Cziybor swiped at them and laughed.

***

With the remains of his breakfast cold on a gilded tray at the edge of his desk, Bel-Tygeon finished the last portion of his letter to King Akabe of Siphra.

…therefore, I beg your forgiveness for my previous actions against you and your country, in particular regarding insults to your queen and your prophet when I removed them to Sulaanc. May Belaal find peace with Siphra as we—

Ebatenai's familiar brisk rap echoed at his bedchamber door. Ty set down his pen and turned over the parchment. "Enter!"

Ebatenai coughed a warning. "The Lady Dasarai, Sire. And… Zaria."

Zaria? Ty stood, frowning. Why was his former consort here? Had Rethae dared to bring her into the palace again as his potential queen?

He studied his sister as she entered the chamber. Rethae's beautiful face was frankly grim, her lips pressed tight as she rapped her gilded palm fan silently against her gown betraying impatience. No, this secretive little visit was clearly not Rethae's idea. Therefore, Zaria must have somehow coerced her.

As Zaria hurried to kneel before him, Bel-Tygeon studied his former favorite. She was as graceful and shapely as ever, and her hair and skin glowed, tempting him to touch her. As he gazed at her, Zaria's bright-dark eyes shone, teasing him and inviting him to remember their many months together.

Or, perhaps to forget. This woman was the very antithesis of Serena, and a mistake he wouldn't repeat. Ty folded his arms. "Zaria, why are you here?"

She blinked, precariously close to fluttering her eyelashes. "I've been waiting for your return, Sire. I've been living in the shadow of your palace, longing every day for you—"

"You've been longing for your own return here," Ty observed. "Never mind who might restore you to your former glorious place."

As she gaped, Ty continued, "If Siyrsun had killed me and offered you his favor, you would have accepted before he finished asking!"

Zaria's back stiffened, and all of her former once-intriguing fire returned. "What could I have said? I would have been compelled!"

"Spare me." Ty cut at the air with one hand. "You would have ensured that Siyrsun compelled you. Do you believe I'm such a fool?

You conspired to kill Araine, discounting her importance to Belaal, and ignoring my own safety while you schemed." He leaned forward, emphasizing each syllable. "I paid your dowry and dismissed you as a wife, and I meant it. I will never again trust you! The only thing you could possibly say to redeem yourself at all would be to bring a living child—my child!—to me this instant!"

Zaria's gaze flickered, betraying defeat. Rethae said, "There is no child. We've had her watched."

Zaria sputtered, "What? Well, then, you'll know my behavior's been exemplary, and worthy—"

Bel-Tygeon cut off her argument with a dismissive wave. "Leave me. I never want to see you again. You should have been executed for conspiring with Siyrsun, so count yourself as spared. Go."

"But, Sire, I love you! My intentions were ever honorable, and I regret—"

"I gave you every possible chance, Zaria, and you failed me. You betrayed me almost to death. Do you believe I'll forget that? Get out! Don't tempt me to lock you away to rot."

Tears shimmered in Zaria's dark eyes. She gathered her veils about herself and then stood and fled the room, crying as she ran. At the door, Ebatenai exhaled loudly in obvious relief, and then he retreated.

As the door closed, Ty lifted an eyebrow at his sister. "Did she harass you?"

"Relentlessly. She was paying for spies among our servants and sending me notes nearly every day." Rethae sighed. "I'm grateful, Sire. You reacted just as I hoped you would."

"Good. If she causes any further trouble I'll order her exiled from Sulaanc." Ty returned to his desk, eager to finish his letter to Akabe of Siphra. His sister lingered, tapping her fan lightly against his desk. Ty pushed a hand through his hair and then smiled at his sister. It *was* good to see her again, even if he longed to break her wretched fan. "What do you wish to say?"

"If Zaria cannot be your queen, then who will?"

"Whomever the Infinite pleases and in His own time. He alone can remove the curse of childlessness from this palace. But I don't want to consider that now. Give me a few months."

Or years.

First, he must try to forget Serena. Impossible…

***

Bracing herself, Serena wiped her tears with her bound hands. She would not shame the Eosyths by weeping and looking pathetic as she was sold. Already, Cziybor had untied the sash from her heavy coat, opening the garment and pushing it back from her rough, short tunic to display her figure as much as possible. Clearly satisfied, Cziybor scooped her up and tossed her into the wagon like refuse. "Stand!"

Serena obeyed, balancing herself against the rough wagon-bed's tilt. Her footing steadied, she lifted her chin and looked toward the spires of rock rimming the opposite side of this valley. Chilled as she was, her face burned with humiliation. How the men were staring! She didn't need to glance down at them. She could almost feel their eager gazes. Ignore them…

Obviously amused, Cziybor called out to the other warriors, "Behold, the most beautiful daughter of Tsir Andris, Lord of Clan Darom!"

A number of the warriors spat on the ground, yet they approached, studying her avidly. Cziybor continued, "As you can see, she's young, strong! *And* she's untouched—avowed so by a pack of jealous women! She carries burdens for days without complaint. She cooks, tends goats, and traps meat for her family. I have witnessed her courage— she is unequaled among women."

Cziybor was talking as if he'd watched her for a considerable time. Serena cast him a wary glance, just as he said, "If I didn't already have too many wives, I would take her for my own!"

As if she'd endure him! She sniffed and glared up at the sky. Only for Miyna's sake… Several warriors laughed and one called out, "I'll give you a colt, two goats, and three pieces of silver!"

Others began to bid variants of the first warrior's offer until a man's big, self-confident voice bellowed, "One four-year-old horse and two weights of gold—from Darzeq!"

Everyone hushed, as if the offer was outrageous. Vsevold snorted, "You didn't have to offer a horse as well, Dalibor."

Unnerved, Serena looked down at Dalibor, who was as brawny and full-bearded as Cziybor, lacking but a few kill-markers. He narrowed his gaze at Serena and said, "Nevertheless, it's my decision."

When no one else offered more, Cziybor laughed. "I accept! Dalibor, give me the weights and you can bring the horse later." He reached up, grabbed Serena's coat, and wrenched her off the cart. Before her booted feet hit the ground, Dalibor was beside her, one hand on her arm, the other hand offering Cziybor two discs of stamped gold. "I'll bring the horse to you later."

"Be sure you do," Cziybor retorted cheerily. "By sunset, or I'll go take my pick of your herd."

Dalibor hissed something that sounded like a curse. Other men crowded near, still eyeing Serena. Someone twisted a lock of her hair and she aimed a backward kick at her unseen tormentor. The man, whoever he was, laughed, and Cziybor chuckled. Leaning down, he muttered, "Have no fear. My wives will cherish your pretty little sister for as long as you obey. Don't try to escape."

Evidently hearing Cziybor's threat, Dalibor tightened his grip on Serena's arm. "I'll be sure she doesn't." He led her away, his pace so swift that she had to trot to keep up with him. Over his shoulder, he yelled at another man, "Djaros, take over the herd and return them to our pens when you've finished watering them."

A younger man's slighter voice called back, "I will."

Dalibor strode onward, weaving his way through the camp. As Serena concentrated on their path and not losing her footing, the man…her owner…heedlessly pulled her along, lifting her bound arms higher, throwing her off balance.

As they reached the southern end of the encampment, Dalibor slowed his pace. "We'll get along with each other, Daughter of Tsir Andris. As long as you obey my every word—spoken or not."

Ha—impossible! She almost told him so, but halted the contemptuous words just in time. No doubt defiance would earn her beatings.

"Remember," Dalibor warned, "say nothing! There's my tent, with the sun-storm signs."

Serena followed his glance toward an impressively pale tent adorned with crimson suns—their rays stylized in curving arcs. No doubt tributes to the god Utzaii.

Dalibor led her to the tent and shoved her inside—placing her face to face with two women who gawked at her as if seeing an alarming oddity. The younger woman, quite pregnant and pretty, backed away. The older woman, however, stared Serena up and down with such affronted boldness that Serena expected a beating. Most likely the first of many.

Dalibor pointed the women toward his tent's low doorway. "Leave us, both of you."

As they retreated, Dalibor wound his fingers into Serena's hair and turned her face upward toward his. He resembled Cziybor enough that she flinched. His eyes were a similar brown, and his beard was riddled with braids and chunks of gold clasped in a similar pattern. Dalibor didn't flaunt as many kill markers as Cziybor, yet…

She froze as Dalibor's scowl intensified. "Smile, woman."

Smile? Was he serious? How? She didn't have a smile left to give. Summoning all possible dignity, Serena bared her teeth at him…and he inspected them as if she were a horse. He was frightfully near, the musky scents of his fur-edged winter garments surrounding her as he grinned. "Very nice. You're the daughter of Tsir Andris, eh? Well… don't hold any mighty thoughts of escape."

He bent to kiss her.

Serena gasped and regretted it. His breath reeked. Didn't he ever scrub or polish his teeth? She must not bite him. Must not stomp his foot. Dalibor *owned* her…a fact she'd weep over for the remainder of her life. *This* was the rescue she'd prayed for?

Ty! She should have run away with Ty.

Chapter 20

As Dalibor kissed Serena and wrenched her closer, she heard the younger woman weeping outside the tent. The girl keened between sobs, "I'm going to kill myself...I will! Oh, let me die...! Eight months a wife and I'm replaced!"

The older woman hovered just beyond the entry and shook its heavy flap-like door in an attention-gaining move, as if she'd just remembered something. "Dalibor! Where did you find this girl? She doesn't look Agocii. Did you buy her?"

Loosening his hold on Serena, Dalibor snarled, "Go away!"

"Huh!" The woman snapped, "Just kill your mother while she's trying to save your life—or at least your good name!"

Dalibor gusted out a horrid breath and shoved Serena onto an open sleeping pallet. "Wait." She sat. And stared as the older woman actually leaned inside the tent, her expression skewed as if she'd caught a whiff of something foul. Given Dalibor's grubbiness, she probably had. The man growled, "Talk, Mother, and then leave us alone!"

Dalibor's mother cinched her lips together like a drawn money pouch and she scowled. When she had her son's full attention, she said, "If you used any of the Darzeq gold weights to purchase this girl, then I must ask... How do you intend to honor your pledge to pay tribute to the elders in support of General Siyrsun as we agreed?"

Dalibor fretted his beard, fraying its ends from their braided strands. "I'll replace the gold—I used only two of the four."

"How?" His mother shoved her way into the tent, slapped down the entry flap and sat. Serena almost loved her that instant. But not quite. Likely the woman was as mean as a starved destroyer. She glared at her son as if she wanted to stomp him. "You've sold all of your best horses, except for the one you ride. There's no way we can scrape together enough gold pieces to fulfill your pledge! Do you think the elders will tolerate your foolishness? What a raw green youth you are! They'll have you beaten, never mind your status! They'll have Liysaii beaten too, and she might lose the child. By the arm of Utzaii, think of what you're doing!"

Dalibor glanced at Serena, and his lips tightened. For an instant, he looked remarkably like his mother. With a beard. "What do you suggest?"

The woman eyed Serena thoughtfully, then nodded. "Give her to me. And give me two guards and Djaros as a driver, *and* your permission to travel. I'll regain your gold within ten days. I know just the man who'll buy her for the markets in Darzeq." When Dalibor hesitated, his mother's voice lowered and turned cold. "You must face the elders next month. With or without the gold you vowed toward Siyrsun's invasion of Belaal."

The Agocii warrior sighed and his gaze went distant as if reminding himself. "Empire."

"Yes—with the Agocii tribes at its heart." His mother drew a dagger from within her mantle, crossed the tent and caught Serena by the back of her coat. "Stand, girl. Walk with me quietly, or I shall kill you."

The dagger's sharpened edge gleamed and then rested thinly cold against her jugular. Undoubtedly, this woman was adept at dispatching livestock. Serena stood. As she passed Dalibor, he threw her a regretful look. A look that made her pause inwardly, though her feet continued to move. Would she face a worse master than Dalibor and his horrid mother?

Infinite, Mighty One…what is about to happen?

***

Every muscle in her body aching, Serena licked her dry mouth, struggled upright, and braced her bound feet against the bottom of the rugged pine cart. Catching her breath, she eyed the double-tracked dirt path ahead. South. Dalibor's mother was taking her farther south. Farther way from Clan Darom and any hope of helping her family.

She had to escape somehow. If not on this journey, then from Darzeq. She'd been to Darzeq only once—to Kiyrem—a tumultuous place. Markets full of noise and bright colors and scents. Though the gazes of so many strangers had made her long to hide...

Dalibor's mother swiped at Serena's hair and snapped, "How many times have I told you to turn away from the sun to avoid more freckles? You're as red as a scaln!"

In all truth, she'd obeyed throughout the journey. Likely she was only pink from struggling to sit up, but best to let the woman yell. Serena averted her face from the sun's comforting warmth in an effort to obey, but Dalibor's mother snorted. "It's too late now."

The slave, Djaros, drew the cart to a bone-jarring halt that sent Serena tumbling over on her side. The remaining two servants rode up alongside the cart—both men heavy-set, braid-bearded and formidably-armed with longswords and bows.

Despite their fierceness, the two men actually eyed Serena with pity. Perhaps a bit more than pity. She lowered her gaze. Particularly as Dalibor's mother spoke to the servants. "Untie her ankles and help her down. If she tries to escape, bind her with chains and then leash her—though that's not how I want to present her to future owners."

The two servants lashed their horses to the cart and then scuffled briefly, until the larger man lunged, reaching over the cart's side rail to snag Serena. "Don't fight, princess of the Eosyths, and I'll give you some water."

Water. How easily she was manipulated. Unwillingly, Serena sighed. "Thank you."

The huskier servant grasped Serena's waist and hefted her over the side of the cart as if she were a sack of food. He set her on her bound feet and held her tight in the crook of one arm. "Steady, are we?" He chuckled and commanded his disgruntled comrade, "Untie the cords while I distract her with water."

As if he was tending an ewe or foal. Serena almost snarled at the thought. Almost. The rude man dangled a water bag before her, shaking it until she heard the water slosh inside. He flipped the bag over the crook of his free arm, unpegged the nozzle with his teeth, and then offered her a drink. This time, he didn't taunt her by lifting it away while she was guzzling the lukewarm water. Instead, he waited until she'd finished, then he re-closed the water skin and muttered into her ear, "How I'll miss you! If I join the coming raids against the Eosyths, princess, I promise I'll look for your sisters and spare them. Do you have sisters?"

Kari. Tessi. Miyna and even Tiphera were at risk. She must not react. She would not speak and certainly not cry. Infinite, please save my family!

From a distance, Dalibor's mother cried, "What are you three dawdling for? Bring her here! Djaros, did you secure the wheels and block the cart? If so, come *here*. Now!"

Serena's guard snarled beneath his breath. "One day, old woman…!"

His comrade stood, flung the leather ankle cords into the cart, and muttered several short, bitter words. He grabbed Serena by the arm, then narrowed his gaze at her. "I ought to be paid a few kisses for guarding you all this way."

Serena tucked her chin and stared at her feet. To speak would only encourage the man. His comrade chuckled. "Never mind—the princess won't talk to you. She knows she belongs to some rich lord in Darzeq. Let's volunteer for the raids and go after the other women in her tribe."

Serena's stomach knotted. If she'd eaten anything, she'd heave it up now. But the men laughed together and while they walked, they discussed the forthcoming attacks as if planning a small hunting trip. Dalibor's mother watched them every step of the way, her fists on her hips. "I can out-walk the three of you together! Hurry."

She marched ahead, leading them toward a small crowd gathered near a showily painted leather tent. Serena scanned the crowd and noticed several other young women much her own age, bound, guarded, and vacant-eyed as if they'd given up all hope of living. The men guarding these girls were focused on a tense, lean, linen-clad man who shook his head as he spoke. Serena caught fragments of their dispute.

"…be realistic. Silver, not gold…"

Dalibor's mother intruded into the conversation, clearly sure of herself. "Here is your prize of the day!"

The linen clad man threw a bored look at the elder woman, but then his gaze rested on Serena and his dark eyebrows lifted. "Bring her here."

Smug, the Agocii woman motioned the guards who led Serena forward. She stood before the slaver, mostly resigned—then shocked as he dug his fingers into her hair, checking her scalp. "This color isn't an herbal wash?"

Dalibor's mother huffed, "Look at her eyebrows and lashes. Do those appear dyed with herbs? I think not! Her price is three pieces of gold—in weights."

"Three weights?" The slaver stared at Serena's eyes. She glared at him, unblinking, her scalp tingling where he'd tugged her hair. The slaver almost smiled—she saw his mouth twitch—but he growled at Dalibor's mother, "Your price is outrageous. Do you believe I'm a lord of Darzeq?"

"You'll sell her to one." The Agocii woman smiled. "She's the daughter of some great Eosyth lord, captured in a raid. There's no fear of revenge upon you, nor hope of rescue for her."

Serena gritted her teeth at the woman's scorn. If she could be freed for an instant, she'd blacken her smug captor's eye.

The slaver checked Serena's teeth, his movements adept as if he'd checked thousands of unwilling slaves—and he probably had. Then he pressed his fingertips along her neck and jaw much as Serena did when testing the children for swellings indicating illness. He tugged at the thin red cord fastened at her throat by Cziybor's wives, then stepped back and studied her again. Lifting his hand sharply, he aimed for Serena's face. "Answer quickly or I'll slap you so hard you'll see stars in daylight—what's your father's name?"

"My lord-father is Tsir Andris, Lord of Clan Darom." Just saying Father's name brought tears to Serena's eyes. She swallowed. Did Father even know about the raid yet? Not likely. Not if he'd traveled as planned, north to Clan Tsahfon, then east to Qedem...

A surprised grimace played over the slaver's lean face. "Is that so?" He lowered his hand and nodded to Dalibor's mother. "Let my servants examine her in the tent—you may accompany them, woman—and then we will determine the price."

By the time Serena was shoved from the tent again, freshly humiliated and wearing a new bright red cord about her throat, the slaver, flanked by two men who were apparently his own guards, was weighing out silver to purchase the last girl. He turned, glimpsed Serena's bright new necklace, and he nodded at Dalibor's mother. "One gold weight, three pieces of silver."

"Robber! Two weights of gold and five pieces of silver—though she's worth three at least!"

The slaver shook his head. "No. Three is her selling price in a large city. We're not there, woman, and I've expenses to meet. One weight of gold and eight pieces of silver. Accept it or take her away. I'm eager but not desperate."

He closed his money chest with a thump and reached for its lock. Dalibor's mother sucked in her breath and then shoved the gangly Djaros forward. "How much for him?"

Djaros gasped his brown eyes huge. "Me? How am I part of the bargain?"

"You're a slave," Dalibor's mother told him. "My son needs money, so off you go. May Utzaii bring you a worthy master." She lifted her squared chin at the slaver and held out her sunstorm-etched money purse. "You can see the mark upon his neck matches my own insignia—he's mine to sell, and he's young. Now...how much for the two of them?"

"Two weights of gold."

"And five silver pieces," the Agocii woman countered, pugnacious.

While his guards moved around the small table to stare down at the ashen Djaros, the slaver paused. His hands toyed with the lock on his money chest as if he wanted to latch it and cease bargaining. Serena trembled inwardly. Darzeq. Could she manage to escape from Darzeq? Surely she could contrive something, if only the Infinite would bless her….

The slaver looked from Djaros to Serena, then sighed. "Two weights of gold, three pieces of silver, and no more."

"Done!" Dalibor's mother accepted the coins and marched away without looking back. Serena glanced over her shoulder in time to see the woman give each of the guards a coin.

Grabbing a pair of manacles from beneath his table, the slaver handed them to his guards, who glared at the dumbstruck Djaros. Indifferent to the young man's shock, the slaver spoke in bored tones. "Hold out your hands. Fight and you'll be scourged."

The youth complied, but blinked at Serena. "Darzeq? We're going to Darzeq?"

Too disheartened to speak, Serena nodded.

A shadow blocked the sun's warmth—the slaver's shadow. Not unkindly, he gripped Serena's bound wrists. "Come, daughter of Tsir Andris. If you must be sold, then trust me there's a worthy place for you in Darzeq. Some nobleman will desire you for his sweetheart, I've no doubt of that."

Some nobleman's sweetheart? Not a wife…never queen of an Eosyth tribe… Her future was dust around her. Serena obeyed as the slaver herded her into the gaudy tent. There, two young women sat side by side on a mat, both red-eyed and puffy-faced as if they'd been crying.

The younger one, slight, pretty and olive-skinned, pleaded with Serena as if she had some power to change their situation. "I don't want to go to Darzeq."

"Neither do I. May the Infinite protect us." A forlorn prayer, to be sure. And her companion slaves looked as doubtful as she felt—their desolate gazes revealing souls long since run dry of prayers.

The bigger girl, robust with a thick gleaming black braid, blooming complexion and bruised circles beneath her dark eyes, muttered, "Can your Infinite be any worse than Utzaii? May He grant your prayer."

Chapter 21

His curiosity sharpening, Ty watched Belaal's former high priest, Ro'ghez, enter the secluded gold and blue antechamber. Why was the man wearing the rough linens endured by the lowest of slaves? Bel-Tygeon had never counted Ro'ghez as a friend, nevertheless he'd rewarded the high priest well for his service, and Ro'ghez had always flaunted the finest clothes befitting his rank. Interesting...

As the female guards left the entry and stationed themselves outside to guard the golden cage-like gate, Ty nodded to the former high priest, cultivating graciousness. "Welcome."

"Thank you, Sire." Ever austere, Ro'ghez now appeared thin to near-skeletal gauntness. Yet his deep-set dark eyes remained calm within his haggard face as he bowed to Bel-Tygeon and then knelt before him. His voice tranquil, the priest said, "It is good to see you've returned in such excellent health. Your subjects will rejoice to see you again."

Was that a hint that Belaal's king must soon present himself publicly? "Yes, and I will be glad to see them, at the proper time."

Ty studied this man whose plots against Araine had undoubtedly fueled Siyrsun's rebellious tendencies. Yet based on the evidence, Ro'ghez had schemed against Araine from misled sincerity. Siyrsun's conniving, however, arose from raw and latent ambition—cloaked by generations of faithful service to Belaal's god-kings.

Bel-Tygeon's humiliating fall from deity had shattered Siyrsun's thin shield of loyalty.

But what had happened to Ro'ghez? What did the man now think of his mortal king? Ty sat back in his chair. "Why did you request this audience?"

"To determine my future, Sire." The former priest glanced toward the entryway. "I was under the impression that the prophet would be here as well—at my request."

Ty straightened. "That's surprising, considering your attempts to have her killed—not to mention Lord Nikaros."

"To my shame and my self-instruction."

In unison, they turned, hearing delicate footsteps and accompanying boot-steps echo briskly against the marble tiles outside. The golden-caged gate beyond the entry clanged open and Araine and Nikaros entered the antechamber, Nikaros bearing a parchment scroll, Araine armed with her gleaming prophet's branch.

Seeing the branch's soft metallic glow, Ty straightened warily. Ro'ghez also shifted, and Bel-Tygeon saw him take a breath and swallow. Had Belaal's prophet and its high priest suffered another clash during his absence?

Nikaros placed a defensive arm around his wife. Araine, however, glanced from Ro'ghez to Ty and smiled, her blue eyes brightening, her expression as endearing as Miyna or one of the twins. It helped Ty to think of her thus. As more of a younger sister. In truth, he'd felt protective toward Araine from the first time he'd glimpsed her in his throne room, a fragile heap, beaten, bloodied and near death. Araine spoke, her voice lilting, joyous. "Sire, good morning!"

She bowed to him—as did Nikaros—and Ty motioned them to approach. The instant she knelt, Araine half-bowed toward Ro'ghez. "Sir, I'm sorry for being late."

Nikaros eyed Ro'ghez. "Because your previous meetings have been less than friendly, I insisted upon accompanying her."

The gaunt priest bowed himself almost to the carpet before Nikaros and Araine. "All the more reason that I am in your debt for your presence now. I have no reason to expect your forgiveness."

Interesting. Ty hid a grin. Were these three about to declare a formal truce? Perhaps now Belaal's priest and prophet might work together. He masked his glee and coughed. "Lord Nikaros. Prophet. Welcome, despite your tardiness. Ro'ghez was about to explain the reason he requested this meeting."

The former high priest cleared his throat. "I will be concise. I begged this meeting, Sire, to confess to you that I've become a heretic and no longer fit for my role as Belaal's priest. First, my temple vanished and with it my strength of faith. Then..." he nodded toward Araine, "This girl-prophet appeared from nowhere and all my efforts to rid Belaal of her influence and her Infinite failed spectacularly. Therefore, as I cannot deny what I have seen and experienced, I worship the Infinite, and not Belaal's god-kings. According to our traditions, my penalty is death. I now await your verdict and sentence."

Such a solemn confession deserved a more solemn judge. Ty passed one hand over his face and summoned dignity. "Ro'ghez, you have a problem. Your offense should be tried in a sacred court, not a civil one. Your most recent god-king, the ruler of your faith, no longer exists. Moreover, if Belaal has no high priest, then you'll have a long wait." He nodded toward Araine. "Perhaps Belaal's prophet has a solution."

Araine shook her head. "No, Sire, I don't. However, the Infinite does." She leaned forward. "Ro'ghez, pray to the One you now serve. Remember, too, that—because you have expressed true remorse—I forgive you, as your Creator has forgiven you."

She glanced at the silent Nikaros and he handed her the frayed scrolled parchment. Tenderly, she unfurled the ancient document. "Sire, when I became Belaal's prophet, you asked me when the Infinite would restore your temple. He declares that now is the time. However, it won't be your temple—you will build it for your people. Here are the plans."

She offered Ty some of the sacred verses she'd nearly died to save. Two years ago, Bel-Tygeon the god-king would have accepted this ancient parchment carelessly, though with some curiosity. Now, he hesitated. Did he imagine this fray-edged document's subtle glow toward him? He certainly felt the impetus of its verses. Whose hands had first inked this parchment? Surely compared to that person, he was unworthy. "Prophet... do you have a copy of these books?"

"Yes, Sire. I've copied several for study. It's been my main task while you were gone."

"I would welcome a copy." As he gently unfurled the gleaming document, Ro'ghez coughed discreetly—a bid for his attention.

"Sire, I have a copy. I will send it to you the instant I return to my rooms."

Ro'ghez had truly changed. Ty grinned. "You've been studying, Ro'ghez?"

"Yes, Sire…to bide my time and quiet my soul as I awaited your verdict. Or, rather, the Infinite's verdict."

Her glance sparkling with obvious enjoyment, Araine told Ro'ghez, "Sir, here is the Infinite's verdict. Abide with your Creator and study with all your might. For by the time His temple is finished, you will be His first high priest in Belaal."

Ty laughed at the priest's stupefaction and then sobered as he finally glanced down at the ancient scroll. At building plans. Descriptions of fabric. Sacred utensils. His own duties…which would span years. "Compose yourself, Ro'ghez. We've a lifetime of work ahead of us."

***

Nikaros watched and listened, restraining his impulse to carry his wife away from this antechamber. His fear that Ro'ghez might be feigning remorse seemed unfounded. And the king had clearly accepted Nik's marriage to Araine.

Why, then, am I so uneasy? Infinite, reveal the reason, I beg You.

While he waited, he would remain calm and quiet—and continue his plans for the coming war. Even as Nik's thoughts sped into the documents he must write today, Bel-Tygeon asked, "Prophet, have you any word from the Infinite concerning this war we're supposed to wage? Where will I be leading my army?

Nik admired his wife's exquisite face as a delicate crease formed between her brows and she shook her head. "Sire, the Infinite remains silent, therefore we must wait and pray."

The king shifted in his chair, clearly wrestling his impatience over her frustratingly brief answer. "No doubt our destination will lead us to Siyrsun." He snapped a look at Nikaros now. "Any clues as to his whereabouts?"

Aware of Ro'ghez—once Siyrsun's ally—Nikaros shook his head. "No, Sire, not enough to commit an army to march toward. The most-heard and accepted rumor is that he fled to Darzeq to hide himself amid the turmoil there."

As if discerning Nik's hesitation, Bel-Tygeon said, "We'll speak at archery practice this afternoon. Be ready. Meanwhile, order our spies to persist. I want Siyrsun caught, and this matter ended."

To practice in earnest and to discuss any further rumors of Siyrsun, Nik had no doubt.

Where are you? He asked Siyrsun inwardly. Are you truly in Darzeq? Or have you indeed crept into Agocii lands to build an army as our spies have hinted?

Old Dreki, what are you planning?

***

Serena gasped as the cart thudded into a muddy hollow in the road. And even Djaros—a bound, huddled heap in the cart's far corner—yelped and looked around. Their driver cursed and urged the oxen forward. The instant the cart lumbered ahead, Serena relaxed. Until Trazios rode up beside the cart, scowling as if he could beat her within a breath. "Where's your veil? Put it on again before I stop the cart and have you whipped!"

Why the fuss over a veil? She lowered her chin to hide her rebellion. "Forgive me. It slid off two jolts ago."

One of her companion-slaves, the fragile and owl-eyed Malia, whispered, "Scoot over. I'll help you."

As Trazios rode ahead, Serena bent, waiting as Malia struggled to pick up and shake out her fallen veil—no easy feat with bound hands. While they worked together, tweaking the veil's gauzy folds in place, Serena hissed, "Why are these slavers so obsessed with veiling us?"

Malia remained fearfully silent, but their older companion, Cecaii, shook her luxuriant dark-braided hair and muttered, "The veils protect our skin and save our families from the disgrace of revealing our identities." Even through their veils, Serena saw Cecaii's shadowed frown. "Eosyth princess, you sheltered creature, do you think Trazios will sell you to a nobleman? No! It's true that you'll be sold to a wealthy man. But that man's wealth will be gained from selling women—captives like us—over and over, every day, for countless men to use as they wish! You'll become a common prostitute, longing to die."

Was this true? For all of Trazios' fine words about making her a Darzeq nobleman's sweetheart, did he actually intend to sell her as a…prostitute? Serena shivered.

"If there's a chance to escape, we must snatch it," Cecaii muttered.

Turning one shoulder against the fuming Cecaii, Malia whispered to Serena, "I prefer the veil. It hides my tears."

Serena felt her own tears stinging along her eyelids. To be sold over and over… Oh, Infinite, if You are truly there…rescue us! Give us a chance to escape!

Despite her struggle for courage, she wept silently until the cart jolted to a halt just before midday. Trazios rode around the cart, grumbling and tapping his coiled whip against his restless gold-hued horse. "Where is he? He should have been waiting for us!" To his cart driver, he said, "If he's not here at noon, we make camp."

"Yes, sir." The cart driver sounded glum, obviously envisioning another boring night alongside this tortuous road.

Just as Serena's feet were falling asleep, and she and her companions were squirming with discomfort, three riders approached all looking weathered and exhausted. Their bronzed and burly leader hailed Trazios. "Sir! Excuse our delay, but we bring you news!"

Serena sniffled and peered through the mists of her veil. The burly rider huffed as he goaded his horse toward Trazios. "There's disaster in Darzeq! Again! No one's buying anything except food, Trazios, believe me—the whole country's in confusion and everyone's holding onto their silver. You'll have to sell these women elsewhere, but leave us out of your dealings. We're done and worn out. Mercenaries tried to—"

"I don't care about the mercenaries!" Trazios spewed out a stream of harsh, furious syllables that made Serena long to cover her ears. "Do you expect me to ride all the way to Belaal? They're not buying as many there either."

"Will you regain your costs by selling these slaves at the roadside?" the first man argued. "I doubt it! You could try Siphra. Their markets should be opening now that the country's recovered from its revolution."

Trazios growled. "Spare me the Siphrans! The few that buy slaves there offer copper, not silver—and don't even mention gold to them—bunch of parsimonious farmers! You're sure about Darzeq?"

Another of the men spoke up now, his tone that of a man pushed beyond endurance.

"Are we *sure*? By the nostrils of Utzaii, yes! The Darzeq mercenaries stole our coins and nearly skinned us alive, and the capitol's a wreck. Fires everywhere! Take your slaves to some other market, Trazios— I'm done! I'll go home and be a parsi-whatever farmer, and thanks!"

He turned aside his horse and rode off—the other two following him eastward.

Trazios spat after them and cursed again. Then, he snapped to the driver and their three guards, "Set up camp! We'll decide our next destination tonight." To Serena and the others, he snarled, "What am I to do with you?"

What indeed? So softly that only her companion-slaves heard, Serena whispered, "Infinite, Mighty One, save us! Give us hope…"

Trazios unbound them, and his men stood guard impatiently as Serena and her companion captives drank water and tended their needs at a nonexistent privy. After a meal of dried fruit and coarse grain cakes, Trazios shoved them into a tent and tied them up again.

During the night, Cecaii twisted and squirmed, clearly trying to loosen her bonds. Could she? Serena shifted quietly, working the cords until she found a hair's width of ease. Still not enough. She paused and listened in the darkness. Outside two men were snoring, and Trazios' grumbling voice rose and fell in unintelligible fragments.

If they entered the tent, she'd pretend to be asleep. Until then… She squirmed her way over to Cecaii and muttered, "We work together. Sit up. Back to back."

Cecaii obeyed. Serena worked at the knots over Cecaii's wrists until her own wrists burned and her thoughts chafed with impatience. More than once, she had to shove aside Cecaii's own frazzled hair braid, which fell in her way.

At last, she tugged a vital cord and eased it loose. Cecaii whispered, "I have it!" Cecaii freed herself, then paused as if deliberating whether or not to free Serena. As if the escape of one woman would be more successful than all three. Serena gritted her teeth and threatened beneath her breath. "Free us, or I'll scream!"

"Be still!" Cecaii wrenched at the knots and Serena's bonds soon fell. While she wrenched at the cords on her ankles, Cecaii freed Malia.

Hardly daring to breathe, Serena tucked the cords inside her coat, picked apart a back seam of the tent—flimsy compared to Eosyth tents—and then opened a space just wide enough for the three of them to scoot out. After listening for the snores and grumbles of their captors, they crept into the darkness.

Though all her impulses urged her northward, Serena resisted. Dalibor and Cziybor stood between her and Clan Darom. She must gather her resources and then make plans and weapons. Until then… She threaded her way through the darkened meadow, parallel to the silent Cecaii and Malia—then ran.

Chapter 22

Serena stared up at the fading stars and morning's first violet-gold hues, then exhaled her uncertainty. Infinite...Lord of her father, was she following the safest course? Away from Trazios and a potentially brief and unbearable lifetime of horrifying enslavement? If so, then why did fears plague her now?

Cecaii halted ahead of her, Malia at her side. "What's wrong? Has our Eosyth lady turned coward?"

"No. But I'm uneasy." Serena followed Cecaii and Malia down a slope, into a rugged ravine of rock formations and winter-bare trees mingled with evergreens that sheltered sparse shrubs and a decaying carpet of leaves.

As they descended, Serena heard the lulling rush of water from within the ravine. This place strongly resembled the ravine she'd been checking when she'd first met Ty. And where she'd first been confronted by Cziybor.

Ice-picks of fear stabbed through Serena's being. Studying Cecaii's intended path, she called to Malia, "Wait! Do you know this land? What lies ahead?"

Malia hesitated, her slender oval face a pale blur against her muted, tangled brown hair. But Cecaii heard and spun about to face Serena. "I don't know about this particular gorge. All I can say is that it's further away from Trazios!" Before Serena could speak, Cecaii continued, all defiance, "I am going to Siphra—no one will sell me there, and I can work for some farmer's wife. If you're so determined to find your family then your safest course is to travel north along Siphra's border."

"Unless we die of our own foolishness before reaching the border," Serena pointed out. "Cecaii, we've hiked for most of the night without stopping to cover our tracks. We can run until we drop, but Trazios and his men have horses, and if one of the guards is a tracker, then they'll find us soon—unless we take care to hide our paths now."

Cecaii's dark brown eyes flicked right, then left as she pondered Serena's words. What was there to consider? Of course they must disguise their paths and hide. Serena persisted, "We're tired. Let's work at covering our tracks for a while, and then find a place to hide and rest while we make plans. We've no food, we need sleep, and we must create weapons and tools."

Malia stepped a bit closer to Serena. "I...agree. I'm tired and hungry."

Cecaii flung a pained glance to the dawn lit heavens, but then she shrugged and faced Serena. "How do you propose we hide our tracks?"

"When we reach the water below, if it's safe, we remove our boots and walk downstream. We'll need to watch for a stone path out of the stream—and a place to rest."

"I'd give anything for a fire right now," Malia quavered.

"No fire," Serena chided gently. "Not until we know we've escaped Trazios."

But at the slope's base, the startlingly wide torrent made Serena catch her breath. Cecaii stepped back, and Malia shook her head, raising her voice. "I'm not going in there!"

Understandable. They'd probably die of the cold within a few breaths of entering the water. That current was too deep, fast and snow-chilled. Therefore... Serena stepped onto the nearest stone edging the torrent's bank, then glanced around for her next step. As her companions stared, she called to them, "Watch out for moss— you don't want to touch it or leave any sort of trail. And you don't want to fall in!"

They followed her cautious lead until the sun gleamed in the sky above, and the ravine had become a chasm. Malia called out, "I need to rest!"

Serena nodded toward an extensive-upslope of rock formations and mixed forest. "There. Let's climb up the embankment and look for some shelter."

They climbed the stone embankment and the rough hillside beyond, then entered a fringe of trees. Serena searched for a cave. Even a low rock overhang hidden by coarse foliage and trees could serve as a shelter. If they withdrew too far into the wood, away from the torrent, then they could gouge trees and tap them for water. She could bash stones to create blades…

"There." Cecaii nodded toward an ancient fallen moss-and-fern-covered tree—a natural barricade for the small recess in the stones beyond, which were veiled with tangles of roots from trees growing above.

Serena sighed. If they huddled together inside the alcove and piled old branches and leaves over the entrance, it might prove safe enough to allow them some sleep. Also, the moss looked safe…not witches' moss, though the alcove would be uncomfortable. "At least we won't have to worry about chasing out any crested lizards. But speaking of beasts, we should forage a bit and then sleep and stay hidden until after dark to avoid Trazios."

Cecaii huffed. "Someone should set beasts on him!"

Together, they found small handfuls of food—sproutling-sized patches of fading winterberries, pine needles, and small black trumpet mushrooms. Malia wrinkled her nose, reminding Serena of Tessi or Kari, without the silent speech. "Those look evil! I won't touch them—we won't be full anyway, so why bother?"

"Some food is better than none," Serena told her. They huddled together, chewing on pine needles. Gradually, they warmed and fell asleep.

Serena awoke to soft glimmers of afternoon light and to Cecaii's shadowed form as she crept from their miniature cave. Reluctant to wake Malia, who was leaning against her, Serena drifted back into sleep until distant shrieks and snarling voices reached their small alcove. Malia sat up. "Cecaii! Should we go to her?"

Before Serena could answer, a shadow darkened their hideaway. A man's big hand pushed aside the tangle of roots and branches.

Trazios lifted his coiled riding whip and raged, "I could kill you both!"

He wrenched Malia from the alcove and flung her toward a guard, who dragged her over the mossy log and then slapped her. Trazios bellowed, "Not the face or throat!"

Malia began to scream.

Even as Trazios turned toward Serena again, she scooted from their root-curtained hiding place and stood, summoning dignity, though her feet were numbed and tingling, causing her to sway. Trazios grabbed her by one shoulder, spun her around and began to thrash her with the whip's blunt end. Digs, gouges and furrows of pain jarred her, layer upon layer of hurt until even her heavy coat no longer cushioned her from the beating.

When she tumbled face-down, Trazios beat the backs of her legs— vulnerable where her short boots and coat gapped. By the time he stopped beating her, she was sobbing. Trazios kicked at her. "Stand!"

Stand…? She could hardly breathe.

Trazios dragged her over the mossy log and down slope, her steps skidding and jolting all the way down. At the slope's base, on the rocks edging the winter-chilled torrent, a guard stood beside Cecaii, gripping her arm. The young woman's face was puffy, with oozing bloodied cuts, and her brown eyes were reddened with weeping. She looked from Malia to Serena and cried, "I—I'm sorry! I—"

Cecaii twisted from her guard's hold, flung herself into the current, and was swept downriver, lost amid the foaming, wild torrent.

Malia wailed. Trazios and his guards swore, and Serena cried, "Oh, Mighty One, no! Can't she be rescued?"

Trazios snarled, "She's not worth our lives. Close your mouth and move!"

***

Just outside a small town, the cart creaked and groaned to a halt, giving Serena's bruises and torn muscles one last rude bump. Malia sat up beside her, both of them too oppressed to speak. At the previous halt, they'd been bathed from scalp to toes in an open stream, and once again Trazios had inspected them like livestock for purchase. Fitting, because ever since their failed escape, they'd been leashed and pegged down at night like animals to mourn and shiver in the darkness—and they'd been fed coarse scraps and shoved about like despised beasts. Surely there'd be nothing human left of their former selves by the time this journey was done.

However this was only the beginning. Had Cecaii known and been through all these indignities before? Mighty One, if there's a chance that she's alive...help her to freedom!

Trazios thumped the cart's side with his whip. "Stand! Now!"

One of the guards pulled Serena from the cart, set her down, and then reached for Malia. Trazios squeezed Serena's shoulder and gave her a short, fierce shake. "Listen to me, Eosyth princess! Whatever happens, you remain silent and obedient or I'll repay you tenfold! Do you hear me? Nod, 'yes'."

She nodded. Trazios swiped off her veil, wadded it into her bound hands, and then tugged at her coat, loosening it and pushing it open to reveal her throat and shoulders. He shook out her hair, briefly groomed it as he would a horse's mane, and then he pinched her cheeks. "Bite your lips and then show your teeth, both of you. Good. Now, close your mouths and say nothing unless you are asked a question."

Trazios guided them to the nearby encampment, which was situated at the edge of a walled city. Within the encampment, Trazios led Serena and Malia directly to a pale, three-peaked leather tent. A tall, thin, blue-clad man stood before the tent in the shade of its awning, his long arms crossed, his fingers tapping impatiently against his robe's blue sleeves. His voice astonishingly deep, the blue-clad man bellowed, "Trazios, are you finally visiting us again? What have you brought me this time?"

All oozing geniality, Trazios laughed and said, "Only the best, Rileon! Only the best. Look at these two jewels."

His dark eyes narrowing in his tanned face, Rileon approached Malia, smoothed her hair, and checked her eyes, teeth, throat, and figure. Finished, he stepped back and nodded. "Pretty."

Rileon puckered his lips thoughtfully, faced Serena, and then paused. He looked her up and down twice, tugged gently at the corners of her eyes, pushed down on her chin and checked her teeth, and then ran his fingers down both sides of her throat and finally rested his hand against the rough crimson cord encircling her neck. "What origin?"

"Eosyth," Trazios said, smirking a little.

"It's rare that we acquire an Eosyth—I haven't for years." Rileon wound a long strand of Serena's hair around his thin tanned fingers, then smoothed it and checked her scalp. As if she might have ticks. Lice. Fleas... "This is natural color. She's a beauty."

Trazios' smirk broadened to a grin. "Four gold weights."

"No-no," Rileon protested. "No bargaining for this one yet. We must examine her first."

Glancing over his shoulder, he spoke to a massively built servant who looked as if he ate whole animals for dinner. "Take her into the tent."

Another examination?

Humiliation heated Serena's face. The servant wrapped his big fingers around her upper arm—coat and all—as if grasping an easily-snapped twig. He shoved her inside calling out good-naturedly, "Biriya, Mother Liliyn, here's another one! Call me if you need help."

Ugh! Reason to behave.... Serena winced, and waited as her eyes adjusted to the tent's shaded interior. Two women stood before her, one looking perturbed, the other bored. Somehow, the boredom was more difficult to accept. Serena protested, "You all behave as if I'm no longer human! Why can't anyone trust anyone else, least of all trust me when I declare that I'm healthy and I've never been with a man?"

The bored woman's expression eased a bit and she chuckled. "Too much gold is involved, so there's no honor here. As for being human, no." She pointed to a mat. "You're only a slave, so come here or we'll call to Pitaros for help."

Remembering the hulking servant's offer, Serena shuddered and obeyed.

***

As they settled into their new owner's straw and wool cushioned cart, Malia stared through their mutual veils at Serena. "Did I hear right? You earned Trazios three weights of gold, and two silver?"

Mortified, Serena slumped beside Malia in the straw. "It's shameful."

Her voice mournful, Malia said, "At least I'm worth one piece of gold. Trazios paid ten pieces of silver for me." Softly, she added, "Trazios paid eight pieces for Cecaii. I would like...to think that she survived. That she's walking to Siphra now, a free woman."

"I pray it's so." Forcing words from her tightening throat, Serena asked, "Did you hear where they're taking us?"

"No... Did you?"

Serena shook her head. "No. Why tell a mere slave anything?"

She was nothing now, with all her dazzling childhood plans trampled about her bleak and fragile as grayed ashes...utterly without hope.

Infinite, do I still exist in Your sight? Remember me! And Malia, Cecaii, Miyna...my family...

***

A breath of warm humid air slid beneath the cart's small canopy, stirring Serena from a restless sleep. Sweat started over her skin and then trickled downward irritatingly. If only she could fling away this veil, unfasten her coat, and be rid of the ropes chafing at her wrists and halting the blood in her feet.

Beside her, Malia slept, her veil crumpled beneath her head as a meager pillow, her face so young and vulnerable that Serena couldn't help comparing her to one of the twins. Was it true that she and Malia would be sold over and over again?

Cecaii had evidently thought so. If only—

Rileon's voice cut into her thoughts. "There's Sulaanc. We'll camp beside that stream for the night. Mother Liliyn, Biyra, as soon as your tent is standing, take the girls and be sure they're presentable by morning. I want them adorned and…"

Whatever else the slaver said, it slid by Serena in a vague jumble of noise. She would enter Sulaanc tomorrow morning. Josias and Lije had said that Nikaros still lived there. Might she somehow reach him? Her heartbeat quickened and she nudged the bewildered Malia awake, hissing, "Listen! My brother-in-law is in Sulaanc. Help me and we might be safe by nightfall!"

Chapter 23

His elbow on the temporary writing table, Bel-Tygeon rested his chin in his hand and eyed the first document in the heap before him. An errant morning breeze snatched the document's edge, and Ty slapped down the parchment. If he had to sit here until noon, then he would use the time to do some work.

He would not look into the private courtyard below. He would not meet the hopeful gazes of the countless young women as they each crossed the courtyard's marble pavings, stood before him for two breaths of time, and then departed—motioned away by Ebatenai.

He would not forgive Rethae for at least a week after she'd presumed to arrange such a viewing. His thoughts were too full of Serena, his grief too fresh. Moreover, his previous unofficial consorts had been untrustworthy and ultimately wearisome with all their pleas, ploys, and plots. There was something to be said for mourning his loss in peace.

"Sire," Ebatenai's thin voice entreated, "only look at this young lady walking in now—she's charming."

She wasn't Serena. Ty crushed a frustrated growl. "Ebatenai. I promised the Lady Dasarai that I would sit here until mid-morning, but I intend to work. Thank you."

"Alas," Ebatenai sighed, "She's gone."

"And I'm reading." Ty flourished a document at his meddlesome household steward. "Military recognitions and then promotions. I *must* concentrate."

"Forgive me, Sire."

Ty scowled, but nodded. He wasn't ready for this. At their noon meal, he would make it very clear to Rethae that he was in mourning. He would tell her about Serena.

If he could trust himself to speak of Serena.

Now, however, he must concentrate upon his work and ignore the parade of young women in the courtyard below. He flicked through the heap of parchments, frowned at an omission, and beckoned Ebatenai. "I was told that Commander Utthreates has been serving as Belaal's lord-general in my absence."

"He has, Sire. Is there a problem?"

Bel-Tygeon straightened the documents. "Where is the official order of his promotion?"

Ebatenai's eyebrows lifted. "I'll have it brought immediately, Sire." He motioned to an attendant who waited at the open corridor's entry and hissed, "Haste-haste…!"

Ty grimaced, rested his forehead against his propped-up fist, and returned to his reading.

***

Shivering, Serena hugged the veil shawl-like about her bare shoulders and thin tunic as she merged into the shuffling crowd of young women. Beside her, Malia was staring up at the massive blue-tiled gate, with its depictions of menacing beasts, some mythical, many all too real.

Behind them, Rileon said, "Hear me, you two. I will be waiting at the far gate. Whether you are purchased or not, you will return to me until matters are settled. Do *not* force me to retrieve you! Now, walk quietly after the other women. And pray to your gods that the king or his servants buy you both."

Or that Nikaros was yet here. As they walked together, Serena leaned toward Malia. "Remember…my brother-in-law's name is Nikaros, son of Lord Levos. I am Serena of Clan Darom."

Malia nodded, eyeing the next guard who stood watch on her side of the long tunneled gate. Clearly gathering her courage, she swallowed, then leaned toward the man and pleaded, "Sir, tell Nikaros, son of Lord Levos, that his sister-in-law Serena is among the slaves."

Though his expression didn't change, the guard cast a glance at them both. Malia pointed to Serena and babbled, "She's Eosyth! Clan Darom—sister-in-law to Lord Nikaros."

The guard glanced away and motioned them to move on. Didn't he believe them? Malia mourned, "I said it wrong! I called him 'Lord Nikaros' and he's no such thing. I'm sorry, Serena."

"At least you tried. It's my turn now." The next guard at the end of the tunnel-like gateway stood nearest her. As Serena approached the man, she looked up at him, allowing her fear to show. "Sir, please tell Nikaros, son of Lord Levos, that his sister-in-law Serena is among the slaves." To her shame, tears threatened. She took a quick breath and finished as she passed him, "I was captured from Clan Darom and sold by the Agocii!"

Like the first guard, he stared and then turned away. As if he would do nothing. Serena slid a hand over her face, fighting despair. She would not cry.

"We tried," Malia whispered.

"We're not finished trying!"

They walked into a wide courtyard, where numerous officials waited, all in blue robes or tunics and mantles rich in comparison to her coarse attire. Several must have been scribes like Detzios, for they pressed thin wooden styluses on wax-layered wooden tablets as four or five others waved the young women to the right and left.

One official motioned Serena to the left as another gestured for Malia to turn right and join a small crowd of captives. A second official eyed Serena and pointed her toward an open stone-arched gateway. One young woman stood there ahead of her, and Serena watched her silent, graceful progress through the courtyard ahead— her gliding walk and tentative turn halfway through, with the nervous obeisance toward a covered portico above the open courtyard. There, in the raised portico, a richly clad, dark-haired man sat before a low stone wall-like rail, clearly too absorbed with reading a parchment to even glance at the young woman waiting below.

Serena watched the young woman's hopeful pause, and then her swaying subtly drooping posture of defeat, just as a portly man leaned over the stone wall and motioned for her to leave the courtyard. The instant the disappointed girl reached the gate, the stout man lifted his chin at Serena, silently urging her forward.

What did it matter? The great man seated above never once looked away from his reading—the bad-mannered thing. By the richness of his apparel, the rings on his partially visible hand, and the heavy gold edging his mantle, he must be the king. Bel-Tygeon. Serena pressed her lips together, resisting the wish to spit toward him for the greed-induced famine he'd inflicted upon the Eosyths two years past. For taking Josias, Lije, and Nikaros captive. For inspiring two years of despairing prayers...

Yet something about his posture made her pause before she bowed in silence. Besides his gleaming black hair, though neatly groomed, reminded her of Ty.

Oh...Ty, if only it could be true! A ridiculous thought.

More so because he was too proud and busy to even glance at her. Serena straightened and turned, then nodded at the stocky servant who motioned her toward the far gate.

For the rest of her life she would regret not spitting at Belaal's tyrant god-king.

***

Ty lifted a hand toward the swift-moving sound of footsteps, toward Nik's voice as he said quietly, "Sire, here is the order for Commander Utthreates' pro..."

Nikaros halted mid-word and dropped the scrolled parchment—a total loss of dignity. Ty glanced up to snap a sarcastic comment at Nik, but the Eosyth was gaping at the courtyard below, his expression profoundly shocked. "Serena?" He leaned over the low balustrade and yelled, "Serena!"

Had the Eosyth lost his mind? Ty huffed. "You're seeing things."

Nik shook his head, looking ready to leap over the balustrade. "It's her! Don't you think I'd recognize my own sister-in-law?" To the eunuch guarding the far gate, he yelled, "That last young woman—catch her! Buy her!"

Infinite grant me patience! "Son of Levos, you overstep! I'm not buying—!"

"It was her! Sire—"

"Impossible!" Ty slammed a hand on his writing table, half-ready to throw Nik over the stone rail himself, with Ebatenai, who was silently cheering. "Are you insane? You could be imprisoned for such presumption! Go down there and rescind that order!"

Nikaros hesitated and then swallowed, bowed, and *almost* glared. "Yes, Sire. Forgive my presumption."

Ty snorted and returned to his documents. The effrontery! Had Nikaros been drinking? No, Nikaros didn't drink.

Nevertheless…if only it could be Serena. Might it have been her? No.

Impossible and impermissible!

His motions short and savage with regal displeasure, Bel-Tygeon snatched up and signed the official order of Commander Utthreates' promotion to Lord-General.

***

Rescind the order! Nikaros gritted his teeth as he stalked to the end of the open corridor. Oh, yes, he'd rescind the order. But he'd speak with this young woman first and be very sure of his decision. If she was not Serena, then Serena had a twin in Belaal.

Yet, if she was Serena… Nik's pace slowed amid his growing horror. If she was Serena, then some disaster had occurred. Mighty One, let me be wrong!

At the corridor's end, he halted as a eunuch-guard bowed humbly, but blocked his path, stout as a never-to-be-moved boulder. "Lord Nikaros, please forgive me, but you cannot proceed. This entry leads to the Women's Palace and you are now forbidden here on pain of death."

Nik paused. Death if he continued or imprisonment if he failed to rescind the order. Then he'd be imprisoned. Unless— He smiled at the guard. "Thank you for warning me that the death-order has been reinstated. But I'm acting upon an order from the king and I need your help. A young woman was just purchased down in the courtyard. The king wishes to rescind her purchase. However, I wish to purchase her as an attendant for my wife. Also, please send a message to the prophet and ask her to meet me here."

No matter how this situation was resolved, Araine must know what had happened.

As for Serena... Infinite, how should I pray?

Work Your will!

***

Dazed, Serena watched as Rileon gloated and accepted ten gold coins from the palace official. She was being purchased. In Belaal... by the king whom she'd nearly spit at.

Infinite, this is how You save me?

Which reminded her— Where was Malia? As the servants herded her toward a small chair that was ludicrously set between two long carrying poles, Serena threw a desperate glance at the royal servant who'd handled her purchase. "Sir, please, ask for Malia! Please, purchase the young woman who was with me—Malia!" To Rileon, she cried, "Don't you dare hurt her or sell her! Rileon, do you hear me?"

Rileon gave her a disgusted look. But if he replied, she couldn't hear, for the servants shoved her into the chair and she was lifted and carried into the palace. As if she'd suddenly become a fragile creature incapable of walking...into a grand blue and gold marble corridor so spectacular that she must be feverish and hallucinating its splendor....

Serena sagged into the chair and stared about as the burly servants hauled her through a series of golden doors and gates, each guarded by scowling, suspicious guards—several of whom were women. Women who could have possibly thrashed Father, or at least Uncle Zeddi.

"Unreal…" She whispered the thought aloud, but she might as well have remained silent, for the bearers sped along through corridor after fantastical blue and gold corridor as if they'd not heard. They finally set down the chair in a large, echoing garden, which was enclosed by the ornate buildings around it. Yet enough light filtered down that innumerable plants flourished, brightening this place— their dazzling colors and fragrances so sweet that Serena's stomach growled from hunger. By now, she was so hungry that she'd gladly eat these flowers.

One of the brawny chair-bearers motioned her to stand as the other bearer rapped furtively on a nearby door—a golden door so tall and dazzling that Serena's gaze swam just looking at it.

She stood there, shivering and watched by her guards until the door opened and a woman entered the garden area. And not just any woman. Her heavily embroidered robes and proud glance proclaiming her to be *someone.* A someone to be obeyed. For although she was delicate, pale and beautiful, the woman's dark eyes glittered formidably. She surveyed Serena and her sculpted black eyebrows drew together in a frown, which she aimed at the servants like a weapon. "This is all? One hopes the king has decided upon others!"

Serena's guards both bowed, and the slightly heftier one answered meekly in a girlish voice that made Serena stare. "Lady, this is the only woman he purchased." The larger man nudged Serena. "Bow to the Lady Dasarai."

Who? Serena bowed. But the Lady Dasarai still looked displeased. She waved at the guards and then at a handful of servants who were now gathering nearby. "Take charge of her. Bathe her, have the physician attend her, and then bring her to me. Hurry."

Before the proud Lady Dasarai lowered her hand, another door opened and a female guard strode in and bowed. "Lady, please excuse me, but the king has rescinded his order to purchase this girl."

Dasarai's nearly perfect features became pinched as if she'd inhaled something offensive. When she finally spoke, her words should have been carved in ice. "Very well. The king has rescinded his order. I will purchase her for him instead. Meanwhile, accept my orders!"

By now, the handful of waiting servants had become a small and impatient mob. They swept around Serena and all but carried her into a spacious, starkly beautiful marble room. Their haste and silence unified to remind her that she was merely a slave. She might have been a carving of wood as they ruthlessly stripped, scrubbed, and oiled her, and then attacked her damp hair with combs and fans, chilling her despite the fresh robe they'd provided.

A woman's cool, authoritative voice interrupted the hair-combing. "Do we finally have a candidate? Step back, all of you." The servants obeyed, bowing to the woman, who was thin, silver-haired, and stern-faced. Yet her gaze was acute and even a bit kind as she smiled at Serena. "Don't be frightened, young lady. I am Cythea, the Women's Palace physician. Let's see if you are in good health and a suitable prospect, shall we?"

Another examination? Serena closed her eyes, praying for patience.

***

Followed by Nikaros and Araine, Ty stormed into his antechamber. The instant the guards closed the gates beyond the entry, Bel-Tygeon pivoted on one heel to face his prophet and her defiant husband. "What is the use of returning to Belaal if my every order is countermanded? First you, Nikaros, then my sister! And you, Araine! Why are you interceding? What can you—"

A guard rattled at the outer gate, indicating that the interruption was important. Ty scowled and shouted across the antechamber. "What?"

Visibly shaken, the guard bowed inside the entry door. "Sire, an astonishing message—two messages—for Lord Nikaros."

"Say them, and then leave," Bel-Tygeon commanded. "Surely Lord Nikaros isn't keeping further secrets from me!"

Nik shook his head, clearly baffled. "I'm not, Sire. Let both messages be spoken."

Moistening his lips, the guard coughed, then faltered, "Lord Nikaros, the two messages are the same, from a palace guard and from Commander Vioc. Your sister-in-law Serena was captured and taken from Clan Darom. She's among the slaves."

Serena...the girl was indeed Serena... Ty's fury faded, replaced by shock and a fear that sank into his soul, insidious as poison. He gaped at Nikaros, who appeared equally appalled, while Araine closed her eyes as if in prayer. Ty growled, "Cziybor! If he's yet alive, I'll kill him!"

He charged for the gate, chased by Nikaros and Araine.

Chapter 24

Serena shivered again as the physician led her into an astonishingly beautiful room that flaunted high, pale columns draped with sheer blue curtains and lavishly carved, gilded tables, curved benches and footstools. As they walked, Serena's footsteps were muted by a thick carpet and hampered by a heavy gold band that a female guard had welded about her ankle, marking her as a slave. A slave. How had this happened? Infinite, why?

Serena hugged her thin undergarments to herself for warmth. When would the other slaves bring her actual clothes? Would she meet the king? Not that she wanted to—awful man! No doubt he'd be furious with the Lady Dasarai for defying his order.

However, Dasarai was evidently the ruler of the Women's Palace. Surely the king must respect or at least hear her reasons for buying Serena against his wishes.

Clinging to hopes of reason and calm, and following Cythea's example, Serena knelt on the thick carpet, adjusting her gold-weighted ankle band. Eventually, perhaps if she became a favored slave, the king might at least listen to her and consider sending help to Clan Darom. But if he was truly furious … if Serena caused her own death while pleading for her people…

So be it. No matter what, she would beg Belaal's hostile god-king for his help—even if she ultimately died. Wasn't this her duty? Any queen of the Eosyths was duty-bound to sacrifice herself, if need be, for the sake of family and clan. Infinite, bless me! Let me gain favor with the king. Let Clan Darom and the Eosyths be rescued in time!

Servants entered the room almost noiselessly, bearing cushions, a low, dark, incredibly carved table, and trays of food, including a pure white cup containing clear pink liquid, which the physician offered to Serena. Trying to compose herself, Serena studied the fragrant roseate drink. One of the prettiest decoctions she'd ever seen. "What's this?"

The physician, Cythea, smiled thinly. "This is a tisane of flower petals, rose hips, and fruit, prepared by Belaal's prophet to improve your health and speed the healing of your bruises. You will drink this for several weeks, therefore the prophet and I hope you enjoy its flavor. Drink the whole cupful."

That was a command. Serena sipped the brew of rose petals and fruit and waited for the outer robes she presumed would be brought. Instead, when the servants finally opened the doors, the elegant Lady Dasarai entered the room and settled gracefully onto the largest cushion. When the servants closed the doors again, she studied Serena. "Your appearance is much improved—indeed, you are beautiful, even without cosmetics."

"Thank you, Lady."

Dasarai shrugged, waved a shimmering fan, and then questioned gently, "Where did you come from? What are your usual habits?"

Courage. Serena set down the remainder of the brewed rose beverage and looked the formidable woman in the eyes. "I'm an Eosyth. From Clan Darom. I—"

A loud thud stopped her. The doors opened and a stunningly handsome man rushed inside, his garments flaring, his smooth-shaven face pale, his black hair mussed, his dark eyes huge. His eyes... Serena gasped. "Ty!"

Even as she questioned her shocked sanity, Serena intuitively crossed her arms, hugging herself again, mortified by her inappropriately thin garments. How could this be? "Ty?"

He paused, seeming incapable of speech while he stared. Serena cringed and looked away, blushing at the intensity of his gaze and her own shame. Within a breath, he hurried across the chamber his garments rustling. "Serena!"

He removed his mantle and swept it around her shoulders, its fabric heavy, warmed by his own body and richly scented with spices and fragrances she couldn't begin to name. But the added warmth didn't stop her sudden tremors. *Was* this man Ty? Or was her fatigue and near starvation causing hallucinations? As the vision-like man knelt beside her, Serena reached between the mantle's edges to touch his face—real as the weight of his mantle. She pitched herself into his arms. "You're truly here. Oh, Infinite, bless You!"

This was how He'd rescued her! How He would save her people... She'd been so ungrateful. So indignant with Him. An invisible leash tightened around Serena's throat as tears burned her eyes. She'd break if she didn't control herself.

Ty rocked her in his arms as if she were Miyna, his voice almost hoarse. "Serena, what *happened*? Was it Cziybor?"

Serena managed a nod. "He and his men found us at Kehb'el four days after you departed, and ... oh, Ty...!" Memories of the Agocii butchery, suppressed for so many days, arose in her thoughts fresh and raw as the day of the attack. She leaned into Ty and sobbed.

***

His emotions warring, Ty held Serena and breathed in the scent of her soft skin and damp hair as she cried. He'd prayed to see her again someday, but not as a slave. Never as a slave.

Unable to restrain himself, he kissed her face, her forehead, her hair, and then he rocked her as she wept. By his own stubbornness, his own foolishness, he'd nearly sent her away to be sold elsewhere. "To think that I didn't see you—I almost lost you. Bless the Infinite for protecting you!"

"Yes ... but, Ty..." Serena huddled against him, shivering violently as she spoke between shattering sobs, "Cziybor ... has Miyna! He sold Iared to another warrior. Aunt Betiya and Detzios ... were killed in the attack! And I don't know if Mother and the other women and children are safe, or if Father's yet alive..."

Cziybor had Miyna? Betiya and Detzios dead! Poor Iared, sold among the Agocii. Had Cziybor sold or killed Ayden as well? Ty caught his breath at the shock, then gently wove his fingers into

Serena's hair and made her look up at him. Her crushed, agonized gaze sliced at his soul. "What of Ayden? Serena, where's Ayden?"

"In the caves. With the twins and Mother and the other women." Serena gulped and then wiped her eyes with an unembroidered portion of his mantle. Just at the edge of his sight-range, Ty saw his sister stiffen. He shook his head to hush her, for Serena was talking again. "I pray they've remained safe and hidden! I've prayed Father found them and Cziybor didn't attack again. Ty—"

She straightened in his arms, pleading, "They'll need help! While I was guarded by Cziybor's wives, Cziybor had a visitor. Someone they called 'Old Dreki'."

"Siyrsun!" Ty growled. How was his former lord-general involved with the attack? Had Siyrsun been skulking in the mountains all these months?

Serena nodded. "Yes, Siyrsun—that was his name. He knows about the gold your men brought to us as thanks, and he's planning to raid more Eosyth settlements to steal their gold. He's joining forces with the Agocii to raise an army against Belaal. The Agocii speak of an empire."

"They won't gain one—the Eosyths will destroy them; I'll see to it."

This was why Araine and Nikaros had prepared Belaal for war. Ty bowed his head over Serena's, kissing her fiercely, near-blinded by his own rage.

Infinite, Mighty One, I see how You planned to thwart our enemies! Thank You…

Serena heaved a shaky, desolate sigh and Ty rocked her as if she were Miyna, while he seethed. Rethae spoke into the silence, sounding genuinely perplexed. "Sire, she calls you 'Ty'?"

Dread-stricken, Bel-Tygeon froze, mute. Serena stiffened in his arms and then drew away. He watched her glance from his embroidered mantle to the rings on his fingers, then to his hair and his face. "Ty." Serena shook her head. "You cannot be *him*!"

The awful tone of that word *him* lingered in the air.

Ty waited, allowing his own stricken silence to confess the truth. He was indeed *him*, the tyrant who'd harassed and starved the Eosyths to soothe his own petty god-king indignation.

Serena closed her eyes. Her complexion turned so ghastly that the only color left on her face was the scattering of tiny freckles over her nose.

The Women's Palace physician, Cythea, warned, "Sire, she's going to faint."

Ty grabbed Serena before she fell over. Rethae scurried to help, fluttering the fan toward Serena's ashen face to create a breeze.

As Ty rubbed Serena's cold hands and patted her face, his sister said, "Ty, one would think you actually love her."

"Yes. One would." Ty briefly abandoned patting Serena's face, snatched Rethae's annoying fan and flung it across the room where it snagged in a curtain then clattered to the floor. "Cythea, please, dismiss the servants, but send for Nikaros and Araine—I command them to be brought here. I must talk with them."

Cythea bowed. Gently scolding them as their lifelong physician, she said, "With your permission, Sire, and Lady Dasarai, I'll also depart to mix a soothing remedy for this poor girl. You've added fresh shocks to everything she's already suffered. She must rest and eat."

***

Consciousness returned to Serena amid a blissful fog of dreaminess and a low hum of voices. A woman's delicate, vaguely familiar voice was saying, "…just to fade them a bit."

Ty answered sharply enough to command Serena's few wits. "Don't touch her freckles! They're perfect. Listen, all of you. She's saved my life more than once, and she's the daughter of an Eosyth lord who also saved my life. She's to be honored as much as I've honored any of you. Treat her as you would my own younger sister, and give her whatever she wants—short of an army to invade Agocii lands. I'll lead that attack myself!"

"Sire," another woman whispered, her voice sweet and soothing, "The day the Infinite restored your sanity, I prayed that you'd live as a mortal, and it's clear you that you have and *are*. She's lovely."

"Pray now that she's willing to speak to me, Prophet," Ty muttered. "Nevertheless, Lord Nikaros, how long until Belaal is prepared to march?"

"We can leave within ten days, Sire." Nikaros drew out his words, his familiar voice low and cautious. "Ideally, we should plot a route through the western DaromKhor Hills to hide our army from the Agocii for as long as possible."

Drawing out his answer, clearly pondering, Ty said, "We'll indeed travel through the hills. But we'll remain as close to the Siphran border as possible, then cut over to Eosyth lands at the last. I'll send a courier bird to Munra to alert Siphra's king that we're on the move to capture Siyrsun and kill Cziybor."

"Thank you, Sire." Nikaros added, "Forgive me, but I've just sent riders after the men you ordered out yesterday. They won't survive a battle in the mountains if Siyrsun has an army."

By now, Serena felt recovered enough to stir. It would be rude of her to pretend unconsciousness while listening in on a private conversation. She opened her eyes. Nikaros leaned into view. Perfectly straight-faced and more ruggedly attractive than ever, he said, "There you are, sister. I received your messages."

Serena worked up a smile and managed to sit up, but she huddled within Ty's royal mantle. "Thank you."

"Of course. You're family." Nik nodded to a beautiful blue-eyed young woman kneeling beside him. "Serena, this is Araine—Belaal's Prophet and my beloved wife. She'll take care of you now."

"You presume to own Serena," the Lady Dasarai sniffed. "But you do not. I do."

"Officially," Ty murmured, "I own her."

He owned her? Serena flicked an uncertain glance at Ty...no, Bel-Tygeon.

Ty's lean, smooth-shaven face—more handsome than ever—turned cold, and his voice became distant. "Serena, I understand if you hate me for any perceived deception. Nevertheless, I give you my word that for the Eosyths and Belaal, we'll chase Siyrsun and Cziybor to death. I won't rest easily until your people are safe."

Unapproachably cool, he nodded to Nikaros. "Your official protection from the death penalty ends the instant I leave the Women's Palace, so walk out with me now, or fight your way out later. Whatever you decide, I must send that message to Akabe of Siphra."

"I'll heed your advice, Sire." Nikaros kissed his pretty wife.

She gave him a light hug, then teased as they stood, "Go, my lord. I don't welcome the thought of battling guards today."

Serena watched Nikaros and Ty … Bel-Tygeon … depart. Had she lost the man she loved? Fresh grief cut into her heart's wounds. She'd thought of Ty as a *someone*. A great lord. But not the tyrant of Belaal. Was Bel-Tygeon so great a man that her beloved Ty didn't actually exist?

And the things she'd probably said about Bel-Tygeon to Ty … Serena's empty stomach took a sickly drop. If she hadn't fainted already, she would faint now—to her humiliation.

She rubbed a hand over her face and tried to think of something else. Someone else. The Lady Dasarai and Nik's wife were both watching her with concern and pity. She bowed toward them and pleaded, "May I ask a favor? Another girl was with me this morning—her name is Malia. Is there any way to free her, or at least bring her here?"

The Lady Dasarai pointed to her fan, which had somehow ended up on the floor at the base of a wall. Nik's wife, Belaal's prophet, retrieved the golden article and Serena caught a sparkling hint of mischief as if the prophet considered accidentally demolishing the gleaming ornament. However, she knelt beside Serena, bowed to Dasarai, and offered her the fan. Armed with her elegant shield, the Lady Dasarai straightened, all the more dignified. "Is this Malia quiet, tidy, and diligent?"

"Yes, Lady. She's not at all like me." Best to warn Dasarai now that Belaal's newest slave wasn't all meekness.

Dasarai stared, then laughed rustily, as if unused to teasing. But her fan fluttered, dispelling Serena's discomfort, and her haughty voice thawed to warmth. "Therefore, my lord-king cannot love her as he loves you. Nevertheless, we shall send for her."

A light tap at the door announced the physician's return, followed by several servants bearing trays of food. The Lady Dasarai nodded them inside, and then smiled at Serena. "It's good that you have a sense of humor, young lady. You will need it. Come—it's time for the midday meal and your medicines. Eat and rest. Then we'll show you through the Women's Palace as you await the perfect Malia."

Malia would be rescued! Serena sighed, releasing her fears for the girl. "Thank you, Lady!" She hesitated and drew Ty's mantle closer. "May I ask one more thing? When will I receive actual clothes?"

**

Nikaros hurried, adjusting his pace to match Bel-Tygeon's while remaining one step behind the king, who now talked rapidly—a man sifting through a mountain of thoughts. "I'll kill Cziybor if Tsir Andris and his people haven't done so already! He's all but crushed her spirit—can you see the difference in her?"

"Yes, sire. She's mourning, which must be expected."

The king slashed the air with an impatient hand. Ahead of them the female guards retreated—their eyes wide as Bel-Tygeon snapped, "I'll execute him, and I don't care how! I want him dead!" He stalked through one of the gleaming, elaborately gilded gates, and then halted and eyed Nikaros. "I doubt you've heard everything. Son of Levos, I'm sorry. Cziybor and his men killed Detzios and Serena's Aunt Betiya. Cziybor also kept Serena's youngest sister, Miyna—probably as a hostage."

Nik's mind reeled. Miyna captive and helpless. And...Detzios... Dead. Betiya too—that loveable tyrant of a woman. She'd probably fought Cziybor. Nik stopped in the corridor, clenching his fists, struggling to master his grief. "I'll kill Cziybor myself!"

Bel-Tygeon turned and gripped his shoulder hard. "We'll repay Cziybor and the Agocii, be sure of it! And Siyrsun." The king's grasp tightened and he shook Nikaros as a friend trying to hearten a friend. "Are you with me? I'd wager all my gold that Siyrsun has been secretly courting the Agocii chieftains and feeding them visions of an empire. He'll betray them as soon as he's in power. The 'empire' will be his alone unless we can stop him."

Nik sucked in a composing breath. "I'm sure you're right, sire."

"I am." Clearly rueful, the king swept a hand through his hair. "I've watched Siyrsun for my entire life. I'm sure that the only reason he didn't assassinate me and claim my throne is because he was raised to consider me as a god. The instant I failed, he rebelled. However—"

Bel-Tygeon almost smiled. "I have one consolation in all this bad news. Serena's *here*! Everything's changed—I hope." He landed a fist on Nik's shoulder, hard enough to jolt him to clarity. Almost hard enough to leave a bruise. "Let's hurry! We've a war to attend."

Chapter 25

Araine watched her mantle-swathed sister-in-law survey the main corridor of the Women's Palace, with its crowded tiers of small, rich apartments.

Serena's smooth, harmonious features took on the shadows of this oppressive place, her gloom deepening the more she looked around. At last, Serena faced Araine. Her beautifully varied voice lowered, betraying dejection. "How many women...lived here?"

Infinite, clearly this is another shock—I beg courage for Serena.

Bracing herself, Araine told the truth. "By my count, more than three hundred. I don't know how many unofficial wives the king actually claimed. But he was never granted the only woman he desired—his queen. The beloved wife who would bear him children."

Serena absorbed this in silence—still much too pale. Was she about to faint again?

Araine wrapped an arm around her, just in case. "Let's return to the garden area and rest. Later I'll ask permission to take you out to the royal garden for some fresh air."

Serena nodded. But then she faltered, pausing to look around again. "The king's had so many wives. Whether they had children or not...how could I ever match any of them? I've lived in a wilderness by comparison."

Araine hugged her overwhelmed new relative. "Remind yourself that in addition to your amazing character and looks, you have the one thing that none of the king's consorts could claim. You have Bel-Tygeon's love. I pray with all my might that you'll become his queen."

Serena answered with a half-hearted nod. But she appeared ill—quite ready to run away.

Araine smiled and guided her onward toward the enclosed garden's sitting area. "Be brave! Pray and seek the Infinite's will. Also…be careful in asking favors of the king. Because he loves you, he will grant your requests. You don't want to regret the consequences."

***

Freshly clad in soft layers of blue and cream, but still wearing Ty's own gold-embroidered blue mantle, Serena stepped from the carrying chair and gazed at the vast, luxurious evening-lit garden. So many flowers this early in the year and so many varieties, not to mention the ornamental trees, each seeming to contend with the other for the most brilliant display of blossoms and leaves, all framed by the rugged woods beyond.

Her beloved mountains, despite their untamed magnificence, could not offer such a variety of colors and scents. How rustic the Eosyths must have appeared to Bel-Tygeon. How primitive. She'd understand if the king had been secretly laughing at them all throughout the winter.

"Infinite, how do I cope with such grandeur and not feel like a fool?"

Light footsteps clicked behind her, and Araine approached, so refined and sweet with those wide blue eyes and exquisite features that Serena felt like an ox by comparison. Araine offered Serena a glowing smile. "You look overwhelmed. Don't be. The king, his lady-sister, and all their glorious ancestors are and were mortals, just as we are—though they often needed reminding. Too much power addles the senses."

She linked an arm through Serena's and guided her toward a well-tramped clay path. "Let's walk until the Lady Dasarai arrives. I'll show you my favorite place—the bridge."

As Serena walked down the path with Araine, gleaming silver-feathered birds flew from the trees above them, their calls bell-like and exquisite—wholly befitting this dreamlike garden. At the wonderfully curved bridge, Araine stopped and leaned against the rail, gazing into the water, and then looking up at the birds chiming above. "This garden has a music all its own. Choirs of birds and a symphony of sounds. Do you like music?"

"I...sing," Serena admitted. "But only inside my lady-mother's tent. Unless it's a formal occasion."

Araine's beautiful blue eyes shone as if Serena were the most wonderful sister-in-law ever. "You *must* sing for me! I play the harp and I'd welcome some vocal accompaniment."

A sharp whistle, quite mortal and male, made them both turn. Nikaros grinned at them—from one pace behind Bel-Tygeon.

Despite herself, Serena sighed like any love-struck girl. Here in his own realm, Ty was beyond compare. Elegant, lean and graceful in his rich garments, his dark hair lustrous and his mouth so delightful—as perfect as any of the glories within his palace.

This was the truth, then. Despotic oppressor of Eosyths or not, he was yet her Ty, though her love for him now seemed traitorous.

Grim-faced, Bel-Tygeon reached for her hand. "Walk with me. We must discuss your future."

***

Ty didn't release her hand as they walked together. Instead, he led her along a sunlit path beyond the bridge—a wild meadow flaunting a carpet of green grass and yellow flowers. Nikaros and Araine followed at a discreet distance, as if ordered, Araine hugging Nik's arm.

It was so easy to pretend she was walking with Ty, not Bel-Tygeon, despite his gloominess. At last, he looked down at her. "Serena, do you hate me?"

Startled by his abruptness, she shook her head. "No. Love isn't destroyed by one tempest. I can be unhappy for a time, yet still love you. In fact..." Serena gathered her courage and poured out her fear, "—after riding through Sulaanc, and then walking through your palace, I'm sure you must despise me and loathe Clan Darom. We're rustics."

"Rustics? That's rubbish!" Ty scoffed, his derision eased by an irreverent grin that set her heartbeat racing. He halted and clasped her hands in his, warming her fingers. "You've forgotten what I was when you first met me. I had nothing but my restored sanity and the Infinite. *I* was the rustic, but you loved me nevertheless, and I'm grateful."

Well, when he phrased it that way... She smiled, remembering the dead mouse in his hair, though she wasn't about to remind him of that.

Ty continued, "I spoke to my sister earlier. Were you overly distressed by the Women's Palace?"

"What young woman wouldn't be? You've had so many wives. I can't compare to them."

"They cannot compare to you," Ty argued. "You're perfect! You're a jewel and they were dull stones. I couldn't trust any of them—not as I trust you." She laughed at his foolishness. He grinned and dragged her into his embrace. "You're distracting me with that beautiful smile, and I must remain clear-headed. I've so much to tell you!"

He kissed her hair and sighed. "Serena, my past cannot be undone. I cannot help what I've been. However, what I am now and what I'll become...those things are within my control. You—and our Creator—may call me to account for my future failings."

Future? Was he planning their future? Before she could ask, he said, "Do you remember when I told you that marriage would be impossible for us? That I would never ask you to make dire sacrifices in order to satisfy my country's legal requirements?"

She nodded against his shoulder, and then leaned back to stare him in the eyes. "Yes. What are you asking now that's going to be so dire?"

"There's nothing more to ask. Serena, you've fulfilled the requirements! You've become a slave—the property of Belaal. Your parents have no claims to power within my country. *Against* my country, undoubtedly, but that's another matter."

She'd fulfilled his country's impossible legal requirements? His wife… "Belaal's queen…must be chosen from among the slaves, without status or wealth of their own? These are your country's laws? They're ridiculous! *Why?*"

"To better ensure the queen's loyalty to Belaal and its king. And to mitigate most threats of civil conflict through the king's marriage. Not that the law has helped in some situations." Ty frowned slightly as if remembering some distant trouble. He released Serena from his embrace, but clasped her hands once more. "What I am trying to say is…after we've captured Siyrsun and repaid Cziybor, I'll offer you a choice. Remain with your family in the mountains, or return here as my wife—my only wife—and, I pray, my queen. If you prefer, I'll exchange vows with you before all of Clan Darom. The marriage won't be enforceable in Belaal, but I'll sign legal pledges here for your protection in Belaal."

Could she? Leave her family to marry Ty? Bel-Tygeon… "You're serious."

"I am." Ty bent, kissed her cheek lightly, then led her onward through the meadow. "Consider what I've said. I won't coerce you."

Marry him…bid farewell to her family, and live farther away from her parents than even Tiphera…"I— I'll consider it."

"I'll ask nothing more, I give you my word. Now, let me show you around some of the garden. Perhaps we should begin with my parents' tomb. If you decide to become my wife and—ultimately, I pray, my queen—you must understand the risks."

Ty turned her around, toward the bridge again. Serena glimpsed Nikaros and Araine clasping each other in a protective embrace, both of them gazing at the meadow, as if they weren't seeing it at all. They broke their mutual hold and half-bowed. Ty passed them briskly. "We're going to the tomb."

Araine's delicate eyebrows lifted in apparent alarm. "Sire, are you prepared to confront that day again?"

"I believe so, Prophet." He led them all at an easy pace over the bridge and down a shaded path that was divided here and there by puddles. Ty swung Serena over a particularly large puddle and then—as she gathered her dazed senses—he released her and smiled. "Araine fears that I'll be upset. My parents' tomb, the family tomb, is where I rebelled against the Infinite and went insane. Whatever happens to me, I count that day as a blessing."

"So do I. Sire."

"Ty," he corrected. "When we're alone together, call me 'Ty'. Are we walking too fast? Do you need to rest?"

"No. Thank you, Ty." The trampled clay path soon merged into a graveled walk, and they entered another meadow, this one smaller, but more sculpted than the meadow beyond the bridge. At the meadow's center stood a majestic blue marble-columned building, its interior shadowed and dark. Ty led Serena to a roughened black marble slab embedded in the white pavings before the blue marble tomb. There, he halted and ground his boots deliberately against the roughened black slab. Serena lifted an eyebrow at him. "Is this a tradition? Should I do the same?"

"If you wish." He stepped off the roughened slab, allowing her room. "Beneath this slab lies the body of Zlateon, my uncle. He assassinated my parents and then tried to kill me."

Serena stared down at the roughened, scarred black marble, becoming nauseated. "Your uncle tried to kill you? To seize power?"

"Yes. I was five." Ty's handsome mouth tightened. "My sister killed him just as he attacked me."

The Lady Dasarai had killed a man? Serena blinked, trying to imagine the delicate Dasarai attacking a prince of Belaal. But that prince had tried to kill Ty. Serena straightened. "Then she acted honorably."

Ty scowled at the pitted black slab. "She was fifteen, and besotted with him. Therefore, he never expected that she would defend me."

"But she did, and I'm grateful." Serena ground her leather-clad feet against the dark stone and stepped away. Ty kissed her hand, then led her up the steps into the tomb. Six raised marble crypts rested in the building's center, four blue, two white, their presence making Serena shiver. "Your parents are entombed here?"

He nodded and touched their white marble crypts. "I remember them clearly. They loved each other. Few kings are so blessed. But my lord-father was blinded to his brother's ambition." Ty's voice echoed in the open marble chamber, as if they were in a cave. Serena looked upward, into the tomb's high, exquisitely vaulted dome. Definitely cave-like. A beautiful covering for such tragedy. Ty continued, "We were together as a family that morning. Until Zlateon slashed my lord-father's throat, then my mother's...before turning on me. Rethae stabbed him from behind with our lord-father's dagger."

He'd been five—her poor love! "I'm so sorry!"

He clasped her hand again, his fingers now chilled. "Will you sing the Eosyth Lament for them? And for Detzios and your Aunt Betiya?"

He'd included Detzios and Aunt Betiya in the same breath as his royal parents. More proof that he'd remained her own Ty. The two white marble coffins blurred before Serena's gaze. She nodded and drew in a sharp breath to endure the grief.

***

Trying to console himself, Nikaros wrapped an arm around Araine's shoulders as they approached the royal tomb. Her sweet presence covered his raw emotions like a balm, easing the shock of Serena's news.

Detzios killed. Betiya butchered...their people besieged...Miyna and Iared enslaved.

Mighty One, save my people! Let my service here in Belaal ensure their survival.

Araine hugged him as they walked along the pavings. "My lord, I love you! I wish I could take some of your grief. I'm so sorry about your friend."

"You would have liked him." Nikaros exhaled. He'd dreamed of taking Araine up to the mountains and introducing her to his family and friends. Detzios would have been as smitten by Araine as he'd been with Serena.

They halted before the pale marble steps leading up into the tomb, and Nik kissed his wife's soft hair, inhaling its delicate floral scent. "I bear a portion of blame for future attacks against my people. Giving that reward of gold ingots to Clan Darom was a mistake. I should have asked you to consult the Infinite."

Araine hugged him again and then scolded tenderly. "Why are you blaming yourself? You provided that gold from our revenues as a reward for Eosyth hospitality and compassion. It's not your fault that wicked men repaid your kindness with their evil."

From the edge of his sight, Nikaros glimpsed the Lady Dasarai being carried formally in her gold chair, into the clearing. Behind Belaal's princess, borne in another gilded chair, was a frail-looking girl, who stared about the clearing, wide-eyed and fearful. Araine straightened in Nik's arms. "That must be Serena's fellow-captive, Malia."

"I don't recognize her; she's not Eosyth," Nik murmured. He was about to guess that she was Agocii and scorned for her apparent frailty, but a wordless tune stopped him. A woman's vibrant yet haunting voice echoed from among the blue marble pillars in the tomb above. Serena... mourning Eosyth losses with song, crying the Lament of generations past.

As the Lament enfolded him, Nik shut his eyes hard. He'd never expected to hear the traditional dirge again. He wasn't prepared to face it now. For Detzios, Betiya, and Clan Darom...

He sucked in a quick breath, adding his silent grief to the Lament.

***

Araine hugged her husband and listened to the haunting perfection of Serena's voice. Her vocalizations were flawless and her song's soaring resonance lingered, touchingly girlish and young, yet ageless, evoking eons of sorrow.

With each breath, Serena sent her voice impossibly higher, gaining power, making Araine hold her own breath. A hand gripped Araine's arm—startling her into the present.

The Lady Dasarai stood beside Araine now, staring up into the tomb, open-mouthed, clearly astounded as Serena's notes lifted into a final piercing cry of loss. Serena's voice silenced. Beside Araine, Nikaros exhaled, bowed to Belaal's princess, then bent and kissed Araine. Without looking at either of them, he walked toward the nearby trees, obviously seeking solitude.

Dasarai watched him depart, then she crept up the marble steps. Araine followed, hardly daring to breathe.

There, within the hushed column-edged mausoleum, Bel-Tygeon held Serena as she wept quietly—his eyes closed, his dark head resting protectively over hers, a man fiercely in love.

Here was the answer to Araine's prayer…Belaal's fallen god-king living as a mortal.

She retreated, feeling like an intruder. But she prayed as she descended the steps and smiled at the fearful Malia.

Infinite, my own Creator, what will happen to the king and Serena? To us?

Listen!

His answer swept over her in a torrent, causing her to sit down hard, clutching the marble steps for support as she stared into the onrushing tide of chaos.

Chapter 26

Bel-Tygeon swayed with Serena, hugging her until her weeping subsided. Her fears for her family, for Miyna and young Iared, all revealed his own. If he failed— Impermissible! "We'll find them! Give us one week to gather the army and assure our supplies."

Serena nodded and straightened, wiping her face. "Thank you!"

Ty smoothed her hair and then stepped away from her, physically and emotionally, willing himself to be composed. After months of hopelessly desiring Serena, her nearness was almost too tempting to resist. He'd been worshiped for more than twenty years as a god-king, and he'd indulged himself for more than ten years with hundreds of wives. Nevertheless he *would* master himself now. "Let's return to the others. You should rest."

"I rested earlier. I'm not fragile."

"Nor are you invulnerable. What good will you be to your family and the Eosyths if you ruin your health?" He kissed her hand, and then turned her toward the steps once more. Serena gave a small start—just as Ty caught sight of Rethae standing in the open entry, her eyebrows raised.

Obviously his sister was perplexed by something and longing to rap him with her fan. He raised his voice as he urged Serena toward the entry. "Ideally, I should allow my commanders more than a week to finish off details and plan our strategies, but we'll hurry things along lest the Agocii and Siyrsun attack sooner than we expect. Until then, I expect you to obey Cythea and recover from your ordeal."

"You're so bossy," she complained, sounding like one of her siblings as they left the tomb. Ty grinned, restraining himself from kissing her again.

Rethae bowed to him and smiled as they met her above the steps. "We will be sure she rests, Sire." But she studied Serena as if seeing her anew. "Your voice is remarkable, young lady. One hopes you intend to pursue singing—such a gift is rare."

Serena inclined her head. "Thank you, Lady. It's a traditional dirge known by all Eosyths." She hesitated, gazing down at Araine, who sat huddled on the bottom step as if ill. "Please excuse me. I must speak with my sister-in-law."

She descended the steps without waiting for permission— definitely not behaving like a proper slave. Ty hid a smile as Rethae sighed and shook her head. "She needs training, Sire. Nevertheless, she is intriguing and truly beautiful. One quite understands your love for her. Will you send for her tonight or tomorrow?"

Temptation beckoned. Bel-Tygeon forced himself to shake his head and deny his former god-king impulses. Low-voiced he said, "No. I won't take advantage of her grief and her vulnerabilities. I pledged to Serena's lord-father that I would behave honorably toward her."

Rethae shrugged. "He's not here now."

"Yet my pledge remains, and I take it seriously. Meanwhile let's find out what ails our prophet."

"Ty," his sister chided, sounding frustrated that she must remind him of an indisputable reality, "Tsir Andris is not your lord."

"And I am not his god, nor am I his king," Ty corrected her. His sharpness actually drew Serena's attention. Though she sat beside Araine and was clearly fretting over Belaal's prophet, Serena looked over her shoulder at Ty. Her brown-green eyes were so wide and solemn, and her dark auburn hair glistened with mesmerizing fiery hues in the evening light. He craved nothing more than to smooth that hair, to touch Serena's soft skin, and to claim her as his unofficial wife tonight. Nevertheless… "My Lord and Creator sees me, so please don't tempt me to dishonor her or my pledge."

His sister frowned, clearly planning to detain him in order to win an argument against him, which was another thing he'd never understood. If he'd been considered a god, why had his sister so often dictated to him? Dotingly, he must admit, yet she'd still interfered with his life on a daily basis. As she was now, arguing, "Ty, how is your favor a dishonor to her, or to anyone? You are the lord-god of—"

Ty raised a warning hand. "No, Rethae! *Never* say that again, to me or to anyone. I'm not a god! The Infinite alone is our Creator and Lord, and I bless Him for it! You must forget my false-god status."

She lowered her fan and winced as if he'd struck her. Worse, she remained silent. How could he win her from this delusion that she'd been trained to believe from infancy? This delusion she'd dutifully fostered in him, believing it as truth.

Ty bent and kissed her cheek. "You know that I revere you, and I hate seeing you so unhappy. But we *are* mortal. Only the Infinite rules the heavens. After all that's happened, you must acknowledge that He rules us."

Rethae refused to look at him. "You'll destroy our kingdom."

Bel-Tygeon sighed. "What will convince you that He *is*, and that He cares enough to correct me when I'm wrong in order to save my kingdom?"

At once, she lifted her fan and her chin. "When I hold your healthy, thriving firstborn. Then I will believe."

Did she believe that holding his future child was such an impossibility? He grinned. "Then I pray for the chance to remind you of this pledge, and I'll hold you to your word." Even as he spoke, Bel-Tygeon's thoughts merged into prayer. Blessed Infinite, let Rethae's pledge come to irrefutable life! Give me an heir, with Serena as my queen.

But not yet. Not until he'd requested her parents' blessings. Mastering himself, Bel-Tygeon bent to stare his sister in the eyes. "Listen to your king's next command. Serena, the daughter of the Lord of Clan Darom, is to be honored according to her rank despite her status as a slave, and she will live with her in-laws while she is here. Now," he nodded toward Araine, "I wish to know why my prophet is so distressed."

***

Serena sat on the marble steps before the royal tomb and leaned toward Belaal's prophet. How fearful and wondrous to call this young woman her sister-in-law—yet Araine's kindness and sweet nature invited her as kindred. Cautious, she pleaded, "Araine, can I bring you some water, or some sort of remedy?"

Araine shook her head and then straightened and inhaled, as if gathering her senses. "Thank you, no. However..." She nudged Serena. "My revelation had everything to do with you, Serena, much as I fear it. Remember that you've been brought to Belaal for our Creator's purpose—to summon an army against your people's enemies. But you won't escape the war."

Serena swallowed. Would she face Cziybor again? Infinite, Mighty One, help me... She braced herself. "I didn't expect to escape the war. But what will I face?"

Araine's clear blue eyes misted as she met Serena's gaze. "The enemy you face won't be the enemy you expect. Therefore, the Infinite warns you to have courage and prepare to confront death. If you take the easy course, your losses will be more than you can endure."

The king's voice interposed from above them, "Meaning *what*, Prophet?" He sat beside Serena on the steps and frowned at Araine as if he would make her withdraw her words. "Is Serena in danger?"

"Sire," Araine said gently, "Once we leave Belaal, there's no safety for any of us. Those who wish to remain sheltered can stay behind, but if the Infinite has called you to defend the Eosyths, then it's wisest to go, despite the danger."

Ty argued, "I'm not thinking of myself; I'm thinking of Serena. If she's in danger—"

Rebellion stirred Serena to protest, "Ty, I must return to my family. You *won't* leave me here!"

He widened his dark eyes and pretended to cringe in fear. "Trust me, I wouldn't dare!" But then he grinned and tweaked her hair. "Even so, I'll be sure you're protected."

The Lady Dasarai sauntered down and settled on the step above them, fanning herself gently. Despite her soft, idling movements her gaze cut toward them, blade-sharp. "One hopes you three are not keeping secrets. If you intend to abandon me again, so soon after returning, my lord, then I must know what is happening. Wait…" She motioned to Malia, who lingered uncertainly near the bottom steps. "Child, go tell those chair-men that we won't tarry long, and then remain with them."

Serena stiffened slightly, longing to reach for Malia and to shield her from any distress. Obviously noticing her movement, Ty clasped her hand—a calming gesture. But the Lady Dasarai tapped her fan lightly on Serena's shoulder. "We realize that you two suffered much together. However, trust must be earned here. We dare not bestow it lightly. You have proven yourself to my lord. She has not. Give us time."

As if she had time to give. Even so, serving the proud Lady Dasarai was clearly preferable to whatever plans the slavers had for her and Malia. Furthermore, wasn't she, Serena—daughter of Tsir Andris— also a slave? "Yes, Lady. Thank you."

Nikaros returned, crossing the clearing from the woods surrounding the royal tomb, his face settled into the first wearied lines of an older man. He halted before the steps, bowed to Bel-Tygeon, then seated himself beside Araine and cast a perceptive look at all their faces. "Is this a secret meeting, Sire?"

"Yes." Ty gently wound a strand of Serena's hair around his fingers, and then released it, his touch so careful that she held her breath. But instead of looking at her, he lifted an eyebrow at Araine. "Tell me, Prophet, will I win this war?"

She stiffened, as if bracing herself. "No, Sire. Yet you'll survive despite everything."

Horror stabbed Serena in slivers, one after another as a multitude of awful imaginings swept her thoughts. They wouldn't win? The Agocii would prevail? Miyna and Iared would remain captives and the Eosyths must again retreat to caves— "What do you mean we won't win? After everything we've been through…is it all for nothing? Won't the Infinite help us?"

Araine's perfect little face turned fierce, and her blue eyes took on the sheen of pale other-realm fire. "Lady, after everything we've been through, how can you believe the Infinite *won't* help us? Don't allow your fear to shake what you know is the truth: He cares! He loves us, and He will work for justice on our behalf—in His own time and His own way, it *will* happen!"

Her ferocity shook Serena inwardly, and her heart near-halted in fear.

Infinite, forgive me.

***

Serena knelt before the low table, staring at the overabundance of food. Fruits, bread, meat, sauces, all so plentiful, and she hadn't worked for even one grain of this meal. Clan Darom would consider this a lifetime feast, yet this was an ordinary meal to Ty and the Lady Dasarai. Even Nikaros—who knew better—seemed to accept this feast as ordinary. Araine, too, looked as if this wasn't an appalling amount of food for five people.

Guilt weighed on Serena, almost stifling her appetite. Ty deliberately set a dish of minced meat smothered in a red glistening sauce before her. "Taste this. Tell me what you think of it."

He dipped a thin, crisp sliver of bread into the dish, scooped up a generous bite, and ate it. By his pleased expression, Serena guessed this sauced meat was one of his favorites. Very well… She followed his example, scooped up a generous portion, and chewed the entire bite at once. The meat was so tender that it nearly dissolved as she chewed, but its fiery spices brought tears to her eyes. She had to sniffle like a child trying to hold back a runny nose. "Sire, you should have warned me!"

And yet hints of smoky sweetness enticed her to take a second bite. She snuck a second sliver of bread and scooped up another portion. While she chewed the meat, a portly man rapped at the room's doorframe, his eyes bright, his thin voice elated. "Sire, forgive me, but *this* has finally arrived."

The man flourished a plain wooden box as if it were gold. Ty raised an eyebrow. "Ebatenai, refresh my memory. Am I expecting some new treasure?"

Ebatenai looked hurt. "Sire, four years ago, you requested that we procure an azurnite weapon from the Tracelands. This is the weapon."

Bel-Tygeon grimaced. "Well, that was quick. But that box isn't long enough to contain the sword I requested."

"It's a dagger," Ebatenai confessed, approaching humbly. "Short of committing murder, this was the only azurnite your agent could acquire—at great cost, I might add."

Ty accepted the box. "Tracelanders are overly protective of their azurnite. Understandable if its properties are everything the rumors suggest." He opened the box and removed a sheathed dagger, its simple lines and plain black leather-wrapped grip contradicting its great cost. Serena swallowed and almost shrugged, unimpressed. Until Ty pulled the dagger from its sheath and lifted the weapon, showing them all an intensely blue blade, its water-patterned metal glistening in the lamplight like a jewel.

"It's beautiful," Serena murmured. "A true treasure."

Ty rewarded her praise of the weapon with a dazzling smile, and he handed it to her. "Keep this for me, Lady."

Did he know a dagger's significance to her as an Eosyth? If she accepted this weapon, then she accepted responsibility for his safety and his future family's safety, as well as pledging faithful stewardship of all his belongings and his own happiness. This gift of a dagger was a veritable marriage vow. Unless... "You're *not* actually giving me this treasure, Sire."

His handsome face as solemn as she'd ever seen it, he said, "If you wish to own this treasure, Lady, you need only tell me, and it will be yours."

He knew. And judging by the silence around the table, and Nik and Araine's raised eyebrows, they all knew. Even the Lady Dasarai and the portly Ebatenai. The king must be deadly-serious to offer her marriage twice in one day. Serena hesitated, and then chose her words carefully. "Sire, I'll gladly guard this treasure for you. But I wish for nothing else until my people are safe."

Ty lifted a lock of her hair and kissed it, then smiled. "Until then."

***

Seated at his desk, Bel-Tygeon signed the final Order of Relief with a flourish, and then waited as Nikaros sealed the command with a pool of blue wax and the royal signet. If this excursion turned into a full-fledged war, then the soldiers' families would be provided for in the army's absence. "Finished!"

"As you say, Sire." Nikaros recorded the document and handed it to Ebatenai, who placed it among the official records. Satisfied, Ty stretched briefly, then opened an official notification from Siphra.

Akabe of Siphra's royal seal, stood out like a pool of congealed blood on the crisp parchment. King Akabe's order, however, was anything but blood-thirsty. *By my hand, it is ordered that the army of Bel-Tygeon, Lord-King of Belaal, shall be permitted access to the lands along our western border without hindrance for the good of the Eosyth nation against its aggressors, the Agocii. Let peace be established among those nations, according to the Infinite's will.* At the document's lower edge, Akabe had scrawled just beside his signature, *I hope to hear good news concerning this situation upon your return to Sulaanc.*

Ty grinned at the casual yet legible script. Might they yet establish trust and trade between their nations, despite his own past misdeeds? A discreet cough summoned his attention.

Ebatenai held out a flat wooden box for Bel-Tygeon's approval. Nikaros stood, then bowed—a servant with a plea. "Sire, when Belaal took me as a hostage, my lord-father sent all the gold he possessed, hoping to ensure my safety. Included among the gold was his torq, which is the mark of his authority among the Eosyths. May I redeem this for twice its weight in gold from my own revenues and then return the torq to him?"

Ty opened the box and studied the freshly polished torq—a simple yet powerful piece of gold work. He'd seen it two years past and hadn't suffered the least twinge of guilt for possessing the Eosyth treasure. Now, shame ate at him—feasted upon his raw conscience and made him flinch. He couldn't even look at Nikaros. "Take it, my lord. You've more than redeemed it by your service."

Nikaros accepted the plain wooden box from Ebatenai, and when he finally spoke, his voice was hoarse, his words clipped tight as if he could barely trust himself to speak. "Sire, thank you."

***

Trailed by Malia, Serena followed Araine down a long corridor. Ahead of them, other slaves backed away, and then bowed as Araine and Serena approached. Did they fear Belaal's sweet prophet so much?

Jangling a collection of bronze keys, Araine worked at a lock, slid aside a bar, and then she led Serena and Malia into a large, but dim room. A veritable battlefield of fragrances struck Serena's senses, the odors almost strong enough to leave their tastes upon her tongue. Standing behind Serena, Malia sneezed. Araine laughed. "Poor Malia! Don't worry, we won't be here for long, and then I'll prepare a remedy for your sneezes. I just need a few more items for our journey."

Evidently encouraged by the prophet's kindness, Malia said, "I wish you weren't all leaving tomorrow. I'll feel lost without you."

Serena almost said, 'Don't worry; we'll return soon.' But that might not be true. Instead, she encouraged her fragile comrade. "Just devote yourself to the Lady Dasarai and you'll be safe. Pray for us as…" Her cheering little speech trailed off as Araine raised her lamp, revealing a shockingly large and dark chamber, its walls and cabinets wholly filled with ornate wooden drawers and boxes, all blue with polished golden latches—each one painted with separate images of the spices contained within. So many spices…

Serena inhaled the fragrance again, still amazed. "Does this palace contain everything in the world?"

Araine laughed. "Quite a bit of it—some of it actually terrifying. You haven't seen the drekar yet, have you?"

"Drekar?" Malia squeaked, "You mean the king owns giant water serpents?"

"Magnificent blue-tinged ones," Araine told her. "Don't worry. They're held in an underground pool at the far corner of the palace. Usually only Belaal's priests tend them." Araine began to open drawers and measure spices into small cloth bags in preparation for their journey. "If you want to see the creatures, I'm sure the king or Lady Dasarai would arrange a viewing."

As Malia made a small noise of denial, Serena winced in the muted light. View a swarm of water-drekar? No, not really. "I think I've seen too much already, but thank you."

Araine sighed, sounding relieved. "Oh, good! Ro'ghez and General Siyrsun had me thrown into the pool just before Siyrsun rebelled, so I'm not eager to see the starved creatures again, even if the Infinite did hold the beasts at a distance. It all started with Ro'ghez, you see. His intentions were honorable in their own way...."

Listening to Araine's light voice describing betrayal, treachery, and starving near-legendary beasts, Serena bit her lip. Did she truly wish to leave her family in the mountains and live here, amid such splendid horrors? Infinite, save her, she'd rather not.

Chapter 27

Bleary from too little sleep, Serena waited with Ty, Nikaros, and Araine in the huge courtyard. Golden dawn light gleamed against Ty's hair and added glints to his eyes, and reflected off his gilded, stunningly-sculpted plate armor and the rich embroideries on his ceremonial cloak. As if he needed anything to emphasize his spectacular looks.

Evidently pleased to catch her admiring him, Ty grinned at Serena. "I should scold you for staying awake too late to visit with Araine."

Serena lifted her chin in taunting defiance. "At *your* command, Sire. I'm enjoying her company. She told me about General Siyrsun's plot with Ro'ghez, when they threw her to the drekar."

A flick of anger crossed Ty's face—though not aimed her. "Did Araine tell you that I tried to save her, but was forced to bow to my country's laws? Very un-godlike, don't you agree?"

"She told me that you tried. She's grateful, Sire."

"Yes, I intend to repay Siyrsun for that day and for his rebellion."

Servants led horses into the private courtyard now, and Ty offered Serena a hand. "Are you ready? I'm eager to show you off."

"As a trinket?"

"*No!*" He looked wonderfully offended. "I'm showing you off as a beloved friend and defender, whom I'm delighted to have in my company." He studied her critically now, becoming Belaal's ceremony-conscious king.

Placing one hand on the azurnite dagger slung about her waist, Serena straightened her too-elaborate blue and gold riding apparel, its voluminous skirts concealing leggings and sturdy, fleece-padded boots, which were practical despite their stamped gold emblems and jaunty tassels. Her veiled hair was a matching combination of showiness and practicality, flowing down from an array of sparkling gold pins filigreed with exquisite gem-dusted flowers and leaves provided by the Lady Dasarai. And the formerly simple red cord about her throat, marking her as Belaal's property, had been replaced with a sparkling gold-embroidered crimson band, hung with a large bejeweled gold pendant. More elaborate, to be sure, but still revealing her enslaved status despite Bel-Tygeon's protective blue and gold mantle.

As Bel-Tygeon nodded his lordly approval, the Lady Dasarai approached, leading serving women who bowed and offered Serena embroidered gloves, and then adjusted her veils to better-shield her skin against the sun. Belaal's princess lifted her fan warningly. "One hopes you will accept advice and wear the veil and gloves as you travel, young lady."

Serena smiled and pretended to cower beneath the fan's threat. "Lady, I'll obey. I might even practice reading and writing on the journey." Dasarai and Nikaros insisted that she must learn. Though reading and writing hadn't been vital to her in the mountains. That had been Detzios' task for the clan. Poor Detzios...

Serena's gaze blurred with tears. To cover the sudden pang of grief, she bowed to Dasarai and then allowed the servants to help her mount her horse. Ridiculous, because as any Eosyth, she was quite capable of managing horses alone—yet apparently, she must conform to tradition.

Behind her, Nikaros was helping Araine onto her horse, her gold-pinned veils shading her delicate face flawlessly. The prophet's staff added its intriguing presence like a frail weapon, which Araine gripped as if for reassurance. She rarely rode and had admitted her lack of expertise last night. Serena threw her an encouraging smile, which ebbed away in shock as she saw the growing length of their entourage. So many carts, chariots, and horses...and these didn't include the army...

Unnerved, she looked to the king.

Bel-Tygeon sat astride his horse, his back and shoulders admirably proud and straight, his profile perfect as he threw the Lady Dasarai a grin and called out, "Pray for us, and remember your pledge!"

She flicked her fan at him, dismissive and teasing. He laughed, his joy making Serena smile despite her sorrow. The Lady Dasarai glanced at Serena and then bowed her head slightly, her gaze appraising...approving. On impulse, Serena returned the bow, but more deeply and solemn—a formal salute to Ty's sister.

By the time she straightened, the massive gates were opening, and the king's guards were leading the procession through the deeply shadowed tunnel-like blue archway, and then out to the city beyond. After more than a week of opulent isolation in the palace, the city nearly overwhelmed Serena with its noise and crowds, particularly as the people surged forward on either side of the wide processional street.

She hadn't remembered Sulaanc as being this crowded. This noisy. And certainly not so avidly interested in *her*. Even as the crowds screamed and cheered at the sight of their dashing king, many were staring at Serena. Pointing. Applauding. And the children were waving—bright-eyed and engaging, making Serena long for her siblings.

She beamed at the children and waved in turn, then laughed as they squealed.

The noise lifted to a deafening uproar of delighted cheers. Until someone flung a gleaming metal object at her—a gold weight struck her right shoulder and then fell to the street. A beautiful young woman charged Serena from the crowd, violet veils streaming back from her livid face. She clawed at Serena's robes, trying to drag her off the horse. Serena kicked the young woman back and then hung on as the horse shied away from her attacker's scream. The young woman fell, scrambled to her feet, and then charged to catch up with Serena.

Serena reined in her startled horse and braced herself as the young woman lunged for her again. But guards surrounded the furious lady and dragged her off, captive and screaming amid a frenzy of violet veils and wild dark hair.

Behind Serena, Nikaros yelled at the guards, "Take her to the palace courts and have her judged for attacking royal property!" To Serena, he called, "Are you hurt?"

"No! Who was that?"

Nikaros scowled and Araine drooped a bit, clearly grieved.

Since they weren't offering immediate answers, she must cast about for her own. Serena soothed her nervous mare and pondered the situation. Insanity or jealousy surely provided the young woman's motive. Therefore.... Had the frenzied woman been one of Bel-Tygeon's unofficial wives?

Most likely, poor thing. Was becoming a cast-off wife her own eventual lot?

Serena straightened her shoulders, set her face in a determinedly bright smile, and seriously questioned her future with Ty.

***

Bel-Tygeon walked with his friends through the uncultivated spring-green field, the sunlight and his own temper heating his skin. He'd been so deafened by the crowd that he'd never noticed— "Who attacked Serena?"

Though his question was aimed at Nik and Araine, Serena shrugged lightly. "It's no matter, Sire. I'm well."

"For that, your assailant will be grateful." Drawing Serena protectively nearer, he eyed Araine and Nikaros. "Who was it?"

Araine answered, but Ty noted her reluctance. "Zaria, Sire. She acted on impulse, I'm sure."

Grim-faced, Nikaros said, "I ordered the guards to take her to the palace courts and to be sentenced for attacking royal property. Please forgive me if I overstepped."

"Forgive?" Ty scowled. "You commanded correctly. There's nothing to forgive."

Indeed, the blame for this attack belonged to Belaal's fool-king. How many times had he himself excused Zaria's rebellious tendencies? If he must admit the truth, Zaria's boldness and lack of reverence for his own royal status had initially intrigued him as much as her beauty. Yet her capricious and ultimately devious nature had exacted a toll upon everyone around him.

Serena spoke into the heavy silence, her lovely eyebrows fretted with concern, though she spoke lightly. "Because I'm the attacked royal property, may I ask what will happen to her?"

"Prison. Until I order her released—which won't be for months. Even then, I'll send her straight into exile in the south. She can sweat there for the rest of her life." He'd warned her.

"Sire," Serena protested, "Are Belaal's laws always so harsh? If she was one of your former wives, then she acted on impulse, from jealousy."

Loathing himself, Bel-Tygeon told her the truth. "Three years ago, I would have ordered her death without remorse." As Serena blinked, Ty forged on. "I often ordered such deaths and my decisions were never questioned, for I was defending Belaal's property as Belaal's god-king. Even now, if she'd injured or killed you, then legally her sentence would be death."

He watched as Serena looked away. Was she questioning her future with him? He ached to think of losing her. Yet for Serena's sake, it was best that she accept or reject his offer of marriage armed with full knowledge of what he'd been. Yet, in his defense, he added quietly, "For your sake, and because the Infinite blessed me with mercy when I didn't deserve it, I am being lenient."

***

He was telling her the truth. Serena saw it in his reluctance and his obvious wariness of her reaction. If she chose a future with Belaal's king, then she must reconcile herself to his past.

He'd killed many. He was a tyrant. He'd often scorned and ignored the helpless. She'd judged him rightly before meeting him as a haughty high-born menace.

Could she live with this knowledge for the remainder of her life?

Serena swallowed as war raged within her thoughts.

***

Serena shivered within the curving, evening-chilled shadows of the DaromKhor Hills. Despite the cold air, she liked these hills—they reminded her of home. Had the Eosyths ever claimed these hills as their own? The name was so similar…

From behind her, Ty's voice teased, "Lady, hasn't anyone taught you that to survive in a wilderness, you must have a proper coat?"

Before she could turn and look, he wrapped her in his own coat that she and Mother had created for him this past winter. Its scent and texture, so familiar, brought tears to Serena's eyes. She hugged the precious garment closer and smiled at him. "You kept your coat! The slaver who brought me to Belaal—Rileon—took mine. He's probably burned it by now."

"If he didn't burn it, then we'll fetch it for you." As if ordering a cup of water, Ty called to a wiry blue-clad servant and showed him the embroidered coat Serena had made. "Send word to Ebatenai that he must find Rileon, the slaver who sold the Lady Serena in Sulaanc. He has her coat, which is much like this one. When it's found, bring it to us for her."

The servant bowed and ran, calling for a horse and supplies as if his life depended upon retrieving her lost coat. Serena gaped at Ty. "From this distance? Just like that?"

Bel-Tygeon grinned at her. "Just like that. It's his job. If the coat still exists, my servant will be abundantly rewarded for returning it to you, and he knows it."

Serena shook her head. "That would be wonderful, but my coat's likely been burned by now."

"It's probably been sold as art. Meanwhile, where's your hope for this one small thing? Hasn't the Infinite blessed you and brought you through your troubles thus far? Praise Him and wait."

She looked up at him, admiring his assurance, and the joy his expression revealed. This man, her Ty...*this* man she could love forever. Even if he sent unfortunate servants off on nonsensical errands for old coats that might no longer exist.

***

Near the foothills of the mountains, the king ordered an early halt to allow his men some rest before they entered Eosyth lands. Serena understood the necessity of Bel-Tygeon's order. They were all tired from nearly two weeks of travel, and Ty expected his army to face battle soon, therefore it was vital that everyone rest and eat well, while he and his commanders surveyed the land and pondered tactics.

Yet she chafed at the long evening before her. Home was so near that she could almost inhale the scent of the trees and hear the mild bleats of her neglected flock. To manage her frustration, Serena joined Araine to grind and mix their grain and oil rations, and to tend their evening's allowance of firewood, obtained from one of the supply carts—during this campaign, they'd decided to share as much of the work as possible to maintain morale.

Around them, the army resounded with its usual clatter of weapons and armor being stored, tent poles being braced, tack clinking and creaking, and hatchets and mattocks thudding against the cold ground to dig waste pits and clear space around hearths. Among the men, low conversations and occasional outbursts of taunts and laughter broke the sounds of their work.

While Serena heated the iron griddles, Araine poured some olive oil into their flour ration, then added vinegar, water, and seasonings, and worked the mixture into coarse dough. As if reading Serena's thoughts, Araine said, "You're almost home—you and my lord-husband. Do you recognize any landmarks?"

Serena smiled at her sister-by-marriage, then nodded toward the distant horizon. "The farthest, highest peaks frowned down upon me as a child when I played in the meadows below. Those I recognize, but of course I've never seen them from here; they're beautiful."

Araine gazed at the view, bright-eyed, yet wistful. "Yes, they're grand indeed. I completely understand why Nikaros has missed them almost as much as his own family."

A sharp whistle drew their attention. Nikaros neared, lifting his eyebrows at Serena, while Ty grinned like a mischievous boy. Beside him—looking sadly bedraggled and ready to drop to the ground for sleep—was the thin young servant carrying her coat in his arms.

Ty nodded to his servant and the man bowed to Serena. "Lady, please excuse my delay. I guessed that a man like Rileon would sell your coat before leaving Sulaanc, therefore I persuaded Ebatenai to offer a reward, which was called through the marketplace. Your coat was returned that very day. However the Lady Dasarai believed it should be brushed and mended, with the sash replaced—otherwise I would have returned yesterday."

All this for her coat? She blinked at Ty, longing to ask...was this sort of errand perfectly normal to him? And yet, the servant was listening, and offering Serena *her* coat, the work of her own hands with some help from her mother and sisters. She smiled at him and accepted the dark coat and its new blue sash. "Thank you! I never dreamed I would see this again. May the Infinite bless you and grant you rest after such a long journey."

The youth turned crimson and bowed. "Lady, thank you."

The instant the servant was dismissed and staggered away to rest, Serena turned to Ty. "Thank you, but such a fuss for a coat—that poor man!"

"Poor, nothing," Ty snorted. "He'll have a reward and another story to tell when he's an old man. Besides, Ebatenai sent him back to us with two servants and four fresh horses, not to mention supplies. He's suffered nothing but a lack of sleep, and you'll have your coat for your return to your family."

Serena's breath caught. Soon—perhaps in two days—she would see her family! They'd rescue Miyna and Iared, and then chase Cziybor until the brute surrendered to despair.

***

Serena reined in her horse, halting it almost alongside Ty's. Together, they stared at the charred and battered landscape, and Serena swallowed her tears. Clan Darom's traditional southernmost encampment lay heaped with ashes and stones—its surrounding trees now charred spikes clawing toward a frozen sky.

When had the Agocii attacked this place? Was her family dead? Captured and sold?

Fighting for calm, Serena sniffed back tears and glanced at Ty.

His dark eyes reflected the bleak ashes, even as he silently asked the question she feared to voice. What now?

By his waiting silence, she understood that he would direct his army by her decision. Therefore, she must determine rightly.

Serena willed down tremors of fear and closed her eyes. Infinite, give us wisdom and clarity!

All her impulses flew toward rescuing Miyna in the south while inflicting absolute destruction upon Cziybor and the Agocii. Yet... to turn south toward the Agocii was to risk abandoning Clan Darom and its kindred encampments to more devastating massacres that might be underway. Even now, Cziybor and Siyrsun could be approaching Clan Darom...encircling it.

She breathed all her prayers and self-control into a single word. "North."

Chapter 28

Nikaros willed himself to relax astride his horse as he led the way down the tree-edged trail into a western valley. Yet he secured his hold on his bow and its waiting arrows as all his senses heightened, alarmed by the certainty that he was being watched.

But by whom? The Agocii or Eosyths? Let it be the Eosyths! This was their largest, most central gathering place for all the clans. Surely they would recognize him and Serena, or even the king, as Ty, for they were each wearing their heavy goat-hair fringed coats.

Riding behind Nik with Bel-Tygeon, Serena said, "At least none of the trees here are burned. Perhaps Clan Darom is near."

"I pray so," Bel-Tygeon agreed. "Nevertheless, we must settle for tonight. Nikaros," he lifted his voice toward Nik. "Is this next valley large enough to accommodate our forces?"

"More than enough, Sire. This valley is a central meeting place— it borders all four clans. To the west is Clan Ma'rawb, ruled by Tsir Davor. North is Clan Tsahfon. To the east, Clan Qedem...my lord-father's lands."

As he spoke, Nikaros glanced over his shoulder, beyond the king, at Araine. Visibly wearied, she lifted her chin at Nik, then smiled— making him long to steal her off that horse and ride away with her. The king dispelled Nik's impulse to flirt with Araine. "Son of Levos, this evening, you'll direct messengers toward all four clans. By now, they must realize we're here."

"If not, Sire, they'll see the smoke from our campfires this evening. Yet I'm sure we're being watched."

He led them around a tree-fringed red rock spire, then lifted a hand to warn everyone, "Ride single file! The trail narrows in a downhill slope." Despite its narrowness, the trail was beautiful. Misted clouds seemed to rest on the ledges below, veiling the trees that fringed this valley.

Nik inhaled the cold air, relishing the mingled fragrances of those trees—pines and deciduous trees just hinting at this year's leaves. Soon this area would be awash in color, bright with grasses and wildflowers.

How he'd missed the mountains! Each day of his captivity, he'd longed to see his family. May the Infinite, the Mighty One, protect them all against the Agocii and General Siyrsun's gathering forces!

Shelter my people, who have bowed to You...

He had just reached the bottom of the trail, and entered the trees below, when three men stepped into his path, all rough-bearded, wary, and wearing plain, heavy goatskin coats.

Nikaros lifted a warning hand to alert the king and his men. But he smiled at the three, who were definitely not Agocii. "Good evening! I'm Nikaros, second son of the High Lord, Levos." He nodded toward the king, Serena, Araine, and the army behind him. "Here are friends who are interested in helping the Eosyths subjugate the Agocii and their new allies."

The eldest of the three—his beard silver—lifted his grizzled eyebrows and snorted. "Nikaros! Even if you're prettified, I'd know your father's features...which aren't appealing!"

Nik eyed the grizzled man, then laughed, recognizing him. When had this dark-haired lord turned gray? "Tsir Mikial!"

Tsir Mikial's nineteen-year-old heir, Lije, of Clan Tsahfon, had been taken as a hostage with Nikaros, then released. "Lord of the hidden north, how is Lije? Where's my lord-father—and have you seen Tsir Andris? His daughter Serena is here."

Tsir Mikial puffed out a shocked breath. "Serena? But we'd heard she was captured by Cziybor!" He peered past Nikaros, who glanced back just in time to catch Serena leaning out from her horse to bestow a radiant smile upon the Eosyth's northern lord. Mikial spluttered, "Now, as I breathe, what's the Infinite done? It *is* Serena, and as lovely as ever!"

Clearly exultant, Tsir Mikial stepped aside and motioned his men off the trail. "Nikaros, you sluggard—lead this army into the valley! We'll join forces and make our plans to crush the Agocii. I'm sending word to your lord-father; you'll see him before dusk. He's already on his way."

Father. Controlling himself tightly, Nikaros nodded. He half-turned and offered the silent, watchful Bel-Tygeon a respectful nod, and then urged his now-restless horse down the tree-edged trail.

As they descended, Tsir Mikial lifted a polished brown hunting horn to his lips and blared a triumphant long-winded call, summoning all Eosyths present to the valley's clearing.

***

Araine sighed and stretched cautiously as one of the soldiers gripped her horse's halter and held it still, signaling that it was time for her to descend. She lifted the prophet's branch from its allotted place—a javelin-holder fastened alongside her saddle—and then she smiled, seeing her husband hurry to meet her. Dear Nikaros, her love, ever trying to spare her from all difficulties, as if she were fragile.

If Nik could see the monsters in her dreams…the battles and absolute desolation in a world she could barely comprehend, much less describe…he would swiftly realize that a few weeks of riding were trivial compared to everything she'd experienced within her thoughts.

Furthermore, these past weeks had given her plenty of time to pray and ponder over certain symptoms that mightn't be trivial in the palace of a childless king. She wouldn't confide her fears to Nikaros now. Not with the Eosyths gathering for war—and not while she was unsure.

Nik grinned as she met his gaze, and she sighed, ridiculously infatuated. How dark and inviting his eyes were—as the pine forest around them. Araine started to practice a graceful dismount, but Nikaros looped an arm around her waist and swooped her off with undignified delight. "My lord-father's on his way! But you knew that, didn't you, Prophet?"

"No…" Araine leaned against Nik for balance as he set her firmly on the ground. "Obviously, the Infinite takes pleasure in planning surprises for me. Furthermore, I must seek a privy-place. Immediately."

She rushed off to the woods, her discomfort multiplying with each hasty step. Yes, definitely a symptom Cythea had mentioned. Well, two or three symptoms meant nothing. Best to remain silent.

By the time she returned to the clearing, the servants were already setting up her tent, and Nikaros was stacking their gear in meticulous order near their planned entryway. He shot her a look and grinned. "Do you feel better?"

"Yes, my lord, but *you* won't if you tease me too much."

Bel-Tygeon led Serena to meet her, seeming regally impatient. "What took you so long? We could have carved out a privy pit waiting for you. Are you ill?"

"Just tired, Sire, thank you." Araine changed the subject. "What can I do to help?"

"Be our prophet," the king answered, his lean, handsome face intense. "Before we meet with the others, tell me the Infinite's plans. Have you heard any word from Him? Where are our enemies?"

Araine couldn't help raising her eyebrows at the king. He wanted to use the Infinite as his spy? Very well. What could she risk by asking Him? She rested her face against the prophet's branch and prayed. Beloved Creator…if it's Your will—

Even as Araine formed the thought, He answered in a flow of images—jagged rocks and sharp-cut valleys that swept up to a high mountain grotto and left her dizzied. If her eyes hadn't been already closed she would have shut them now in an attempt to blot out the sight of bloodied weapons and sacrifices. The drugged, bound young girls…their mortal blood spilling over altar stones…

Trembling, she absorbed the vision's impact and then straightened, speaking despite her tears. "Sire, you'll find your enemies in the largest valley to the south of Clan Darom. As we speak, they're offering sacrifices to Utzaii...all young women."

And she could do nothing to stop them. The victims were so young and vulnerable—so like her when she'd been given up to the goddess Atea. If only she could blot away the sight of Utzaii's victims. Yet evil must be faced and acknowledged.

Nikaros enfolded her in his arms, smoothing her hair, empathy in his silence.

Softly, Bel-Tygeon said, "As soon as we know of Clan Darom's plans, we'll take the armies south. I'd prefer to work with the Eosyths as unobtrusively as possible, yet if my army must stand alone, so be it."

***

Ty had to look away from Araine. Her stricken look was too raw, too near to the expressions of sufferers from his past, during his time as a god. How many times had he, in his arrogance, caused such sorrow?

Infinite, my Lord and Creator, bless You for granting me mercy. I don't deserve to live! I can only attempt reparations for the harm I've inflicted upon others...

From a distance, Tsir Mikial bellowed cheerily, "Nikaros, is this what scribes and scholars do—stand still and talk? Useless lot! Why are...you...?" His voice and good cheer faded, and he threw the mournful Araine a bemused glance. "Bad news, lady?"

"A vision. Nothing that can be helped, my lord." Araine sniffled and straightened, seemingly determined—more so when Serena offered a consoling hug. Whatever Serena had been prepared to say faded as several hunting horns blared in unison from the eastern edge of the fog-veiled valley.

Horsemen emerged from the mist. Ty recognized wild-bearded Josias of Clan Ma'rawb—riding ahead of his father, Tsir Davor, who was accompanied by High Lord Levos, leader of Clan Qedem and all the Eosyths and... Serena gasped. "Father!"

She ran to Tsir Andris, heedless as any child, hitching up her garments beneath her heavy coat until Ty glimpsed the tops of her boots. He started to follow her, but Nikaros cut him off, rushing by to greet his own father, Lord Levos.

The two Eosyth lords turned to survey the commotion. As one, their eyes widened when they recognized Serena and Nikaros. They flung themselves off their horses and ran to snatch their children in ferocious embraces—Tsir Andris weeping and swaying as he held Serena, Lord Levos laughing and hammering his fists against Nik's back and shoulders. Levos finally held Nik at arm's length and frowned...looking up at him. "You're taller."

Nik laughed. "Is that a problem, my lord?"

"Yes, I'll have to think twice before challenging you. But may the Infinite be praised, you're here!" He hugged Nik again, then straightened. "Listen, I've brought courier birds—send word to your mother at once that Serena's alive and you've both returned. She'll treasure a note from your own hands." The Eosyth high lord looked past his son and raised an eyebrow at Bel-Tygeon. A prickling of wariness coursed over Ty's skin as Levos mused aloud, "You...Ty..."

Ty inclined his head. "At the Infinite's command, I returned home and found my army almost fully prepared to defend my adoptive clan. Then, when Serena appeared and told us of Cziybor's attack, we departed as soon as possible."

All three lords were studying him, and then eyeing Nikaros, Serena, and Ty's army, fully arrayed along the southern end of this valley. Clearly the Eosyth lords were piecing together the truth. Ty waited, masking his fears with coolness. If the Eosyths rejected him, his plans would remain unchanged. He'd still hunt down Cziybor and Siyrsun. What he feared most was to lose his friends, and Serena. If she rejected him...

Araine approached, beautiful and surprisingly formidable as she planted the prophet's branch between Ty and the Eosyth lords. The thin, subtly-twisted staff of vinewood gleamed, taking silvery fire as she spoke. "My lords, your suspicions are true. Belaal has arrived in Eosyth lands—as true allies. The Infinite has made His plans. If you're wise, you'll follow His lead now as He brings eternal good from mortal evil."

**

Nik waited, but kept one arm around his lord-father's shoulders to restrain him if he attacked Belaal's king—Levos certainly looked indignant enough. Yet Araine had commanded his attention as she spoke of the Infinite. Ever cool-headed, Father held himself in check. But he muttered to Nikaros, "Who is that young lady?"

Mighty One, let Father accept this news. Nik cleared his throat. "Araine is the Infinite's prophet of Belaal…and your daughter-in-law."

Levos looked up at Nik, gaping, as if hearing an incredible, impossible tale. "No…"

**

Breathless, still hugging her father, Serena demanded, "Where's Mother? Are she and the children and other survivors safe?"

"Safe as they can be for now." Father glared down at her, his proud face harsh with rage. "They're with Tiphera in Clan Qedem. They walked north, driving the herds for days after the attack—all of them starved much of the way. They're suffering nightmares and they cry for you and Miyna and Iared. Your Uncle Zeddi will be along soon. He's grieving for Betiya and Siyos deeply enough to bury himself. As I live, I'll kill Cziybor!"

"You'll have to fight others for that privilege, my lord."

Serena felt him tense as he stared past her at Ty. Yet, despite his obvious misgivings, Tsir Andris hesitated, glancing from Bel-Tygeon to Araine and the prophet's glowing branch. Father exhaled. "So he *is* the king! As I suspected once or twice last winter. But who is that young woman defending him and speaking for the Infinite?"

Serena smiled, as proud of Araine as she would be of a sister. "She's Nik's wife, and Belaal's prophet. Isn't she wonderful?"

"I hope she's wonderful," Father growled beneath his breath, clearly wary of the shimmering vinewood in Araine's hand. "Otherwise we're all in trouble!"

He gave Serena a protective shake. "Are you well?"

"Yes. Once Nikaros and Ty bought me, I was treated very well. Like a too-indulged younger sister. Father, Ty's been perfect— amazingly kind. Please don't be angry with him!"

"They *bought* you?"

"They rescued me. Cziybor sold me to another chieftain, then I was resold twice...." Her explanation faded as Lord Levos marched toward Araine and Ty, clearly a lord determined to have answers. Father hauled Serena after them, never loosening his grip. Serena matched her father's stride and walked with him to meet Belaal's king and its lovely, fearsome prophet. To forge an understanding between Belaal and the Eosyths.

And to launch a war.

***

Araine waited, watching the Eosyth lords approach. By now, she and Bel-Tygeon were surrounded—the ruggedly-clad Eosyths framing the northern edge of the impromptu meeting place, the king's men nearing protectively from the south. Araine glanced at her shimmering, now metallic prophet's branch, resting her thoughts with the Infinite.

Let them behave wisely! Let them seek Your will and set aside their own grievances...

Finished with her prayer, Araine looked up and met the skeptical gaze of her father-in-law, Lord Levos. Her courage ebbed, sinking like a broken shell in an ocean. The Eosyth high lord was now so bestirred that his scar stood out pale against his tanned, livid face. Did he consider her to be some sort of enchantress who'd snared his son? Did he believe that she and Bel-Tygeon were scheming to conquer the Eosyths?

Quietly, as nearby Eosyths rested their hands on daggers or shifted their bows and arrows, Levos, lord of the Eosyths, eyed her and Bel-Tygeon, then snapped out his challenge. "Offer us proof that I should allow my people to heed you!"

Chapter 29

Araine re-gathered her courage. *My own Creator, give me Your words to ease this lord's fears. Let me honor him as my husband's father. But what should I say?*

I declare the truth; I am his Creator and you are My prophet, who must speak My truth or die...

For the merest breath, He, Creator of All, placed her spirit within an earlier time and she saw the Eosyth lord's most terrible instant of fear—his gashed face bloodied, his unmoving gaze that of a man facing divine wrath. As Araine stared into that time-fragment, her father-in-law's horror slashed into her soul, knife-cold. She gasped, flinching at the impact.

Drawn into the present again, she studied Nik's father. "Lord Levos, the Infinite declares the truth. He is your Creator, and I am His prophet. I must speak the truth on His behalf, or I'll die. Didn't you see His hand at the siege of Parne? Didn't you see Him strike those who scorned His warnings and plotted to kill His children of dust the instant Parne's wall was broken? You were among those who brought forces against Parne. Yet He spared you with only the gash on your face as a remembrance! And," Araine bowed toward Bel-Tygeon, "He spared Belaal's king. Not because either of you were perfect, but because He comprehended your hearts and saw what you would become."

Levos closed his eyes for a brief instant and then opened them—looking so much like his son that Araine melted and softened her tone. "You remember Parne every day, my lord, but I'll tell you this: Your Creator remembers you every instant, as a father remembers

His beloved child. Don't doubt Him now, not when He's moved an entire nation on behalf of your people!"

She'd been so focused on the Eosyth lord that she hadn't noticed his son. Nikaros stood beside her now, adding his silent testimony to her words. Nik clasped Araine's hand, entwining his warm fingers with hers, comforting her with his calm unspoken support.

Levos exhaled. "May the Infinite forgive me. But it's a leader's role to be certain he's chosen the correct path before leading his people onto it."

Unable to stop herself, Araine quipped, "And it's a prophet's role to chase the Infinite's faithful from an incorrect path—even if the chase requires severity."

Serena and her father neared, as did Tsir Mikial and another man who must be Tsir Davor, for Nik's friend, Josias, approached and stood at attention to his right—their somber, waiting expressions reflecting each other's too closely to be a coincidence.

Araine sobered. "My lords, all four of you bowed to the Infinite at Parne, therefore listen. This past winter, Tsir Andris and Clan Darom sheltered an unexpected guest and protected him, for which he is grateful. Belaal's king wishes to prove his gratitude by driving our mutual enemies from your lands—and by returning Serena safely to her lord-father after Cziybor stole her and sold her to another man. Was any of this a surprise to the Infinite? Have no doubt it was not."

"It was indeed the Infinite's plan." Nikaros gave all four lords, including his father, a sweeping, determined glance. "He warned Belaal many months ago to prepare for war. This is why we've arrived here just as your people are gathering their forces to fight the Agocii and the rebels from Belaal who have raided and burned Clan Darom's encampments."

Serena added, "Without Belaal's help, we could be overrun and destroyed."

Tsir Davor grunted. "Belaal won't overrun and destroy us instead?"

Clearly offended, Serena's lovely features hardened, as did her voice. "Belaal's king—who was sheltered all winter by my lady-mother and my lord-father—has behaved honorably toward me and toward us, since the first day we brought him into our tribe. By all our laws, my lords, he is still protected as our guest. You may trust him! I pledge this on my life."

Nikaros nodded. "On mine as well."

Two men quietly shouldered themselves into the circle amid the Eosyth lords. Araine recognized them immediately—Josias and Lije, the heirs of Tsir Davor and Tsir Mikial, both rugged, bearded, leather-clad, and death-serious. Almost in unison, they crossed the circle to stand with Nikaros and Bel-Tygeon.

Josias lifted his chin at his father, Tsir Davor, and Lije said, "We agree. We lived in Sulaanc for more than a year, and we'll testify that Belaal's king can be trusted to do what he says in any situation." With a wry, sidelong glance at Bel-Tygeon, Lije added, "Whether we like what he says, or not."

Lord Levos didn't quite laugh, but his eyes glittered. "Then, let us hope we like what Belaal's king says now."

Aware of the silent, listening king, Araine shifted the subtly glowing branch out of his path and then stepped back—into her husband's arms. Nikaros pulled her closer, as if he must protect her while Bel-Tygeon spoke. The king began with a mocking grin at Lije, promising unspoken retribution for the young man's taunt. But then his smile faded. "You're all wise to be wary, given my past dealings with your people. I don't deserve your trust. I know that I must prove myself worthy to you all in the coming weeks—and I'll gladly do so. Whatever happens, know that I'm grateful to Tsir Andris for his compassion upon a grubby madman-beggar this past winter. He had no reason to concern himself with me, just as the Infinite has no reason to concern Himself with us, yet I'm grateful. May the Infinite be blessed, and let us deal with each other in peace." His gaze turned fierce, and he raised his bow and arrows in one fist. "After we've routed our enemies, rescued the captives, and repaid Cziybor!"

Whistles, and ferocious yowls of agreement lifted from among the Eosyths, while many clattered their swords, shields and bows. Araine felt her husband's profound sigh. When she looked up at him amid the clamor, Nik kissed her, and then rested a warm hand on her face.

Weariness stole over her, stealthy as night. She leaned against Nikaros in the deepening mist and prayed. He held her, and when she straightened, he grinned. "Now I can return the Eosyth Torq to my lord-father!"

***

Standing inside his tent amid pallid morning rays of sunlight, Ty waited as his armorer checked his golden plate mail, the greaves, the buckles, and each rivet and loop of his protective gear. Tedious work, but it must be done—he hadn't donned this armor for years, and he couldn't afford to be distracted during battle by gear that no longer fit him.

At last, his armorer opened the final case and stood, holding Bel-Tygeon's sculptured helmet. Ty gazed at the extraordinary piece and went sick inside. He'd forgotten this helm. The elaborate gilding and that gold crown welded in a protective circlet across its brow were perfectly acceptable, but that golden formidably emotionless god-mask below—an idealized rendition of his former god-king glory— No.

Impermissible. He would not ride into battle masked as a false god.

"Can you unhinge that mask and have it melted down?"

The armorer blinked up at him, clearly aghast. "Indeed, Sire, but your face won't be protected!"

Remembering the vivid gash on Lord Levos's face, Ty shrugged. "Let the Infinite protect my face. I cannot wear that mask."

The armorer's shoulders sagged, but he obeyed, carefully working the pins out of the mask's concealed hinges. At last, the armorer stood, checked the leather and wool padding within the gold-crowned helm, and offered it to Ty. As Ty donned the helm and adjusted it, voices drifted to him from outside the tent. Feminine voices. He cut a glance toward the open entrance. Serena and Araine peeked inside, both looking bright-eyed and prepared to face the day. Ty flung them his most intentionally charming grin. "Wait!"

He turned, testing the helm, his greaves, armguards and the plate mail. Granted, battle gear would never be wholly comfortably, but the fit was satisfactory. Even the armorer seemed pleased. For once, the fussy man nodded, hands becalmed. Eager to meet with Serena and Araine, Ty began to unlatch every fastener and buckle he could find. "Are we finished? Get me out of this gear."

Freed from his accoutrements, Ty dragged on his Eosyth coat, wound the belt around his waist, grabbed his bow and arrows and the loathsome gold mask, then ducked outside. By now, Serena was pacing, Araine was leaning against the prophet's branch as if she could have napped because he'd taken so long to abandon his gear, and Nikaros was approaching with Josias and Lije in tow. Ty pretended a scowl in their direction. "Is this a meeting I didn't request?"

Nikaros bowed. "A convergence, Sire. We've come to report our decision." He nodded at Josias and Lije. "As soon as we reach the southern border, we're planning a spying expedition to find Cziybor's tribe and to study the area."

Serena's eyes widened. "Perhaps you'll find Miyna! I'm going with you."

"No," Ty argued. "You're not! Clan Darom has suffered enough losses; we won't risk your life."

"Ty, I'm—"

Nikaros motioned toward her—a quieting motion. "For your lord-father's sake, no. You can travel with us to the border and wait in the camp there with Araine. You'll be well-protected. And we'll hurry back to you with news."

For an instant, Ty longed to thrash Nikaros. Who was he to be giving orders and making plans? Before Ty could say a word, Nik half-bowed toward him. "Forgive me, Sire; I didn't want a loud quarrel. We're hoping to keep this foray as near-secret as possible. There's no sense in risking lives for lack of solid information, therefore we should sneak in, and then retreat again as swiftly as possible with any news. We wanted to inform you of our decision."

Serena sniffed. But then she aimed a dart of a look at Nikaros. "Give me your word that Araine and I can accompany you to the border."

"Did I agree to this?" Araine demanded, her blue eyes widening with indignation.

Ty almost laughed at her. "Of course you did." Prophets were marvelous mental weapons. Parne's prophet, Ela Roeh, had yelled threats at him from the city's wall—to his amusement, and then his fury. She'd been a lovely deterrent, and the Parnians had been foolish to not appreciate her worth as he appreciated Araine's. Ty added, "Prophet, I need you to chaperone Serena and keep matters settled in the camp. Have no fear; you'll both be encircled by Belaal's army while we're gone to spy out the land."

Ever forthright, Lije huffed at Ty, "Sir, *you* weren't a part of our plan."

"I am now."

Serena looked doubtful, clearly mistrusting his impulsive decision to accompany Nikaros and Josias and Lije. Was she worried that he might be injured or killed on the jaunt into Agocii lands? Ty handed the gold mask to her—glad to distract Serena and to be rid of the mask. "Might your Uncle Zeddi melt this down? Is he here?"

"Yes, he rode in with the supply horses last night." She shifted the mirror-perfect gold mask—studying the idealized mimicry of his features. "I'll give this to him when I see him. Promise me…that you'll be safe."

"As safe as I can be in enemy lands."

With Siyrsun eager to slaughter him and take Belaal's throne.

Infinite, Victor of Parne, intercede here, and protect us all.

***

Inside her lord-father's tent, Serena handed the perfect gold mask to Uncle Zeddi, hoping she'd composed herself enough to mask her own shock. Uncle Zeddi looked so much older. Life-wearied. Indeed, much of his life's joy had vanished with Betiya and his firstborn, Siyos. "Uncle, Belaal's king asks if you'd melt this down. He hates what it represented."

Zeddi turned over the mask and shook his head. "It would be such a pity to destroy such a marvel. Even the back is polished..." But then he shrugged, evidently too dispirited to argue in defense of saving such a work of art glorifying a fallen god-king. "Later. Perhaps later."

Busy checking his weapons and battle gear, Father studied Serena. "You were visiting him this morning. Is he behaving properly toward you?"

"Yes, Father. As I said, he's behaved perfectly toward me from the instant I was found in Sulaanc."

For the most part, that was true. Ty had been completely correct with her. Much as she sometimes wished he might misbehave, just a little. She gazed down at the golden mask, so chillingly beautiful on the fleece coverlet. Why had it shocked her this morning to see Ty garbed in full battle gear? They were preparing for war—a battle for their lives, for the survival of their clans. She must remain calm.

She must accept that Ty, Father, Uncle Zeddi, Nikaros, and all the men would fight.

Serena's stomach knotted hard at the thought. She touched the cold mask, then turned away and prayed.

***

The day's lingering fog covered them like an overwhelming veil as Nikaros led the others along the low path at the cliff's base. Even as the dense mist interfered with their spying mission, its persistent gloom sheltered them better than their worn rock-hued leather garments as they edged through this valley. A blessing. The king's presence was concealed, and his safety was Nik's overriding concern on this spying foray. Nikaros, son of Lord Levos, would *not* die as the reviled Eosyth who'd led Belaal's king to a legendary death to be ever retold in tragic verses for generations. Infinite, spare me such infamy!

But this evening or tomorrow, they'd plan a different route for their return to the horses and onward to the camp—no doubt the skies would be clearer then. Nik frowned at himself. Had they left the horses too early in their journey? Was Cziybor's tribe farther away than he'd reckoned? He'd remembered this valley from a youthful hunt and retreat with his lord-father and Tsir Andris…from a time with the Agocii kept a condescending truce with the Eosyths.

From a time when both nations worshiped at shared shrines in these mountains, offering gifts to the god Utzaos and his Atzaia. The Eosyths had routinely offered small perfect gems and malleable gold wafers that Nik suspected the Agocii stole for their own use, never mind that the items were dedicated to the deities. The Agocii had ever-favored this valley…

A hunting horn resounded nearby, its piercing double-note call and accompanying hoof beats and voices announcing an Agocii horde. How many? Nikaros motioned to the king and Lije and Josias, and they hunkered at the cliff's base, the mist blending their presence into the rocks. Behind him, the king looked wary, but alert and calm, his bow and arrows readied. Anyone seeing him for the first time would vow he was an Eosyth—except that his hair was shorter than usual, and he'd recently shaved.

Yowls and Agocii curses echoed up the slopes, mingled with sharp accents Nikaros hadn't heard in years. Men from Darzeq. Mercenaries? Nik exhaled. Surely Cziybor was near.

Nik sidled along the path, praying the fog would linger. Where was Cziybor's encampment? Were other Agocii tribes also gathering? Had Belaal provided enough men to defend the Eosyths?

Another hunting horn's odd rippling soaring notes echoed along the fog-shrouded valley, and the king shifted. Nik glanced his way, then froze. Bel-Tygeon's tensed expression and posture revealed suppressed fury. Nikaros leaned toward him, lifting his eyebrows to question the king silently. Bel-Tygeon breathed one harsh word. "Siyrsun!"

That last hunting call had been Siyrsun's? Undoubtedly, the king would recognize it. If Siyrsun trapped them, they'd all end up hung and gutted. He had to get Bel-Tygeon away.

The king tapped him, then glanced south emphatically. Nik nodded as the hunting party's noises faded into the distance and the mist. Yes. South. The opposite way from the hunters—though they'd have to remain hidden. Infinite, conceal us and save the king!

They continued on, their cautious footsteps accented by occasional nerve-spiking scuffs against stone. Following the cliff's base, Nikaros led them down into a mist-sodden ancient forest of mixed evergreens, crowded with fallen trees, cold-bronzed shrubs, thickets of tangled grasses, and dulled bracken. The icy scouring rush of a spring-thawed stream turned them aside, forcing them into a sheltered curve within the valley.

"How far do we go before turning back?" Josias muttered as they wound their way among the trees. "Belaal's servants aren't familiar with these mountains; they're liable to stretch out on witches' moss tonight."

Nikaros shuddered at the thought. Men had died making such a mistake—welcoming the poisonous moss as a cushion when they should have torched it. He looked over his shoulder at the king. Bel-Tygeon muttered, "We have warned them of the moss. Repeatedly."

But his tone was grim, clearly pondering the implications if his men should make a mistake. Such as a horse being unpegged and led to an infested grazing area.

"Noon," Nikaros said. "Let's be sure we turn back at noon." For safety's sake, they must allow themselves time to reach their horses and Bel-Tygeon's servants by nightfall. Even that might be too long.

They continued hiking until Nikaros caught the low, heavy scent of smoke drifting toward them from an encampment.

***

Moving at a crouch, his bow and arrows in his left hand, Ty prayed as they neared the clearing. If only they could isolate Siyrsun from the hunt and catch him unawares. Sometimes killing an army's leader was the only step needed to confound and scatter the enemy. Being a leader himself, the thought wasn't altogether pleasant. However, it would work in his favor now.

He hunched down near Nikaros and the others amid evergreen shrubs and darkened bracken and stared at the Agocii encampment—the multiple-peaked leather tents testifying to their identities. The camp seemed remarkably calm. Women laughed and chattered in the distance and Ty glanced their way, trying to discern their faces in the mist.

Except for the very youngest members of the tribe, the Agocii were all busy, tending fires, sewing, cooking, and combing and spinning huge tufts of wool into coarse thread.

No sign of any of the men or their horses. Most likely they'd all joined the hunt. Worse, Ty didn't recognize Miyna among the youngest children—search as he might.

If only they could find Cziybor or Siyrsun or both! Unfortunately, the Agocii leader had likely joined Siyrsun's hunting party they'd nearly met. Would this spying mission end in near-failure?

Ty scowled. He was about to nudge Nikaros and motion for them to leave, when a small girl sporting two short crimson-tied braids, stood and held out her little fists to one of the women. Still chattering, the woman nodded to the girl and carelessly waved her off. Pouting slightly, the child meandered from the group and plopped onto the recently grazed ground with a handful of dirty wool fibers, apparently hoping to somehow turn it into thread. Other children scampered off from the women, vanishing into the mist—their games not tempting the little girl in the least.

She turned briefly, and Ty recognized the soft lines of her sweet face. Miyna! Wearing braids. Ty tapped Nikaros on the shoulder, and then motioned to Josias and Lije, breathing one barely audible word. "Miyna!"

If they could steal her back—it would be a victory to lift everyone's spirits and ease some of his own worries.

Ty sought a pebble. A chunk of bark. Anything…anything to throw lightly at the child without frightening her. He checked a nearby moldering stump, pried up coarse lumps of lichen and bark, then hunkered down near the shrubs and pitched a clump softly at Miyna.

She looked at the lichened bark as it tumbled lightly toward her feet. Ty flung another, pleading in frantic silence, Do you remember me?

Miyna glanced over at him, dark eyes wide and curious. Ty grinned at her from the shrubs and made the twins' lowering, patting hush-hush motion with one hand.

The little girl blinked. Had she recognized the twins' signed word? Ty nodded encouragingly and motioned for her to approach him, even as his thoughts pleaded, Remember me! You were my comrade during the milk pox. You wiped your nose on my sleeve. You stole my food!

Remember me!

Chapter 30

Nikaros gaped as Bel-Tygeon motioned to the small girl and offered her a coaxing grin. Did the king believe he could lure her away? Would she—

Clutching the fibers, Miyna stood and trotted toward them, never once looking back at the women who still chattered as they tended the fire, prepared cords, and mended garments. She entered the shrubs and, as Bel-Tygeon scooted backward, Miyna approached him and held out her hands, displaying two messy clumps of fiber twined with splinters of bark and pine needles. Ty chuckled beneath his breath and whispered, "Clever girl! Good work!"

He shouldered his bow and arrows and then swept her into a hug, kissing her hair and motioning to her silently, making her smile.

Nik suppressed a snort. Just like that, Bel-Tygeon had reclaimed Miyna. The king's charm would be disgusting if it weren't so useful now, though Miyna had seemed to recognize the king. Grinning, Nik waved to Josias and Lije. Their footsteps muffled and swift, they crept away from the Agocii encampment, bows and arrows readied to defend the king and Miyna.

Before they reached the coursing, rushing stream, Nikaros heard the Agocii women clamoring in the distance, calling Miyna's name.

***

As they hurried through the trees, Ty managed to tuck Miyna partway into his heavy coat. He was sweating, elated by the unexpected Miyna-snatching, and warmed by their swift pace. Miyna seemed remarkably accepting of the whole adventure, brave girl.

Only once did she seem to question her decision to flee the Agocii. As Ty hugged her close, she leaned backward in the crook of his arm and stared up at him quizzically. He smiled at her. Miyna wrinkled her small nose and then huddled against him, establishing tenacious fist-holds on Ty's tunic beneath his Eosyth coat—reassuring gestures of trust. But what had she done with the fistfuls of wool and bark filaments? Had she discarded them inside his coat?

His answer soon came with the chafing-stabbing of minuscule wood splinters that promised to scour layers of skin just above his coat's heavy wool belt while he ascended the incline from the forest.

His discomfort gradually increased as he followed Nikaros up a slope and into a narrow defile that—despite its treacherous rocks—promised some protection from being seen.

Time ground on with their wary footsteps. The rocky defile merged into an odd tawny canyon, which twisted sinuously, its curved walls making even their breath sound louder than normal. Ty's distress multiplied into acute misery—no longer just from the splinters. He'd downed half his ration of water and its effects were pressing, particularly with Miyna's weight inside his coat. He must find some type of makeshift privy. And, to judge by her squirming and signed gestures of grumpiness, so did Miyna.

Ty whispered harshly, "Nik! We need to stop. Now!"

"Sire, with all respect—"

No. He would not carry Miyna through this wilderness with both of them soaked, sour, and splinter-chafed. He eyed the canyon's oddly twisted walls and spied a curved hollow of a niche perfect for sheltering an increasingly desperate child. Aided by memories of Serena tending her youngest sister, Ty set Miyna down inside the niche and bent to remove her small rough-stitched coat, so she could crouch unhindered. "Here's a good place. Careful, Miyna…"

He hadn't reckoned on the niche's sloped stone floor and the resultant stream against his boots. Ty released a breath and a plea. Infinite? Let the leather not soak through….

Voices echoed from high above at the canyon's narrowed rim—men's raucous distant laughter and curses. Ty looked up, a shiver lifting every hair on his scalp. Agocii? Within a breath, Nikaros, Josias, and Lije crowded into the niche with Ty and Miyna as best they could to avoid being seen by the men above. Ty wrapped Miyna in her coat, then lifted her in his arms to keep her quiet. Clearly obsessed with the same idea, Josias pushed a chunk of dried meat at the little girl.

Miyna's mossy-brown eyes shone. She grasped the dried meat, plugged an edge of the leathery chunk into her mouth and gnawed as their enemies clattered high above them at the canyon's rim.

Ty gritted his teeth against his own misery and stood still.

***

In her lord-father's morning-lit tent, Serena knelt, unable to stand as Ty's messenger— ashen-faced with alarm—bowed and addressed the gathered Eosyths. "My lords, the king and your sons haven't returned. I've been sent to request your help in a search."

Ty…missing. With Nikaros and two Eosyth heirs…

Cold fingers touched Serena's hand, summoning her from the initial shock. Araine, her eyes huge with fear for her husband and the king, scooted over to Serena and hugged her.

Lord Levos stood, big and authoritative as he addressed the Eosyth lords. "Two of us stay and two of us go. Who stays?"

"A lord is responsible for his guests," Tsir Andris said. "These are my lands. I'll go."

"I'll go," Serena added. "I know those valleys well enough."

Father shook his head. "Your mother would kill me if I survive. No. You stay here."

Before Serena could argue, Araine murmured, "As they search, we'll pray that the Infinite shields them all—our task is equally important; don't doubt it. The Infinite's realm is moved by prayers."

Serena whispered, "You speak as one who's walked in that realm."

"I have and will again."

***

Sweating in the afternoon sunlight, Nikaros prayed his fears aloud as they approached the designated meeting place, just inside Clan Darom's borders. "No corpses! Let there be no corpses."

The lack of circling Aeryons and other scavenging winged beasts reassured him. But they were a full day late and without a doubt everyone in Belaal's encampment was now alarmed and planning an invasion to retrieve Bel-Tygeon...and possibly to kill Nik for endangering the king.

Nik's first scan of the encampment wasn't promising. No servants and no horses waited. Yet neither did any corpses. Behind Nikaros, Josias exhaled loudly, and Lije said, "I vote we rest and find food."

"There's no voting here," Bel-Tygeon huffed, sounding grimly amused. "We are not in the Tracelands! I *decree* that we rest and find food. Who would think that such a little girl could weigh as much as a destroyer?"

He studied the ground and then set Miyna on a patch of coarse winter-dried grass. The child beamed as she looked around, bright-eyed and happy—the only one among them who'd eaten well and slept soundly since leaving the Agocii encampment. Nik envied her energy. But he didn't envy the king.

The instant Bel-Tygeon sat down, rubbing his hands over his fatigue-dazed face, Miyna pounced on him like a tiny cub on its parent.

Bel-Tygeon opened one eye and then laughed and jostled her, tweaking her charmingly frazzled braids. "Have you no mercy, lady? You've ruined my boots, eaten my food, splintered my hide, stretched my arms out of their sockets, and now you expect me to play?"

A horse's rumbling warning rippled through the air, making Nikaros tense his fingers around his bow and arrows. Josias and Lije set arrows within their bows and kept watch, while the king crouched holding Miyna—a man guarding living treasure.

An entire regiment rode into the clearing, led by Tsir Andris, Commander Utthreates, and Nik's lord-father. All three men looked grim...until they saw Nikaros, and then the king, Josias, and Lije. Within a blink, Tsir Andris gasped and dropped off his horse at a run, heading for Bel-Tygeon and Miyna. "Mighty One be blessed forever! You found her! Miyna…!"

Heedless of the king, Tsir Andris snatched his youngest child from her protector's arms and swayed, kissing her and weeping. Less than enthusiastic, Miyna leaned away from him, clearly suspicious until recognition lit her small pretty face. She grabbed her lord-father's hair and hugged him for a long, fierce instant. But then she hesitated and reached for Bel-Tygeon again. Beside Nik now, Lord Levos chuckled. "Clearly she holds divided loyalties." He cuffed Nikaros on the back. "You had us worried, but I see you were delayed for the best of reasons."

"Indeed, my lord." Nik returned his father's grin. "We've much to tell you as soon as we've returned to camp."

Commander Utthreates stifled a grin and knelt before the king. "Sire, by your leave, please allow your servants to escort you to your forces again. We've feared you were dead."

The king motioned his commander to stand, but he seemed regally pleased. "I've not departed yet, Commander. Moreover, we now know who we face. Let's go draw maps and make our plans. Several plans."

***

Serena hesitated at the entrance of the beautiful heavily-quilted white pavilion Bel-Tygeon's servants had set up for her. She hadn't bothered to inspect the tent yet. Somehow it seemed to belong to someone else, not her. She'd sheltered with Nik and Araine during their journey, and since arriving in camp, she'd been caring for Father's guests in his tent and visiting Araine's tent during her spare time. Should she inspect this place and take charge of it?

No… Already, she wore robes Ty had provided, as well as the gold anklet and the bejeweled crimson cord around her throat, marking her as a slave of Belaal. She also still guarded the precious azurnite blade for Ty, though she'd never shown it to Father. If she accepted full ownership of the blade and this tent, Father would certainly believe that she'd given herself and her future to Belaal's king.

If Ty was still alive.

If she lost him… Serena's breath snagged in her throat as her heartbeat skittered its fear. Trying to deal with the hurt, she gripped a gilded pole that supported the tent's canopied entry.

A hunting horn's exultant blare, and shouts and laughter, made her turn. "Ty!" Father, too. Serena clutched her robes close and ran to encampment's main gathering area. As Belaal's soldiers filed off on either side of the encampment, Father and Lord Levos rode into the camp's center, both looking jubilant as children who'd brought home their first hunt-harvest. Riding behind them, Nikaros, Josias and Lije seemed to be guarding Bel-Tygeon, who managed his horse's reins with one fist. For in his other arm, he held—

"Miyna!" Serena screeched like a child herself and ran to seize her sister.

Ty leaned down, his smile beautiful in his dark-whiskered face. "The Infinite blessed us with a gift—a chance we stole."

"Bless Him!" Serena pulled Miyna from Ty's arms, allowing him to dismount his horse. She kissed her baby sister and laughed at Miyna's braids. "Oh, you look so grown up! Miyna—"

Miyna gave her a blank look and deliberately turned away. An obvious rejection. Heart-cut, Serena pleaded, "Miyna, what's wrong? Are you upset with me?"

Try as she might, Serena could not persuade her little sister to meet her gaze.

Instead, Miyna held out her arms for Ty, who took her—though he had the grace to appear uncomfortable. He eyed Serena, then tenderly chided Miyna, "Look at your sister. You can't be angry with her…it wasn't her fault that Cziybor stole you. She loves you."

Miyna answered with a small fist-strike in the air. Ty kissed Miyna's mussed hair and handed her to Serena once more. "I'm sorry if you're not happy, little girl, but you'll have to accept Serena's apologies. We've a battle to plan."

***

Dawn emerged wan and gray from a sullen mist-shrouded night that had offered Serena little sleep. She'd longed for this day—the day Cziybor would be repaid for his crimes against the Eosyths. Yet vengeance might cost the Eosyths more loved ones. Infinite, spare us further losses...

A futile request, she was sure. Didn't battle guarantee fatalities? Cuddling Miyna close, she walked beneath Belaal's gleaming gold and blue banners as the men prepared their horses and gear. Father stood near his horse, waiting with Uncle Zeddi and other Eosyths. She hurried to meet him.

Father bent to kiss Serena's cheek and Miyna's once more as she offered him a hug. His tone understandably preoccupied, he said, "Nikaros has sent word north that our battle is for today. Pray that we take down Cziybor and drive the Agocii far from our borders! And have food waiting for us when we return."

"Yes, my lord."

Ty was equally distracted, resplendent in full battle gear and evidently absorbed in plotting final tactics with Lord Levos, Commander Utthreates, Commander Vioc, and Nikaros—for they were eyeing the mountains to the south, and Bel-Tygeon's elegant hands swept through the air as if evaluating the landscape and their encampment. But he noticed Serena and Miyna. His dark eyes shone and he beckoned them. Serena's entire being faltered in a mingling of delight and fear. Had any man ever been so handsome—so enthralling with such a tender glance and breathtaking smile? She longed for an acceptable excuse to kiss him farewell in front of everyone. Even as she walked toward the king, Serena prayed.

Infinite, bless him and bring him safely through the battle! Please, Mighty One...return all of these men to us victorious!

Miyna lunged at Ty. He grinned and scooped her into a hug, kissing her clean hair. When Ty finally straightened, adoration and regret mingled within the glance he gave Serena. "If I could survive it, lady, I'd kiss you as well!"

"I'm praying for you," Serena said, gently shifting the topic. "For you and for all our men. "Return unharmed!"

"With the Eosyths avenged." Uncle Zeddi grazed his knuckles over Miyna's tender cheek, which two months before had been marked with Aunt Betiya's blood. Watching Zeddi, and no doubt remembering Aunt Betiya and Detzios, Ty's face settled in cold, grim lines, making him look older. "May they indeed be avenged!" He nodded to Serena now, brisk as he held Miyna toward her. "We hope to return by nightfall—tomorrow morning at the latest."

By tomorrow morning? That was much too long. Serena gently took hold of Miyna again. "We'll be watching, my lord."

Ty nodded toward the servants and royal guards tending the encampment. "Let them keep watch. You two rest."

Such a dictatorial tone! Serena smiled. "Yes, Sire."

Araine approached them now, her lovely complexion pallid, her gaze lacking its usual sparkle as she hugged Nik in farewell. While the men mounted their horses and prepared to ride away, Serena kissed Miyna's hair and then whispered, "Prophet, what's about to happen?"

"I don't know." Araine gazed after her husband in obvious desolation as she whispered the words. "May the Infinite guard us all."

***

Araine longed to call back Nikaros—to call back the entire army. Why? Of course they must go to war. They'd known this day would arrive. Infinite, why can't I see what will happen to my beloved? To his family?

Was it more than she should request? Perhaps, a prophet shouldn't know everything. She rested a hand on Serena's arm, admiring little Miyna for the thousandth time. "Come with me. Let's pray and wait together as the Infinite fulfills His will."

***

His gilded armor dimmed by the relentless mist that hung suspended above the valley and above the steady clinking and creaking of their advancing army, Ty rode between Tsir Andris and Lord Levos. To his left, Commander Utthreates led half of Belaal's horsemen. Directly behind Ty, Tsir Mikial had charge of the Eosyths, all readied with arrows clenched in their fists, and to Ty's right, Nikaros and Tsir Davos led the other half of Belaal's horsemen and a contingent of Eosyth horsemen, armed with bows and blades.

The combined forces of Belaal and the Eosyths formed a wall that cut off any escape through the main valley. Soon, the Agocii encampment would be isolated. Bless the Infinite that He'd placed Miyna in Eosyth hands and away from the coming battle…

Quietly, Lord Levos said, "Spring mists and rains may green the fields, but I'd welcome brown grass today, in exchange for a clear sky."

Ty nodded. "I agree, my lord. Even so, may the Infinite provide us with sight."

A warning blast from an unseen watchman's horn carried through the fog above them. Not an Agocii cry—that was the long two-note blare Siyrsun favored when calling his men to battle. Ty frowned. Siyrsun's men were guarding this section of the valley. And if he knew his former general…

Alarms lifted in an outlying disharmony of shouts and clashing metal. Battle trumps resounded along the valley before them. Ty called to his men, "Hold back! Wait for our enemies to gather so we can take them all! Hold back!"

Chapter 31

Ty held himself coldly in check, serving as an example to his men despite his longing to charge through the valley and obliterate Cziybor and Siyrsun. Men swarmed the mist-canopied valley before the Eosyths and Belaal's army, clustering into bristling formations of javelins and swords. Far more men than the Agocii alone could have provided.

Araine's warnings, and Nik's spies all proved true—not that Ty had doubted them.

Had Siyrsun hired every surviving mercenary from the previous chaos in Darzeq?

As his men waited, Ty called out, "Bless the Infinite for bringing us to this place! This day, He will remember all our names as we face our foes—let Him defend His name to His glory and our joy!" Glancing over his shoulder, Ty yelled, "Clan Darom!"

The Eosyths met his call with fierce howls, lifting their bows, prepared to strike at his prearranged signal. Ty lifted his Eosyth bow and saluted them.

By now, Cziybor and Siyrsun were riding up to the forefront of their allied forces—Cziybor from the left, Siyrsun from the far right. Cziybor bellowed, all arrogance and boasting. "Who is this Infinite? May Utzaii cleanse that name from your mouths with your own blood! May our lord of the high places feed our pastures with your rotting corpses! But first—" He motioned to the Eosyths. "Clan Darom! Are you so eager to take vengeance when I've only served Utzaii according to our traditions, which you abandoned? Tsir Andris! Come meet me now and let us see who wins! The Infinite against Utzaii!"

Behind Ty, Zeddi growled, "Why should he dictate our terms? Let's give him the same terms he offered Clan Darom! For Betiya!"

Zeddi lifted his bow and he sent a swift unsanctioned succession of arrows arced high over Ty's head. The arrows descended upon Cziybor, lodging with visible thumps in his protective coat of thick boiled leather, the last arrow embedding deeply into his chest. Cziybor froze, wavered in his saddle, then scoffed. His movements betraying pain, the Agocii chieftain angled a spear toward the Eosyths, as all his men set their arrows. "Aim—"

Before Cziybor could cry out his order, Ty released his first signaling arrow. Instantly Eosyth arrows rained over Cziybor and the Agocii exclusively, attesting to Clan Darom's aim. Cziybor fell, his corpse bristled with Clan Darom's strikes. Siyrsun called out, "Agocii! Avenge this treachery! Outcasts of Darzeq, kill them and seize all you wish! Onward!"

Agocii warriors surged forward on foot, obeying Siyrsun, but their charge faltered amid a stormfall of Eosyth arrows, as all the clans set then released the third and fourth arrows held within their bow-fists.

Multiple screams lifted in the air as the canopy of mist drifted upon the battle like a pall and horse-hooves shook the ground. A trump-call blared—Siyrsun's usual trump call, with an added rising note. What that final note signaled, Ty could only guess. His movements a controlled and trained rush, he fanned more arrows within his left fist, raised his bow, then sent one arrow after another toward the Agocii and their allies.

When their scattering forces became mere shadows within the surrounding mist, Ty finally drew his sword and yelled, "Belaal, forward! Let no man escape!"

Glaring into the mist, alert for his first foe, Bel-Tygeon goaded his horse ahead.

***

Spying an Agocii warrior charging toward him battle axe upraised, Nikaros dropped his bow over his saddle's high pommel, drew his long sword, and unleashed the blade in a wide semicircle against his yowling attacker, catching him mid-shoulder with such force that the warrior's knees buckled. The Agocii battle axe fell to the damp ground amid the warrior's own blood. Nikaros lifted his stained sword and sucked in a sharp breath, seeing yet another warrior turn his way, running, teeth bared in savage war-induced fury, one arm upraised—a javelin poised to strike Nik from his horse.

Two arrows slashed the air from Nik's left with lethal accuracy, embedding themselves in the warrior and taking him down. Beyond Nik, his lord-father roared a triumphant battle cry. Nik lifted his shield from alongside his horse and thrust his arm through its straps—readied to face another onslaught.

Infinite...strengthen me!

He urged his horse forward, peering through the mist, searching for Siyrsun—and cutting down any foe who dared to cross him. But soon, every man he faced was Agocii. Where were Siyrsun's soldiers? And the Darzeq mercenaries? Had they regrouped for a fresh attack?

The death-cries and clamor finally faded, leaving a hush as morbid as the glooming mist. Nik called over to his father, "My Lord! Any sight of Siyrsun? Should I call our men to regroup?"

Father loathed Siyrsun—a distrust stemming from dealings with the ruthless general during the siege of Parne. Weapons poised Levos shook his head. "I saw him only once during the battle. Yes, sound a call for the clans to regroup! We'd best prepare for another attack."

Nikaros pressed his lips together and forced the summoning call through his polished metal-banded ram's horn. As the call faded, Commander Vioc rode toward him, followed by the blood-spattered Josias and Lije—all three looking mistrustful of the battle's outcome. Lije yelled, "Nik! Most are on the run, but Vioc suspects trickery."

"So do we." *Mighty one, what is wrong?*

***

Flanked by his guards, wary of an impending ambush, Bel-Tygeon rode through the lifting mist. Scents of smoldering fires reached him, and he nodded Utthreates toward the odors. "We're approaching at least one camp. We'll need to search for others."

A muddle of overturned pots, ruined food, felled tents, smoldering ashes, and hoof-printed mud pointed to hasty abandonment. Not a soldier or camp slave in sight. Ty frowned. "Keep your weapons readied and keep the men in their assigned formations. Siyrsun's liable to attack at any time."

Vioc called from the camp's edge, "Sire, beyond this camp is another—Agocii and empty. They're running!"

Serena's uncle rode up to Ty, his wearied face lined and fretted with concern. Zeddi asked, "Will you spread word among your men to keep some survivors for questioning? If my younger son is among the Agocii, then one of the survivors might know where. The man's name was Vsevold. I'd be willing to ransom Iared."

Ty called to Vioc. "Commander, spare any Agocii who are willing to surrender. We're looking for an Eosyth captive named Iared—this man's son."

He sent Zeddi with Vioc and his men. Infinite…let them not ride into a trap! At least the mist had lifted and they could now see.

Where was Siyrsun?

***

Keeping her movements soft, Serena covered the dozing Miyna. Brave little sister—she was so glad to be among Eosyth tents again that she fought sleep. Serena kissed Miyna's hair, and then whispered to Araine, "While she's resting, I'll go search the spare tent for fresh clothes and more food."

"I'll watch over her," Araine murmured. "She makes sleep look so inviting."

"Sleep then. I'll cook. May I borrow a kettle for our evening meal?"

Araine smiled. "Gladly. I trust your cooking more than mine."

Serena lifted an empty kettle from the hearth, retreated from Araine's tent, and covered its entry. While planning their meal, she argued with herself about raiding the white tent for clothes and food. Just because she was borrowing items and occupying its interior for an evening didn't mean she'd claimed the tent. But should she kindle a fire in its portable iron hearth?

Drawing her mantle close, Serena crossed the camp and knelt on a rocky perch at the rushing spring. As she filled the kettle, she spied a worrisomely dingy-green clump clinging to the base of a stone near the water's edge. Witches' moss. Treacherous stuff! How had the servants missed it while preparing the site?

Ah, well. She'd burn the infested area as soon as possible. Hefting the kettle in her arms, Serena proceeded to the borrowed tent—nodding pleasantly to the royal servants and guards. "Sirs, warn everyone to check the camp's boundaries. I saw witches' moss near the stream."

The lead guard saluted her. "Yes, Lady. I'll spread the word."

Smiling, Serena entered her temporary realm. Everything seemed perfect—the bright carpets, gilded storage chests, new metal and clay lamps, baskets of fragrant wood, stacked iron pots, and rolled sleeping pallets stacked with puffy new pillows... It was a lovely spacious tent.

Did she want to possess this place, and later live in the palace in Sulaanc?

Could she leave these mountains for Ty? She weakened with longing for a glimpse of his brilliant dark eyes, the touch of his hands...a kiss... No. Just thinking of him would dash her resolve to make a rational, unemotional decision.

Serena placed the kettle on the cold portable hearth, checked its protective rings of stones, angled kindling, and bark resins beneath the iron grate, then struck her flint and sent sparks into a puffy nest of dried grass. She blew the fire into warming life, slid the burning nest amid the kindling and resins within the hearth and gradually built up the wood.

While the water heated, she arranged the carpets in a more comfortable fashion, rummaged through the chests, changed into fresh, bright garments and a warmer mantle. Satisfied, she donned

Ty's azurnite dagger, and then found her palace-allotted stash of food—including the dried pink fruit tisane prescribed by the palace physician, Cythea.

Perfect! Tonight, she'd brew this for their meal. Miyna would enjoy the drink's rosy color and tart-sweet taste.

As soon as the water boiled, she stirred lentils, seasonings, and dried vegetables into the kettle. The camp's dried meat, unfortunately, was better gnawed on as a snack.

Now...to destroy the moss. Serena checked the fire, grabbed a lamp, and then ducked through the entry and marched toward the nearest outdoor fire. She'd ask the guards to check on her tent's hearth-fire during her brief departure, then she'd light the lamp and burn the moss.

A voice bellowed from amid the other tents, "Foreign soldiers riding toward us! Arm yourselves!"

"Lady!" Bel-Tygeon's lead guard cut off her path to the fire and herded her back. "To your tent again, I beg you, for your own safety!"

"I'll go to my sister's tent—"

"No!" The lead guard shoved her at the tent. "There's no time! I'll be dreki food if I live and you die! Lady, *hide*! We'll guard the prophet and your sister."

Other guards swarmed about, grabbing their weapons and shields. A thunderous herd of hoof-beats echoed throughout the camp, accompanied by hair-raising war cries. Serena dashed into the tent again, set down the lamp and dropped to her knees, pleading, Not again! Oh, Infinite...

Let Miyna remain asleep. Protect Araine! Guard Ty and Father and the other men!

Outside, numerous horses huffed, stomped, and snorted as they circled her tent, sending shudders through the soil beneath Serena's feet. Battle cries and weapons clashed beyond the tent's quilted exterior, the violent ringing of metal against metal, so near that Serena cowered. Would the battle demolish her tent? At last, his voice hoarse, Bel-Tygeon's lead guard cried in a fading voice, "We surrender—! Please spare our charges...they're defenseless."

A coarse, deep, vaguely familiar voice commanded, "Spare any women and children. Execute the guards. Hide the bodies, but take their gear. Hurry!"

Execute the guards? No! As Serena stood and turned toward the entry, men's sudden cries and agonized groans cut through the air. She emerged from the tent just as the last two guards were run through by multiple attackers wielding bloodied swords and spears.

Serena screamed in anguished protest. She tore her gaze from the fallen guards and the cluster of terrified surviving servants, to the invaders...who now stared at her, their avid, lecherous gazes freezing Serena where she stood.

The oldest warrior—a burly blunt-featured man with a deeply scarred face and thick silvering hair—shoved her inside the tent once more and followed her. As Serena skittered backward across the carpets and fought for footing, he eyed her, clearly intrigued. Rough-voiced, he asked, "What have I found? Are you a palace treasure saved for Bel-Tygeon's victory celebration?"

Before she could answer, he leaned outside the tent and snapped, "Find food, all of you and keep watch as you rest! They'll follow soon enough."

They? Was he talking about Ty, Father, Uncle Zeddi and the others?

Forcing down her panic, hating the tremor in her voice, she asked, "Sir...who are you?"

He looked her up and down again. His gaze rested on the gold-embroidered crimson cord around her throat, and then he laughed. "I'm your new master, and I *know* what that red ornament signifies. He hasn't touched you yet—and that's in your favor. Obey me, and I'll deal well with you, Lady. In fact you'll prefer me to Belaal's former god-king. You're wasted on that madman!" He laughed again, richly amused. "As soon as he's dead, and I take his place, you'll learn what I mean."

She recognized his laugh now. She'd heard him in Cziybor's tent nearly two months past.

"You're General Siyrsun."

Siyrsun leaned toward her, his smile half-gloating, half-leering. "Yes. And until now, I was frustrated to learn that the king's yet alive. But what a gift he's left to me...my first consort."

Mortifying weakness forced her to kneel.

Inwardly, however, her resolve steadied itself as the scheming man sat uninvited on the carpets she'd just arranged. How eager his stare was. How self-assured. She knew what he saw. To him, she was the king's current amusement—a well-clad young woman brought into the wild mountains from the palace in Sulaanc. But what he saw was not the woman he actually possessed. Pretending meekness, she bowed her head toward him.

Eosyth woman to invading enemy.

Chapter 32

For a brief instant, she thought of Miyna. Someday, Miyna would understand what had happened tonight. Serena, daughter of Tsir Andris, would follow Eosyth traditions, even at the cost of her life.

Siyrsun scattered her thoughts, snapping an order at her. "Get me something to drink! Anything warm. What's in that kettle?"

"Lentil soup, my lord. I've just set it to simmer."

Gathering every scrap of her audacity, she studied the man. His garments were bloodstained and sodden. He also appeared to be cold and—though he'd never admit it, tired and sore. "Sir? If you would permit me, I'll hurry to the spring for more water to prepare a warming brew." She slid the small dish of dried fruits, petals, and leaves toward him. "The palace physician, Cythea, has ordered me to brew this every day, and…"

He lunged forward, grabbed her wrist, and then dragged her toward him, making her gasp. His coarse voice low, he muttered, "Listen, for I will do as I say. My men will be watching you. If you run, I'll order this entire camp slaughtered, then I'll kill you myself—and not swiftly! Do you hear me?"

She allowed him to see her fear…allowed herself to shiver within his grasp. "Yes, Lord. I won't risk others' lives." Only hers. And his. "I promise you. Just to the stream and back again."

Clutching her mantle around her clean clothes, and praying Ty's azurnite dagger would remain concealed, Serena bowed again, retrieved a small pot from atop a storage chest, and scooted from the tent. Instantly, a rough-hewn leather-clad soldier stood and followed her as if he'd heard every word of the general's threat. His looming, lurking presence sent a fresh shudder through Serena, particularly when his shadow crept over her back. He was too near. Clasping her mantle close, she whirled about and threatened him with a wave of the small pot, "*You* remain ten paces away from me! Your commander's made his intentions clear, and your attentions won't be welcomed."

Condescending, the soldier halted and smiled, but he placed one hand on his sword's hilt. "So you say. But if his plans change, you'll deal with me."

A fine speech for a grubby-looking soldier. Though he'd meant what he said. If Siyrsun cast her out of the tent, still alive, this man would claim her. Infinite, she was going to vomit.

Mastering her nausea, she turned and stalked toward the stream. Toward the patch of witches' moss.

She prayed as she knelt beside the stream. As she scraped the pot's rim against the damp moss, loosened it and tipped it inside the small iron vessel. Gently, lest the moss escape, she allowed fresh water to trickle into the pot, then she stood and marched past the smirking guard, heading directly to her tent.

Siyrsun raised an eyebrow as she entered. "Hurry. That madman could arrive at any time before sunset."

It was a good thing that the former general didn't know how much it irked her to hear him call Ty a madman. How determined she was to protect her beloved's life. Feigning meekness, Serena knelt and placed the small pot near the kettle on the hearth. Infinite…please allow this moss to be enough. Let Siyrsun not look inside the kettle!

She'd obscure the moss with the tisane… As she reached for the dish of dried fruits and petals, Siyrsun grunted. "I've met the worthy Cythea. That looks to be one of her more tolerable concoctions."

Serena forced herself to speak mildly as she slid the dried fruits and petals into the small pot of water. "It's the finest tisane I've ever tasted. The fruit and petals are sweet even after they've been brewed."

"Then I'll eat them." He watched as she fed slivers of dried wood into the fire. Only once, his hand shifted to his sword as if debating whether or not he'd kill her. His movement, that deliberate hesitation as he closed his broad fingers around the sword's gold-banded hilt, sent a punch of fear into Serena's stomach. Had he guessed? But then he relaxed, and began to talk—a braggart dreaming aloud. "Yes, you'll do well... With one such as you by my side, I'll found an empire! Belaal will praise the death of its king, then bow to me, and I'll take this world, country by country. Boldness alone is enough to conquer cowards, lady! Otherwise, bloodshed will do the job. The world *will* fear me, and if my words become your law and you please me, you'll share my glory."

Feigning docility, she stirred the simmering lentils, which weren't yet softened. The tisane finally began to steam, and she gently swirled the fruit and petal garnished liquid. But as she returned it to the hearth, Siyrsun snapped, "Pour that and bring it to me! I'll drink it while I wait for the soup."

It might be unwise to appear eager. Serena objected, "Sir..."

Her pretend-protest faded amid genuine fear as Siyrsun threw her an 'I-shall-kill-you-for-arguing' glare. She closed her mouth, retrieved the largest red-glazed cup available, and poured the steaming ruddy liquid, careful to prevent the largest bits of moss from sliding into the cup. As she offered him the tisane, Siyrsun all but snatched it from her hand. "I've not eaten since dawn."

He drained the hot tisane more quickly than she'd anticipated and then frowned at her. "Well?"

"Sir?" What did he want? Did he suspect...?

He motioned at the pot—his blunt hand cutting through the air. "Serve me the fruit!"

"Forgive me." Serena hurriedly wiped off the soup spoon and served him every bit of fruit she could scrape from the small pot without touching it herself. He downed the violet-pink concoction in one mouthful, swallowed, then flopped over onto the carpets and turned on his left side, facing her. "Wake me the instant that soup is cooked. If you try to escape, my men will chase you down—you'd be good sport."

Serena tried to speak calmly. "Thank you for the warning, Sir, but I won't leave." When would the poison take effect? She'd heard rumors of witches' moss poisoning—the paralysis. The gradual suffocation as the skin became mottled and flushed. Perhaps she could escape before witnessing his travail.

Pretending to be his humble captive-slave, she draped the general's cloak over his shoulders to cover his arms and hands. He'd have to fling it aside and turn to draw his sword. Perhaps she could slash her way out the back of the tent as she'd done during the escape from Rileon. Perhaps she might—

Siyrsun grabbed at Serena's mantle, his hand a vicious claw as he suddenly writhed. She hadn't reckoned on the tisane's quickness, nor on Siyrsun's strength—his swiftness as he wrenched her down beside him on the carpet. She gasped, "Sir!"

His writhing fit eased and he stared into her eyes…knowing… accusing… murderous. His untrimmed fingernails suddenly gouged bloody crescents into her wrist as if he wished his nails were talons tearing into her heart.

Serena gritted her teeth and fumbled for the azurnite dagger, expecting Siyrsun to bellow for his guards. He didn't. Instead his breath became an indistinct wheeze as if his throat had constricted beyond speaking or drawing more than a thread of breath. Spittle flecked at one corner of his mouth. He tightened his hold on her wrist, dragging her nearer. Yet he made no effort to use his left arm, which he partially rested upon. Was his arm paralyzed?

Perhaps. However, if a man's glare could slaughter her—

Serena twisted her hand from his grasp and drew her dagger. His now-reddened eyes shifted in their sockets, his gaze rapt as if briefly bedazzled by the azurnite. Then, again he clawed toward her, snagging her hair, scratching furrows in her scalp and face, making her sweat in pain and panic.

Might he catch his breath and scream? She lunged at Siyrsun and struggled to trap him once more within his cloak, finally pinning him again on his left side. A shudder wracked his entire body. He writhed in obvious torment, then thrashed, striving mightily to fling her off in between his thin barely audible gasps for air—his strength terrifying.

Serena finally pinned his arms within his cloak. As he wheezed, then quieted and closed his eyes, she whispered, "I'm sorry! But you've attacked the Eosyths, my people, who worship the Infinite! And you've threatened your king, whom I love!"

Siyrsun's eyes flashed open. He shoved Serena violently with his head and shoulders, and then kicked against her legs viciously with his right leg, clearly fighting to overthrow her. Might he be resistant to the poison? In despair, she pressed her cheek hard against his right temple, wove her fingers into his hair, and dragged the azurnite blade across his throat with all her might.

A tremor shook him once more, and then he stilled as his blood sprayed, then pooled over the carpets.

Was he dead? Infinite...had she killed him? Had she actually killed a man?

His reddened brown eyes stared, dulled, and his blue-tinged mouth went slack. Serena retreated from his body, muffling her frantic breaths and blinking down tears as she watched him for signs of life.

When he didn't move, she finally closed his eyelids and covered him with another carpet to hide his wound and the growing pool of blood beneath him. In a whisper, she begged, "Infinite...save me..."

She'd killed a man. And not just any man—she'd killed Siyrsun! But he'd invaded her tent and mistreated her. He'd offended all Eosyth traditions. He'd threatened Ty! Stop...

Serena inhaled. She must calm herself and plan how to survive this disaster. Siyrsun's men would slaughter her the instant they realized their commander was dead.

Then they'd kill Araine and Miyna and everyone else in the encampment.

Hands shaking, Serena slid the bloodied azurnite blade into its scabbard, and then hid it beneath sash within her mantle. Its hilt was also coated with blood as was her right hand, and her sleeve. There would be no hiding her role as Siyrsun's murderer. Serena snatched a small towel from the tent's supplies, dipped it in the still-watery surface of the lentil soup, and scrubbed at the blood. While she worked, she prayed beneath her breath, "Infinite, Mighty One...I know You see what I've done to save Your people and my beloved. Save me now!"

***

Araine hugged the warm, sleep-tousled Miyna and frowned up at the soldier who once again leaned into her tent. "Sir! You've been commanded to spare us—I heard the order—and I presume that not torturing or tormenting captives was included within that order, so behave yourself. Otherwise I must bring you to order myself, and you *don't* want me to take such drastic action!"

Her ferocity was diminished by a sudden hiccough, which she failed to squelch entirely. The guard snickered at her. "His order'll change and I'm not the only man who'll watch you—b'lieve me."

"Oh, just—!" She hiccoughed again, then mustered dignity and glared at the man, imperious as the Lady Dasarai. "Go away!" At least the man hadn't recognized her as Belaal's prophet. Siyrsun would order her death at once, unless he killed her himself.

Yet if she must disclose her identity to save Miyna and the others, she would. Until then, Araine briefly closed her eyes and prayed between hiccoughs. "Beloved Creator...protect Serena!"

Miyna stirred at the mention of Serena. When Araine looked down at the little love, Miyna made tiny deliberate hand motions— her secret language according to Serena. Araine smiled at the child's earnest expression. "I wish I might learn your words! I'd welcome knowing your thoughts. Please, oh please—won't you talk to me?"

Unfortunately, she'd never tended a child before. Well, beyond doubt, it was time she learned. Surely Miyna would enjoy hearing a tune from Araine's harp...but no. Hiccoughs notwithstanding, Siyrsun might recognize the music at once. "M-Miyna, are you hungry? Would you enjoy some dried meat?"

Miyna's soft green-brown eyes brightened and her hands fluttered enthusiastically—no translation needed. Araine sighed and handed the little girl a leathery strip of dark meat. "I know you can talk. Won't you teach me your signs?"

Araine hiccoughed again. Miyna shook her head and laughed, teasing. "No-ooo…!"

"Aha!" Araine lifted the child until they were nose-to-nose. "I say 'yes'!"

A sudden warning shiver and an appalling image propelled Araine to stand. She shifted Miyna to her hip and pleaded, "Infinite, will You shield us?"

His answer lit in her hand, forming the Prophet's Branch—so swift and dazzling that Miyna squeaked. Araine kissed the child, paused for another hiccough, and then said, "Miyna, we're going to be brave! We're going to protect Serena!"

Careless of her loose hair and rumpled garments, Araine hugged Miyna close, charged through the entry, and sped toward Serena's allotted tent. The soldiers whistled and started after her, until an outcry and a clashing of swords against shields rang from the southern edge of the encampment. A blaring war-trump resounded and the grimy soldiers yelled to each other, "They've returned! Weapons—to your horses!"

Wielding the branch, Araine dashed aside the entry flap to Serena's tent and ducked inside. As she'd seen, the former Lord-General Siyrsun lay as if sleeping beneath a heavy carpet. Serena huddled near his corpse, her bright blue and gold mantle closed over her garments, covering even her hands. A soldier charged into the tent after Araine and she slashed the branch at his face. "Out!"

He gasped, checked his seared face for blood, and then scurried from the tent as if escaping death. Battle cries and the united thuds of multiple horse-hooves ricocheted through the encampment. Serena's beautiful face paled and tensed. She whispered frantically, "I couldn't remove all the blood! If Siyrsun's men see me—"

All the Infinite's own reassurance manifest itself in Araine's words. "He is your shield, lady—praise your Creator! And bless you for having the courage to destroy our enemy. May He repay you a thousand times over!"

She set down Miyna, and the little girl skittered around Siyrsun's prostrate form, as if she recognized him and knew better than to disturb Belaal's former Lord-General while he slept. Her lovely eyes brimming with tears, Serena welcomed her little sister and Miyna settled in her lap. Battle cries and metal clashing against metal lifted outside and Serena wept. Miyna looked around, listened to the clamor outside, then patted Serena and soothed her in clear, consoling tones, her small voice sounding remarkably old. "Don't cry. We here now."

***

Ty screamed out his rage as he urged his men through the encampment. "Spare no invaders! Find Siyrsun—I want his body!"

Clearly his own guards and servants had been attacked and butchered. If anyone had touched Serena— "Infinite, I beg You... where is she?" His desperation grew with every sign of slaughter throughout the camp as the battle wore on. Pools of blood, evidence of looting...

Guiding his horse without reins, he pressed his right leg to turn the wearied beast left, then intuitively lifted his shield arm as another rider charged at him. A mercenary, likely bent on glory. Ty snarled at the man, received the blow to his shield then rained his own sword-strikes on the man's shield, splintering its wooden surface.

The mercenary's arms were as long as his own, promising a protracted fight, not a swift felling—a reality the mercenary strove to defy as he clouted at Ty with blow after thudding blow. A stinging swipe whisked along Ty's face warning him that his altered helm left him vulnerable. He retaliated viciously, pouring all his strength into his attacks as he sought some way around the man's shield. His longsword snagged once upon a crack in the shield, but the blade's perfect gleaming lines flexed as Ty wrenched it free.

Two strikes later, the mercenary's sword dug a fissure into Ty's shield and the stained blade snapped. Ty turned and lunged, sending a sword thrust around the vulnerable man's shield and taking him in the side.

As the man toppled from his horse, Ty heard Josias screaming from his right. Josias drew back on his bow and sent arrow after arrow beyond Ty—to a man who'd evidently struck down Tsir Mikial. Another mercenary rode toward Josias, sword upraised. Ty bellowed, "Josias…!"

Ty charged the mercenary, caught the man's blow on his own shield, then thrust his sword directly beneath the man's chest plate taking him down.

Accompanied by Tsir Andris, Commander Utthreates rallied his forces to chase after a band of retreating mercenaries, and the battle finally ebbed, allowing Ty a chance to breathe. He could almost hear his own heartbeat thrumming in distress. This unplanned clash had done far more harm than the rout against the Agocii.

By now, Lord Levos was kneeling with Josias beside the fallen Tsir Davos, obviously mourning. Vioc was also down, his men desperately tending a wound to his thigh. Lije had been bashed from his horse and was holding his no doubt broken ribs. And Nikaros approached Ty on foot, as hurriedly as a limp would allow. He bowed and eyed Bel-Tygeon warily. "Sire, your face is gashed. Are you well?"

"Well enough for a mortal! At least we've won. We need to find Serena and Araine. Where's your horse?"

"Struck from beneath me." Nik's face contorted briefly, and he said, "I've been looking and calling through the other side of the camp. Araine's tent is empty."

Praying inwardly, Ty yelled, "Serena! Miyna! Araine! Answer me! Where are you?"

Chapter 33

"Serena! Miyna! Araine! Answer me! Where are you?"

"Ty!" Serena turned toward his voice as Miyna squirmed from her lap. At the tent's entry, Araine breathed, "Infinite, thank you! He's alive! Please let Nikaros be with him!"

She pushed aside the tent's entry flap, but Miyna skittered outside first. Immediately, she rushed inside again, wringing her small hands, her green-brown eyes huge as she sheltered behind Araine. Before she could find words or motions to explain her panic, Ty charged inside.

His sword and his handsome face were bloodied, and he looked frantic but otherwise— Serena's very soul leaped. She sighed her profound relief and cuddled Miyna, who now sought refuge in her lap. "Ty! Oh, Infinite, thank You! Where's my lord-father and Nikaros?"

"Tsir Andris and my men are hunting down the renegades who fled. Nikaros is fine." Ty looked around, then his gaze fixed on Siyrsun's corpse. "Serena, Araine, what happened?"

From outside, Nik's voice arose, unusually agitated. "Am I permitted inside?"

As Araine gasped and rushed outside to her husband, Ty studied Serena's stained garments and her scratches. He returned his long sword to its scabbard, then circled Siyrsun's corpse and hissed beneath his breath, "Serena, answer me please! How did you receive those scratches? Did he attack you? I'd kill him once more myself, if I could!"

"No, my lord." Serena rocked Miyna as the little girl trembled at his barely suppressed ferocity. "Siyrsun was amused. He thought I was a victory celebration you'd brought with you from Sulaanc.

However, he was hungry and thirsty, so while he waited to kill you, I brewed Cythea's tisane with witches' moss. When he realized he'd consumed poison, he clawed and fought me, and I..." Unable to finish the sentence, Serena removed her borrowed mantle and unbuckled the azurnite dagger, still in its scabbard. "I hope I didn't ruin the blade."

"The blade is unimportant." Ty partially removed the azurnite dagger, studied its dark bloodstained surface and concealed it again. "I wish you hadn't been compelled to kill him. But for all our sakes, thank you! I praise the Infinite that you are all unharmed."

He knelt beside Serena. Lifting her hand, he kissed it, then touched her scratched cheek. "It's as Araine predicted: I didn't win. You'll be revered as Siyrsun's executioner—and credited for winning this battle. At least the victory's given to someone whose courage I'll admire for all my life."

Nearly undone by his tenderness, Serena sniffled back tears. "I couldn't let him touch you! He forfeited his life when he entered this tent and scorned all tradition by making demands and threats. I'm sorry." She fought for composure. "I need to scrub my hands, and that dagger, then burn the carpet—and purify anything that held the moss."

"Not yet." Bel-Tygeon shook his head. Miyna stirred, clearly feeling safer. Ty patted the air. "Miyna, wait! Please, both of you, remain seated there. Trust me, it's important."

He hurried from the tent, but chased Nikaros and Araine inside again, followed soon after by the grim Lord Levos and...in single file...every subordinate commander from Belaal who wasn't wounded or chasing renegades. Serena eyed the silent, somber men—all battle-wearied and bloodied—and realization struck her like a dart. These men were official witnesses who would testify to Siyrsun's death. These men would name her as Siyrsun's executioner.

Followed by Nikaros, Lord Levos paced around Siyrsun's corpse, then half-knelt before Serena and bowed his head, silently honoring her. Fresh tears burned, threatening her composure as Nikaros and all Belaal's subordinate commanders followed his example.

Just as the final commanders were departing, bowed out into the dusk by Nikaros, Tsir Andris entered the tent, looking like a man who has received news too appalling to believe. He stared from Nik and Araine to Serena. Then he looked down at Siyrsun and exhaled. "Infinite, I never thought I'd say this, but bless You for creating that plagued moss!"

He knelt before Serena, bowed, and gathered her with Miyna into his arms, kissing them, and smiling through his sudden tears. "You're both alive...may our Creator be forever praised! Now, let our people live in peace."

***

Serena lifted the carved and polished wooden comb, then frowned at her little sister. "Miyna, you must hold still!"

Miyna shook her head, perfectly self-certain. "No, I mustn't."

"Yes, you must!" She scooped the stubborn child into her lap. "It's clear that you've decided to talk just to annoy others. But we love you anyway. Sit."

"No...thank you."

A welcoming trump-blast resounded outside, alerting everyone within earshot to visitors. As others outside greeted visitors with news of the victory—and undoubtedly her own clash with Siyrsun, Serena set the wriggling half-combed Miyna on her feet and warned, "Don't think you've won!"

Miyna laughed at her, then shot from the tent swift as a released arrow. She'd be trampled if anyone was riding into the encampment. "Miyna, wait!"

She reached her little sister and scooped her up just as a procession of winter-shaggy horses entered the encampment.

Nik's mother, the Lady Zinaya, rode up, followed by Adelia, the twins, and Ayden, who was sharing his horse with Serena's older sister. "Tiphera!"

Serena's joyous call caught everyone's attention. The Lady Zinaya laughed, but Adelia cried as the twins, Ayden, and Tiphera tumbled from their rough-coated horses and attacked Serena and Miyna with hugs. Joining the twins, who'd locked their thin arms around Serena and Miyna, Ayden whooped, "I was afraid you were gone forever! Is Cziybor dead?"

"Yes, but Uncle Zeddi struck him first; I had nothing to do with Cziybor's death."

"Yet everything to do with another," Tiphera whispered offering Serena a fierce hug. "It's horrifying, but we're proud of you for upholding tradition!"

"Thank you! I'm glad you don't think it's glorious. I'm sickened thinking of it." She hugged her older sister again. "Are you well?"

Smiling, Tiphera opened her coat and revealed her secret. "I'm due in about five months—finally! Aleon's already planning on a son."

As Serena hugged her older sister and laughed, Lady Zinaya beckoned, then caught her attention. "Serena, well done. Thank you."

Appropriately solemn, Lady Zinaya formally bowed her braid-crowned head, then straightened and rode on, followed by a string of pack-ponies carrying crates and blanketed cages of courier birds. Adelia leaned across the younger children to enfold Serena and Miyna in a fierce hug. "Here's my little wild one and her older twin!" Adelia kissed Serena and eyed her scratches. "They're not festering?"

Serena shook her head. "Don't worry, Mother, I've scrubbed them and Nik's wife has been checking them constantly. Have you heard about Ty?"

"Yes." Adelia's lovely eyes glittered and her mouth hardened. "We guessed his secret, didn't we—just not grandly enough! What are his plans for you?"

Holding her own secret tight, Serena shrugged, "I'm not certain, Mother. He's been very quiet since Siyrsun's death, so I'm making plans of my own."

***

Followed by Araine, Nikaros hurried to meet his mother and her attendants. She'd arrived so swiftly. She must have departed from Clan Qedem the same evening his courier bird had alighted. He stared, startled by her thinness, by the distressed lines etched about her eyes and mouth, and those first glimmers of silver threaded through her braided crown. His fault.

Though she was teary-eyed, Zinaya started talking the instant she broke their embrace of greeting. "Look at you—you've grown! Are you taller than your lord-father? Oh, what he must think of that! Is this your wife?" Zinaya paused and stared at Araine, who bowed gracefully, then straightened, offering a smile.

Before Nikaros could begin to fear that his mother would—for some obscure reason—protest against his marriage, Zinaya hugged Araine, studied her again, and then asked, "Are you ill, or simply nervous about meeting me? Tell me the truth."

Araine's color faded so swiftly that Nik caught her by the arm. She'd been unusually tired and preoccupied these past few days. Was she traumatized by meeting his mother? "Araine, are you ill?"

"Not precisely. I straightened too quickly." She flung Nik a wary little glance that wrung his heart. "I need to eat. Please, Lady, let's rest and visit inside the tent. I…do have news."

Zinaya picked at Nik's sleeve and whispered, "I believe I like her, and she's beautiful. I've also brought you two crates of courier birds to take with you to Belaal."

He would have laughed, except that he was shocked. "What? You're prepared to send me off again?"

"I have my spies," Zinaya murmured. "I've been informed of your situation, and I understand. I only ask that you inform us of matters from time to time and visit when you can. Now…I'm very interested in your wife's news."

***

Standing with her parents, Serena bit down tears as she watched her cousin Iared cross the rocky, snow-dusted field to meet Uncle

Zeddi. Beyond Iared, his former master, the Agocii chieftain Vsevold, watched the youth as well. But Vsevold clawed the fringes of his flowing gold-clasped warrior-beard, perturbed as if he'd released Iared under compulsion from other tribal leaders.

Had Vsevold actually adopted Iared? For a slave, Iared looked remarkably well-fed and wonderfully garbed in heavy boots and a fine fur-edged coat that all seemed fitted to him. More telling, he paused once and offered Vsevold a respectful parting salute—a polite motion that visibly affected the small band of Agocii witnesses observing from behind Vsevold. Their sullen heavily bearded faces seemed to relax, if not actually brighten.

Cziybor's death, and Siyrsun's obvious betrayal in battle had added to the Agocii sense of defeat and grudging submission. Serena prayed their compliance would last. For now at least, Iared's return promised peace. The boy pitched himself into Zeddi's embrace. They hugged each other, and then Zeddi brought his surviving son to stand near Tsir Andris, who nodded to Lord Levos.

Brawny and impressive in his furs, his heavy gold torq gleaming about his throat, Lord Levos picked up a field stone and marched to the center of the declared neutral field between the two peoples. There, amid the blanched, matted, winter-chilled grasses, he planted the stone as if it were a tree. One by one, in a silent, solemn parade, the Eosyths each added a stone to the memorial, marking the boundary between Clan Darom's territories and Agocii lands.

While the Eosyths built their memorial to this uncomfortable peace, the Agocii gradually disbanded and retreated among the stone spires and cliffs that edged their lands' northern boundaries.

Leading her siblings, Serena placed her own rock on the pile, wedging it into place, adding to the memorial's strength. Even Miyna added a small pebble of her own. Even so, every Eosyth here would gladly forget this memorial and endure Cziybor still-living and stalking around these mountains if only Betiya, Siyos, Detzios, and all the others could yet be alive and unscathed.

Serena turned, prepared to follow her parents into the encampment. Until Ty walked up and deliberately stood to the right of her intended path. Handsome, but wearing that remote expression he used as a mask for his true feelings, he said, "My men and I must leave in the morning."

Serena stared. Was this the beginning of an ultimatum? If so, then he must endure a rude shock. She handed Miyna to the twins and lifted her chin at Ty, challenging him to walk with her among her siblings.

***

Ty hid his reluctant smile at Serena's audacious glance. How beautiful she was, his love, his weakness. If she refused to accompany him… If she was determined to stay with her family…

Infinite, please, give me strength.

"Serena—" He started to explain why he and his men must leave. Their carefully calculated provisions would fail if they tarried. His men would become restless and perhaps unintentionally break discipline, causing strife or even offense to the Eosyths. He would help to enforce the peace with the Agocii…

Serena interrupted before he could say more. "I want to burn that tent."

The tent he'd given her? The tent she'd never actually used until she killed Siyrsun? Misery gnawed into his heart and ate at his soul. Thus she rejected him. He'd be a lifetime recovering from her refusal. But he must try to accept her decision with dignity…

She flung him a beautiful, heart-wounding look. "Then, I want *your* tent and that dagger, though I'll have to scrub both."

His tent? And the precious azurnite dagger? Ty drew in a breath of disbelief and halted, staring at her while the other Eosyths walked past them on their way to the encampment. "You're very demanding today! One would think you presume yourself to be a queen."

She gave him the smallest hint of that dazzling smile, but her eyes were serious. "Might I be, Sire?"

Bless You, Infinite! "Lady, are you asking me to marry you? Or are you accepting my previous proposal?"

"Both. Do you agree?"

Did he agree? How could she even ask? She'd cut a dead flattened mouse from his hair when he was a just-recovered madman. She'd loved him when he was nothing but a beggar, and she wondered if *he* would agree? He was going to kiss her and scandalize his men and the Eosyths! Controlling himself, Bel-Tygeon allowed her a grin. "As you say. When?"

Serena faltered. She looked around the beautiful, snow-dusted valley and then up at him. "If you're leaving tomorrow, then the ceremony must be tonight. You've already given my family the gold. You've already proven yourself to us—you know our ways. I'll speak to my parents. I doubt they'll be surprised."

She began to walk again and Ty kept pace with her, talking quietly to encourage her to abandon any second-guessings over her decision. "Nikaros and Araine are returning with us, so you'll have family in the palace. The Lady Zinaya also brought him a crate full of courier birds, so you'll both be able to send notes to your families. We'll have to meet now and then to exchange the Eosyth birds for the birds from Belaal, and I'll be sure your family can visit—"

By now, the twins were motioning to each other, swift eager signs, while Miyna patted at them for attention. Ayden, wearing a gold pendant—one of Cziybor's kill-markers—hammered the air with one fist and then huffed, "You're all talking too fast! Slow down!"

Kari bounced Miyna in her arms and squealed, "Serena's going to marry Ty!"

"Finally!" Ayden whooped, causing Serena's parents and every Eosyth within earshot to turn, stare, and then smile as the twins danced and hugged Ty and Serena.

∗∗∗

Serena folded the last of her Eosyth garments, tucked them into a storage chest, closed its lid, and then stood. Finished dressing, Ty crossed their tent, his footsteps muted by the heavy carpets. Smiling, he looped a beautiful blue-corded gold pendant over her head and settled it about Serena's throat as she tugged her hair out of the way. He adjusted the pendant, then slid his arms around Serena and kissed her, his lips warm, tender, and as ardent as the most perfect bridegroom ever to live.

Sighing, Serena lost herself in her husband's warmth, the blissful sweetness of his kiss, until he finally straightened. "Beloved…my perfect wife! Do you know how much I adore you?" Before she could answer, he swung her into another hug and rained kisses over her hair and her face, making her laugh. Between kisses, he breathed, "I love you! I want to marry you again and again—according to the customs of every known nation! I'll give you a ring from Darzeq! A contract from the Tracelands! Even an armband from Siphra! I'll give you all these in addition to my pendant. Later, if you give me a child…" He held his breath over the words. "Then, I'll crown you my queen…"

If she should give him a child.

Serena clung to him, kissed his neck, and then his lips. When they finally stepped apart she touched his handsome, whisker-roughened face. "May the Infinite grant you everything you desire through me. I love you! Your kisses are sweeter than I ever imagined—I could hold you forever!"

Ty laughed and murmured, "Lady, I'm your willing captive." He clasped her hand and she led him out into the early springtime light, to return with him to their home, to the song-filled gardens and palace in Sulaanc.

Chapter 34

Cradling her nursing three-month-old daughter, Betiyana, Serena willed herself to relax and to study the official gold-edged scroll on the polished table beside her. For Betiyana would not be hurried for all the realm. Not even for her impatient royal father, whom she adored. At least the unexpected wait gave Serena the chance to finally review this very wordy petition in her slow, learning-to-read fashion. A request from the citizens of Sulaanc that she sponsor a children's school. Serena smiled, pleased by the idea. In a few years, after it was built, and when she'd mastered her studies well enough to not shame Ty, she'd visit with...

Ty swept into the sunlit chamber, his blue and gold robes glittering with every movement. "Is she finished? At this rate, it'll be sunset before she's done. She must be on Eosyth time!" But his expression softened, utterly captivated as he gazed down at his dark-haired daughter.

Betiyana finally sighed, snuggled against Serena, and dozed. Ty grinned. "At last." He kissed Serena's bared throat and grinned. "Hurry, love. I'll be waiting for you."

She reached up and caressed his perfect face. "We won't be long, beloved."

As her husband sped from the chamber, Serena handed Betiyana to her attendant, the delighted, ever watchful Malia, and then she stood. From the other side of the chamber, the Lady Dasarai beckoned, "Haste, Malia! Serena, we've everything ready."

"Lady," Serena murmured, resisting the impulse to tease, "I'm at your command." She accompanied Malia, smiling as she placed Betiyana on the embroidered blue covers beside her bright-eyed twin brother, Rian. Clad in a simple white tunic, the infant boy glanced up at Serena and offered her a sudden flirting smile, so like his father that Serena laughed and swooped down to kiss his tenderly rounded face. Beside her, Dasarai sighed, "Isn't he perfect? Aren't they both beyond compare?"

"I bless the Infinite that they're healthy," Serena agreed.

"Yes," Dasarai murmured dotingly, "bless the Infinite for hearing us at last. But we must hurry. One mustn't forget duty."

While Dasarai and the servants swooped in to groom and swaddle the twins, Serena allowed her attendants to dress her. They re-pinned her heavy undergarments, fastened her gleaming blue gown and its protective mantle, hooked a weighty gemstone collar around her throat, added matching earrings, then secured a sheer blue and gold-edged veil to her smoothly sculptured hair, coiled and pinned high upon her head.

As the final touch, they fastened the azurnite dagger—graced with a new gem-studded ivory hilt—around Serena's waist. Serena endured the weapon, but suppressed a shudder at all it represented. How had this thing become her emblem? This morning, Ty had laughed at her dismay and teased, "You're legend, beloved, and you're not even old."

Outside in the corridor, more attendants waited. Serena smiled at them. "I hope you're not tired of waiting. The princess refused to rush through her midday feeding."

The courtiers laughed and applauded the richly swaddled babies who were being carried by Dasarai and Malia.

As they'd rehearsed, they paraded outside into the vast formal courtyard. There, Serena settled into her gold-canopied, richly-cushioned carrying chair, and the babies were snugged in her arms.

The porters carried the golden chair through the massive opening gates, and the tumult began. The waiting crowd's cheers of greeting and celebration lifted to an almost deafening roar. In Serena's arms, the swaddled babies twitched and blinked, both of them turning their heads and staring, their lustrous dark hair as wonderfully thick as their royal father's.

Carried amid a procession of dignitaries and banners, Serena nodded and smiled all along Sulaanc's parade route, and then through the vast crowded plaza. At the end of the plaza, the Lady Dasarai and Malia took the babies, and Serena stood. Servants arranged her robes, then escorted her up the stairs to the site of the Infinite's future temple in Sulaanc, where Ty waited with his high priest, Ro'ghez, and Belaal's beautiful prophet, Araine. Just beyond Araine, Nikaros stood watch over the proceedings, with Serena's family, who'd been brought down from the mountains and into Sulaanc by an honor guard this past month.

Father looked somber, but Mother and the children laughed to see her.

Serena inclined her veiled head toward them. The Lady Dasarai and Malia handed her the twins again, then Serena looked up at Ty and caught her breath.

Her beloved. He was worth all she'd suffered during her captivity and the battle. And through him, she'd been blessed.

Yet, she would give up this honor, the gem-laden crown in his hands if it should be the Infinite's perfect will. The ambitions of the girl she had been were dust to her now—nothing compared to His love.

Ty placed the crown on her head, and Serena straightened, bearing its weight as she smiled at him…prepared to serve Belaal.

To serve You, she promised the Infinite as Ro'ghez and Araine blessed her.

For You brought me to this place through my trials, according to Your plan. Nothing in this realm of dust can purchase the love You have granted me! I will sing to You for as long as I live…

***

Bel-Tygeon gazed at his wife…his queen…and his heart constricted for an instant as she smiled at him alone. His courageous, dazzling Serena, holding their children. Here was his most cherished dream.

Proof of the Infinite's blessing and Divine mercy as the everlasting Sovereign. Who could withstand Him?

Infinite, Ruler of the Eternal realm and all realms beyond, let me remain Your servant forever as I praise You for all You have done!

Oblivious to the crowd, Bel-Tygeon bent and kissed his beguiling, long-desired queen.

***

Araine, prophet of Belaal, gently nuzzled her sleeping infant daughter, Zinaya, then tucked her into the ridiculously large cradle given by the Lady Dasarai. However, Zinaya—exquisite living sunshine in baby form—loved the gold-embossed blue monstrosity. Therefore the oversized, overdecorated cradle would shelter her as long as her dreams remained sweet and she greeted the dawn happily, the perfect love.

Smiling, Araine returned to bed and snuggled beside her husband. Nikaros slumbered on, exhausted. But Araine closed her eyes and stepped into her dreams, into a world of darkness she couldn't fathom even now.

Cold, gleaming cities near-wild with chaos. Oceans of blackened blood birthing creatures of fire...a monster-dreki beyond her imaginings, its red and gold scales lit from within by the fury of hate, as souls cried out to the Infinite for rescue.

Infinite, what is the truth about these creatures—about everything I've seen?

What do all these things mean?

These are not for your generation, but for times to come. Don't be afraid, My Child of Dust.

From the corner of her eye, an immortal warrior approached, tranquil, yet alight with joy and the Infinite's reflected glory. Araine looked into the warrior's eyes and retreated, glimmers of recognition stirring fear. But he smiled and said, "Don't be afraid. I am His servant. His eternal warrior! And we've a battle to wage."

He strode toward the chaos, armed with their Creator's might. To Araine, the Infinite murmured, *Take up the weapons I have given you, and follow.*

Armed with His golden Word, and the prophet's branch, she followed the warrior into the vision, into His realm, the branch glowing reflecting her soul, alive in the presence of her Creator

Follow Me.

***

Worn out by the day's festivities, but too restless to sleep, Ty sat down at his desk and pondered briefly, rubbing his fingers over the faint battle scar marring his jaw. Enhancing it, Serena ever argued. Wonderful of her to think so. Smiling, he lifted a pen, and wrote.

To all nations, rejoice with me, for the Infinite has proclaimed His glory through what has befallen me. I, in my pride, was brought low and driven to madness as His prophet foretold…

Character List

In approximate order of appearance:

Araine \Ah-**Rain**\ Prophet of Belaal. Wife to Lord Nikaros.

Belaal \Bell-**A**-el\ Kingdom south of Siphra, southeast of the highlands.

Bel-Tygeon \Bell-**Ty**-jee-on\ King of Belaal.

Agocii \Ah-**goss**-ee\ Nation of warrior tribes south of the Eosyths

Eosyths **E**-o-siths\ Confederation of highland clans who joined Belaal and the Agocii in the failed siege of the ruined city-state of Parne.

Darom \Daw-**rome**\ Southern clan of the Eosyths.

Siyrsun **Seer**-sun\ Belaal's former General of the Army. Also known as Old Dreki.

Serena \Seh-**ree**-na\ Daughter of Clan Darom's ruler, Tsir Andris.

Tsir Andris \Sir **An**-dris\Ruler of Clan Darom. Follower of the Infinite. Destroyed Eosyth altars to Utzaos.

Utzaos \Oot-**zay**-aws\ Former Eosyth god of the sun.

Utzaii \Oot-**zah**-ee\ Agocii god of the sun. Named among the Eosyths as Utzaos.

Miyna **Mee**-nah\\Serena's baby sister.

Betiya \\Beh-**tee**-ah\\ Serena's aunt.

Nikaros **Nik**-kehr-aws, servant and scribe to Bel-Tygeon. Son of the Eosyth high lord, Levos.

Clan Tsahfon \\Tsah-**fone**\\ Northern Eosyth Clan, ruled by Tsir Davos, father of Josias.

Clan Ma'rawb \\Mah-**rawb**\\ Western Eosyth Clan, ruled by Tsir Mikial, father of Lije.

Clan Qedem \\Keh-**dem**\\ Eastern Eosyth Clan, ruled by High Lord Levos, father of Nikaros.

Ebatenai \\E-**bat**-en-ay\\ Bel-Tygeon's household steward.

Rethae Dasarai \\Reth-**ay** Da-**Sar**-ay\\ Princess of Belaal. Bel-Tygeon's sister. Sovereign of Sulaanc's Women's Palace.

Cziybor **Sea**-bor\\ An Agocii chieftain.

Rtial Vioc **Reh**-tee-al Vee-**oak**\\ A commander of Belaal.

Cecaii \\Seh-**sah**-ee\\ Agocii slave.

Ela Roeh **El**-ah **Roe**-eh\\ Prophet of the vanquished city-state of Parne.

Queen Acknowledgements

Thank you to all my wonderful readers, and my dear, patient husband, who encouraged me to persist through a tumultuous year as I wrote Queen. Hugs to my beloved sons.

Special thanks to Brianna Anderson for cheerfully submitting to the photo session with Katharin Fiscaletti for the cover—zero retouches!

To Deb Haggerty, editor and reader for Exiles and Queen, you are a blessing and fun—thank you!

Jim Hart, bless you for courageously taking me on as a client and for waiting so patiently as I finish current projects. I appreciate your encouraging notes!

Scott Rodgers and the Falcon 1644 team, hey, what can I say? You're the most awesome crew! Thanks for putting up with me.

Readers, thank you again for your notes and your questions, and for all who have stopped by at my Facebook page (www.facebook.com/RJLarson.Writes) and on Pinterest to monitor my progress as I wrote Exiles and Queen! Keep after me, all of you! These stories are yours, and I'm blessed to write them for you.

Ever yours,

R. J. Larson

P.S. check out my website for the map, sample chapters, and vocabulary lists! http://www.rjlarsonbooks.com

Made in the USA
San Bernardino, CA
13 March 2018